"In an interesting mash-up of fairy tales and science fiction, the book is a cross between Cinderella, *The Terminator*, and *Star Wars*."
—*Entertainment Weekly* on Cinder

"Action packed."
—*The Horn Book*

Praise for the Lunar Chronicles

A *New York Times* Bestseller · An Amazon Best Book of the Year
A *Publishers Weekly* Best Book of the Year
An IRA Young Adult Choices Master List Selection

★ "Meyer's brilliance is in sending the story into an entirely new, utterly thrilling dimension." —*Publishers Weekly*, starred review

"Terrific." —*Los Angeles Times*

"In an interesting mash-up of fairy tales and science fiction, the book is a cross between Cinderella, *The Terminator*, and *Star Wars*."
—*Entertainment Weekly*

"Author Marissa Meyer rocks the fractured fairy-tale genre with a sci-fi twist on Cinderella." —*The Seattle Times*

"Fairy tales are becoming all the rage." —USAToday.com

"Cinderella is a cyborg in this futuristic take on the fairy tale."
—*The Wall Street Journal*

"Spellbinding." —VOYA

"Singing mice and glass slippers are replaced with snarky androids and mechanical feet in this richly imagined and darkly subversive retelling of Cinderella." —*BCCB*

"This is one buzzed novel that totally delivers." —Stacked Books Blog

"Debut author Meyer ingeniously incorporates key elements of the fairy tale into this first series entry." —*The Horn Book Magazine*

"Offers a high coolness factor by rewriting Cinderella as a kickass mechanic in a plague-ridden future." —*Kirkus Reviews*

Praise for the Lunar Chronicles

A *New York Times* Bestseller • A Kids' Indie Next Top Ten Title
A *VOYA* Perfect Ten Title • An Amazon Best Book of the Month
A YALSA Best Fiction for Young Adults

★ "It's another Marissa Meyer roller-coaster ride, part science fiction/fantasy, part political machination with a hint of romance."
—*Booklist*, starred review

★ "A great choice for all ages, with strong appeal for both girls and boys, these novels will be read and enjoyed—repeatedly."
—*VOYA*, starred review

★ "Returning fans of Meyer's *Cinder* will gladly sink their teeth into this ambitious, wholly satisfying sequel."
—*Publishers Weekly*, starred review

"The author has stepped up the intrigue and plot from the first novel, and readers will be eagerly awaiting the next." —*School Library Journal*

"Further development of this futuristic world plus plenty of action, surprises, and a fast pace will keep readers invested in their journey."
—*The Horn Book*

"The sci-fi elements are stronger than the fairy-tale allusions this time out, but the story remains just as absorbing. . . . Readers will be thrilled to discover that this steampunky fairy-tale/sci-fi mashup promises more installments." —BCCB

Praise for the Lunar Chronicles

Cress

A *New York Times* Bestseller
A *USA Today* Bestseller
A Kids' Indie Next Top Ten Title

★ "Meyer continues to show off her storytelling prowess, keeping readers engaged in a wide cast of characters while unfolding a layered plot that involves warring governments and a fast-spreading plague. The momentum Meyer built in the first two books continues to accelerate as the stakes grow higher for Cinder and her friends. The next installment cannot come fast enough."
—*Publishers Weekly*, starred review

"As always, Meyer excels at interweaving new characters that extend beyond the archetypes of their fairy tale into the main story. Readers will eagerly await the final installment of this highly appealing and well-constructed series." —*School Library Journal*

"Once again, Meyer offers up a science fiction-fantasy page-turner that salutes women's intelligence and empowerment.... Old and new romances, unfinished story lines, and the prognostication of wartime horrors all pave the way for Meyer's much anticipated next installment." —*Booklist*

"This multilayered, action-packed page-turner is sure to please series fans." —*The Horn Book*

Cress's story continues...

The Lunar Chronicles

Cinder

Scarlet

Cress

Winter

And don't miss Levana's story in...

Fairest

Book Three

Cress

The Lunar Chronicles

WRITTEN BY

Marissa Meyer

SQUARE
FISH

An Imprint of Macmillan
175 Fifth Avenue
New York, NY 10010
macteenbooks.com

Square Fish books may be purchased for business or promotional use.
For information on bulk purchases, please contact the Macmillan Corporate
and Premium Sales Department at (800) 221-7945 x5442 or by e-mail
at specialmarkets@macmillan.com.

Library of Congress Cataloging-in-Publication Data Available
ISBN 978-1-250-00722-3 (paperback) / ISBN 978-1-250-05318-3 (e-book)

Originally published by Feiwel and Friends
First Square Fish Edition: 2015
Square Fish logo designed by Filomena Tuosto

10 9 8 7 6 5 4 3 2 1

AR: 6.0 / LEXILE: 840L

For Jojo, Meghan, and Tamara
high fives

BOOK
One

When she was just a child, the witch

locked her away in a tower that

had neither doors nor stairs.

One

HER SATELLITE MADE ONE FULL ORBIT AROUND PLANET EARTH every sixteen hours. It was a prison that came with an endlessly breathtaking view—vast blue oceans and swirling clouds and sunrises that set half the world on fire.

When she was first imprisoned, she had loved nothing more than to stack her pillows on top of the desk that was built into the walls and drape her bed linens over the screens, making a small alcove for herself. She would pretend that she was not on a satellite at all, but in a podship en route to the blue planet. Soon she would land and step out onto real dirt, feel real sunshine, smell real oxygen.

She would stare at the continents for hours and hours, imagining what that must be like.

Her view of Luna, however, was always to be avoided. Some days her satellite passed so close that the moon took up the entire view and she could make out the enormous glinting domes on its surface and the sparkling cities where the Lunars lived. Where she, too, had lived. Years ago. Before she'd been banished.

As a child, Cress had hidden from the moon during those achingly long hours. Sometimes she would escape to the small washroom and distract herself by twisting elaborate braids into her hair. Or she would scramble beneath her desk and sing lullabies until she fell asleep. Or she would dream up a mother and a father, and imagine how they would play make-believe with her and read her adventure stories and brush her hair lovingly off her brow, until finally—finally—the moon would sink again behind the protective Earth, and she was safe.

Even now, Cress used those hours to crawl beneath her bed and nap or read or write songs in her head or work out complicated coding. She still did not like to look at the cities of Luna; she harbored a secret paranoia that if she could see the Lunars, surely they could look up beyond their artificial skies and see her.

For more than seven years, this had been her nightmare.

But now the silver horizon of Luna was creeping into the corner of her window, and Cress paid no attention. This time, her wall of invisi-screens was showing her a brand-new nightmare. Brutal words were splattered across the newsfeeds, photos and videos blurring in her vision as she scrolled from one feed to the next. She couldn't read fast enough.

14 CITIES ATTACKED WORLDWIDE
2-HOUR MURDER SPREE RESULTS IN 16,000
EARTHEN DEATHS
LARGEST MASSACRE IN THIRD ERA

The net was littered with horrors. Victims dead in the streets with shredded abdomens and blood leaking into the gutters. Feral men-creatures with gore on their chins and beneath their fingernails and staining the fronts of their shirts. She scrolled through them all with one hand pressed over her mouth. Breathing became increasingly difficult as the truth of it all sank in.

This was her fault.

For months she had been cloaking those Lunar ships from Earthen detection, doing Mistress Sybil's bidding without question, like the well-trained lackey she was.

Now she knew just what kind of monsters had been aboard those ships. Only now did she understand what Her Majesty had been planning all along, and it was far too late.

16,000 EARTHEN DEATHS

Earth had been taken unaware, and all because she hadn't been brave enough to say no to Mistress's demands. She had done her job and then turned a blind eye to it all.

She averted her gaze from the pictures of death and carnage, focusing on another news story that suggested more horrors to come.

Emperor Kaito of the Eastern Commonwealth had put an end to the attacks by agreeing to marry Lunar Queen Levana.

Queen Levana was to become the Commonwealth's new empress.

The shocked journalists of Earth were scrambling to determine their stance on this diplomatic yet controversial arrangement. Some were in outrage, proclaiming that the Commonwealth and the rest of the Earthen Union should be preparing for war, not a wedding. But others were hastily trying to justify the alliance. With a swirl of her fingers on the thin, transparent screen, Cress raised the audio of a man who was going on about the potential benefits. No more attacks or speculations on when an attack might come. Earth would come to understand the Lunar culture better. They would share technological advances. They would be allies.

And besides, Queen Levana only wanted to rule the Eastern Commonwealth. Surely she would leave the rest of the Earthen Union alone.

But Cress knew they would be fools to believe it. Queen Levana was going to become empress, then she would have Emperor Kaito murdered, claim the country for her own, and use it as a launching pad to assemble her army before invading the rest of the Union. She would not stop until the entire planet was under her control. This small attack, these sixteen thousand deaths… they were only the beginning.

Silencing the broadcast, Cress set her elbows on her desk and dug both hands into her hive of blonde hair. She was suddenly cold, despite the consistently maintained temperature inside the satellite. One of the screens behind her was reading aloud in a child's voice that had been programmed during four months of insanity-inducing boredom when she was ten years old. The voice was too chipper for the material it quoted: a medical blog from the American Republic announcing the results of an autopsy performed on one of the Lunar soldiers.

> *The bones had been reinforced with calcium-rich biotissue, while the cartilage in major joints was infused with a saline solution for added flexibility and pliability. Orthodontic implants replaced the canine and incisor teeth with those mimicking the teeth of a wolf, and we see the same bone reinforcement around the jaw to allow for the strength to crush material such as bone and other tissue. Remapping of the central nervous system and extensive psychological tampering were responsible for the subject's unyielding aggression and wolf-like tendencies. Dr. Edelstein has*

theorized that an advanced manipulation technique of the
brain's bioelectric waves may also have played a role in—

"Mute feed."

The sweet ten-year-old's voice was silenced, leaving the satellite humming with the sounds that had long ago been relegated to the back of Cress's consciousness. The whirring of fans. The thrumming of the life support system. The gurgling of the water recycling tank.

Cress gathered the thick locks of hair at the nape of her neck and pulled the tail over her shoulder—it had a tendency to get caught up in the wheels of her chair when she wasn't careful. The screens before her flickered and scrolled as more and more information came in from the Earthen feeds. News was coming out from Luna too, on their "brave soldiers" and "hard-fought victory"—crown-sanctioned drivel, naturally. Cress had stopped paying attention to Lunar news when she was twelve.

She mindlessly wrapped her ponytail around her left arm, spiraling it from elbow to wrist, unaware of the tangles clumping in her lap.

"Oh, Cress," she murmured. "What are we going to do?"

Her ten-year-old self piped back, "Please clarify your instructions, Big Sister."

Cress shut her eyes against the screen's glare. "I understand that Emperor Kai is only trying to stop a war, but he must know this won't stop Her Majesty. She's going to kill him if he goes through with this, and then where will Earth be?" A headache pounded at her temples. "I thought for certain Linh Cinder had told him at the ball, but what if I'm wrong? What if he still has no idea of the danger he's in?"

Spinning in her chair, she swiped her fingers across a muted newsfeed, punched in a code, and called up the hidden window that she checked a hundred times a day. The D-COMM window opened like a black hole, abandoned and silent, on top of her desk. Linh Cinder still had not tried to contact her. Perhaps her chip had been confiscated or destroyed. Perhaps Linh Cinder didn't even have it anymore.

Huffing, Cress dismissed the link and, with a few hasty taps of her fingertips, cascaded a dozen different windows in its place. They were linked to a spider alert service that was constantly patrolling the net for any information related to the Lunar cyborg who had been taken into custody a week earlier. Linh Cinder. The girl who had escaped from New Beijing Prison. The girl who had been Cress's only chance of telling Emperor Kaito the truth about Queen Levana's intentions should he agree to the marriage alliance.

The major feed hadn't been updated in eleven hours. In the hysteria of the Lunar invasion, Earth seemed to have forgotten about their most-wanted fugitive.

"Big Sister?"

Pulse hiccupping, Cress grasped the arms of her chair. "Yes, Little Cress?"

"Mistress's ship detected. Expected arrival in twenty-two seconds."

Cress catapulted from her chair at the word *mistress*, spoken even all those years ago with a tinge of dread.

Her movements were a precisely choreographed dance, one she had mastered after years of practice. In her mind, she became a second-era ballerina, skimming across a shadowy stage as Little Cress counted down the seconds.

00:21. Cress pressed her palm onto the mattress-deploy button.

00:20. She swiveled back to the screen, sending all feeds of Linh Cinder beneath a layer of Lunar crown propaganda.

00:19. The mattress landed with a thunk on the floor, the pillows and blankets wadded up just as she'd left them.

00:18. 17. 16. Her fingers danced across the screens, hiding Earthen newsfeeds and netgroups.

00:15. A turn, a quick search for two corners of her blanket.

00:14. A flick of her wrists, casting the blanket up like a wind-caught sail.

00:13. 12. 11. She smoothed and tugged her way to the opposite side of the bed, pivoting toward the screens on the other side of her living quarters.

00:10. 9. Earthen dramas, music recordings, second-era literature, all dismissed.

00:08. A swivel back toward the bed. A graceful turning down of the blanket.

00:07. Two pillows symmetrically stacked against the headboard. A flourish of her arm to pull out the hair that had gotten caught beneath the blanket.

00:06. 5. A glissade across the floor, dipping and spinning, gathering up every discarded sock and hair tie and sending them into the renewal chute.

00:04. 3. A sweep of the desks, collecting her only bowl, her only spoon, her only glass, and a handful of stylus pens, and depositing them into the pantry cabinet.

00:02. A final pirouette to scan her work.

00:01. A pleased exhalation, culminating in a graceful bow.

"Mistress has arrived," said Little Cress. "She is requesting an extension of the docking clamp."

The stage, the shadows, the music, all fell away from Cress's thoughts, though a practiced smile remained on her lips. "Of course," she chirped, swanning toward the main boarding ramp. There were two ramps on her satellite, but only one had ever been used. She wasn't even sure if the opposite entrance functioned. Each wide metal door opened up to a docking hatch and, beyond that, space.

Except for when there was a podship anchored there. Mistress's podship.

Cress tapped in the command. A diagram on the screen showed the clamp extending, and she heard the thump as the ship attached. The walls jolted around her.

She had the next moments memorized, could have counted the heartbeats between each familiar sound. The whir of the small spacecraft's engines powering down. The clang of the hatch attaching and sealing around the podship. The vacuum as oxygen was pushed into the space. The beep confirming that travel between the two modules was safe. The opening of the spacecraft. Steps echoing on the walkway. The whoosh of the satellite entrance.

There had been a time when Cress had hoped for warmth and kindness from her mistress. That perhaps Sybil would look at her and say, "My dear, sweet Crescent, you have earned the trust and respect of Her Majesty, the Queen. You are welcome to return with me to Luna and be accepted as one of us."

That time had long since passed, but Cress's practiced smile held firm even in the face of Mistress Sybil's coldness. "Good day, Mistress."

Sybil sniffed. The embroidered sleeves of her white jacket fluttered around the large case she carried, filled with her usual provisions: food and fresh water for Cress's confinement and, of course, the medical kit. "So you've found her, have you?"

Cress winced around her frozen grin. "Found her, Mistress?"

"If it *is* a good day, then you must have finally completed the simple task I've given you. Is that it, Crescent? Have you found the cyborg?"

Cress lowered her gaze and dug her fingernails into her palms. "No, Mistress. I haven't found her."

"I see. So it isn't a good day after all, is it?"

"I only meant…Your company is always…" She trailed off. Forcing her hands to unclench, she dared to meet Mistress Sybil's glare. "I was just reading the news, Mistress. I thought perhaps we were pleased about Her Majesty's engagement."

Sybil dropped the case onto the crisply made bed. "We will be satisfied once Earth is under Lunar control. Until then, there is work to be done, and you should not be wasting your time reading news and gossip."

Sybil neared the monitor that held the secret window with the D-COMM feed and the evidence of Cress's betrayal to the Lunar crown, and Cress stiffened. But Sybil reached past it to a screen displaying a vid of Emperor Kaito speaking in front of the Eastern Commonwealth flag. With a touch, the screen cleared, revealing the metal wall and a tangle of heating tubes behind it.

Cress slowly released her breath.

"I certainly hope you've found *something.*"

She stood taller. "Linh Cinder was spotted in the European Federation, in a small town in southern France, at approximately 18:00 local ti—"

"I'm well aware of all that. And then she went to Paris and

killed a thaumaturge and some useless special operatives. Anything else, Crescent?"

Cress swallowed and began winding her hair around both wrists in a looping figure eight. "At 17:48, in Rieux, France, the clerk of a ship-and-vehicle parts store updated the store inventory, removing one power cell that would be compatible with a 214 Rampion, Class 11.3, but not notating any sort of payment. I thought perhaps Linh Cinder stole...or maybe glamoured..." She hesitated. Sybil liked to keep up the pretense that the cyborg was a shell, even though they both knew it wasn't true. Unlike Cress, who was a true shell, Linh Cinder had the Lunar gift. It may have been buried or hidden somehow, but it had certainly made itself known at the Commonwealth's annual ball.

"A power cell?" Sybil said, passing over Cress's hesitation.

"It converts compressed hydrogen into energy in order to propel—"

"I know what it is," Sybil snapped. "You're telling me that the only progress you've made is finding evidence that she's making repairs to her ship? That it's going to become even more difficult to track her down, a task that you couldn't even manage when they were on Earth?"

"I'm sorry, Mistress. I'm trying. It's just—"

"I'm not interested in your excuses. All these years I've persuaded Her Majesty to let you live, under the premise that you had something valuable to offer, something even more valuable than blood. Was I wrong to protect you, Crescent?"

She bit her lip, withholding a reminder of all she'd done for Her Majesty during her imprisonment. Designing countless spy systems for keeping watch on Earth's leaders, hacking the communication links between diplomats, and jamming satellite signals to allow the queen's soldiers to invade Earth undetected, so that now the blood of sixteen thousand Earthens was on her hands. It made no difference. Sybil cared only about Cress's failures, and not finding Linh Cinder was Cress's biggest failure to date.

"I'm sorry, Mistress. I'll try harder."

Sybil's eyes narrowed. "I'll be very displeased if you don't find me that girl, and soon."

Held by Sybil's gaze, she felt like a moth pinned to an examination board. "Yes, Mistress."

"Good." Reaching forward, Sybil petted her cheek. It felt almost like a mother's approval, but not quite. Then she turned away and released the locking mechanisms on the case. "Now then," she said, retrieving a hypodermic needle from the medical kit. "Your arm."

Two

WOLF PUSHED HIMSELF OFF THE CRATE, HURTLING TOWARD her. Cinder braced herself against the instinctive panic. The anticipation of one more hit tightened every muscle, despite the fact that he was still going easy on her.

She squeezed her eyes shut moments before impact and *focused.*

Pain shot through her head like a chisel into her brain. She gritted her teeth against it, attempting to numb herself to the waves of nausea that followed.

The impact didn't come.

"Stop. Closing. Your. Eyes."

Jaws still clenched, she forced one eye open and then the other. Wolf stood before her, his right hand in mid-swing toward her ear. His body was still as stone—because she was holding him there. His energy was hot and palpable and just out of reach, the strength of her own Lunar gift keeping him at bay.

"It's easier to have them closed," she hissed back. Even those few words put a strain on her mind, and Wolf's fingers twitched. He was struggling against the confines of her control.

Then his gaze flickered past her, as a thump between her

shoulder blades sent Cinder tumbling forward. Her forehead collided with Wolf's chest. His body released just in time for him to steady her.

Behind her, Thorne chuckled. "It also makes it easier for people to sneak up on you."

Cinder spun around and shoved Thorne away. "This isn't a game!"

"Thorne is right," said Wolf. She could hear his exhaustion, though she wasn't sure whether it came from the constant melee or, more likely, his frustration at having to train such an amateur. "When you close your eyes, it makes you vulnerable. You have to learn to use the gift while still being aware of your surroundings, while still being active within them."

"Active?"

Wolf stretched his neck to either side, eliciting a few pops, before shaking it out. "Yes, active. We could be facing dozens of soldiers at a time. With any luck, you'll be able to control nine or ten—although that's optimistic at this point."

She crinkled her nose at him.

"Which means you'll be vulnerable to countless more. You should be able to control me while still being fully present, both mentally and physically." He took a step back, pawing at his messy hair. "If even Thorne can sneak up on you, we're in trouble."

Thorne cuffed his sleeves. "Never underestimate the stealth of a criminal mastermind."

Scarlet started laughing from where she sat cross-legged on a plastic storage crate, enjoying a bowl of oatmeal. "'Criminal mastermind'? We've been trying to figure out how to infiltrate the royal wedding for the past week, and so far your biggest contribution has been determining which of the palace rooftops is the most spacious so your precious ship doesn't get scratched in the landing."

A few light panels brightened along the ceiling. "I fully agree with Captain Thorne's priorities," said Iko, speaking through the ship's built-in speakers. "As this may be my big net debut, I'd like to be looking my best, thank you very much."

"Well said, gorgeous." Thorne winked up toward the speakers, even though Iko's sensors weren't sensitive enough to pick up on it. "And I would like the rest of you to note Iko's proper use of *Captain* when addressing me. You could all stand to learn a thing or two from her."

Scarlet laughed again, Wolf raised an eyebrow, unimpressed, and the cargo bay's temperature clicked up a couple degrees as Iko blushed from the flattery.

But Cinder ignored them all, downing a glass of lukewarm water while Wolf's admonishments spun through her head. She knew he was right. Though controlling Wolf strained every ability she had, controlling Earthens like Thorne and Scarlet usually came as easy to her as replacing a dead android sensor.

By now, she should have been able to do both.

"Let's go again," she said, tightening her ponytail.

Wolf slipped his attention back to her. "Maybe you should take a break."

"I won't get a break when I'm being chased down by the queen's soldiers, will I?" She rolled her shoulders, trying to re-energize herself. The pain in her head had dulled, but the back of her T-shirt was damp with sweat and every muscle was trembling from the effort of sparring with Wolf for the past two hours.

Wolf rubbed his temple. "Let's hope you never have to face off against the queen's real soldiers. I think we stand a chance going up against her thaumaturges and special operatives, but the advanced soldiers are different. More like animals than humans, and they don't react well to brain manipulation."

"Because so many people do?" said Scarlet, scraping her spoon against the bowl.

His glance flickered toward her, something in his eyes softening. It was a look Cinder had seen a hundred times since he and Scarlet had joined the crew of the Rampion, and yet seeing it still made her feel like she was intruding on something intimate.

"I mean they're unpredictable, even under the control of a thaumaturge." He returned his focus to Cinder. "Or any other Lunar. The genetic tampering they undergo to become soldiers affects their brains as much as their bodies. They're sporadic, wild . . . dangerous."

Thorne leaned against Scarlet's storage crate, fake-whispering to her, "He does realize that *he's* an ex–street fighter who still goes by 'Wolf,' right?"

Cinder bit the inside of her cheek, smothering a laugh. "All the more reason for me to be as prepared as possible. I'd like to avoid another close call like we had in Paris."

"You're not the only one." Wolf started to sway on the balls of his feet again. Cinder had once thought this indicated he was ready for another sparring match, but she'd lately begun to think that's just how he was—always moving, always restless.

"Which reminds me," she said, "I'd like to get some more of those tranquilizer darts, whenever we land again. The fewer soldiers we have to fight or brainwash, the better."

"Tranquilizer darts, got it," said Iko. "I've also taken the liberty of programming this handy countdown clock. T minus fifteen days, nine hours until the royal wedding." The netscreen on the wall flickered to life, displaying an enormous digital clock counting down by the tenth of a second.

Three seconds of staring at that clock made Cinder sick with anxiety. She tore her gaze away, scanning the rest of the netscreen and their ongoing master plan for putting a stop to the wedding between Kai and Queen Levana. A list of needed supplies was jotted down the left side of the screen—weapons, tools, disguises, and now tranquilizer darts.

In the middle of the screen was a blueprint of New Beijing Palace.

On the right, a ridiculously long preparation checklist, none of which had yet to be checked off, though they'd been planning and plotting for days.

Number one on the list was to prepare Cinder for when she would inevitably come face-to-face with Queen Levana and her court again. Though Wolf hadn't said it outright, she knew her Lunar gift wasn't improving fast enough. Cinder was beginning to think that item could take years to reach satisfactory completion, and they had only two more weeks.

The rough plan was to cause a distraction on the day of the wedding that would allow them to sneak into the palace during the ceremony and announce to the world that Cinder was truly the lost Princess Selene. Then, with all the world's media watching, Cinder would demand that Levana relinquish the crown to her, ending both the wedding and her rule in one fell swoop.

Everything that was supposed to follow the wedding blurred in Cinder's mind. She kept imagining the reactions of the Lunar people when they discovered that their lost princess was not only cyborg, but also entirely ignorant of their world, culture, traditions, and politics. The only thing that kept her chest from being crushed by the weight of it all was the knowledge that, no matter what, she couldn't possibly be any worse of a ruler than Levana.

She hoped they would see it that way too.

The glass of water sloshed in her stomach. For the thousandth time, a fantasy crept into her thoughts of crawling beneath the covers of her crew-issued bunk bed and hiding until all the world forgot there had ever been a Lunar princess in the first place.

Instead, she turned away from the screen and shook out her muscles. "All right, I'm ready to try again," she said, settling into the fighting stance that Wolf had taught her.

But Wolf was now sitting beside Scarlet and polishing off her oatmeal. Mouth full, he dipped his eyes to the floor and swallowed. "Push-ups."

Cinder dropped her arms. "What?"

He gestured at her with the spoon. "Fighting isn't the only type of physical exertion. We can build your upper body strength and train your mind at the same time. Just try to stay aware of your surroundings. Focus."

She glowered for five full seconds before dropping to the ground.

She'd counted to eleven when she heard Thorne push himself away from the crate. "You know, when I was a kid, I was tricked into thinking that princesses wore tiaras and hosted tea parties. Now that I've met a real princess, I must say, I'm kind of disappointed."

She didn't know if he meant it as an insult, but these days the word *princess* set every one of Cinder's nerves on edge.

Exhaling sharply, she did just as Wolf had instructed. She

focused—easily picking up on Thorne's energy as he passed by her on his way toward the cockpit.

She was lowering into the fourteenth push-up when she forced his feet to stall beneath him.

"Wha—"

Cinder pushed up and swung one leg forward in a half circle. Her ankle collided with the back of Thorne's calves. He cried out and fell, landing on his backside with a grunt.

Beaming, Cinder glanced up at Wolf for approval, but both he and Scarlet were too busy laughing. She could even see the sharp points of Wolf's canine teeth that he was usually so careful to keep hidden.

Cinder stood and offered Thorne a hand. Even he was smiling, though it was coupled with a grimace as he rubbed his hip.

"You can help me pick out a tiara when we're done saving the world."

Three

THE SATELLITE SHUDDERED AS SYBIL'S PODSHIP DISCONNECTED from the docking clamp, and Cress was left alone again in the galaxy. Despite how Cress yearned for companionship, it was always a relief when Sybil left her, and this time even more than usual. Normally her mistress only visited every three or four weeks, just often enough to safely take another blood sample, but this was the third time she'd come since the wolf-hybrid attacks. Cress couldn't remember her mistress ever seeming so anxious. Queen Levana must have been growing desperate to find the cyborg girl.

"Mistress's ship has detached," said Little Cress. "Shall we play a game?"

If Cress hadn't been so flustered from yet another visit, she would have smiled, as she usually did when Little Cress asked this question. It was a reminder that she wasn't *entirely* without companionship.

Cress had learned, years ago, that the word *satellite* came from a Latin word meaning a companion, or a minion, or a sycophant. All three interpretations had struck her as ironic, given her solitude, until she'd programmed Little Cress. Then she understood.

Her satellite kept her company. Her satellite did her bidding. Her satellite never questioned her or disagreed or had any pesky thoughts of her own.

"Maybe we can play a game later," she said. "We'd better check the files first."

"Certainly, Big Sister."

It was the expected response. The programmed response.

Cress often wondered if that's what it would be like to be truly Lunar—to have that sort of control over another human being. She would fantasize about programming Mistress Sybil as easily as she'd programmed her satellite's voice. How the game would change then, if her mistress was to follow *her* orders for once, rather than the other way around.

"All screens on."

Cress stood before her panorama of invisi-screens, some large, others small, some set on top of the built-in desk, others bracketed to the satellite walls and angled for optimal viewing no matter where she was in the circular room.

"Clear all feeds."

The screens went blank, allowing her to see through them to the satellite's unadorned walls.

"Display compiled folders: Linh Cinder; 214 Rampion, Class 11.3; Emperor Kaito of the Eastern Commonwealth. And . . ." She paused, enjoying the rush of anticipation that passed through her. "Carswell Thorne."

Four screens filled up with the information Cress had been collecting. She sat down to review the documents she'd all but memorized.

On the morning of 29 August, Linh Cinder and Carswell Thorne escaped from New Beijing Prison. Four hours later, Sybil had given Cress her orders—*find them*. The command, Cress later discovered, came from Queen Levana herself.

Scrounging up information on Linh Cinder had taken her only three minutes—but then, almost all the information she'd found was fake. A fake Earthen identity written up for a girl who was Lunar. Cress didn't even know how long Linh Cinder had been on Earth. She'd simply popped into existence five years ago, when she was (supposedly) eleven years old. Her biography had family and school records prior to the "hover accident" that had killed her "parents" and resulted in her cyborg operation, but that was all false. One had to follow Linh Cinder's ancestry back only two generations before they hit a dead-end. The records had been written to deceive.

Cress glanced at the folder still downloading information on Emperor Kaito. His file was immeasurably longer than the others, as every moment of his life had been recorded and filed away— from net fangroups to official government documentation. Information was being added all the time, and it had exploded since the announcement of his engagement to the Lunar queen. None of it was helpful. Cress closed the feed.

Carswell Thorne's folder had required a bit more legwork. It took Cress forty-four minutes to hack into the government records of the American Republic's military database and five other agencies that had had dealings with him, compiling trial transcripts and articles, military records and education reports, licenses and income statements and a timeline that began with his certificate of birth and continued through numerous accolades and awards won while he was growing up, through his acceptance into the American Republic military at age seventeen. The timeline blinked out after his nineteenth birthday, when he removed his identity chip, stole a spaceship, and deserted the military. The day he'd gone rogue.

It started up again eighteen months later, on the day he was found and arrested in the Eastern Commonwealth.

In addition to all the official reports, there was a fair amount of swooning and gossiping from the many fangroups that had sprouted in the wake of Carswell Thorne's new celebrity status. Not nearly as many as Emperor Kai had, of course, but it seemed that plenty of Earthen girls were taken with the idea of this handsome rake on the run from the law. Cress wasn't bothered by it. She knew that they all had the wrong idea about him.

At the top of his file was a three-dimensional holograph scanned in from his military graduation. Cress preferred it to the infamous prison photo that had become so popular, the one in which he was winking at the camera, because in the holograph he was wearing a freshly pressed uniform with shining silver buttons and a confident, one-sided grin.

Seeing that smile, Cress melted.

Every. Time.

"Hello again, Mr. Thorne," she whispered to the holograph. Then, with a giddy sigh, she turned to the only remaining folder.

The 214 Rampion, Class 11.3. The military cargoship Thorne had stolen. Cress knew everything about the ship—from its floor plan to its maintenance schedule (both the ideal and the actual).

Everything.

Including its location.

Tapping an icon in the folder's top bar, she replaced Carswell Thorne's holograph with one of a galactic positioning grid. Earth shimmered into existence, the jagged edges of its continents as familiar to her as Little Cress's programming. After all, she had spent half her life watching the planet from 26,071 kilometers away.

Encircling the planet flickered thousands of tiny dots that indicated every ship and satellite from here to Mars. A glance told Cress that she could look out her Earth-side window right then and spot an unsuspecting Commonwealth scouting ship passing by her nondescript satellite. There was a time when she would have been tempted to hail them, but what would be the point?

No Earthen would ever trust a Lunar, much less rescue one.

So Cress ignored the ship, humming to herself as she cleared away all the tiny markers on the holograph until only the Rampion's ID remained. A single yellow dot, disproportionate in the holograph so that she could analyze it in the context of the planet below.

It hovered 12,414 kilometers above the Atlantic Ocean.

She called up the ID of her own orbiting satellite. If one were to attach a string from her satellite to the center of the Earth, it would cut right through the coast of Japan Province.

Nowhere near each other. They never were. It was a huge orbiting field, after all.

Finding the coordinates of the Rampion had been one of the greatest challenges of Cress's hacking career. Even then, it had taken her only three hours and fifty-one minutes to do it, and all the while her pulse and adrenaline had been singing.

She had to find them first.

She had to find them first.

Because she had to protect them.

In the end, it had been a question of mathematics and deduction. Using the satellite network to ping signals off all the ships orbiting Earth. Discarding those with trackers, as she knew that the Rampion had been stripped. Discarding those that were clearly too big or too small.

That left mostly Lunar ships, and all of those were, of course, already under her dominion. She'd been disrupting their signals and confusing radar waves for years. There were many Earthens who believed Lunar ships were invisible because of a Lunar mind trick. If only they'd known that it was actually a worthless shell causing them so much trouble.

In the end, only three ships were orbiting Earth that fit the criteria, and two of them (no doubt illegal pirating ships) wasted no time in landing on Earth once they realized there was a massive space search going on that they were about to be caught in the middle of. Cress, out of curiosity, had later scanned Earthen police records in their proximity and found that both ships had been discovered upon re-entering Earth's atmosphere. Silly criminals.

That left only one. The Rampion. And aboard it, Linh Cinder and Carswell Thorne.

Within twelve minutes of pinpointing their location, Cress scrambled every signal that posed any risk of finding them using the same method. Like magic, the 214 Rampion, Class 11.3, had vanished into space.

Then, nerves frazzled from the mental strain, she'd collapsed onto her unmade bed and beamed deliriously at the ceiling. She'd done it. She had made them invisible.

A chirp resounded from one of the screens, pulling Cress's attention away from the floating dot that represented the Rampion. Cress spun toward it, flinching when a strand of hair caught in the chair's wheels. She yanked it out with one hand and nudged the screen out of hibernation with the other. A flick of her fingers and the window was enlarged.

CONSPIRACY THEORIES OF THE THIRD ERA

"Not another one," she muttered.

The conspiracy theorists had been slobbering over themselves ever since the cyborg girl had disappeared. Some said that Linh Cinder was working for the Commonwealth government, or Queen Levana, or that she was in cahoots with a secret society determined to overthrow one government or another, or that she was the missing Lunar princess, or that she knew where the Lunar princess was, or that she was somehow tied to the spread of letumosis, or that she had seduced Emperor Kaito and was now pregnant with a Lunar-Earthen-cyborg *thing*.

There were almost as many rumors surrounding Carswell Thorne. They included theories on the *real* reason that he was in prison, such as plotting to kill the last emperor, or how he'd been working with Linh Cinder for years prior to her arrest, or how he was connected to an underground network that had infiltrated the prison system years ago in preparation for the day when he would require their assistance. This newest theory was suggesting that Carswell Thorne was, in fact, an undercover Lunar thaumaturge meant to assist Linh Cinder with her escape so that Luna would have an excuse for starting the war.

Essentially, nobody knew anything.

Except for Cress, who knew the truth of Carswell Thorne's crimes, his trial, and his escape—at least, the elements of the escape she'd been able to piece together using prison surveillance video and the statements from the on-duty guards.

In fact, Cress was convinced that she knew more about Carswell Thorne than anyone else alive. In a life in which newness and novelty were so rare, he had become a fixture of fascination to her. At first, she was disgusted by him and his apparent greed and recklessness. When he'd deserted the military, he'd left half a dozen cadets and two commanding officers stranded on an island in the Caribbean. He had stolen a collection of second-era goddess sculptures from a private collector in the Eastern Commonwealth and a set of Venezuelan dream dolls on loan to a museum in Australia to potentially never be seen in public again. There were additional claims of an unsuccessful robbery of a young widow from the Commonwealth who owned an extensive collection of antique jewelry.

Cress had continued to dig, entranced by his path of self-destruction. Like watching an asteroid collision, she couldn't look away.

But then, strange anomalies had begun to creep up in her research.

Age eight. The city of Los Angeles spent four days in panic after a rare Sumatran tiger escaped from the zoo. Video surveillance of the cage showed the young Carswell Thorne, there on a field trip with his class, opening the cage. He later told the authorities that the tiger had looked sad locked up like that, and that he didn't regret it. Luckily, no one, including the tiger, had been hurt.

Age eleven. A police report was filed by his parents claiming they'd been robbed—overnight, a second-era diamond necklace had gone missing from his mother's jewelry chest. The necklace was traced to a net sales listing, where it had recently sold for 40,000 univs to a buyer in Brazil. The seller was, of course, Carswell himself, who had not yet had a chance to send off the necklace, and was forced to return the payment, along with an official apology. That apology, made public record to prevent other teens from getting the same idea, claimed that he was only trying to raise money for a local charity offering android assistance to the elderly.

Age thirteen. Carswell Thorne was given a weeklong school suspension after fighting with three boys in his grade, a fight he had lost according to the school's med-droid report. His statement proclaimed that one of the boys had stolen a portscreen from a girl named Kate Fallow. Carswell had been trying to get it back.

One situation after another was brought to Cress's attention. Theft, violence, trespassing, school suspensions, police reprimands. Yet Carswell Thorne, when given a chance to explain, always had a reason. A *good* reason. A heart-stopping, pulse-racing, awe-inspiring reason.

Like the sun rising over Earth's horizon, her perception began to change. Carswell Thorne wasn't a heartless scoundrel at all. If anyone bothered to get to know him, they would see that he was compassionate and chivalrous.

He was exactly the kind of hero Cress had been dreaming about her entire life.

With that discovery, thoughts of Carswell Thorne began to infiltrate her every waking moment. She dreamed of deep soul connections and passionate kisses and daring escapades. She was certain that he simply had to meet her, just once, and he would feel the same way. It would be like those epic love affairs that exploded into existence and burned white hot for all eternity. The type of love that time and distance and even death couldn't separate.

Because if there was one thing Cress knew about heroes, it was that they could not resist a damsel in distress.

And she was nothing if not in distress.

Four

SCARLET PRESSED A COTTON PAD TO THE CORNER OF WOLF'S mouth, shaking her head. "She may not get in many hits, but when she does, she makes them count."

Despite the bruise creeping around his jaw, Wolf was beaming, his eyes bright beneath the medbay's lights. "Did you see how she tripped up my feet before she swung? I didn't see it coming." He rubbed his hands giddily on his thighs, his feet kicking at the side of the exam table. "I think we might finally be getting somewhere."

"Well, I'm glad you're proud of her, but I think it would be nice if next time she hit you with her nonmetal hand." Scarlet pulled the cotton away. The wound was still bleeding where Wolf's lip had broken on his upper canine, but not as bad as before. She reached for a tube of healing salve. "You might be adding a new scar to your collection, but it kind of matches the one on this side of your mouth, so at least they'll be symmetrical."

"I don't mind the scars." He shrugged, his eyes taking on a mischievous spark. "They hold better memories now than they used to."

Scarlet paused with a dab of ointment on her fingertip. Wolf's attention had affixed itself to his own knotted hands, a hint of color on his cheeks. Within seconds, she was feeling extra warm herself, remembering the night they'd once spent as stowaways aboard a maglev train. How she'd traced her fingers along the pale scar on his arm, brushed her lips against the faint marks on his face, been taken into his arms . . .

She shoved him on the shoulder. "Stop smiling so much," she said, dabbing the salve onto the wound. "You're making it worse."

He quickly schooled his features, but the glint remained in his eyes when he dared to look up at her.

That night on the maglev remained the only time they'd kissed. Scarlet couldn't count the time he'd kissed her while she was being held captive by him and the rest of his special operative "pack." He had used the chance to give her an ID chip that ultimately helped her escape, but there had been no affection in that kiss, and at the time she'd despised him.

But those moments aboard the maglev had caused more than one sleepless night since coming aboard the Rampion. When she had lain awake and imagined slipping out of her bed. Creeping across the corridor to Wolf's room. Not saying a word when he opened the door, just pulling herself against him. Curling her hands into his hair. Wrapping herself up in the sort of security that she'd only ever found in his arms.

She never did, though. Not for fear of rejection—Wolf hadn't exactly tried to conceal his lingering gazes or how he leaned into every touch, no matter how trivial. And he had never taken back what he said after the attack. *You're the only one, Scarlet. You'll always be the only one.*

Scarlet knew he was waiting for her to make the first move.

But every time she found herself tempted, she would see the tattoo on his arm, the one that marked him forever as a Lunar special operative. Her heart was still broken from the loss of her grandmother, and the knowledge that Wolf could have saved her. He could have protected her. He could have prevented it all from happening in the first place.

Which wasn't fair to him. That was before he'd known Scarlet, before he'd cared. And if he had tried to rescue her grandmother, the other operatives would have killed him too. Then Scarlet really would be alone.

Maybe her hesitation was because, if she were honest with herself, she was still a little afraid of Wolf. When he was happy and flirtatious and, at times, adorably awkward, it was easy to forget that there was another side to him. But Scarlet had seen him fight too many times to forget. Not like the restrained brawls he and Cinder had, but fights where he could ruthlessly snap a man's neck, or tear an opponent's flesh from his bones using nothing but his own sharp teeth.

The memories still made her shudder.

"Scarlet?"

She jumped. Wolf was watching her, his brow creased. "What's wrong?"

"Nothing." She called up a smile, relieved when it didn't feel strained.

Yes, there was something dark inside him, but the monster she'd seen before was not the same as the man seated before her now. Whatever those Lunar scientists had done to him, Wolf had shown time and again that he could make his own choices. That he could be different.

"I was just thinking about scars," she said, screwing the cap back onto the ointment. Wolf's lip had stopped bleeding, though the bruise would last a few days.

Cupping his chin, Scarlet tilted Wolf's face away from her and pressed a kiss against the wound. He inhaled sharply, but otherwise became as still as rock—an unusual feat for him.

"I think you'll survive," she said, pulling away and tossing the bandage into the trash chute.

"Scarlet? Wolf?" Iko's voice crackled through the wall speakers. "Can you come out to the cargo bay? There's something on the newsfeeds you might want to see."

"Be right there," said Scarlet, stashing away the rest of the supplies as Wolf jumped down from the exam table. When she glanced over at him, he was grinning, one finger rubbing against the cut.

In the cargo bay, Thorne and Cinder were seated on one of the storage crates, hunkered over a deck of paper cards. Cinder's hair was still a mess from her recent semi-victory over Wolf.

"Oh, good," said Thorne, glancing up. "Scarlet, tell Cinder she's cheating."

"I'm not cheating."

"You just played back-to-back doubles. You can't do that."

Cinder crossed her arms. "Thorne, I just downloaded the official rulebook into my brain. I know what I can and can't do."

"Aha!" He snapped his fingers. "See, you can't just download stuff in the middle of a game of Royals. House rules. You're cheating."

Cinder threw up her hands, sending cards fluttering throughout the cargo bay. Scarlet snatched a three out of the air. "I was taught that you can't play back-to-back doubles either. But maybe that was just how my grandma played."

"Or maybe Cinder's cheating."

"I am not—" Clenching her jaw, Cinder growled.

"Iko called us out here for something?" said Scarlet, dropping the card back onto the deck.

"*Oui*, mademoiselle," said Iko, adopting the accent that Thorne often imitated when talking to Scarlet, though Iko sounded much more authentic. "There's breaking news coming out on the Lunar special operatives." The netscreen on the wall flickered, as Iko hid the ticking clock and palace blueprint and replaced them with a series of vids—reporters and grainy footage of armed military personnel coaxing half a dozen muscular men into a secured hover. "It seems that since the attack, the American Republic has been conducting investigations into the operatives, and a sting operation is going down right now in the three Republic cities that were attacked: New York, Mexico City, and São Paulo. They've already rounded up fifty-nine operatives and four thaumaturges, to be held as prisoners of war."

Scarlet stepped closer to the screen, which was showing footage from Manhattan Island. It appeared that this particular pack had been hiding out in an abandoned subway line. The operatives were bound at their hands and ankles and each one had at least two guns trained on him from the surrounding troops, but they all looked as carefree as if they were picking wildflowers in a meadow. One even flashed an amused grin at the camera as he was herded past. "Do you know any of them?"

Wolf grunted. "Not well. The different packs didn't usually socialize, but I'd see them in the dining hall, and sometimes during training."

"They don't seem too upset," said Thorne. "Evidently they've never tasted prison food."

Cinder came to stand beside Scarlet. "They won't be there for long. The wedding is in two weeks, and then they'll be released and sent back to Luna."

Thorne hooked his thumbs in his belt loops. "In that case, this seems like a pretty big waste of time and resources."

"I disagree," said Scarlet. "The people can't keep living in fear. The government is trying to show that they're doing something to keep the massacres from happening again. This way, they can feel like they have some sort of control over the situation."

Cinder shook her head. "But what happens when Levana retaliates? The whole point of the marriage alliance was to hold her temper in check."

"She won't retaliate," said Wolf. "I doubt she'll even care."

Scarlet glanced at the tattoo on his forearm. "After all the work she's gone through to create you ... them?"

"She wouldn't jeopardize the alliance. Not for the operatives, who were only meant to serve one purpose to begin with—to launch that first attack and remind Earth that Lunars can be anyone, anywhere. To make them afraid of us." He began to shuffle restlessly from foot to foot. "She's done with us now."

"I hope you're right," said Iko, "because now that they've discovered how to track the operatives, everyone expects the rest of the Union to follow suit."

"How *did* they find them?" asked Cinder, adjusting her ponytail.

A sigh of air whooshed through the cooling system. "It turns out, Lunars have managed to reprogram a bunch of the med-droids stationed at plague quarantines all over the world. They've been harvesting ID chips from the deceased and shipping them off to these operatives to be reprogrammed and inserted into their bodies, so they could blend in with society. Once the government figured out the connection, they just had to follow the trail of the ID chips, and they were led straight to the packs' operation bases."

"Peony ..." Cinder shifted closer to the netscreen. "That's why the android wanted her chip. You're telling me it would have ended up inside one of *them*?"

"Spoken with true derision for our canine friends," said Thorne.

Cinder massaged her temple. "I'm sorry, Wolf. I don't mean you." She hesitated. "Except . . . I do, though. Anyone. She was my *little sister.* How many people have died from this disease, only to have their identities violated like this? Again, no offense."

"It's all right," said Wolf. "You loved her. I would feel the same if someone wanted to erase Scarlet's identity and give it to Levana's army."

Scarlet stiffened, heat rushing into her cheeks. He certainly wasn't insinuating . . .

"*Aaaaw,*" squealed Iko. "Did Wolf just say that he *loves* Scarlet? That's so cute!"

Scarlet cringed. "He did not—that wasn't—" She balled her fists against her sides. "Can we get back to these soldiers that are being rounded up, please?"

"Is she blushing? She sounds like she's blushing."

"She's blushing," Thorne confirmed, shuffling the cards. "Actually, Wolf is also looking a little flustered—"

"*Focus,* please," said Cinder, and Scarlet could have kissed her. "So they were taking ID chips from plague victims. Now what?"

The lights dimmed as Iko's giddiness diminished. "Well, it won't be happening anymore. All American androids assigned to the quarantines are being evaluated and reprogrammed as we speak, which will no doubt carry into the rest of the Union."

On the screen, the last operative in Manhattan was being loaded into the armored hover. The door clanged and locked shut behind him.

"It does take care of one threat, at least," said Scarlet, thinking of the pack that had kept her prisoner. That had killed her grandmother. "I hope Europe hunts them down too. I hope they kill them."

"I hope they don't think their job is done after this," said Cinder. "Like Wolf said, the real war hasn't even begun yet. Earth should be on high alert right now—preparing for anything."

"And we should be making sure we're ready to stop this wedding and put you on the throne," added Scarlet, noting how Cinder flinched at the mention of becoming queen. "If we can pull this off, the war may never go any further than it already has."

"I have a suggestion," said Iko, replacing the news story of the Lunar operatives with an ongoing report for the upcoming wedding. "If we're going to be sneaking into New Beijing Palace while Levana is there, why don't we just assassinate her? Not to be all cold-wired murderer about it, but wouldn't that solve a lot of our problems?"

"It's not that easy," said Cinder. "Remember who we're talking about here. She can brainwash hundreds of people at once."

"She can't brainwash me," said Iko. "Or you."

Wolf shook his head. "It would take an army to get close enough. She'll have countless guards and thaumaturges with her. Not to mention all the Earthens she could use as shields, or turn into weapons themselves."

"Including Kai," Cinder said.

The ship's engine sputtered, causing the walls to quake. "You're right. We can't risk that."

"No, but we can tell the world that she's a fraud and a murderer." Cinder planted her hands on her hips. "They already know she's a monster. We just need to show them that no one is safe if she becomes empress."

Five

"SCREEN FOUR," SAID CRESS, SQUINTING AT THE GRID OF ICONS. "High Jack to . . . D5."

Without waiting for the animated jester to cartwheel to his new space, she shifted her attention to the next game. "Screen five. Claim rubies and daggers. Discard crowns."

The screen sparkled, but she had already moved on.

"Screen six." She paused, chewing on the tips of her hair. Twelve rows of numbers filled up the screen, some slots left blank, some tinted with colors and patterns. After her brain twisted around an equation she wasn't sure she could have done a second time, the puzzle lit up before her, the solution as clear as a moonrise over Earth. "3A, insert yellow 4. 7B is black 16. 9G is black 20." The grid melted away, replaced with a second era singer swooning into a microphone, the audience swelling with applause.

"Congratulations, Big Sister," said Little Cress. "You won!"

Cress's victory was short-lived. She rolled onto her side and reassessed the first game. Seeing the move that Little Cress had made since her last turn squelched her pride. She'd backed herself into a corner. "Screen one," she murmured, swooping her hair over one shoulder and mindlessly knotting the dampened ends around her fingers. Five knots later and her victory on screen six was forgotten. Little Cress was going to win this one.

She sighed and made the best move she could, but it was immediately followed by Little Cress's king moving to the center of the holographic labyrinth and claiming the golden chalice. A laughing jester appeared, gobbling down the rest of the game board.

Cress groaned and pulled her hair off her neck, waiting for whatever task her younger self would randomly select for her.

"I won!" said Little Cress, once the holograph had disappeared back into the screen. The other games automatically locked themselves. "You now owe me ten minutes of country-western line dancing, as guided by the following video, followed by thirty jump-squats. Let's begin!"

Cress rolled her eyes, wishing she hadn't been quite so perky when she'd recorded the voice. But she did as she was told, sliding off the bed as a mustached man in a large hat appeared on the screens, thumbs hooked into his belt loops.

A couple years ago, upon realizing that her living accommodations offered few opportunities to be active, Cress had gone on a fitness kick. She'd installed all the games with a program that chose from a variety of fitness activities, which she would be required to perform from every time she lost. Though she'd often regretted the program, it did help keep her from becoming cemented to her chair, and she kind of enjoyed the dancing and yoga routines. Although she was not looking forward to those jump-squats.

Just as the twang of a guitar announced the start of the

dance, a loud chime delayed the inevitable. Thumbs locked into her pretend-belt loops, Cress glanced around at the screens.

"Little Cress, what—"

"We have received a direct communication link request from Unknown User: Mechanic."

Her insides spun as if she'd just done a backflip.

Mechanic.

With a cry, she half stumbled, half fell toward the smallest screen, hastily tapped in the fitness-routine override code, checked the firewall and privacy settings, and saw it. A D-COMM request, and the most innocent of questions.

ACCEPT?

Mouth dry, Cress smoothed both palms over her hair. "Yes! Accept!"

The window faded away, replaced with blackness, and then—

And then—

There he was.

Carswell Thorne.

He was tilted back in a chair, the heels of his boots propped up in front of the screen. Three people stood close behind him, but all Cress could see were the blue eyes staring back at her, *directly* back at her, beginning to fill with the same breathless awe she felt.

The same wonder.

The same enchantment.

Though they were separated by two screens and vast amounts of empty space, she could feel the link being forged between them in that look. A bond that couldn't be broken. Their eyes had met for the first time, and by the look of pure amazement on his face, she knew he felt it too.

Heat crept up into her cheeks. Her hands began to shake.

"Aces," Carswell Thorne murmured. Dropping his feet to the ground, he leaned forward to inspect her closer. "Is that all *hair*?"

The bond snapped, the fantasy of one perfect true-love moment disintegrating around her.

Sudden, overwhelming panic clawed up Cress's throat. With a squeak, she ducked out of view of the camera and scrambled beneath the desk. Her back struck the wall with a thud that rattled her teeth. She crouched there, skin burning hot and pulse thundering as she took in the room before her—the room that he was now seeing too, with the rumpled bedcovers and the mustached man on all the screens telling her to grab her imaginary partner and swing them around.

"Wha—where'd she go?" Thorne's voice came to her through the screen.

"Honestly, Thorne." A girl. Linh Cinder? "Do you ever think before you speak?"

"What? What did I say?"

"'*Is that all hair?*'"

"Did you see it? It was like a cross between a magpie nest and ball of yarn after it's been mauled by a cheetah."

A beat. Then, "A cheetah?"

"It was the first big cat that came to mind."

Cress hurriedly tried to finger-comb the tangles around her ears. Her hair hadn't been cut since she'd been put into the satellite and now hung past her knees, but Sybil didn't bring sharp objects into the satellite and Cress had long ago stopped worrying about keeping it neatly braided. After all, who was going to see her?

Oh, to have styled her hair that morning. To have worn the dress that didn't have a hole in the collar. Had she even brushed her teeth since she'd eaten breakfast? She couldn't remember, and now she was sure that she had bits of spinach from her freeze-dried eggs Florentine stuck between them.

"Here, let me speak to her."

Shuffling from the screen.

"Hello?" A girl again. "I know you can hear me. I'm sorry my friend is such a wing nut. You can just ignore him."

"That's usually what we do," said the other feminine voice.

Cress searched hastily for a mirror or anything that could pass for one.

"We need to talk to you. I'm . . . This is Cinder. The mechanic who fixed the android?"

The back of Cress's hand smacked into her clothes hamper. It collided with her wheeled chair, which was launched halfway across the room where it hit the far desk and sent a half-full cup of water tipping and wobbling. Cress froze, her eyes going wide as the glass teetered toward the memory drive that housed Little Cress.

"Um, hello? Is this a good time?"

The cup came to rest straight and still once more, not a drop having spilled.

Cress slowly exhaled.

This was not how this meeting was supposed to go. This was not the fantasy she'd dreamed up a hundred times. What had she said in all those dreams? How had she acted? Who had that person been?

All she could think of was the burning mortification of the country-western dancer (*now face your partner and do-si-do!*) and her magpie-nest hair, her sweating palms and her deafening pulse.

She squeezed her eyes shut and forced herself to focus, to *think.*

She was not a silly little girl hiding beneath her desk. She was—she was—

An actress.

A gorgeous, poised, talented actress. And she was wearing a sequined dress that sparkled like stars, one that would mesmerize anyone who saw her. She was not one to question her own power to charm those around her, any more than a thaumaturge would question her ability to manipulate a crowd. She was breathtaking. She was—

Still hiding under the desk.

"Are you there?"

A snort. "Yeah, this is going really well." Carswell Thorne.

Cress flinched, but her breaths were becoming less sporadic as she cocooned herself in the fantasy. "This is a drama set," she whispered, quiet enough that they couldn't hear her. She forced it into her imagination. This was not her bedroom, her sanctuary, her prison. This was a drama set, with cameras and lights and dozens of directors and producers and android-assistants milling about.

And she was an *actress.*

"Little Cress, pause fitness programming."

The screens halted, the room going silent, and Cress crawled out from beneath the desk.

Cinder was sitting before the screen now, with Carswell Thorne hovering over her shoulder. Cress glanced at him long enough to catch a smile that was perhaps meant to be apologetic, but only served to make her heart skitter.

"Hi," said Linh Cinder. "Sorry to surprise you like that. Do you remember me? We spoke a couple weeks ago, on the day of the coronation and—"

"Y-yes, of course," she stammered. Her knees started to shake as she surreptitiously dragged her chair back toward her and sat down. "I'm glad you're all right." She forced herself to focus on Linh Cinder. Not on Carswell Thorne. If she only refrained from meeting his gaze again, she would manage. She would not fall apart.

And yet the temptation to fix her eyes on him was still there, tugging at her.

"Oh, thanks," said Cinder. "I wasn't sure…I mean, do you follow Earthen news? Do you know what's been happening since—"

"I know everything."

Cinder paused.

Cress realized her words had come out all mushed together, and she reminded herself to enunciate when she was playing such a sophisticated role. She forced herself to sit up a bit straighter.

"I follow all the newsfeeds," she clarified. "I knew you were spotted in France, and I've been tracking your ship, so I knew it hadn't been destroyed, but I still didn't know whether you'd been injured, or what had happened, and I've been trying to establish the D-COMM link but you never responded." She deflated a little, her fingers tying knots into her hair. "But I am glad to see that you're all right."

"Yes, yes, she's fine, we're fine, everybody's fine," said Thorne, perching an elbow on Cinder's shoulder and leaning toward the screen with furrowed brows. Meeting his eyes was unavoidable, and an involuntary squeak slipped past her lips—a sound she'd never heard herself make before. "Did you just say you've been *tracking* our ship?"

She opened her mouth, but shut it a moment later when no sound followed. Finally, she managed a brittle nod.

Thorne squinted at her as if trying to figure out if she were lying. Or merely an idiot.

She longed to crawl back beneath the desk.

"Really," he drawled. "And who do you work for again?"

You are an actress. An actress!

"Mistress," she said, forcing the word. "Mistress Sybil. She ordered me to find you, but I haven't told her anything—and I won't, you don't have to worry about that. I—I've been jamming the radar signals, making sure surveillance satellites are faced the other way when you pass, that sort of thing. So no one else could find you." She hesitated, realizing that four faces were gaping at her as if all her hair had just fallen out. "You must have noticed that you haven't been caught yet?"

Lifting an eyebrow, Cinder slid her gaze over to Thorne, who let out a sudden laugh.

"All this time we thought Cinder was casting some witchy spell on the other ships and it's been *you*?"

Cinder frowned, but Cress couldn't tell who her annoyance was directed at. "I guess we owe you a huge thanks."

Cress's shoulders jerked into an uncomfortable shrug. "It wasn't that difficult. Finding you was the hardest part, but anyone could have figured it out. And sneaking ships around the galaxy is something Lunars have been doing for years."

"I have a price on my head large enough to buy the Province of Japan," said Cinder. "If anyone could have figured it out, they would have by now. So, really, thank you."

A blush crept down her neck.

Thorne jabbed Cinder in the arm. "Soften her up with flattery. Good strategy."

Cinder rolled her eyes. "Look. The reason we're contacting you is because we need your help. Evidently more than I realized."

"*Yes*," Cress said emphatically, unwrapping the hair from her wrists. "Yes. Whatever you need."

Thorne beamed. "See? Why can't you all be this agreeable?"

The second girl smacked him on the shoulder. "She doesn't even know what we want her to do yet." Cress really looked at her for the first time. She had curly red hair, a collection of freckles over her nose, and curves that were unfairly exaggerated next to Cinder, who was all angles in comparison. The man beside her dwarfed them both and had brown hair that stuck up in every direction, faded scars that hinted at more than his share of scuffles, and a recent bruise on his jaw.

Cress tried her best to look confident. "What do you need help with?"

"When I talked to you before, on the day of the ball, you told me that you've been spying on Earth's leaders and reporting back to Queen Levana. And you also knew that once Levana became empress, she planned on having Kai assassinated so she could have total control of the Commonwealth and use that power to launch a full-scale attack on the other Earthen countries."

Cress nodded, perhaps too vigorously.

"Well, we need the people of Earth to know what lengths she's willing to go to in order to stake claim to Earth, not just the

Commonwealth. If the other leaders knew that she's been spying on them all this time, and that she has every intention of invading their countries the first chance she gets, there's no way they would condone this wedding. They wouldn't accept her as a world leader, the wedding would be canceled, and...with any luck, that'll give us a chance to...er. Well, the ultimate goal is to dethrone her entirely."

Cress licked her lips. "So...what do you want me to do?"

"Evidence. I need evidence of what Levana's planning, of what's she's been doing."

Pondering, Cress sank back in her chair. "I have copies of all the video surveillance from over the years. It would be easy to pull up some of the most incriminating vids and send them to you over this link."

"That's perfect!"

"It's circumstantial, though. It would only prove that Levana is interested in what the other leaders are doing, not necessarily that she plans on invading them, and I don't think I have any documentation about her wanting to murder His Majesty, either. It's largely my own suspicions, and speculation on the things my mistress has said."

"That's fine, we'll take whatever you have. Levana already attacked us once. I don't think Earthens will take much convincing that she would do it again."

Cress nodded, but her enthusiasm had waned. She cleared her throat. "My mistress will recognize the footage. She'll know it was me who gave it to you."

Cinder's smile began to fade, and Cress knew she didn't need to clarify her point. She would be killed for her betrayal.

"I'm sorry," said Cinder. "If there was any way for us to get you away from her, we would, but we can't risk coming to Luna. Getting through port security—"

"I'm not on Luna!" The words tumbled out of Cress, coaxed on by a twist of hope. "You don't have to come to Luna. I'm not there."

Cinder scanned the room behind Cress. "But you said before that you couldn't contact Earth, so you're not…"

"I'm on a satellite. I can give you my coordinates, and I checked weeks ago if your Rampion has compatible docking gear and it does, or at least the podships that come standard with it do. You…you still have the podships, right?"

"You're on a satellite?" said Thorne.

"Yes. Set to a sixteen-hour polar orbit around Earth."

"How long have you been living in a satellite?"

She twisted her hair around her fingers. "Seven years… or so."

"Seven *years*? By yourself?"

"Y-yes." She shrugged. "Mistress restocks my food and water and I have net access, so it isn't so bad, but…well…"

"But you're a prisoner," said Thorne.

"I prefer damsel in distress," she murmured.

One side of Thorne's mouth quirked up, into that perfect half smile he'd had in his graduation photo. A look that was a little bit devious, and all sorts of charming.

Cress's heart stopped, but if they noticed her melting into her chair, they didn't say anything.

The red-haired girl leaned back, removing herself from the frame, though Cress could still hear her. "It's not like we can do anything that will make Levana want to find us even more than she already does."

"Plus," said Cinder, exchanging looks with her companions, "do we really want to leave someone in Levana's care who knows how to track our ship?"

Cress's fingers began to tingle where her hair was cutting off circulation, but she hardly noticed.

Thorne tilted his head and peered at her through the screen. "All right, damsel. Send over those coordinates."

Six

"MOVING ON TO THE DINNER SERVICE. HER LUNAR MAJESTY did approve the traditional eight-course feast following the ceremony since last we spoke. For that, I suggest we begin with a quartet of sashimi, followed by a light soup. Perhaps imitation shark's fin soup, which I think would strike a nice balance between old traditions and modern sensibilities." The wedding planner paused. When neither Kai, who was laid out on his office's sofa with one arm draped across his eyes, nor his chief adviser, Konn Torin, offered any objections, she cleared her throat and continued, "For our third course, I thought a nice braised pork belly with green mango relish. That would then lead into our vegetarian entrée, for which I recommended *potol* with poppy seeds on a bed of banana leaves. For the fifth course I was going to talk to the caterers about some sort of shellfish curry, maybe with a vibrant coconut-lime sauce. Does Your Majesty have any preference on lobster, prawns, or scallops?"

Kai peeled his arm off his face, just enough to peer at the wedding coordinator through his fingers. Tashmi Priya must have been well into her forties, and yet she had the sort of skin that hadn't aged a day past twenty-nine. Her hair, on the other hand, was making a slow transition into gray, and he thought it might have accelerated over the past week, as she was the one person in charge of communicating the bride's wishes to the rest of the wedding coordinators. He didn't for a moment underestimate the stress she was under to be working with Queen Levana.

Luckily, it seemed to him that she was very, very good at her job. She'd accepted the role of planning the royal wedding without a moment's hesitation, and hadn't balked once at Levana's demands. Her professional perfectionism was evident in every decision she made, even in how she presented herself, with deceptively subtle makeup and not a hair astray. This simplicity was set against a wardrobe of traditional Indian saris, lush silk shot through with jewel tones and complicated embroidery. The combination gave Priya a regal air that Kai knew, at that moment, *he* was lacking.

"Scallops, lobster . . . ," he murmured, struggling to pay attention. Giving up, he covered his eyes again. "No, I have no preference. Whatever Levana wants."

A brief silence before he heard the click of fingernails against her portscreen. "Perhaps we'll come back to the feast menu later. As for the ceremony, do you approve of the queen's choice of Africa's Prime Minister Kamin as your officiant?"

"I can think of no one more suitable."

"Excellent. And have you given any thought to your wedding vows?"

Kai snorted. "Delete anything that has to do with love, respect, or joy, and I'll sign on the dotted line."

"Your Majesty," said Torin, in that way he had of making the title of respect sound like a chastisement.

Sighing, Kai sat up. Torin was in the seat opposite Priya, his hand wrapped around a short glass filled with nothing but ice cubes. He was not normally one to imbibe, which reminded Kai that these were trying times for everyone.

He slid his attention back to Priya, whose expression was professionally impassive. "What do you suggest, for the vows?"

Her eyelids crinkled at the corners, almost apologetically, and he detected something horrible about to come his way. "Her Lunar Majesty has suggested that you write your own vows, Your Majesty."

"Oh, stars." He fell back down into the cushions. "Please, anything but that."

A hesitation. "Would you like me to write them for you, Your Majesty?"

"Is that in your job description?"

"Ensuring that this wedding goes smoothly *is* my job description."

He peered up at the ornate tasseled chandeliers that lined the ceiling. After a complete sweep of the office that had taken his security team a week to complete, they had found a single recording device, smaller than his fingernail, embedded in one of those chandeliers. It was the only device they had found. There was no question that it was Lunar, and that Kai had been right all along—Levana was spying on him.

His personal quarters had also been swept, though nothing had been discovered there. To date, these were the only rooms where he allowed himself to speak freely about his betrothed, though there was always a warning hum in his head. He really hoped the security detail hadn't missed anything.

"Thank you, Tashmi-jiě. I'll think on it."

With a nod, Priya stood. "I have an appointment with the caterer this afternoon. I'll see if he has any input on the remaining courses."

Kai forced himself to stand, though the action was surprisingly difficult. The stress of the past weeks had caused him to lose a few pounds, and yet he felt heavier than ever, as if the weight of every person in the Commonwealth were pressing down on him.

"Thank you for everything," he said, bowing while she gathered her color swatches and fabric samples.

She returned his bow. "We will speak again in the morning, before Thaumaturge Park's arrival."

He groaned. "Is that tomorrow already?"

Torin cleared his throat.

"I mean—fantastic! He was such a joy to have around the first time."

Priya's smile was fleeting as she slipped out the door.

Restraining a melodramatic sigh, Kai crumpled back onto the sofa. He knew he was being childish, but he felt he had the right to lash out occasionally, especially here in the privacy of his own office. Everywhere else he was expected to smile and proclaim how much he was looking forward to the wedding. How beneficial this alliance would be for the Commonwealth. How he had no doubt that his marriage to Queen Levana would serve to unite the people of Earth and Luna in a way that hadn't been seen for centuries and would no doubt lead to greater appreciation and understanding of each other's cultures. It was the first step toward doing away with years of hatred and ignorance and who on Earth did he think he was fooling, anyway?

He hated Levana. He hated himself for giving in to her. He hated that his father had managed to keep her and her threats of war at bay for years and years, and within *weeks* of Kai taking the throne, he'd let everything fall apart.

He hated that Queen Levana had probably been planning

this from the moment it was announced that Emperor Rikan, Kai's father, was ill, and that Kai had played right into her hands.

He hated that she was going to win.

The ice in Torin's glass clacked and popped as he leaned forward. "You look pale, Your Majesty. Is there anything I can assist you with? Anything you would like to discuss?"

Kai pushed his bangs off his forehead. "Be honest, Torin. Do you think I'm making a mistake?"

Torin considered the question for a long moment, before setting the glass aside. "Sixteen thousand Earthens were killed when Luna attacked us. Sixteen thousand deaths in only a few hours. That was eleven days ago. I cannot fathom how many lives were spared because of the compromise you made with Queen Levana." He steepled his fingers over his lap. "And we cannot forget how many lives will be saved once we have access to her letumosis antidote."

Kai bit the inside of his cheek. These were the same arguments he'd been repeating to himself. He was doing the right thing. He was saving lives. He was protecting his people.

"I know the sacrifice you're making, Your Majesty."

"Do you?" His shoulders tensed. "Because I suspect she's going to try to kill me. Once she has what she wants. Once she's been coronated."

Torin inhaled sharply, but Kai got the impression that this wasn't news to Torin after all. "We won't let that happen."

"Can we stop it?"

"Your wedding will not be a death sentence. We have time to figure out a way. She . . . still wants an heir, after all."

Kai couldn't stifle a grimace. "Very, very small consolation."

"I know. But that makes you valuable to her, at least for the time being."

"Does it? You know the reputation Lunars have. I'm not sure Levana cares one bit who fathers a child, as long as someone does. And wasn't Princess Selene born without anyone knowing who her father was? I'm really not convinced Levana needs me for anything other than saying 'I do' and handing her a crown."

Much as he hated to admit it, the thought was almost a relief.

Torin didn't try to argue against him. He just shook his head. "But the Commonwealth does need you, and they will need you that much more once Levana becomes empress. Your Majesty, I won't let anything happen to you."

Kai recognized an almost fatherly tone. There was affection there, where normally there was only patience and veiled frustration. In some ways, he felt like Torin had become the true emperor once his father had passed away. Torin was the solid one, the decisive one, the one who always knew what was best for the country. But looking at his adviser now, that impression began to shift. Because Torin had a look that Kai had never seen directed toward himself before. Respect, maybe. Or admiration. Or even trust.

He sat up a little straighter. "You're right. The decision has been made and now I have to make the best of it. Waiting to be trampled under Levana's whims won't help anything. I have to figure out how to defend myself against her."

Torin nodded, just shy of a smile. "We will think of something."

For a moment, Kai felt peculiarly bolstered. Torin was not an optimist by nature. If he believed there was a way, then Kai would believe it too. A way to stay alive, a way to protect his country even after he'd cursed them all with a tyrant for an empress. A way to protect himself from a woman who could control his thoughts with a bat of her lashes.

Even as her husband, he would continue to defy Levana for as long as he could.

Nainsi, Kai's android assistant, appeared in the office doorway, holding a tray with jasmine tea and hot washcloths. Her sensor light flashed. "Daily reports, Your Majesty?"

"Yes, thank you. Come in."

He took one of the washcloths off the tray as she rolled by, chafing his fingers with the steaming cotton.

Nainsi set the tray on Kai's desk and turned to face him and Torin, launching into the day's reports that blissfully had nothing to do with wedding vows or eight-course dinners.

"Lunar Thaumaturge Aimery Park is scheduled to arrive tomorrow at 15:00, along with fourteen members of the Lunar Court. A list of guest names and titles has been transferred to your portscreen. A welcome dinner will commence at 19:00, to be followed by evening cocktails. Tashmi Priya will be in attendance at both the dinner and cocktail reception to begin communicating wedding plans to Thaumaturge Park. We've extended an invitation for Her Lunar Majesty to join us via netscreen conferencing, but our offer was not accepted."

"How disappointing," Kai drawled.

"We are expecting a resurgence of protestors outside the palace with the arrival of the Lunar court, which will likely continue through the date of the wedding ceremony. We have arranged for military reinforcements, beginning tomorrow morning, to ensure the security of our guests. I will alert you should any protests become violent."

Kai stopped cleaning his hands. "Are we expecting them to be violent?"

"Negative, Your Majesty. The head of palace security has stated this is only a precaution."

"Fine. Go on."

"The weekly letumosis report estimates thirty thousand plague-related deaths during the week of 3 September throughout the Commonwealth. The palace research team did not have any progress to report on their ongoing search for an antidote."

Kai traded withering looks with Torin. *Thirty thousand deaths.* It almost made him wish the wedding were tomorrow, so he could get his hands on Levana's antidote that much sooner.

Almost.

"We have received word that the American Republic, Australia, and the European Federation have all instituted manhunts for the Lunar soldiers responsible for the attacks, and claim to be holding multiple suspects as prisoners of war. So far, Luna has not threatened retaliation or made any attempt to bargain for their freedom, other than the previously made agreement that all soldiers will be removed from Earthen soil following the coronation ceremony on the twenty-fifth."

"Let's hope it stays that way," Kai muttered. "The last thing this alliance needs are more political complications."

"I will keep you posted on any developments, Your Majesty. The last item to report is that we've received word from Samhain Bristol, parliament representative from Toronto, East Canada Province, United Kingdom, that he has declined his invitation to attend the wedding ceremony, on behalf of his refusal to accept Lunar Queen Levana as a suitable world leader within the Earthen Union."

Torin groaned, as Kai rolled his eyes toward the ceiling. "Oh, for all the stars. Does he think *anyone* feels like she would be a suitable leader?"

"We can't blame him for this position, Your Majesty," said Torin, though Kai could hear the irritation in his tone, "or for wanting to make this statement. He has his own people to be concerned with."

"I'm aware of that, but if this starts a trend among the Union leaders, Levana will be livid. Can you imagine her response if *no one* shows up for the wedding?" Kai dragged the now-cool washcloth down his face. "She'll see this as a personal offense. If we're trying to avoid another attack, I don't think angering her is the way to do it."

"I agree," said Torin, standing and adjusting his suit jacket. "I will schedule a comm with Bristol-dàren and see if we can't come to a compromise. I suggest we keep this information close for the time being, as to avoid giving our other invited guests any wayward ideas."

"Thank you, Torin." Kai stood and matched Torin's bow, before his adviser slipped out of the office.

Kai barely resisted the urge to collapse back on the sofa. He had another meeting in thirty minutes, and there were still plans to review and reports to read and comms to respond to and—

"Your Majesty."

He started. "Yes, Nainsi?"

"There was one additional report that I thought might be best to discuss with you in private."

He blinked. There were very few subjects that he didn't discuss with Torin. "What is it?"

"An association was recently discovered by my intelligence-synapses. It involves Linh Cinder."

His stomach dropped. It would be that topic—that one topic that he couldn't talk to even his most trusted adviser about. Every time he heard her name, he was filled with barely constrained panic, certain that Cinder had been found. She had been taken into custody. She had already been killed. Even though he should have been glad that his country's most-wanted fugitive had been captured, the thought made him ill.

"What about her?" he said, tossing the washcloth back onto the tray and perching on the arm of the sofa.

"I may have deduced the reason that she was in Rieux, France."

The tirade of worried thoughts evaporated as quickly as they had come. Sensing a headache, Kai massaged the spot above his nose, relieved that one more hour had come and gone and Cinder was still missing. Which meant she was still safe.

"Rieux, France," he said, reorienting himself. Everyone had known that the ship Cinder was on would need to return to Earth eventually, for fuel and possible maintenance. Her choice of a small town—*any* small town—had never struck him as suspicious. "Go on."

"When Linh Cinder removed the D-COMM chip that had temporarily shut down my programming, I transmitted information to her about Michelle Benoit."

"The pilot?" Kai had practically memorized the information Nainsi had gathered regarding everyone who had even the most tenuous connection to the missing Princess Selene. Michelle Benoit had been one of their top suspects for someone who had possibly helped to hide the princess.

"Yes, Your Majesty. Linh Cinder would have known her name and her previous affiliation with the European military."

"So?"

"After retiring, Michelle Benoit purchased a farm. That farm is located near Rieux, France, and it was on that property where the stolen ship first landed."

"So Cinder went there because . . . do you think she was looking for Princess Selene?"

"That is my assumption, Your Majesty."

He jumped to his feet and began pacing. "Has anyone spoken to Michelle Benoit? Has she been questioned? Did she see Cinder, talk to her?"

"I am sorry, Your Majesty, but Michelle Benoit disappeared over four weeks ago."

He stalled. "Disappeared?"

"Her granddaughter, Scarlet Benoit, has gone missing as well. We know only that she boarded a maglev train in Toulouse, France, en route for Paris."

"Can't we track them?"

"Michelle Benoit's ID chip was found in her home the day she went missing. Scarlet Benoit's ID chip, it appears, has been destroyed."

Kai slumped. Another dead-end.

"But why would Cinder go there? Why would she care about finding Princess . . ." He hesitated. "Unless she's trying to help me."

"I cannot follow your reasoning, Your Majesty."

He faced Nainsi again. "Maybe she's trying to help me. Cinder knows that if she finds the princess, it could be the end of Levana's rule. I wouldn't have to marry her. She would probably be executed for treason. Cinder risked her life going to that farm, and she did it . . . she may have done it for me."

He could hear Nainsi's fan whirring, before she said, "I might suggest the alternate explanation that Linh Cinder's motives stem from Queen Levana's desire to have her found and executed, Your Majesty."

Face flushing, he dropped his gaze to the hand-woven rug beneath his feet. "Right. Or that."

But he couldn't shake the feeling that Cinder's new objective was about more than self-preservation. After all, she'd come to the ball to warn him against marrying Queen Levana, and that decision had nearly gotten her killed.

"Do you think she found anything? About the princess?"

"I have no way of discerning that information."

He paced around his desk, staring thoughtfully at the vast city beyond his office window, glass and steel glinting in the afternoon sunlight. "Find out everything you can about this Michelle Benoit. Maybe Cinder is onto something. Maybe Princess Selene is still out there."

Hope fluttered again, brightening with every moment. His search for the princess had been abandoned weeks ago, when his life had become too tumultuous to focus on anything other than keeping war at bay. Pacifying Queen Levana and her temper. Preparing himself for a life at her side, as her husband . . . and that, only if he was lucky enough not to be murdered before their first anniversary.

He'd been so distracted that he'd forgotten the reason he'd been searching for Princess Selene in the first place.

If she was alive, she would be the rightful heir to the Lunar throne. She could end Levana's reign.

She could save them all.

Seven

DR. DMITRI ERLAND PERCHED ON THE EDGE OF HIS HOTEL BED, with the worn cotton quilt pooling around his ankles. All his attention was on the battered netscreen on the wall, the one where the sound cut out randomly and the picture liked to tremble and flicker at inopportune moments. Unlike the last time a Lunar representative had come to Earth, this time the arrival was being internationally broadcast. This time, there was no hiding the purpose of the visit.

Her Majesty, the Queen, had gotten what she wanted. She was going to become empress.

Though Queen Levana herself would not be arriving until closer to the ceremony date, Thaumaturge Aimery Park, as one of her closest lackeys—er, *advisers*—was coming early as a show of "goodwill" to the people of the Commonwealth and planet Earth. That, and to ensure all wedding arrangements were being made to suit Her Majesty's preferences, no doubt.

The shimmering white spaceship with its decorative runes had landed on the launchpad of New Beijing Palace fifteen minutes ago, and still showed no sign of opening. A journalist from the African Union was droning on and on in the background about trivial wedding and coronation details—how many diamonds were in the empress's crown, the length of the aisle, the number of expected guests, and of course, yet another mention that Prime Minister Kamin herself had been selected as the ceremony's officiant.

He was glad for one thing to result from this engagement, at least. All this ballyhoo had taken the media's attention off Miss Cinder. He'd hoped that she would have had the sense to take this serendipitous distraction and come find him, *quickly*, but that had not yet happened. He was growing impatient and more than a little worried for the girl, but there was nothing he could do but wait patiently in this forsaken desert and continue with his research and plan for the day when all his hard work would finally come to fruition.

Growing bored of the broadcast, Dr. Erland removed his spectacles and spent a moment huffing on them and rubbing them down with his shirt.

It seemed that Earthens were quick to forget their prejudices when a royal wedding was involved, or perhaps they were simply terrified to speak openly about the Lunars and their tyranny, especially with the memory of the wolf-hybrid attacks so fresh in the collective memory. Plus, since the announcement of the royal engagement, at least two members of the worldwide media who had declared the alliance a royal mistake—a netgroup administrator from Bucharest-on-the-Sea and a newsfeed editor from Buenos Aires—had committed suicide.

Which Dr. Erland suspected was a diplomatic way of saying "murdered by Lunars, but who can prove it?"

Everyone was thinking the same thing, regardless of whether

or not they would say it. Queen Levana was a murderer and a tyrant and this wedding was going to ruin them.

But all his anger was eschewed by the knowledge that he was a hypocrite.

Levana was a murderer?

Well, he had helped her become one.

It had been years—a lifetime, it seemed—since he was one of the leading scientists on Luna's genetic engineering research team. He had spearheaded some of their greatest breakthroughs, back when Channary was still queen, before Levana took over, before his Crescent Moon was murdered, before Princess Selene was stolen away to Earth. He was the first to successfully integrate the genetics from an arctic wolf with those of a ten-year-old boy, giving him not only many of the physical abilities that they'd already perfected, but the brutal instincts of the beast as well.

Some nights he still dreamed of that boy's howls in the darkness.

Erland shivered. Pulling the blanket over his legs, he turned back to the broadcast.

Finally, the spaceship door lifted. The world watched as the ramp hit the platform.

A gaggle of Lunar nobility arose from the ship first, bedecked in vibrant silks and flowing chiffons and veiled headdresses, always with the veiled headdresses. It had become quite the trend during Queen Channary's rule, who, like her sister, refused to reveal her true face in public.

Erland found himself leaning closer toward the screen, wondering if he could identify any of his long-ago peers beneath their cloaks.

He had no luck. Too many years had passed, and there was a good chance that all those telling details he'd memorized were glamour created anyway. He, himself, had always given off the illusion of being much taller when he was surrounded by the narcissistic Lunar court.

The guards were next, followed by five third-tier thaumaturges, donning their embroidered black coats. They were all handsome without any glamours, as the queen preferred, though he suspected that few of them had been born with such natural good looks. Many of his coworkers on Luna had made lucrative side businesses offering plastic surgery, melatonin adjustments, and body reconstruction to thaumaturge and royal guard hopefuls.

In fact, he'd always been fond of the rumor that Sybil Mira's cheekbones were made out of recycled plumbing pipes.

Thaumaturge Aimery came last, looking as relaxed and smug as ever in the rich crimson jacket that so well complimented his dark skin. He approached the waiting Emperor Kaito and his convoy of advisers and chairmen, and they shared a mutually respectful bow.

Dr. Erland shook his head. Poor young Emperor Kai. He had certainly been thrown to the lions during his short reign, hadn't he?

A timid knock rattled the door, making Dr. Erland jump.

Look at him—wasting his time with Lunar processions and royal alliances that, with any luck, would never be realized. If only Linh Cinder would stop gallivanting about Earth and space and start following directions for once.

He stood and shut off the netscreen. All this worrying was going to give him an ulcer.

In the hallway was a squirrelly boy who couldn't have been more than twelve or thirteen, with dark hair cut short and uneven. His shorts hung past his knees and were frayed at the hems and his sandaled feet were coated in the fine sand that covered everything in this town.

He was holding himself too tall, like he was trying to give the impression that he wasn't at all nervous, not one little bit.

"I have a camel for sale. I heard you might be interested." His voice trembled on the last word.

Dr. Erland dropped his spectacles to the end of his nose. The boy was scrawny, sure, but he didn't appear malnourished. His dark skin looked healthy, his eyes bright and alert. Another year or so, and Erland suspected he'd be the taller of the two of them.

"One hump or two?" he asked.

"Two." The boy took in a deep breath. "And it never spits."

Erland tilted his head. He had had to be careful about who he told this code language to, but news seemed to be spreading quickly, even into neighboring oasis towns. It was becoming common knowledge that the crazy old doctor was looking for Lunars who would be willing to help him with some experimentation, and that he could pay them for their assistance.

Of course, the spreading knowledge of his semi-celebrity status, complete with Commonwealth want ads, hadn't hurt either. He thought many people who came to knock on his door were merely curious about the Lunar who had infiltrated the staff of a real Earthen palace...and who had helped the true celebrity, Linh Cinder, escape from prison.

He would have preferred anonymity, but this did seem to be an effective method for gathering new test subjects, which he needed if he was ever going to copy the letumosis antidote the Lunar scientists had discovered.

"Come in," he said, stepping back into the room. Without waiting to see if the boy followed, he opened the closet that he had transformed into his own mini laboratory. Vials, test tubes, petri dishes, syringes, scanners, an assortment of chemicals, all neatly labeled.

"I can't pay you in univs," he said, pulling on a pair of latex gloves. "Barter only. What do you need? Food, water, clothing, or if you're willing to wait on payment for six consecutive samples, I can arrange one-way transportation into Europe, no documentation required." He opened a drawer and removed a needle from the sterilizing fluid.

"What about medication?"

He glanced back. The boy had barely taken two steps into the room.

"Shut the door, before you let in all the flies," he said. The boy did as he was told, but his focus was now caught on the needle. "Why do you want medicine? Are you sick?"

"For my brother."

"Also Lunar?"

The boy's eyes widened. They always did when Dr. Erland threw out the word so casually, but he never understood why. He only asked for Lunars. Only Lunars ever knocked on his door.

"Stop looking so skittish," Dr. Erland grumbled. "You must know that I'm Lunar too." He did a quick glamour to prove himself, an easy manipulation so that the boy perceived him as a younger version of himself, but only for an instant.

Though he'd been tampering with bioelectricity more freely since he'd arrived in Africa, he found that it drained him more and more. His mind simply wasn't as strong as it used to be, and it had been years since he'd had any consistent practice.

Nevertheless, the glamour did its job. The boy's stance relaxed, now that he was somewhat sure that Dr. Erland wouldn't have him and his family sent to the moon for execution.

He still didn't come any closer, though.

"Yes," he said. "My brother is Lunar too. But he's a shell."

This time, it was Erland's eyes that widened.

A shell.

Now that had true value. Though many Lunars came to Earth in order to protect their non-gifted children, tracking those children down had proven more difficult than Erland had expected. They blended in too well with Earthens, and they had no desire to give up their disguise. He wondered if half of them were even aware of their own ancestry.

"How old?" he said, setting the syringe down on the counter. "I would pay double for a sample from him."

At Erland's sudden eagerness, the boy took a step back. "Seven," he said. "But he's sick."

"With what? I have pain killers, blood thinners, antibiotics—"

"He has the plague, sir. Do you have medicine for that?"

Dr. Erland frowned. "Letumosis? No, no. That isn't possible. Tell me his symptoms. We'll figure out what he really has."

The boy looked annoyed at being told he was wrong, but not without a tinge of hope. "Yesterday afternoon he started getting a bad rash, with bruises all over his arms, like he'd been in a brawl. Except he hadn't. When he woke up this morning he was hot to the touch, but he kept saying he was freezing, even in this heat. When our mother checked, the skin under his fingernails had gone bluish, just like the plague."

Erland held up a hand. "You say he got the spots yesterday, and his fingers were already turning blue this morning?"

The boy nodded. "Also, right before I came here, all those spots were blistering up, like blood blisters." He cringed.

Alarm stirred inside the doctor as his mind searched for an

explanation. The first symptoms did sound like letumosis, but he'd never heard of it moving through its four stages so quickly. And the rash becoming blood blisters . . . he'd never seen that before.

He didn't want to think of the possibility, and yet it was also something he'd been waiting for years to happen. Something he'd been expecting. Something he'd been dreading.

If what this boy said was true, if his brother did have letumosis, then it could mean that the disease was mutating.

And if even a Lunar was showing symptoms . . .

Erland grabbed his hat off the desk and pulled it on over his balding head. "Take me to him."

Eight

CRESS HARDLY FELT THE HOT WATER BEATING ON HER HEAD.
Outside her washroom, a second-era opera blared from every screen. With the woman's powerful voice in her ears, swooning over the incessant shower, Cress *was* the star, the damsel, the center of that universe. She sang along at full volume, pausing only to prepare herself for the crescendo.

She didn't have the full translation memorized, but the emotions behind the words were clear.

Heartbreak. Tragedy. Love.

Chills covered her skin, sharply contrasted against the steam. She pressed a hand to her chest, drowning.

Pain. Loneliness. *Love.*

It always came back to love. More than freedom, more than acceptance—*love.* True love, like they sang about in the second era. The kind that filled up a person's soul. The kind that lent itself to dramatic gestures and sacrifices. The kind that was irresistible and all-encompassing.

The woman's voice rose in intensity with the violins and cellos, a climax sung up into the shower's downpour. Cress held the note as long as she could, enjoying the way the song rolled over her, filling her with its power.

She ran out of breath first, suddenly dizzy. Panting, she fell against the shower wall.

The crescendo died down into a simple, longing finale, just as the water sputtered out. All of Cress's showers were timed, to ensure her water reserves wouldn't run out before Mistress Sybil's next supply visit.

Cress sank down and wrapped her arms around her knees. Realizing there were tears on her cheeks, she covered her face and laughed.

She was being ridiculously melodramatic, but it was well deserved.

Because today was the day. She'd been following the Rampion's path closely since they'd agreed to rescue her nearly fourteen hours before, and they had not deviated from their course. The Rampion would be crossing through her satellite's trajectory in approximately one Earthen hour and fifteen minutes.

She would have freedom, and friendships, and purpose. And she would be with *him*.

In the next room, the operatic solo began again, quiet and slow and tinged with longing.

"Thank you," Cress whispered to the imaginary audience that was going mad with applause. She imagined lifting a bouquet of red roses and smelling them, even though she had no idea what roses smelled like.

With that thought, the fantasy disintegrated.

Sighing, she picked herself off the shower floor before the tips of her hair could get sucked down the drain.

Her hair weighed heavy on her scalp. It was easy to ignore when she was caught up in such a powerful solo, but now the weight of it threatened to make her topple over, and a dull headache was already creeping up from the base of her skull.

This was not the day for headaches.

She held up the ends of her hair with one hand, taking some pressure off her head, and spent a few minutes ringing it out, handful by soaking handful. Emerging from the shower, she grabbed her towel, a ratty gray thing she'd had for years, worn to holes in the corners.

"Volume, down!" she yelled out to the main room. The opera faded into the background. A few last droplets from the shower-head dribbled onto the floor.

Cress heard a chime.

She pulled her hair through her fists again, gathering another handful of water and shaking it out in the shower before wrapping herself in the towel. The weight of her hair still tugged at her, but was feeling manageable again.

In the main room, all but the single D-COMM screen were showing the theater footage. The shot was a close-up of the woman's face, thick with makeup and penciled eyebrows, a lion's mane of fire-red hair topped with a gold crown.

The D-COMM screen held a new message.

FROM USER: MECHANIC. ETA 68 MINUTES.

Cress was buoyed by giddiness. It was happening. They were really coming to rescue her.

She dropped the towel to the floor and grabbed the wrinkled dress she'd been wearing before—the dress that was a little too small and a little too short because Sybil had brought it for Cress when she was only thirteen, but that was worn to the perfect softness. It was Cress's favorite dress, not that it had a lot of competition.

She pulled it over her head, then rushed back into the

bathroom to begin the long process of combing out her wet tangles. She wanted to look presentable, after all.

No, she wanted to look *irresistible*, but there was no use dwelling on that. She had no makeup, no jewelry, no perfume, no properly fitting clothes, and only the most basic essentials for daily hygiene. She was as pale as the moon and her hair would dry frizzy no matter how she coddled it. After a moment of staring at herself in the mirror, she decided to braid it, her best hope for keeping it tamed.

She had just divided it into three sections at the nape of her neck when Little Cress's voice squeaked. "Big Sister?"

Cress froze. She met her own wide-eyed gaze in the mirror. "Yes?"

"Mistress's ship detected. Expected arrival in twenty-two seconds."

"No, no, no, *not today,*" she hissed.

Releasing her wet strands of hair, she rushed out into the main room. For once, her few belongings weren't strewn across the floor and tabletops, because they were all packed neatly inside a pulled-out drawer that sat on top of her bed. Dresses, socks, and undergarments neatly folded alongside hair combs and barrettes and what food packs she still had from Sybil's last visit. She'd even nestled her favorite pillow and blanket on top.

All evidence that she was running away.

"Oh stars." She swept forward and grabbed the drawer with both hands, pulling it off the bed. She tore out the blanket and pillow and tossed them onto the mattress, before dragging the heavy drawer over to the desk she'd taken it from.

00:14, 00:13, 00:12, sang Little Cress as she wrestled the drawer back into place. It wouldn't shut.

Cress squatted beside it, eyeing the rails to either side of the drawer. It took seven more seconds of harried finagling before she managed to slam the drawer shut. Sweat, or water from her still-wet hair, dripped down the back of her neck.

Tugging out a lock of hair that had gotten caught in the drawer, she hastily straightened the bed as well as she could.

"Mistress has arrived. She is requesting an extension of the docking clamp."

"I'm getting there," Cress responded, darting toward the boarding ramp screen and entering the code. She turned back to the room as the clamp extended outside her walls, as Sybil's ship attached, as oxygen filled the space.

The opera singer was still there, and Mistress would be annoyed at Cress's waste of time, but at least it wasn't—

She gasped, her eyes landing on the one screen that stood out from the rest, and the single bright green message on a field of black.

FROM USER: MECHANIC. ETA 68 MINUTES.

She heard Sybil's steps approaching as she launched herself across the room. She shut down the screen just as the satellite door whistled open.

Heart in her throat, Cress spun around and smiled.

Sybil met her gaze from the doorway. She was already glaring, but Cress thought her eyes narrowed even more in that moment between seeing Cress and noting her brilliant grin.

"Mistress! What a surprise. I just got out of the shower. Was just...listening to some...opera." She gulped, her mouth suddenly dry.

Sybil's eyes darkened and she cast them around the room, at

the screens still quietly transmitting the opera singer engrossed in her song. Sybil sneered. "*Earthen* music."

Cress chewed on her lower lip. She knew there were musicians and plays and all sorts of entertainments for the Lunar court, but they were rarely recorded, and Cress didn't have access to them. Lunars generally disliked having their true appearances transmitted for all the galaxy to see. They much preferred live performances where they could alter the audience's perception of their skills.

"All screens, mute," she murmured, trying to stop shaking.

In the wake of silence, Sybil stepped inside, allowing the door to shut behind her.

Cress gestured to the familiar metal box Sybil carried. "I don't believe I'm in need of any supplies, Mistress. Is it time for another blood sample already?" she asked, knowing it wasn't.

Sybil set the box on the bed, sparing a distasteful glance for the rumpled blankets. "I have a new assignment for you, Crescent. I trust you noticed that one of our primary feeds from New Beijing Palace was disabled last week."

Cress willed herself to look natural. Collected and unworried. "Yes—the recorder from the emperor's office."

"Her Majesty found it to be one of the more lucrative feeds we've placed on Earth. She wants another programmed and installed immediately." She opened the box, revealing a collection of chips and recording devices. "As before, the signal should be untraceable. We don't want it drawing any attention to itself."

Cress nodded, perhaps too enthusiastically. "Of course, Mistress. It won't take long. I can have it finished tomorrow, I'm sure. Will it be disguised in a light fixture, like the last one?"

"No, we risked too much by brainwashing the maintenance attendant before. Make it so that it can be more easily hidden. Able to embed on a wall hanging, perhaps. One of the other thaumaturges will likely handle the installation themselves during our upcoming visit."

Cress's head was still bobbing. "Yes, yes, of course. No problem."

Sybil scowled. Perhaps Cress was being too agreeable. She stopped nodding, but it was difficult to focus as a clock ticked in her head. If Cinder and the others spotted the Lunar podship attached to her satellite, they would think Cress had led them into a trap.

But Mistress Sybil never stayed long. Surely she would be well gone before the hour was up. Surely.

"Is there anything else, Mistress?"

"Have you anything to report on the other Earthen feeds?"

Cress strained to think about any news she may have heard in the past few days. Her skills in cyber espionage went beyond research and hacking into Earthen feeds and databases, or programming spy equipment to be strategically installed in various homes and offices of high-ranking officials. It was also one of her responsibilities to monitor those feeds and report anything interesting back to Sybil and Her Majesty.

It was the most voyeuristic part of her job, which she hated. But at least if Sybil was asking her about it now, it meant that she and the queen hadn't had time lately to monitor the feeds themselves.

"Everyone's focused on the wedding," Cress said. "Lots of talk of travel arrangements and scheduling diplomatic meetings while so many representatives are together in New Beijing."

She hesitated before continuing, "A lot of the Earthens are questioning Emperor Kaito's decision to enter into the alliance and whether or not it will really signal an end to the attacks. The European Federation recently placed a large order from a weapons manufacturer. It seems they're preparing for war. I . . . I could find the specifics of that order if you want."

"Don't waste your time. We know what they're capable of. Anything else?"

Cress searched her memory. She considered telling Mistress Sybil that one UK representative, a Mr. Bristol something, was trying to make a political statement by rejecting his invitation to the royal wedding, but she determined that his decision might still change. Knowing Her Majesty, she would want to set the man up as an example, and Cress didn't want to think what she would do to him. Or his family.

"No, Mistress. That's all."

"And what about the cyborg? Any progress there?"

She had told the lie so many times, it was effortless on her tongue. "I'm sorry, Mistress. I haven't found anything new."

"Do you suppose, Crescent, that her ability to go without detection is due to a similar technique we use to disguise our ships?"

Cress pulled her damp hair away from her neck. "Perhaps. I understand she's a talented mechanic. Her skills may include software jamming."

"And if that's the case, would *you* be able to detect it?"

Cress opened her mouth, but hesitated. She most likely could, but telling Sybil that would be a mistake. She would only wonder why Cress hadn't thought of doing it sooner. "I-I don't think so, Mistress, but I'll try. I'll see what I can find."

"See that you do. I'm sick of making excuses for you."

Cress tried to look regretful, but her fingers were tingling with relief. Sybil always said some variation of this line when she was preparing to leave. "Of course, Mistress. Thank you for bringing me this new work, Mistress."

A chime sang through the room.

Cress recoiled, but instantly attempted to morph her expression into nonchalance. Just another chime. Just another non-suspicious alert for one of Cress's non-suspicious hobbies. Sybil had no reason to question it.

But Sybil's attention had swerved to the single black screen that had awoken with the alert.

A new message had appeared.

MESSAGE RECEIVED FROM MECHANIC: ETA 41
MINUTES. NEED FINAL COORDINATES.

The satellite tilted beneath Cress—but, no, it was her own balance leaving her.

"What is this?" Sybil said, nearing the screen.

"It's—it's a game. I've been playing it with the computer." Her voice squeaked. Her face was warming, cooled only where her damp hair clung to her cheeks.

There was a long silence.

Cress tried to feign indifference. "Just a silly game, imagining the computer is a real person . . . you know how my imagination can be, when I get lonely. Sometimes it's nice to have someone to talk to, even if they're not—"

Sybil grabbed Cress's jaw, shoving her against a window that overlooked the blue planet.

"Is it her?" Sybil hissed. "Have you been lying to me?"

Cress couldn't speak, her tongue heavy with terror, as if she were pinned by a glamour. But this was not magic. This was only a woman strong enough and angry enough to tear Cress's arms from their sockets, to break her skull against the corner of the desk.

"You had better not even think to lie to me, Crescent. How long have you been communicating with her?"

Her lips trembled. "S-since yesterday," she half sobbed. "I was trying to earn her trust. I thought if I could get close enough, I could tell you and—"

A slap sent the world spinning and Cress hit the floor. Her cheek burned and her brain took a moment to stop rattling inside her skull.

"You hoped she was going to *rescue* you," said Sybil.

"No. No, Mistress."

"After all I've done for you. Saved your life when your parents meant to have you slaughtered."

"I know, Mistress. I was going to bring her to you, Mistress. I was trying to help."

"I even allowed you net access to watch those disgusting Earthen feeds, and this is how you repay me?" Sybil eyed the screen, where the message still lingered. "But at least you've finally done something useful."

Cress shuddered. Her brain began to cloud with the instinctual need to run, to escape. She shoved herself off the floor, but tripped on her hair and landed hard against the closed doors. Her fingers sought out the keypad, punching in the command. The doors zipped open. She did not wait to see Sybil's reaction. "Close door!"

Cress flew down the corridor, lungs burning. She couldn't breathe. She was hyperventilating. She had to get out.

Another door loomed before her, an identical switch beside it. She barreled into it. "Open!"

It did.

She stumbled forward and her abdomen smacked into a railing. She grunted from the collision, bracing herself before she could topple over it and straight into the cockpit.

She stood, panting and staring wide-eyed at the interior of a small podship. Lights and flashing panels and screens glowed all around her. The windows formed a wall of glass separating her from a sea of stars.

And there was a man.

His hair was the color of golden straw and his body strong and broad in his royal uniform. He looked like he could be threatening, but at that moment he seemed only astonished.

He raised himself from the pilot seat. They gawked at each other as Cress struggled to find words amid her tumbling thoughts.

Sybil did not come alone. Sybil had a pilot that brought her here.

Another human being knew that Cress existed.

No—another Lunar knew that Cress existed.

"Help me," she tried to whisper, gulping when the words couldn't form. "Please. Please help me."

He shut his mouth. Cress's hands twitched on the bar. "Please?" Her voice broke.

The man flexed his fingers and she thought—was it only her imagination?—his eyes seemed to soften. To sympathize.

Or to calculate.

His hand shifted toward the controls. The command to shut the door? To disengage from the satellite? To fly her far away from this prison?

"I don't suppose you killed her?" he said.

The words seemed like they came from a different language altogether. He said them emotionlessly—a simple question. Expecting a simple answer.

Killed her? *Killed her?*

Before she could form a response, the guard's eyes sped past her.

Sybil grabbed a fistful of Cress's hair and yanked her back toward the corridor. Cress screamed and collapsed onto the ground.

"Jacin, we are about to have company," said Sybil, ignoring Cress's sobs. "Separate yourself from this satellite, but stay close enough to have good visual without drawing suspicion. When an Earthen ship draws close, they will likely release one podship—wait until the pilot has boarded this satellite and then rejoin us using the opposite entry hatch. I will ensure the clamp is pre-extended."

Cress trembled, nonsense words falling from her in hopeless pleas.

The man's sympathy and astonishment were gone, vanished as if they'd never been there. Perhaps they never had.

He jerked his head in a nod. No question. No thought to disobey.

Though Cress screamed and kicked, Sybil managed to drag her all the way back to the satellite's main room, tossing her like a bag of broken android parts on the floor.

The door shut behind them, dividing her from the exit, from her freedom, and with its familiar clang she knew.

She would never be free. Sybil was going to kill her, as she was going to kill Linh Cinder and Carswell Thorne.

When Cress pushed back her mess of hair, a sob shook her to the bones.

Sybil was smiling.

"I suppose I should thank you. Linh Cinder is going to come to me, and our queen will be so pleased." Bending down, Sybil grasped Cress's chin in a claw-like grip. "Unfortunately, I don't think you'll survive long enough to receive your reward."

Nine

CINDER GROANED, THE IMPACT OF HER MOST RECENT LANDING still reverberating through her spine. The cargo bay's ceiling spun and wobbled in her vision. "Was that necessary?"

Wolf and Scarlet appeared above her.

"I'm sorry," said Wolf. "I thought you had control. Are you all right?"

"Frustrated and sore, but, yes, I'm fine." She forced herself to take Wolf's outstretched hand. He and Scarlet both helped her to her feet. "You're right. I lost focus. I felt your energy snap out of my hold, like a rubber band." That was moments before Wolf completed the maneuver she'd managed to halt for six whole seconds— grasping her arm and tossing her over his shoulder. She rubbed her hip. "I need a moment."

"Maybe you should call it quits for the day," said Scarlet. "We're almost to the satellite."

Iko chimed in. "Estimated time of arrival is nine minutes, thirty-four seconds. Which, by my estimation, is enough time for Cinder to be defeated and embarrassed in seven more brawls."

Cinder glared up at the ceiling. "Also just enough time to disconnect your audio device."

"Since we have a few minutes," said Scarlet, "maybe we should talk about how to handle this girl. If she's been stuck on a satellite for seven years, with no one to talk to but a Lunar thaumaturge, she might be . . . socially awkward. I think we should all make an effort to be extra welcoming and supportive and . . . try not to terrify her."

A laugh came from the cockpit and Thorne appeared in the doorway, strapping a gun holster around his waist. "You're asking the cyborg fugitive and the wild animal to be the welcoming committee? That's adorable."

Scarlet planted her hands on her hips. "I'm saying we should be aware of what she's been through and try to be sensitive to that. This may not be an easy transition for her."

Thorne shrugged. "The Rampion is going to be like a five-star hotel after living on that satellite. She'll adjust."

"I'll be nice to her!" said Iko. "I can take her net-shopping and she can help me pick out my future designer wardrobe. Look, I found this custom escort shop that has the best accessories, and some discounted models. What would you think of me with orange hair?" The netscreen on the wall switched to an escort-droid sale listing. The image of a model was slowly rotating, showing off the android's perfect proportions, peachy skin, and royalty-approved posture. She had purple irises and cropped tangerine hair and a tattoo of an old-fashioned carousel that rotated around her ankle.

Cinder squeezed an eye shut. "Iko, what does this have to do with the satellite girl?"

"I was getting to that." The screen scrolled through a menu, landing on hair accessories, and dozens of icons clustered together showing everything from dreadlocked wigs to cat-ear headbands to rhinestone-encrusted barrettes. "Just think how much potential she has with hair like that!"

"You see?" said Thorne, nudging Scarlet in the shoulder. "Iko and the imprisoned, socially awkward satellite girl, best friends forever. Now, what *I'm* worried about is how we're going to be dividing the reward money when this is all over. Because this ship is starting to feel awfully crowded and I'm not sure I'm happy with all of you cutting into my profits."

"What reward money?" asked Scarlet.

"The reward Cinder's going to pay us out of the Lunar treasury once she's queen."

Cinder rolled her eyes. "I should have guessed."

"And that's just the beginning. By the end of this escapade, the whole world will see us as heroes. Imagine the fame and fortune, the sponsorship opportunities, the marketing requests, net-dramatization rights. I think we should discuss the profit division sooner rather than later, because I'm considering a 60-10-10-10-10 split right now."

"Am I the fourth ten percent?" said Iko. "Or is that the satellite girl? Because if it's the satellite girl, I'm going on strike."

"Can we discuss this imaginary money later?" said Cinder.

"Like, maybe when there's actual money to discuss?" suggested Scarlet. "Besides, don't you still have to prepare the podship?"

"*Oui*, mademoiselle." With a salute, Thorne grabbed a handgun off a storage crate and sank it into the holster.

Scarlet cocked her head. "Are you sure you don't want me to go? It's going to require some precise manuvering to attach to the docking clamp, and from what Cinder told me about your flying skills..."

"What do you mean? What did Cinder say about my flying skills?"

Scarlet and Cinder shared a look. "Naturally, she told me that you're a fantastic pilot," said Scarlet, grabbing her red hoodie off a crate. Though it had been badly torn in Paris, she'd stitched it up as well as she could. "Absolutely top-notch."

"I think she was practicing her sarcasm," said Iko.

Thorne glared, but Cinder only shrugged.

"I'm just saying," continued Scarlet, threading her arms through the sleeves, "it may not be an easy attachment. You have to dock slowly, and don't leave the pod until you're sure the satellite's system is compatible and you have a secure connection."

"I can handle it," said Thorne. Winking, he reached out and gave Scarlet's nose a tweak, ignoring how Wolf bristled behind her. "But you sure are sweet to be so concerned about me."

THE DOCKING CLAMP ENGAGED ON THORNE'S SECOND attempt, which he thought was pretty good for never having docked with a satellite before. He hoped Scarlet was watching, after she'd so brazenly doubted his abilities. He checked the connection before putting the podship into standby mode and unlatching his harness. Through the window he could see the curving side of the satellite and one of its circular gyrodines whirling lazily overhead, propelling the satellite through space. He could see only the edge of the docking hatch through the ship's windows, but it appeared secure, and his instruments were telling him that the pressure and oxygen levels made it safe to exit his ship.

He tugged his collar away from his throat. He was not, by nature, a paranoid man, but dealing with Lunars gave him more hesitation that he was accustomed to, even young, semi-cute ones.

Young, semi-cute ones who had probably been driven insane by years of solitude.

Thorne unlatched the podship door and it swung upward, revealing two steps up to a ramp edged with a rail, and beyond it a narrow corridor. His ears popped with the change in pressure. The entrance into the main satellite was still shut tight, but as he approached he heard a hissing noise and the doors parted, sliding seamlessly into the walls.

He recognized the room from the D-COMM connection—dozens of flat, clear screens, some overhead storage cabinets, a mussed-up bed with worn blankets, a wash of bluish white light coming from built-in fixtures. A door to the left led to what he assumed was a washroom, and directly opposite him, there was the door to the second podship hatch.

The girl was sitting on the edge of the bed, her hands in her lap, her hair pooling over both shoulders and ending in a bundle of knotted frizz by her shins.

She was smiling, a close-lipped, polite look that was entirely at odds with the nerve-bundled reaction she'd had over the D-COMM.

But that smile faltered when she saw him.

"Oh, it's you," she said, tilting her head to the side. "I was expecting the cyborg."

"No need to look so disappointed." Thorne thrust his hands into his pockets. "Cinder can fix ships, but she's useless at flying them. I'll be your escort today. Captain Carswell Thorne, at your service." He tipped his head toward her.

Rather than swoon or flutter her lashes, as was duly expected of her, the girl looked away and glowered at one of the screens.

Coughing, Thorne rocked back on his heels. Somehow he'd

expected that a girl with no prior human interaction would be a lot easier to impress.

"Are you all packed up? We don't like to loiter in one spot for long."

Her eyes flickered to him, hinting at annoyance. "No matter," she murmured to herself. "Jacin and I will go to her then."

Thorne frowned, feeling a twist of regret at his previous mocking, even if it had only been in his own head. What if the solitude really *had* driven her crazy? "Jacin?"

She stood up, her hair swinging against her ankles. He hadn't been able to tell how tall she was before, but now seeing that she couldn't have been much more than five feet, he felt comforted. Crazy or not, she was harmless.

Probably.

"Jacin, my guard."

"Right. Well, why don't you invite your friend Jacin to join us, and let's get going?"

"Oh, I don't think you'll be getting far."

She stepped toward him, and in that movement, she changed. The nest of hair grew dark and silky as a raven's wing. Her eyes changed from sky blue to slate gray, her pale skin turned golden, and her body stretched upward, becoming tall and graceful. Even her clothes changed, from the plain, worn day dress to a dove-white coat with long sleeves.

Thorne was quick to bury his surprise.

A thaumaturge. Figured.

Not one for denial, he accepted the immediate resignation with a stiffening of his shoulders. It had all been a trap then. The girl had been bait, or perhaps she'd been in on it all along. Funny—he usually had better instincts when it came to these sorts of things.

He stole another glance around the room, but there was no sign of the girl.

Something clanged outside the second entry hatch, shaking the satellite. *Hope.* His crew must have noticed something was wrong. That would be them now, aboard the second podship.

He called up his most practiced, most charming grin, and reached for his gun. He even felt a sting of pride when he managed to get it all the way out of its holster before his arm froze of its own accord.

Thorne shrugged with the one uncontrolled shoulder. "You can't blame me for trying."

The thaumaturge smirked and Thorne's fingers loosened. The gun clattered to the ground.

"*Captain* Carswell Thorne, is it?"

"That's right."

"I'm afraid you won't have claim to the title for long. I'm about to commandeer your Rampion for the queen."

"I am sorry to hear that."

"Additionally, I assume you are aware that assisting a wanted fugitive, such as Linh Cinder, is a crime punishable by death on Luna. Your sentence is to be carried out immediately."

"Efficiency. I respect that."

The second entry door opened behind her. Thorne tried to send mental warnings to his companions—it was a trap! Be ready!

But it was not Cinder or Scarlet or Wolf who stood in the second entry hatch, but a Lunar guard. Thorne's hope began to wither.

"Jacin, we will be boarding the Rampion using its own podship."

"Aah, *you're* Jacin," said Thorne. "I thought she was making you up."

They ignored him, but he was rather used to that.

"Go see that it's ready to disembark as soon as I'm finished here."

The guard respectfully inclined his head and moved to follow her commands.

"Careful," said Thorne. "It wasn't an easy connection. Required some real precise maneuvering. In fact, would you like me to come disconnect the ship for you? Just to make sure you do it right?"

The guard eyed him smugly as he passed, not as empty-eyed as he'd appeared before. But he didn't respond as he slipped into the corridor, heading toward Thorne's podship.

The thaumaturge grabbed a blanket from the bed and tossed it at Thorne. He would have caught it on reflex, but it wasn't necessary—his hands did all the work without him. Soon he found himself wrapping the blanket around his own wrists and tying it into intricate knots, giving the blanket a final yank with his teeth to tighten it into place.

"I look forward to returning to Luna aboard your ship and spreading the good news that Linh Cinder is no longer a threat to our crown."

His eyebrow twitched. "Anything I can do to assist Her Majesty's benevolent cause."

The thaumaturge strode to a screen beside the hatch and entered a command—a security code followed by a complicated set of instructions. "I had at first considered turning off the life support and letting you and Crescent gasp for air as the oxygen was used up. But that could take too long, and I would hate to give you an opportunity to free yourselves and call for assistance. Instead, I will be merciful." Finished, she straightened her long sleeves. "Consider yourself lucky that it will be quick."

"I always consider myself lucky."

Her gaze became hard as sterling and Thorne found himself marching toward the open door that led to the washroom. As he got closer, he saw the girl tied up with a sheet around her hands, knees, and ankles, and a cloth gag in her mouth. Remnants of tears streaked down her blotchy face. Her hair was a tangled mess on the ground all around her, many of the locks caught up in her bindings.

Thorne's gut tightened. He'd been sure that she had betrayed them, but her trembling body and horrified expression said otherwise.

His knees gave way and he landed on the floor with a grunt. The girl winced.

Drawing a sharp breath through his nostrils, Thorne glared up at the thaumaturge. "Is this all necessary? You're scaring the poor girl."

"Crescent has no reason to be upset. It was her betrayal that brought us to this moment."

"Right. The five-foot-tall girl tied up and gagged in the bathroom is always the one to blame."

"Besides," the thaumaturge continued as if he hadn't spoken. "I'm granting Crescent her greatest wish. I'm sending her to Earth." She held up a small shimmering chip, identical to the D-COMM Cinder had been carrying around with her. "I'm sure Crescent won't mind if I keep this. It is, after all, property of Her Majesty."

Her sleeves whipped behind her as she left. Thorne heard her heels clipping down the docking hatch and the doors shut behind her. His podship's engine was muffled, but he felt the slight jolt when they disconnected.

It was only then that he felt the first pang of helplessness.

She'd taken his ship.

That witch had taken his ship.

But the Rampion had a second shuttle. His crew could still come for them. *Would* come for them.

But then he sensed something new—a slight pull, a gentle shift—and the girl whimpered.

The satellite's trajectory had been altered. Gravity was claiming them, drawing them out of their orbit.

The satellite was falling toward Earth.

Ten

"HE'S ATTACHED," SAID SCARLET, WATCHING THORNE'S podship through the cockpit viewing window. "That wasn't too embarrassing."

Cinder propped herself against the door frame. "I hope he's quick about it. We have no way of knowing that this girl isn't being monitored."

"You don't trust her?" said Wolf.

"I don't trust who she works for."

"Wait. Is that another ship?" Scarlet jerked forward, pulling up a radar search on the screen beside her. "Our scanners aren't seeing it."

Wolf and Cinder clustered behind her, peering down at the podship, only slightly larger than Thorne's, as it neared the satellite. Cinder's heart began to pound. "Lunar."

"It has to be," said Scarlet. "If they're blocking the signals—"

"No, look. The insignia."

Wolf cursed. "It's a royal ship. Probably a thaumaturge."

"She betrayed us," Cinder murmured, shaking her head in disbelief. "I don't believe it."

"Do we run?" asked Scarlet.

"And abandon Thorne?"

In the window, the Lunar podship had connected with the satellite's second clamp. Cinder raked her fingers through her hair, her thoughts stumbling through her head. "Comm them. Establish the D-COMM link. We need to know what's going on—"

"No," said Wolf. "It's possible they don't know we're here. Maybe she didn't betray us. If they didn't pick up our ship on radar, there's still a chance they haven't had visual of us."

"They would know Thorne's podship came from some-where!"

"Maybe he'll be able to get away," Iko chimed in, but there wasn't the normal enthusiasm to her tone.

"Against a thaumaturge? You saw how well that worked out in Paris."

"So what do we do?" said Scarlet. "We can't comm them, we can't dock . . ."

"We should run," said Wolf. "They'll come for us next."

They both looked at Cinder and she realized with a jolt that they expected her to take charge. But it wasn't a simple decision. Thorne was down there. He'd walked right into a trap, and this had all been Cinder's idea in the first place. She couldn't leave him.

Her hands began to shake from gripping the chair. Every second of indecision was wasted time.

"Cinder." Scarlet placed a hand on her arm. It only made her squeeze the chair tighter. "We have to—"

"Run. We have to run."

Scarlet nodded. She spun back to the controls. "Iko, prep thrusters for—"

"Wait," said Wolf. "Look."

Beyond the cockpit window, a podship was disconnecting from the satellite. Thorne's podship.

"What's happening?" Iko asked.

Cinder hissed. "Thorne's ship is coming back. Comm him."

Scarlet pulled the comm screen up. "Thorne—report. What happened down there?"

The screen returned only static.

Cinder chewed on the inside of her cheek. After a moment, the static was replaced with a simple text comm.

CAMERA DISABLED. WE'RE INJURED. OPEN DOCK.

Cinder reread the message until the words blurred in her vision.

"It's a trap," said Wolf.

"It might not be," she answered.

"It *is*."

"We don't know that for sure! He's resourceful."

"Cinder—"

"He could have survived."

"Or it's a trap," muttered Scarlet.

"Cinder," Iko broke in, her voice pitched high. "What should I do?"

She swallowed, hard, and shoved herself away from the chair. "Open the dock. Both of you, stay here."

"Absolutely not." Wolf fell into step beside her. She could tell that he was in fight mode—his shoulders hunched near his ears, his hands curled into claws, his stride fast and determined.

"Wolf." Cinder pressed her titanium fist against his sternum.

"Stay here. If there is a thaumaturge on that ship, Iko and I are the only ones who can't be controlled."

Scarlet latched on to his elbow. "She's right. Your presence could do more harm than good."

Cinder didn't wait for Scarlet to convince him. She was already halfway down the ladder that dropped into the ship's lower level. In the corridor between the podship dock and engine room, she stopped to listen. She heard the solid closing of the dock's doors, and the life system pumping oxygen back into the space.

"Dock is secured," said Iko. "Life system stabilized. Safe for entry."

Cinder's retina display was panicking, as it tended to do when she was nervous or afraid. Red diagnostics flared up in the corner of her vision, laced with warnings: BLOOD PRESSURE TOO HIGH; HEART RATE TOO FAST; SYSTEMS OVERHEATING, INITIALIZING AUTO-COOL RESPONSE.

"Iko, what do you see in there?"

"I can see that we need to get some real cameras installed on this ship," she responded. "My sensor confirms that the podship has docked. I detect two life-forms inside, but it doesn't seem that anyone has gotten out of the ship yet."

Maybe they were too injured to get out of the ship.

Or maybe it was a thaumaturge, unwilling to leave the shuttle while there was still a chance they could reopen the docking doors and have everything inside sucked out into space.

Cinder opened the tip of her left pointer finger, loading a cartridge. Though she'd used up all her tranquilizer darts during the fight in Paris, she'd been able to manufacture some weapons of her own—projectiles made out of welded nails.

"We just received another text comm from the ship," said Iko. "It says, 'Help us.'"

Everything inside Cinder's head was screaming at her—*Trap. Trap. Trap.*

But if it was Thorne . . . if Thorne was inside that ship, injured or dying . . .

Clearing her thoughts, she reached up and punched in the dock's access code, then wrenched down the manual lever. The unlock mechanism clunked and Cinder held up her left hand like a gun.

Thorne's podship was sandwiched between the second pod and a wall of cords and machinery bolted to the thick paneling: tools for loading and unloading freight, fueling equipment, jacks, air compressors, pneumatic coils.

She inched toward the ship.

"Thorne?" she said, craning her head. She spotted a lump of fabric in the pilot seat—a body hunched over.

Shaking, she swung open the door before ducking a few steps back and aiming her weapon at the body. His shirt was soaked in blood.

"Thorne!"

Lowering her hand, she reached forward, rolling him toward her. "What hap—"

An orange light brightened in the corner of her vision, her optobionics reminding her that her eyes were a weakness.

She gasped and raised her hand again, just as he shot forward. One hand wrapped around her wrist, the other clamped around her neck, his movements so fast Cinder fell onto the floor. For a moment it was Thorne on top of her, blue eyes surprisingly calm as he pinned her to the ground.

Then he morphed. His stare became cold and crystalline, his hair grew longer and lighter, and his clothes melded into the red and gray uniforms of the Lunar royal guard.

Her instincts seemed to recognize him before her eyes did, flaring with violent hatred. This was not any Lunar guard. This was the guard who had held her captive during the ball, while Levana taunted her and threatened Kai, threatened *everyone*.

But wasn't he—

A fluttery laugh drifted through the air. Cinder squinted against the bright lights as a woman emerged from the podship.

Right. The personal guard to Head Thaumaturge Sybil Mira.

"I had expected more from the galaxy's most-wanted criminal," she said, watching as Cinder pressed her free hand into the guard's chin, struggling to push him away. The thaumaturge smiled, looking like a hungry cat with a new toy. Stars began to speckle Cinder's vision. "Shall I kill you here, or deliver you in chains to my que—"

She cut off, her gray eyes flickering toward the door. A guttural roar was followed by Wolf throwing himself against the thaumaturge and trapping her against the podship.

The guard's hold slackened, indecision flashing across his face as he glanced up at his mistress. Cinder swung her fist toward his jaw. She felt the crunch and he reeled back, his attention back on her.

Cinder pulled her knees up, gaining purchase, and shoved him away. She scrambled to her feet, as Wolf grabbed the thaumaturge and wrenched her back. His lips curled, revealing his implanted fangs.

The guard reached for his holster, drawing Cinder's focus. He pulled the gun out. Cinder raised her hand.

Two shots fired in unison.

Wolf howled in pain as the guard's bullet buried itself beneath his shoulder blade.

The guard grunted as Cinder's projectile found his side.

Cinder pivoted, her aim seeking out the thaumaturge's heart, but Wolf was between them, a dark spot of blood seeping through his shirt.

Sybil's face was disfigured by fury as she placed her palm against Wolf's chest and snarled. "Now then," she hissed. "Let's remind you what you really are."

Wolf snapped his jaw shut. A low growl rumbled through his throat. He spun toward Cinder, his gaze filling with bloodlust.

"Oh, stars," she murmured, backing up until she was pressed against the second podship. She held her hand steady, but she had no hope of hitting Sybil with Wolf in the way, especially now that he was under the thaumaturge's control. Gulping, she reached out with her mind, grasping for the familiar waves of Wolf's energy, his own signature of bioelectricity, but found something brutal and feral clouding around him instead.

Wolf lunged for her.

Cinder switched her target, reaching for the guard instead. It felt natural, the half second it took to claim his willpower and force him into action. In a blink, the guard was between them. He raised his gun, but was too slow as Wolf backhanded him out of the way, sending him sliding between the ship's landing gear. The gun clattered along the row of cabinets.

Cinder skittered around the podship's nose. They made eye contact over its roof and Wolf hesitated, his fangs bared. Cinder's internal warnings were coming so fast they'd blurred together, pointing out escalated heart rates and an unhealthy increase of adrenaline. She ignored them, focused only on keeping the pod-ship between her and Wolf as he prowled back and forth.

But then his entire body flinched. Wolf turned and raced toward Sybil as another gunshot echoed through the dock. Wolf threw himself in front of the thaumaturge, catching the bullet in his chest.

Scarlet screamed from the doorway, a gun in her shaking hands.

Panting, Cinder scanned for a weapon, a plan. The thaumaturge was backed into a corner with Wolf acting as her shield. The Lunar guard was curled up beneath the nearest podship, hopefully unconscious. Scarlet lowered the gun. The thaumaturge would have no trouble controlling her.

Except, the thaumaturge had doubt in her expression and a grimace on her face. A vein was throbbing in her forehead as she cowered behind Wolf.

Cinder realized with some shock that it was almost as difficult for Sybil to control Wolf as it was for her. She couldn't control anyone else so long as she had him, and the moment she released Wolf, he would turn on her and the battle would be over.

Unless.

Unless she killed Wolf and removed him from the equation entirely.

With the blood pooling and dribbling out of his two bullet wounds, Cinder wondered how long that would take.

"Wolf!" Scarlet's voice shuddered. The gun was still aimed at Sybil, but Wolf was still between them.

Another gunshot made Cinder jump, the noise ricocheting off the walls. Sybil cried out in pain.

The guard—not unconscious after all—had grabbed the abandoned gun. And he'd shot *the thaumaturge*.

Sybil hissed, her nostrils flaring as she fell to one knee, one hand pressed against her thigh, already covered in blood.

The guard was kneeling, gripping the gun. Cinder couldn't see his face, but he sounded strained when he spoke. "She's controlling me. The cyborg—"

Cinder's lie detector flickered, unnecessarily. She was doing no such thing, although, had she thought of it before . . .

Sybil shoved Wolf toward the guard. The energy in the room quivered, waves of bioelectricity steaming and shimmering around them. Sybil had released her power over Wolf. The gunshot had weakened her—she could no longer control him.

Wolf collapsed against the guard, and they both crumpled to the ground. The guard grappled for purchase, keeping a tight hold on the gun as he shoved Wolf away. Pale and shaking, Wolf couldn't even fight back. Blood puddled around them, slicking the floor.

"WOLF!" Scarlet raised the gun toward the thaumaturge again, but Sybil had already scrambled up, limping behind the nearest podship.

Cinder dove for Wolf, grabbing him under both arms and dragging him away from the guard. He flailed his legs, his heels slipping on the blood, but otherwise offered no assistance.

The guard rose up to a crouch, panting, covered in blood, his own side bleeding from Cinder's projectile. He still held the gun.

As Cinder stared at him, she saw the choice.

Take control of the guard before he raised the gun and killed her.

Or take control of Wolf and give him the strength he needed to get out of the dock before he bled to death.

The guard held her gaze for one throbbing moment, before he hauled himself up and ran toward his mistress.

Cinder didn't wait to see whether he was going to kill her or protect her.

Clenching her fists, she blocked out everything around them, focusing only on Wolf and the bioelectricity that simmered around him. He was weak. This was not like trying to control him in their mock fights. She found her will slipped easily into his, and though his body protested, she urged him to stiffen his legs. Just enough to take most of his weight off her. Just enough so she could carry him, limping, into the corridor.

She dropped Wolf against the wall. Her palms were sticky with blood.

"What's happening?" Iko wailed over the speakers.

"Keep your sensor on this corridor," said Cinder. "When all three of us are safely out of the dock, shut the door and open the hatch."

Sweat dripping into her eyes, she rushed back into the dock. All she needed was to get Scarlet and let Iko open the hatch. The vacuum of space would take care of the rest.

She spotted the thaumaturge first. Not ten paces in front of her.

She had a clear shot.

Nerves humming with adrenaline, she lifted her hand and prepared a projectile. She took aim.

Scarlet leaped in front of her, her arms out in a T. Her expression was blank, her mind under the thaumaturge's control.

Cinder almost wilted with relief. Without hesitating, she

grabbed Scarlet around the waist with one arm and raised the other to let off a volley of projectiles toward the thaumaturge—more to keep her at bay than in hopes of doing any real damage. The last of her welded nails struck the metal walls as Cinder stumbled and fell back into the corridor.

She noticed the orange light in her vision at the same moment she screamed, "Iko, now!"

As the corridor door zipped shut, she spotted Sybil racing toward the nearest pod, and a glimpse of feet on the other side of the podship.

The guard's feet.

But—

But—

Blue jeans and tennis shoes?

Cinder shoved Scarlet's body away with a scream.

The glamour vanished, along with the orange light in her vision. Scarlet's red hoodie flickered, transforming into the Lunar uniform. The guard groaned and rolled away. He was bleeding from the wound in his side.

She'd grabbed the *guard*. Sybil had tricked her. Which meant—

"No—Scarlet! Iko!"

She threw herself at the control panel and punched in the code to open the door, but an error flashed at her. On the other side, the docking hatch was opening. A curdled scream echoed through the corridor, and Cinder almost didn't realize it was hers.

"Cinder! What's happening? What—"

"Scarlet's in there. . . . She has . . ."

She raked her fingernails viciously along the door's airtight seal, unable to keep away the vision of Scarlet being pulled out into space.

"Cinder, the podship!" said Iko. "She's taking the podship. Two life-forms aboard."

"*What?*"

Cinder looked up at the panel. Sure enough, the room's scanners indicated there was only one shuttle still docked.

The thaumaturge had survived, and she'd taken Scarlet with her.

Eleven

"SHE HAS SCARLET," SAID CINDER. "QUICK—CLOSE THE HATCH!
I'll take the other pod, I'll follow them—"

Her words faltered, her brain catching up.

She did not know how to fly a podship.

But she could figure it out. She could download some instructions and she could . . . she would have to . . .

"Your friend is dying."

She spun around. She'd forgotten about the Lunar guard.

He was pressing a hand to his side, where Cinder's projectile was still embedded, but his attention was on Wolf.

Wolf, who was unconscious and surrounded by blood.

"Oh, no. Oh, no." She ejected the knife in her finger and started cutting the bloodstained fabric away from Wolf's wounds. "Thorne. We need to get Thorne. Then we can go after Scarlet and I . . . I'll bandage Wolf and—"

She glanced at the guard. "Shirt," she said firmly, although the order was more to focus her own thoughts. In seconds, the guard's hands were working at her command, removing the empty gun holster and pulling his own bloodied shirt over his head. She was glad to see a second undershirt as well—she had a feeling they were going to need every bit of "bandaging" she could find to stanch Wolf's bleeding. Eventually they would have to get him to the medbay, but there was no way she could move him in this condition, especially not up that ladder.

She tried to ignore the niggling thought in her head that this was not enough. That not even the bandages in the medbay would be enough.

She grabbed the guard's shirt and bunched it against Wolf's chest. At least this bullet had missed his heart. She hoped the other one hadn't hit anything vital either.

Her thoughts were hazy, repeating over and over in her head. They had to get Thorne. They had to go after Scarlet. They had to save Wolf.

She couldn't do it all.

She couldn't do any of it.

"Thorne—" Her voice broke. "Where's Thorne?" Keeping one hand pressed onto Wolf's wound, she reached for the guard with the other, grabbing his collar and pulling him toward her. "What did you do to Thorne?"

"Your friend who boarded the satellite," he said, as much a statement as a question. There was regret in his face, but not enough. "He's dead."

She shrieked and slammed him into the wall. "You're lying!"

He flinched, but didn't try to protect himself, even though she'd already lost her focus. She could not keep him under her control so long as her thoughts were so divided, so long as this chaos and devastation reigned in her head.

"Mistress Sybil changed the satellite's trajectory, removing it from orbit. It will burn up during entry. It probably already has. There's nothing you can do."

"No," she said, shaking her head. Every part of her was trembling. "She wouldn't have sacrificed her own programmer too."

But there was no telltale orange light in her vision. He wasn't lying.

The guard leaned his head back as his gaze skimmed Cinder from head to toe, as if examining an unusual specimen. "She would sacrifice anyone to get to you. The queen seems to believe you're a threat."

Cinder ground her teeth so hard she felt that her jaw would snap from the pressure. There it was—stated with such blatant simplicity.

This was her fault. This was all her fault.

They'd been after *her*.

"Your other shirt," she whispered. She didn't bother to control him this time, and he removed the undershirt without argument. Cinder grabbed it from him, spotting the end of her own projectile jutting from his skin, just below his ribs.

Looking away, she pressed the second shirt against the wound in Wolf's back.

"Roll him onto his side."

"What?"

"Get him on his side. It'll open the airway, help him breathe."

Cinder glowered at him, but a four-second net search confirmed the validity of his suggestion, and she eased Wolf onto his side as gently as she could, positioning his legs like the medical diagram in her brain told her to. The guard didn't help, but he nodded approvingly when Cinder was done.

"Cinder?"

It was Iko, her voice small and restrained. The ship had become dark, running only on emergency lighting and default systems. Iko's anxiety was clouding her ability to function as much as Cinder's was.

"What are we going to do?"

Cinder struggled to breathe. A headache had burst open in her skull. The weight of everything pressed against her until it was almost too tempting to curl up over Wolf's body and simply give up.

She couldn't help them. She couldn't save the world. She couldn't save anyone.

"I don't know," she whispered. "I don't know."

"Finding someplace to hide would be a start," said the guard, followed by a ripping sound as he tore a shred of material from the hem of his pants. He winced as he yanked out the projectile and tossed it down the corridor, before pressing the fabric against the wound. For the first time, she noticed that he still wore what looked like a large hunting knife sheathed on his belt. He looked up at her when she didn't respond, his eyes sharp as ice picks. "Maybe someplace your friend can get help. As a thought."

She shook her head. "I can't. We just lost both of our pilots and I can't fly ... I don't know how ..."

"I can fly."

"But Scarlet ..."

"Look. Thaumaturge Mira will be contacting Luna and sending for reinforcements, and the queen's fleet isn't as far away as you might think. You're about to have an army on your trail."

"But—"

"But nothing. You can't help that other girl. Consider her dead. But you might be able to help *him*."

Cinder dropped her chin, curling in on herself as the warring decisions in her head threatened to tear her apart. He was being logical. She recognized that. But it was so hard to admit defeat. To give up on Scarlet. To make that sacrifice and have to live with it.

With every passing second, though, she was closer to losing Wolf too. She glanced down. Wolf's face was scrunched in pain, his brow beaded with sweat.

"Ship," said the guard, "calculate our location and relative trajectory over Earth. Where is the closest place we can get to? Someplace not too populated."

There was a hesitation before Iko said, "Me?"

He squinted up at the ceiling. "Yeah. *You.*"

"Sorry, right. Calculating now." The lights brightened. "Following a natural descent to Earth, we could be in central or north Africa in approximately seventeen minutes. A loose thousand-mile radius opens us up to the Mediterranean regions of Europe and the western portion of the Eastern Commonwealth."

"He needs a hospital," Cinder murmured, knowing as she said it that there wasn't a hospital on Earth that wouldn't know he was one of the queen's wolf-hybrids as soon as he was admitted. And the risk she posed to take him there herself, and how recognizable the Rampion would be . . . where could they possibly go that would offer them sanctuary?

Nowhere was safe.

Beneath her, Wolf moaned. His chest rattled.

He needed a hospital, or . . . a doctor.

Africa. Dr. Erland.

She peered up at the guard and for the first time struggled through the sluggish mess inside her head to wonder why he was doing this. Why hadn't he killed them all? Why was he helping them?

"You serve the queen," she said. "How can I trust you?"

His lips twitched, like she'd made a joke, but his eyes were quick to harden again. "I serve my princess. No one else."

The floor dropped out from beneath her. The princess. His princess.

He knew.

She waited a full breath for her lie detector to recognize his falsehood, but it didn't. He was telling the truth.

"Africa," she said. "Iko, take us to Africa—to where the first outbreak of letumosis occurred."

Twelve

THE FALL WAS SLOW AT FIRST, GRADUAL, AS THE PULL OF THE
satellite's orbit was overpowered by the pull of Earth's gravity.

Thorne hiked up his pant leg, using his toe to pry off his left
boot. The knife he'd stashed there clattered onto the floor and he
grabbed for it, awkwardly trying to angle the blade toward the
blanket that was knotted around his wrists.

The girl murmured around her gag and shifted toward him.
Her binds were much more secure and complex than his own. The
thaumaturge had only bothered to have Thorne tie his hands in
front of him, but this girl had binds all down her legs, in addition to
having her wrists fastened behind her and the gag over her mouth.

With no leverage to press the knife against his own binds, he
nodded at the girl. "Can you turn around?"

She flopped and rolled onto her side, pushing off the wall with
her feet to turn herself so her hands were toward him. Thorne
hunkered over her and sawed at the sheet that was cutting into
her arms. By the time he'd hacked it off, there were deep red lines
carved into her skin.

She ripped the gag off her mouth, leaving it to hang around
her neck. A knot of her frayed hair caught in the fabric. "My
feet!"

"Can you untie my hands?"

She said nothing as she snatched the knife from him. Her hands were shaking as she angled the blade toward the binds around her knees, and Thorne thought maybe it was best for her to practice on herself anyway.

Sawing through the sheet, she looked like a madwoman—her brow wrinkled in concentration, her hair knotted, her complexion damp and blotchy, red lines drawn into her cheeks from the gag. But the adrenaline had her working quickly and soon she was kicking away the material.

"My hands," Thorne said again, but she was already grasping for the sink and pulling herself up on trembling legs.

"I'm sorry—the entry procedures!" she said, stumbling out into the main room.

Thorne grabbed the knife and clambered to his feet as the satellite took a sudden turn. He slipped, stumbling into the shower door. They were falling faster as Earth's gravity claimed them.

Using the wall for balance, Thorne rushed into the main room. The girl had fallen too, and was now scrambling to get over the bed.

"We need to get to the other podship and disconnect," said Thorne. "You need to untie me!"

She shook her head and pressed herself against the wall where the smallest of the screens was embedded, the screen that the thaumaturge had meddled with before. Strings of hair were sticking to her face.

"She'll have a security block on the ship and I know the satellite better and—oh, no, no, no!" she screamed, her fingers flying over the screen. "She changed the access code!"

"What are you doing?"

"The entry procedures—the ablative coating should hold while we're passing through the atmosphere, but if I don't set the parachute to release, the whole thing will disintegrate on impact!"

The satellite shifted again and they both stumbled. Thorne fell onto the mattress and the knife skittered out of his grip, bouncing off the end of the bed, while the girl tripped and landed on one knee. The walls around them began to tremble with the friction of Earth's atmosphere. The blackness that had clouded the small windows was replaced with a burning white light. The outer coating was burning off, protecting them from the atmosphere's heat.

Unlike the Rampion, this satellite was designed for only one descent toward Earth.

"All right." Forgetting about his binds, Thorne swung himself over to the other side of the bed and hauled the girl back to her feet. "Get that parachute working." She was still wobbly as he spun them toward the screen and dropped his arms over her, forming a cocoon around her body. She was even shorter than he'd realized, the top of her head not even reaching his collarbone.

Her fingers jabbed at the screen as Thorne widened his stance and locked his knees, bracing himself as much as he could while the satellite shook and rocked around them. He hunched over her, trying to hold his balance and keep her steady while codes and commands flickered and scrolled across the screen. His attention flicked to the nearest window, still fiery white. As soon as the satellite had fallen far enough into Earth's atmosphere, the auto-gravity would shut off and they would be as secure as dice in a gambler's fist.

"I'm in!" she shouted.

Thorne curled the toes of his one shoeless foot into the

carpet. He heard a crash behind him and dared to glance back. One of the screens had fallen off the desk. He gulped. Anything not bolted down was about to turn into projectiles. "How long will it take to—"

"Done!"

Thorne whipped her around and thrust them both toward the mattress. "Under the bed!" He stumbled and fell, dragging her down with him. The cabinets swung open overhead and Thorne flinched as a rain of canned goods and dishes clattered around them. He hunkered over the girl, deflecting them away from her. "Quick!"

She scurried forward, out of the ring of his arms, and pulled herself into the shadows. She backed against the wall as far as she could, both hands pushing against the bed frame to lock her body in place.

Thorne kicked off from the carpet and grabbed the nearest post to pull himself forward.

The shaking stopped, replaced with a smooth, fast descent. The brightness from the windows faded to a sunshine blue. Thorne's stomach swooped and he felt like he was being sucked into a vacuum.

He heard her scream. Pain and brightness exploded in his head, and then the world went black.

BOOK
Two

The witch snipped off her golden hair and

cast her out into a great desert.

Thirteen

CRESS WOULD NOT HAVE BELIEVED THAT SHE HAD THE strength to drag Carswell Thorne beneath the bed and secure his unconscious body against the wall if the proof wasn't in her arms. All the while, cords and screens and plugs and dishes and food jostled and banged around them. The walls of the satellite groaned and she squeezed her eyes shut, trying not to imagine the heat and friction melting through the bolts and seams, trying not to guess at how stable this untested satellite could be. Trying not to think about plunging toward the Earth—its mountains and oceans and glaciers and forests and the impact that a satellite thrown from space would have when it crashed into the planet and shattered into billions of tiny pieces.

She was doing a poor job of not imagining it all.

The fall lasted forever, while her small world disintegrated.

She'd failed. The parachute should have opened already. She should have felt it release, felt the snap back as it caught their descent and lowered them gently to Earth. But their fall was only faster and faster, as the satellite's air grew warmer. Either she'd done something wrong or the parachute hatch was faulty, or perhaps there was no parachute at all and the command was from false programming. After all, Sybil had commissioned this satellite. Surely she'd never intended to let Cress land safely on the blue planet.

Sybil had succeeded. They were going to die.

Cress wrapped her body around Carswell Thorne and buried her face into his hair. At least he would be unconscious through it all. At least he didn't have to be afraid.

Then, a shudder—a sensation different from the drop—and she heard the brisk sound of nylon ropes and hissing and there it was, the sudden jerk that seemed to pull them back up into the sky. She cried out and gripped Carswell Thorne tighter as her shoulder smacked into the underside of the bed.

The fall became a sinking, and Cress's sobs turned to relief. She squeezed Thorne's prone body and sobbed and hyperventilated and sobbed some more.

It took ages for the impact to come and when it did, the jolt knocked Cress into the bed again. The satellite crashed and slid, rolled over and tumbled. They were slipping down something solid, perhaps a hill or mountainside. Cress clenched her teeth against a scream and tried to protect Thorne with one arm while bracing them against the wall with the other. She'd expected water—so much of the Earth's surface was water—not this solid something they'd hit. The spiraling descent finally halted with a crash that shook the walls around them.

Cress's lungs burned with the effort to take in what air they could. Every muscle ached from adrenaline and the strain of bracing for impact and the battering her body had taken.

But in her head, the pain was nonexistent.

They were alive.

They were on Earth and they were alive.

A grateful, shocked cry fell out of her and she embraced Thorne, crying happily into the crook of his neck, but the joy receded when he did not hold her back. She'd almost forgotten the sight of him hitting his head on the bed's frame, the way his body was thrown across the floor, how he'd slumped unnaturally in the corner and made no sound or movement as she'd hauled him beneath the bed.

She pried herself away from him. She was covered in sweat and her hair had tangled around them both, binding them almost as securely as Sybil's knotted sheets had.

"Carswell?" she hissed. It was strange to say his name aloud, like she hadn't yet earned the familiarity. She licked her lips and her voice cracked the second time. "Mr. Thorne?" Her fingers pressed against his throat. Relief—his heartbeat was strong. She hadn't been sure during the fall whether he was breathing, but now with the world quiet and still, she could make out wheezing air coming from his mouth.

Maybe he had a concussion. Cress had read about people getting concussions when they hit their heads. She couldn't remember what happened to them, but she knew it was bad.

"Wake up. Please. We're alive. We made it." She placed a palm on his cheek, surprised to find roughness there, nothing at all like her own smooth face.

Facial hair. It made sense, and yet somehow she'd never worked the sensation of prickly facial hair into her fantasies. She would amend that after this.

She shook her head, ashamed to be thinking of something like that when Carswell Thorne was hurt right before her and she couldn't do any—

He twitched.

Cress gasped and attempted to cushion his head in case he jerked around too much. "Mr. Thorne? Wake up. We're all right. Please wake up."

A low, painful moan, and his breaths began to even out.

Cress pushed her hair out of her face. It fought against her, clinging to her sweat-dampened skin. Long strands of it were pinned beneath their bodies.

He groaned again.

"C-Carswell?"

His elbow lurched, like he was trying to lift his hand, but his wrists were still bound between them. His lashes fluttered. "Wha—huh?"

"It's all right. I'm here. We're safe."

Thorne dragged his tongue around his lips, then shut his eyes again. "Thorne," he grunted. "Most people call me Thorne. Or Captain."

Her heart lifted. "Of course, Tho—Captain. Are you in pain?"

He shifted uncomfortably, discovering that his hands were still tied. "I feel like my brain's about to leak out through my ears, but otherwise, I feel great."

Cress inspected the back of his head with her fingers. There was no dampness, so at least he wasn't bleeding. "You hit your head pretty hard."

He grunted and tried to wriggle his hands out of the knotted blanket.

"Hold on, there was that knife . . ." She trailed off, scouring the clutter and debris around them.

"It fell off the bed," said Thorne.

"Yes, I saw it . . . there!" She spotted the knife handle lodged beneath a fallen screen and went to grab for it, but her hair had gotten so wrapped up around her and Thorne that it yanked her back. She yelped and rubbed at her scalp.

He opened his eyes again, frowning. "I don't remember being tied together before."

"I'm sorry, my hair gets everywhere sometimes and . . . if you could just . . . here, roll this way."

She grabbed his elbow and nudged him onto his side. With a scowl, he complied, allowing her enough movement to reach the knife handle.

"Are you sure it's over—" Thorne started, but she had already draped herself over his side and was sawing through the blanket. "Oh. You have a good memory."

"Hm?" she murmured, focused on the sharp blade. It frayed easily and Thorne sighed with relief as it fell away. He rubbed his wrists, then reached toward his head. When the tangles of Cress's hair tried to hold him back, he tugged harder.

Cress yelped and crashed into Thorne's chest. He didn't seem to notice as his fingers found the back of his scalp. "Ow," he muttered.

"Yeah," she agreed.

"This bump is going to last awhile. Here, feel this."

"What?"

He fished around for her hand, then brought it to the back of his head. "I have a huge bump back here. No wonder I have such a headache."

He did, indeed, have an impressive bump on his scalp, but Cress could think only of the softness of his hair and the way she was practically lying on top of him. She blushed.

"Yes. Right. You should probably, um . . ."

She had no idea what he should probably do.

Kiss her, she thought. Isn't that what people did after they survived thrilling, near-death experiences together? She was sure it wasn't an appropriate suggestion, but this close, it was all she could think about. She yearned to lean in closer, to press her nose into the fabric of his shirt and inhale deeply, but she didn't want him thinking she was odd. Or guessing the truth, that this moment, filled with injuries and her destroyed satellite and being separated from his friends, was the most perfect moment of her entire life.

His brow creased and he picked at a lock of hair that had tightened around his bicep. "We need to do something about this hair."

"Right. Right!" She shifted away, her scalp screaming as her hair was trapped beneath them. She started to untangle the strands, gently, one by one.

"Maybe it would help if we turned on the lights."

She paused. "The lights?"

"Are they voice activated? If the computer system went down in the fall...spades, it must be the middle of the night. Is there a portscreen or something we can turn on, at least?"

Cress cocked her head. "I . . . I don't understand."

For the briefest moment, he seemed annoyed. "It would help if we could *see*."

His eyes were open, but he was looking blankly past Cress's shoulder. He pried away some strands of hair that had gotten twisted around his wrist, then waved his hand in front of his face. "This is the blackest night I've ever seen. We must be somewhere rural...is it a new moon tonight?" His scowl deepened, and she could tell he was trying to remember where Earth was in its moon cycle. "That doesn't seem right. Must be really overcast."

"Captain? It's...it isn't dark. I can see just fine."

He frowned in confusion and, after a moment, worry. His jaw flexed. "Please tell me you're practicing your sarcasm."

"My sarcasm? Why would I do that?"

Shaking his head, he squeezed his eyes tight together. Opened them again. Blinked rapidly.

Cursed.

Pressing her lips, Cress held her fingers in front of him. Waved them back and forth. There was no reaction.

"What happened?" he said. "The last thing I remember is trying to get under the bed."

"You hit your head on the bed frame, and I dragged you under here. And then we landed. A little rocky, but . . . that's all. You just hit your head."

"And that can cause *blindness*?"

"It might be some sort of brain trauma. Maybe it's only temporary. Maybe . . . maybe you're in shock?"

He settled his head on the floor. A heavy silence closed around them.

Cress chewed on her lip.

Finally, he spoke again, and his voice had taken on a determined edge. "We need to do something about this hair. Where did that knife go?"

Before she could question the logic behind giving a knife to a blind man, she had set it into his palm. Thorne reached behind her with his other hand and gathered a fistful of her hair. The touch sent a delicious tingle down her spine.

"Sorry, but it grows back," he said, not sounding at all apologetic. He began sawing through the tangles, one handful at a time. Grab, cut, release. Cress held perfectly still. Not because she was afraid of being cut—the knife was steady in his hand, despite the blindness, and Thorne kept the blade angled carefully away from her neck. But because it was Thorne. It was *Captain Carswell Thorne*, running his hands through her hair, his rough jaw mere inches away from her lips, his brow furrowed in concentration.

By the time he was brushing feather-soft fingers along her neck, checking for any strands he'd missed, she was dizzy with euphoria.

He found a missed lock of hair by her left ear and cut it away. "I think that's it." He tucked the knife under his leg so he would know where to find it and buried his hands into the short, impossibly light hair, working out the remaining tangles. A satisfied grin stretched over his face. "Maybe a little jagged on the ends, but much better."

Cress reached for the back of her neck, amazed at the sensation of bare skin, still damp from sweat, and short-cropped hair that had a subtle wave to it now that all the weight was gone. She scratched her fingernails along her scalp, riveted by the pleasure of such a foreign sensation. It felt as though twenty pounds had been cut from her head. Tightness was fading from muscles that she hadn't even realized was there.

"Thank you."

"You're welcome," he said, brushing away the locks of hair that still clung to him.

"And I'm really sorry . . . about the blindness."

"Not your fault."

"It is kind of my fault. If I hadn't asked you to come rescue me, and if I had—"

"It's *not* your fault," he said again, his tone cutting off her argument. "You sound like Cinder. She always blames herself for the stupidest things. The war is her fault. Scarlet's grandmother is her fault. I bet she'd take responsibility for the plague too, if she could."

Picking up the knife, he shimmied out from beneath the bed, pushing his arms out in a wide circle to nudge away any debris before pulling himself up onto the edge of the mattress. His progress was slow, like he didn't trust himself to move more than a few inches at a time. Cress followed and stood up beside him, shuffling some of the debris around with her bare toes. One hand stayed buried in her hair.

"The point is, that witch tried to kill us, but we survived," said Thorne. "And we'll find a way to contact the Rampion, and they'll come get us, and we'll be *fine*."

He said it like he was trying to convince himself, but Cress didn't need any convincing. He was right. They were alive, and they were together, and they would be fine.

"I just need a moment to think," said Thorne. "Figure out what we're going to do."

Cress nodded and rocked back on her heels. For a long time, Thorne seemed to be deep in thought, his hands clasped in his lap. After a minute, Cress realized they were shaking.

Finally, Thorne tilted his head toward her, though his unfocused eyes were on the wall. He took in a deep breath, let it out, then smiled.

"Let's begin again, with some proper introductions. Did I hear your name was Crescent?"

"Just Cress, please."

He extended a hand toward her. When she gave him hers, he tugged her closer, bent his head, and pressed a kiss against her knuckles. Cress stiffened and swooned, her knees threatening to buckle beneath her.

"Captain Carswell Thorne, at your service."

Fourteen

CINDER FOLLOWED THE PROGRESSION OF THE RAMPION ON her retina display, watching breathlessly as they entered Earth's atmosphere over northern Africa and careened toward Farafrah, a small oasis that had once been a trading post for caravans traveling between the central African provinces and the Mediterranean Sea. It had fallen into poverty since the plague had first struck a decade ago, sending the trade caravans farther east.

She didn't leave Wolf's side. She dressed the wounds as well as she could using the bandages and ointments the guard had thrown down from the ship's upper level. She had already had to change the bandages once, and still the blood soaked through. His face was pale and clammy, his heartbeat growing weaker, each breath a struggle.

Please, please, let Dr. Erland be there.

So far, the guard, at least, had proven trustworthy. He had flown straight and fast—very fast, to Cinder's relief. It was a risk entering Earth's orbit, but a necessary one. She only hoped this oasis would be the safe haven the doctor had believed it to be.

"Cinder," said Iko, "the Lunar is asking where he should land."

She shuddered. She'd been expecting the question. It would be safest, and most prudent, to land outside the town, out in the ruthless desert. But she could never carry Wolf and they didn't have the luxury of being prudent.

"Tell him to land on the main road. On the map it looks like there's only one—a town square of sorts. And tell him not to worry about being stealthy."

If they couldn't hide, then she would draw as much attention as possible. Maybe if they made enough of a spectacle it would draw Dr. Erland out from wherever he was hiding. She had to hope that any civilians would be so distracted by their brazenness, they wouldn't bother alerting the police until it was too late.

It wasn't a good plan, but there wasn't time to come up with anything better.

The ship dove. Normally this was the quiet part of landing, when the engine power switched to magnetic levitation, but it seemed the guard was planning on doing this all manually.

Perhaps the town was so rural, they didn't have magnetic roads at all.

Finally the ship clanked and groaned. Though it was a soft landing, the shock still made Cinder jump. Wolf groaned.

Cinder bent over him and cupped his face in both hands. "Wolf, I'm going to get help. Just stay with us, all right? Just hold on."

Standing, she keyed in the code for the podship dock.

The dock was a sight—blood and destruction everywhere. But she walked past the remaining shuttle and tried to put it all from her thoughts. "Iko, open hatch."

As soon as the doors had parted enough for her to fit through, she crouched on the ledge and jumped down into the street.

A cloud of dust whirled around her as her feet struck the hard, dry ground. The surrounding buildings were mostly single-story structures made of stone or clay or large beige bricks. Some window shutters had been painted blue or pink, and stenciled designs lined the entryways, but the colors had been bleached by the sun and chipped by relentless sand. The road dipped down toward an oasis lake a few blocks to Cinder's right, both sides lined with thriving palm trees—trees that looked too alive for a town that hung with desertion. A few blocks to her left was a stone wall lined with more trees and, beyond it, reddish plateaus disappearing in a sandy haze.

People were emerging from the buildings and around street corners, civilians of all ages, mostly dressed in shorts and light-weight tops to combat the desert heat, though a few wore more concealing robes to keep off the blazing sun. Many were covering their mouths and noses. At first Cinder thought they were pro-tecting themselves from the plague, but then she realized they were simply annoyed at how much dust the ship's landing had kicked up. The cloud was already blowing off down one of the side streets.

Cinder scanned them, searching for a wrinkled face and a familiar gray cap. Dr. Erland would be paler than most of the townspeople, although skin tones ranged from the deepest browns to honeyed tans. Still, she suspected that a little old man with glaringly blue eyes would have drawn some attention in the past weeks.

She opened her hands wide to show she had no weapons and took a step toward the crowd. Her cyborg hand was on full dis-play, and the townsfolk had noticed. They were staring at it openly, though no one shied away as she took another step closer.

"I'm sorry about the dust," she said, gesturing to the cloud.

"But this is an emergency. I need to find someone. A man. This tall, old, wears glasses and a hat. Have any of you—"

"I saw her first!" a girl squealed. She ran out from the crowd, her flip-flops smacking the dirt, and grasped Cinder's arm. Startled, Cinder tried to pull away, but the girl held firm.

Then there were two boys, not older than nine or ten, emerging from the crowd and arguing over who had seen the ship drop out of the sky, who had seen it land, who had seen the docks open, and who had first spotted the cyborg.

"Step away from Miss Linh, you greedy little vultures."

Cinder whirled around.

Dr. Erland was striding toward them, though she almost didn't recognize him. Barefoot and hatless, he wore a pair of khaki shorts and a striped shirt that hung lopsided, as he'd missed a buttonhole and the rest of the buttons were all wrong. His gray hair stuck out along his bald spot like he'd recently been electrocuted.

None of that mattered. She'd found him.

"I suppose you can all *share* the prize for finding her, even though the deal was to bring her to me, not make me come all the way down here in this center-of-the-sun heat." He pulled a bag of gummy candies from his pocket and held it up over the children's heads, forcing them to *promise to share* before he handed it over. They snatched it and ran away squealing.

The rest of the townspeople remained where they were.

Dr. Erland planted his hands on his hips and glared up at Cinder. "You have *much* explaining to do. Do you know how long I've been waiting for you, watching the—"

"I need your help!" she said, stumbling toward him. "My friend . . . he's dying . . . he needs a doctor . . . I don't know what to do."

He scowled, then his attention caught on something over Cinder's shoulder. The Lunar guard emerged at the edge of the ship, shirtless and covered in blood and straining to support Wolf's body.

"What—he's—"

"A Lunar guard," said Cinder. "And Wolf is one of her soldiers. It's a long story, and I'll explain later, but can you help him? He was shot twice, he's lost a lot of blood. . . ."

Dr. Erland raised an eyebrow. Cinder could tell he wasn't at all thrilled with the company she was keeping.

"*Please.*"

Harrumphing, he gestured at some of the onlookers and called out a few names. Three men stepped forward. "Bring him to the hotel," he said. "*Gently.*" With a sigh, he set about redoing the buttons on his shirt. "Follow me, Miss Linh. You can help prepare the tools."

Fifteen

"I SUPPOSE IT'S TOO MUCH TO HOPE THAT WE LANDED ourselves near any sort of civilization," Thorne said, tilting his head to one side.

Cress picked her way through the debris to the nearest window. "I'm not sure we want to be near civilization. You're a wanted criminal in three Earthen countries, and one of the most recognizable men on Earth."

"I am pretty famous now, aren't I?" Grinning, he waved a hand at her. "I guess it doesn't matter what we want. What do you see out there?"

Standing on tiptoes, Cress peered into the brightness. As her eyes adjusted to the glare, they widened, trying to take it all in.

All at once, it dawned on her. She was on Earth. *On Earth.*

She'd seen pictures, of course. Thousands and thousands of photographs and vids—cities and lakes and forests and mountains, every landscape imaginable. But she had never thought the sky could be so impossibly blue, or that the land could hold so many hues of gold, or could glitter like a sea of diamonds, or could roll and swell like a breathing creature.

For one moment, the reality of it all poured into her body and overflowed.

"Cress?"

"It's beautiful out there."

A hesitation, before, "Could you be more specific?"

"The sky is this gorgeous, intense blue color." She pressed her fingers to the glass and traced the wavy hills on the horizon.

"Oh, good. You've really narrowed it down for me."

"I'm sorry, it's just..." She tried to stamp down the rush of emotion. "I think we're in a desert."

"Cactuses and tumbleweeds?"

"No. Just a lot of sand. It's kind of orangish-gold, with hints of pink, and I can see tiny clouds of it floating above the ground, like... like smoke."

"Piled up in lots of hills?"

"Yes, exactly! And it's *beautiful*."

Thorne snorted. "If this is how you feel about a desert, I can't wait until you see your first real tree. Your mind will explode."

She beamed out at the world. *Trees.*

"That explains the heat then," Thorne said. Cress, in her thin cotton dress, hadn't noticed before, but the temperature did seem to be rising. The controls must have been reset in the fall, or perhaps destroyed altogether. "A desert would not have been my first choice. Do you see anything useful? Palm trees? Watering holes? A pair of camels out for a stroll?"

She looked again, noting how a pattern of ripples had been carved into the landscape, repeating for eternity. "No. There's nothing else."

"All right, here's what I need you to do." Thorne ticked off on his fingers. "First, find some way to contact the Rampion. The sooner we can get back on my ship, the better. Second, let's see if we can get that door open. We're going to be baked alive if the temperature keeps rising like this."

Cress studied the mess of screens and cords on the floor. "The satellite was never installed with external communication abilities. The only chance we had of contacting your crew was the D-COMM chip that Sybil took. And even if we did have some way of contacting them, we won't be able to give exact coordinates unless the satellite positioning system is functioning, and even then—"

Thorne held up a hand. "One thing at a time. We have to let them know that we're not dead, and check that they're all right too. I think they're capable of handling two measly Lunars, but it would put my mind at ease to be sure." He shrugged. "Once they know to start looking for us, maybe Cinder can whip up a giant metal detector or something."

Cress scanned the wreckage. "I'm not sure anything is salvageable. The screens are all destroyed, and judging from the loss of temperature regulation, the generator is—oh, no. *Little Cress!*" She wailed and kicked her way to the main databoard that had housed her younger self. It was crushed on one side, bits of wire and plastic dangling from the shell. "Oh, Little Cress..."

"Um, who's Little Cress?"

She sniffed. "Me. When I was ten. She lived in the computer and kept me company and now she's dead." She squeezed the databoard against her chest. "Poor, sweet Little Cress."

After a long silence, Thorne cleared his throat. "Scarlet did warn me about this. Do we need to bury Little Cress before we can move on? Want me to say a few words for her?"

Cress glanced up, and though his expression was sympathetic, she thought he was probably mocking her. "I'm not crazy. I know she's just a computer. It's just...I programmed her myself, and she was the only friend I had. That's all."

"Hey, I'm not judging. I'm familiar with IT-relations. Just wait until you meet our spaceship. She's a riot." His expression became thoughtful. "Speaking of spaceships, what about that other pod, the one the guard docked with?"

"Oh, I'd forgotten about that!" She tucked the databoard beneath its slanted desk and tripped over to the other entryway. The satellite sat at an angle, with the second entry near the lower end of the slope, and she had to clear away countless bits of plastic and broken equipment before she could get to the control screen. The screen itself was down—she couldn't get a flicker of power out of it—so she opened the panel that housed the manual override locks instead. A series of gears and handles had been set into the wall over the door, and while Cress had known they were there for years, she'd never given them much thought before.

The devices were stuck from years of neglect and it took all her strength to pull on the handle, planting one foot on the wall to gain leverage. Finally it snapped down and the doors sprang open, leaving a gap.

Hearing her struggle, Thorne got up and trudged toward her, carefully kicking debris out of his way. He kept his hands outstretched until he bumped into her and together they pried open the door.

The docking hatch was in worse shape than the satellite. Almost an entire wall had been sheared off and piles of sand had already begun to blow in between the cracks. Wires and clamps dangled from the shattered wall panels and Cress could smell smoke and the bitter scent of burned plastic. The podship had been shoved up into the corridor, crumpling the far end of the hatch like an accordion. The docking clamp had been rammed straight through the ship's cockpit control panel, filling the glass with hairline fractures.

"Please tell me it looks better than it smells," said Thorne, hanging on to the door frame.

"Not really. The ship is destroyed, and it looks like all the instruments too." Cress climbed down, holding on to the wall for balance. She tried pressing some buttons to bring the ship back to life, but it was useless.

"All right. Next plan." Thorne rubbed his eyes. "We have no way of contacting the Rampion and they have no way of knowing we're alive. Probably won't do us much good to stay here and hope someone passes by. We're going to have to try and find some sort of civilization."

She wrapped her arms around herself, a mix of nerves and giddiness swirling in her stomach. She was going to leave the satellite.

"It looked like the sun was setting," she said. "So at least we won't be walking in the heat."

Thorne screwed up his lips in thought. "This time of year the nights shouldn't be too cold, no matter which hemisphere we've landed in. We need to gather up all the supplies we can carry. Do you have any more blankets? And you'll want a jacket."

Cress rubbed her palms down the thin dress. "I don't have a jacket. I've never needed one."

Thorne sighed. "Figures."

"I do have another dress that isn't quite so worn as this one."

"Pants would be better."

She glanced down at her bare legs. She'd never worn pants before. "These dresses are all Sybil brought me. I ... I don't have any shoes, either."

"No shoes?" Thorne massaged his brow. "All right, fine. I went through survival training in the military. I can figure this out."

"I do have a few bottles we can fill with water. And plenty of food packs."

"It's a start. Water is our first priority. Dehydration will be a much bigger threat than hunger. Do you have any towels?"

"A couple."

"Good. Bring those; and something we can use for rope." He raised his left foot. "While you're at it, do you have any idea where my other boot ended up?"

"ARE YOU SURE YOU DON'T WANT ME TO DO THAT?"

Thorne scowled, his empty gaze pinned somewhere around her knee. "I may be temporarily blind, but I'm not useless. I can still tie good knots."

Cress scratched at her ear and withheld further comment. She was seated on the edge of her bed, braiding a discarded lock of her own hair to use for rope, while Thorne knelt before her. His face was set in concentration as he wrapped a towel around her foot, then looped the "rope" around her ankle and the arch of her foot a few times before securing it with an elaborate knot.

"We want them to be nice and tight. If the fabric is too loose it will rub and give you blisters. How does that feel?"

She wiggled her toes. "Good," she said, and waited until Thorne had finished the other foot before surreptitiously adjusting the folds of the cloth to be more comfortable. When she stood, it felt strange—like walking on lumpy pillows—but Thorne seemed to think she'd be grateful for the makeshift shoes when they were out in the desert.

Together, they fashioned a bundle out of a blanket, which

they filled with water, food, bedsheets, and a small medical kit that Cress had rarely needed. The knife was safely in Thorne's boot and they'd disassembled part of the busted bed frame for Thorne to use as a walking cane. They each drank as much water as they could stand and then, as Cress gave one last inspection of the satellite and could think of nothing else worth taking, she stepped to the docking hatch and pulled down the manual unlock lever. With a *kathunk*, the door's internal devices released. The hydraulics hissed. A crack opened between the metal doors, allowing Thorne to get his fingers in and push one side into its wall pocket.

A breeze of dry air blew into the satellite—a scent Cress had no comparison for. It was nothing like the satellite or the machinery or Sybil's perfume.

Earth, she supposed, memorizing the aroma. *Or desert.*

Thorne swung the makeshift supply bundle over his shoulder. Kicking some debris out of the way, he reached his hand toward Cress.

"Lead the way."

His hand encased hers and she wanted to savor the moment, the sensation of touch and warmth and this perfect smell of freedom, but Thorne was nudging her forward before the moment had settled.

At the end of the docking hatch was the rail and two steps leading down to where a podship normally attached, but now there was only sand, tinted lavender as night's shadows crept forward. It had already started to blow up onto the second step and Cress had a vision of the satellite being slowly buried beneath it, disappearing forever in the desert.

And then she looked out, past the railing and the dunes, toward the rolling horizon. The sky was a haze of violet, and where that faded away—blue and black and stars. The same stars she'd known all her life, and yet now they were spread out like a blanket over her. Now there was an entire sky and an entire world ready to engulf her.

Her head swam. Suddenly dizzy, Cress stumbled backward, crashing into Thorne.

"What? What is it?"

She tried to swallow down the rising panic, this sensation that her existence was as small and unimportant as the tiniest fleck of sand blowing against her shins. There was a whole world—a whole planet. And she was stuck somewhere in the middle of it, away from everything. There were no walls, no boundaries, nothing to hide behind. A shudder swept over her, goose bumps crawling across her bare arms.

"Cress. What happened? What do you see?" Thorne's fingers tightened on her arms, and she realized she was trembling.

She stammered twice before forcing the thought out of her head. "It—it's so big."

"What's so big?"

"Everything. Earth. The sky. It didn't seem so big from space."

Her pulse was a drum, thundering through every artery. She could hardly take in any air, and she had to cover her face and turn away before she could breathe again. Even then the sensation was painful.

Suddenly she was crying, without knowing when the tears had started.

Thorne's hands found her elbows, tender and gentle. There was a moment in which she expected to be taken into his arms, pressed warm and safe against his chest. She yearned for it.

But instead, he shook her—hard.

"Stop it!"

Cress hiccupped.

"What is the number one thing people die from in the desert?"

She blinked, and another hot tear slipped down her cheek. "Wh-what?"

"The number one cause of deaths. What is it?"

"De-dehydration?" she said, recalling the Survival 101 lecture he'd given while filling up their water bottles.

"And what does crying do?"

It took a moment. "Dehydrates?"

"Exactly." His grip relaxed. "It's all right to be scared. I get that until now most of your existence has been contained in two hundred square meters. In fact, so far you've shown yourself to be saner than I expected."

She sniffed, unsure if he'd just complimented or insulted her.

"But I need you to pull yourself together. You may have noticed that I'm not exactly in prime form right now, and I am relying on you to be aware and observant and help us find our way out of this, because if we don't . . . I don't know about you, but I'm just not fond of the idea of being stranded out here and eaten alive by vultures. So, can I depend on you to hold it together? For both of us?"

"Yes," she whispered, though her chest was about to burst with all the doubts being crammed into it.

Thorne squinted and she didn't think he believed her.

"I'm not convinced that you fully grasp the situation here, Cress. We will be eaten. Alive. By vultures. Can you visualize that for a second?"

"Y-yes. Vultures. I understand."

"Good. Because I *need* you. And those are not words that I throw around every day. Now, are you going to be all right?"

"Yes. Just give me—I just need a moment."

This time, she took in an extra deep breath and shut her eyes and grappled for a daydream, any daydream . . .

"I am an explorer," she whispered, "setting courageously off into the wild unknown." It was not a daydream she'd ever had before, but she felt the familiar comfort of her imagination wrapping around her. She was an archaeologist, a scientist, a treasure hunter. She was a master of land and sea. "My life is an adventure," she said, growing confident as she opened her eyes again. "I will not be shackled to this satellite anymore."

Thorne tilted his head to one side. He waited for three heartbeats before sliding one hand down into hers. "I have no idea what you're talking about," he said. "But we'll go with it."

Sixteen

THORNE PASSED THE MAKESHIFT CANE TO HIS OPPOSITE SIDE
so he could hold Cress's elbow as they stepped out onto the sand.
She kept her head down, carefully choosing each step but also
afraid that if she looked up into the sky, her legs would freeze
beneath her and she would never be able to make them move
again.

When they'd gone a safe distance from the satellite, Cress
tentatively lifted her gaze. Ahead of her was the same eternal
landscape, the sky growing darker.

She glanced back toward the satellite, and gasped.

Thorne's hand squeezed her elbow.

"There are mountains," she said, gaping at the jagged peaks
along the horizon.

He squinted. "Mountains, or glorified hills?"

She considered the question, comparing the site before her
with the photos of mountain ranges she'd seen on the screens.
Dozens of peaks of varying heights disappeared into the blackness of night.

"I think . . . real mountains," she said. "But it's getting dark, and
I can't see any white on top. Do mountains always have snow?"

"Not always. How far are they?"

"Um . . ." They seemed close, but the foothills and sand dunes between them could have been deceiving, and she'd never been asked to judge distances before.

"Never mind." Thorne tapped the cane against the ground. It stirred something in Cress's gut when he didn't let go of her arm, though perhaps he appreciated the tethering sensation as much as she did. "What direction are they in?"

She took his hand and pointed. Her heart was fluttering erratically and she felt herself trapped between elation and terror. Even from this distance, she could tell that the mountains were enormous—hulking, ancient beasts lined up like an impenetrable wall dividing this wasteland. But at least they were *something*, a physical, visual marker to break up the monotony of the desert. They somehow calmed her, even while making her feel as insignificant as ever.

"So that must be . . . south, right?" He pointed in another direction. "The sun set over there?"

She followed his gesture, where a faint green light could still be seen over the rolling dunes, fading fast. "Yes," she said, a shaky smile stretching across her lips. Her first true sunset. She'd never known sunsets could be green, had never known just how quickly the darkness set in. Her thoughts hummed as she tried to pull together every minute detail, to store this moment safely away in a place where she would never, ever forget. Not the way the light turned dull and hazy above the desert. Not the way the stars emerged from the black. Not the way her instincts kept her gaze from wandering too far up into the sky, keeping her panic at bay.

"Do you see any plant life? Anything other than sand and mountains?"

"Not from here. But I can hardly see anything..." Even as they spoke, the blackness was taking over, the once-golden sand turning into shadows beneath her feet. "There's our parachute," she added, noting the deflated white fabric that stretched out over a sand dune. It was already being swallowed up by the shifting sands. A trench had been carved into the dune where the satellite had hit and slid down.

"We should cut off a piece," said Thorne. "It could come in handy, especially if it's waterproof."

They said little as Cress guided him up the dune, the journey made difficult by the unstable ground. Thorne was awkward with the cane, trying to test the ground ahead of him without digging the tip into the hillside and stabbing himself with the other end. Finally they reached the parachute and managed to cut off a square large enough to be used as a tarp.

"Let's head toward the mountains," said Thorne. "It will keep us from walking directly into the sun in the morning, and with any luck they'll offer some shelter, and maybe even water."

Cress thought it sounded like as good a plan as any, but for the first time she noted a tinge of uncertainty in Thorne's tone. He was just guessing. He didn't know where they were or what direction would lead them to civilization. Every step they took could be leading them farther and farther from safety.

But a decision had to be made.

Together, they started up the next dune. The day's heat was fading, and a mild breeze kicked sand at her shins. When they reached the top, she found herself staring into an ocean of nothingness. Night had arrived and she couldn't even make out the mountains anymore. But as the stars grew brighter and her eyes adjusted, Cress realized that the world around her was not pitch-black but tinged with a faint silver hue.

Thorne tripped, yelping as he stumbled and collapsed onto his hands and knees. The makeshift cane was left jutting up from the sand, having narrowly missed impaling Thorne when he fell.

Gasping, Cress dropped to her knees beside him and pressed one hand against his back. "Are you all right?"

Roughly shaking her off, Thorne pushed himself back to sit on his heels. In the dim light, Cress could see that his jaw was clenched tight, his hands balled into fists.

"Captain?"

"I'm fine," he said, an edge to his tone.

Cress hesitated, her fingers hovering over his shoulder.

She watched as his chest expanded with a slow breath, and listened to the shaky, strained exhale.

"I," he began, speaking slowly, "am not happy with this turn of events."

Cress bit her lip, burning with sympathy. "What can I do?"

After a moment of glaring absently toward the mountains, Thorne shook his head. "Nothing," he said, reaching back until his arm hit the cane. He wrapped his fingers around it. "I can do this. I just need to figure it out."

He climbed to his feet and yanked the traitorous cane out of the sand. "Actually, if you could try to give me some warning when we're coming up on a hill, or about to start heading down again, that would help."

"Of course. We're almost to the top of . . ." She trailed off as her eyes left Thorne's face to seek out the top of the dune and caught on the moon, a crescent glowing vivid and white off the horizon. She shriveled away from it, habit telling her to hide beneath her desk or bed until the moon couldn't find her anymore—but there was no desk or bed to crawl beneath. And as the initial surprise wore off, she began to realize that the sight of the moon didn't grip her with terror as it once had. From Earth, it somehow seemed so very far away. She gulped. "... almost to the top of this dune."

Thorne quirked his head to the side. "What's wrong?"

"Nothing. I just ... I can see Luna. That's all."

She let her gaze wander away from the moon, taking in the night sky. She was tentative at first, worried that looking at the sky would once again overwhelm her, but she soon discovered that there was something comforting about seeing the same galaxy she'd always known. The same stars she'd been looking at all her life, seen through a new lens.

The tension in her body released, bit by bit. This was familiar. This was safe. The faint swirl of gasses in the universe, glowing purple and blue. The sparkle of thousands and thousands of stars, as numerous as sand grains, as breathtaking as an Earthen sunrise seen through her satellite window.

Her pulse skipped. "Wait—the constellations," she said, spinning in a circle while Thorne brushed the sand from his knees.

"What?"

"There—there's Pegasus, and Pisces, and—oh! It's Andromeda!"

"What are you ... oh." Thorne dug the cane into the sand, settling his weight against it. "For navigation." He rubbed his jaw. "Those are all Northern Hemisphere constellations. That rules out Australia, at least."

"Wait. Give me a minute. I can figure this out." Cress pressed her fingers against the sides of her face, trying to picture herself looking at these same constellations, how many countless times from the windows of her satellite. She focused on Andromeda, the largest in sight, with its alpha star glowing like a beacon not far off the horizon. Where would her satellite have been in relation to Earth when she was seeing that star, at that angle?

After a moment, the constellations began to spread out like a holograph in her mind. As if she were seeing the shimmering illusion of Earth rotating slowly before her, surrounded by spaceships and satellites and stars, stars, *stars*...

"I think we're in northern Africa," she said, turning around to scan the other constellations that were emerging from the ocean of stars. "Or possibly the Commonwealth, in one of the western provinces."

Thorne's brow knit together. "Could be the Sahara." His shoulders began to slump and Cress saw the moment when he realized that it made no difference what hemisphere they were in, what country. It was still a desert. They were still trapped. "We can't stand here stargazing all night," he said, bending down to pick up the bag of supplies and resituate it on his shoulder. "Let's keep heading toward those mountains."

Cress tried to offer him her elbow again, but Thorne only gave it a gentle squeeze before letting go. "Throws off my balance," he said, testing the length of the cane so he could walk without spearing it into the ground again. "I'll be fine."

Burying her disappointment, Cress started up the dune. She announced the top when they reached it, and continued down the other side.

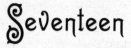

Seventeen

SCARLET WAS PILOTING THE PODSHIP. SHE COULD NOT RECALL how long she had been flying it, or where she had been before, or how she had ended up behind these controls. But she knew very well *why* she was there.

Because she wanted to be.

Because she *needed* to be.

If she did well, she would be rewarded. The thought made her feel joyful. Eager. Willing.

And so she flew fast. She flew steady. She allowed the little ship to become an extension of her. Her hands gripping the controls, her fingers dancing over the instruments. She had never flown so well, not since the day her grandmother had begun teaching her in the delivery ship around the farm. How the ship had warbled under her unskilled hands. How it rocked and sank, its landing gear brushing against the just-tilled dirt, then miraculously drifted back up toward the sky as her grandmother's patient voice talked her through the steps...

The memory disappeared as fast as it had come, snapping her back into the podship, and she could not remember what she had just been thinking. She could only think of this flight. This moment. This responsibility.

She paid no heed to the stars blurring out in all directions. She gave no thought to the planet falling farther and farther behind her.

In the ship's backseat, the woman was hissing and cursing as she tended to her wound. She was upset, and this alone bothered Scarlet, because she wanted the woman to be pleased.

Eventually, the angry muttering died down and then the woman was talking. Scarlet's heart fluttered, until she realized that it was not to her that the woman was speaking. Rather, she had sent out a comm. She heard two words that sent a bolt of panic through her—*Your Majesty.*

She was talking to the queen herself.

It occurred to Scarlet that this knowledge should terrify her, but she couldn't recall why. Rather, she felt embarrassed to be listening in. It wasn't her place to be curious. She tried to ignore the conversation, allowing her mind to muddle and wander. Inside her head, she recited childhood rhymes that she hadn't thought of in years.

It mostly worked. Only when a name broached her consciousness did curiosity overcome her.

Linh Cinder.

"No, I could not capture her. I was overpowered. I am sorry, Your Majesty. I have failed you. Yes, I have already sent the last-known coordinates of the ship to the royal guard. I was able to capture a hostage, Your Majesty. One of her accomplices. Perhaps she has information on where Linh Cinder might go next, or what her plan could be. I know it isn't good enough, Your Majesty. I will make this up to you, Your Majesty. I *will* find her."

The conversation ended and Scarlet's ears burned at having eavesdropped. She was ashamed. She deserved punishment.

In an attempt to make up for her delinquency, she refocused on her task. Flying as smooth and fast as any pilot had ever flown. She thought only of how she must fly well. She thought only of how she must make her mistress proud of her.

She felt no awe as she approached the great, crater-filled Luna with its gleaming white surface and sparkling domed cities.

Cities that were home to countless strangers.

Cities that had been his *home, once...*

She flinched at the intrusive thought. She did not know what it meant. She could not remember who *he* was.

But this was where he came from...

She suppressed the voice out of nervous panic that her mistress would sense her confusion. She did not want that. There was no confusion.

She knew precisely where she wanted to be. Precisely who she wished to be serving.

Scarlet felt no fear as the moon dwarfed the tiny ship, expanded until it was all she could see through the glass.

She paid no attention to the hot tears as they crept down her cheeks and dripped soundlessly into her lap.

Eighteen

IT DIDN'T TAKE LONG FOR CRESS AND THORNE TO FALL INTO A
pattern. As Thorne became more comfortable with the movement of the sand underneath them and the sensation of the cane
in his hand, he grew more confident, and their pace increased.
Three dunes. Five. Ten. Before long, Cress realized that it took a
lot less energy to stay in the valleys between the dunes when they
could, so she began cutting a slower, yet less exhausting zigzag
route across the desert.

As she walked, the towels around her feet began to loosen
and grains of sand slipped in and got caught between her toes,
despite how tight Thorne had tied the ropes of hair. The soles of
her feet began to burn and a cramp was threatening to overtake
her left foot from the constant grab and release of her toes on
the unstable ground. Her legs ached. Cress's body began to rebel
as they rambled up yet another dune. Her thighs would burn as
she crested one more hill—but then her shins would cry out as
they descended the other side. Her silly fitness routines aboard
the satellite hadn't prepared her for this.

But she did not complain. She panted a great deal. She swiped
at the sweat drops on her temples. She clenched her jaw against
the hurt. But she did not complain.

At least she could see, she reminded herself. And at least she didn't have to carry the supplies. She heard Thorne switch shoulders from time to time, but he didn't complain either.

Sometimes when they struck a flat spot, she closed her eyes to see how long she could go without opening them. Vertigo would set in almost immediately. Panic would blossom at the base of her spine and crawl up it until she was sure each new step would bring her in contact with a rock or a small hill and she would stumble face-first into the sand.

The fourth time she did it, Thorne asked her why they kept slowing down. She kept her eyes open after that.

"Do you need to take a break?" Thorne asked, hours later.

"N-no," she huffed, her thighs burning. "We're almost to the top of this dune."

"Sure? No point passing out from exhaustion."

She breathed a sigh of relief upon reaching the top of the dune, but dread quickly took its place. She didn't know why she'd expected this dune to be different from the dozens they'd already crested. She didn't know why she'd been thinking that this must have marked the end of the desert, because she didn't think she could go much farther.

But it was not the end. The world was made of more dunes, more sand, more nothingness.

"Really. Let's take a break," Thorne said, setting down the pack and stabbing the cane into the ground. He spent a moment working the kinks from his shoulders, before hunching over and undoing the bundle's knot. He handed Cress one of the water bottles and took another for himself.

"Shouldn't we ration it?" she asked.

He shook his head. "It's best to drink when we're thirsty, and just try to keep sweating to a minimum—as much as possible.

Our bodies will be better able to maintain hydration that way, even if we do run out of water. And we should avoid eating until we find another water source. Digestion uses up a lot of water too."

"That's fine. I'm not hungry." Which was true—the heat seemed to have stolen what appetite she'd had.

When she'd drank all she could, Cress handed the bottle back to Thorne and fantasized about collapsing into the sand and going to sleep, but she dared not, fearing she would never get up again. When Thorne lifted the pack, she took off down the hill without question.

"What do you think is happening on your ship?" Cress asked as they descended the hill. The question had been echoing in her mind for hours, but the water had finally made her capable of speech. "Do you think Mistress Sybil . . ."

"They're fine," Thorne said, with unrelenting confidence. "I pity the person who goes up against Wolf, and Cinder's made of tougher stuff than people realize." A pause, before a hearty laugh burst through the quiet desert air. "Literally, in fact."

"Wolf. That must be the other man on the ship?"

"Yes, and Scarlet is his . . . well, I don't really know what they call themselves, but he's lunatic-crazy for her. Scarlet's not a bad shot, herself. That thaumaturge had no idea what she was walking into."

Cress hoped he was right. Mistress Sybil had found them because of *her*, and the guilt was as painful as the deep aches in her bones.

"So how did a girl born on Luna get stuck in a satellite and become an Earthen sympathizer, anyway?"

She wrinkled her nose. "Well. When my parents found out I was a shell, they gave me up to be killed, because of the infanticide laws. But Mistress saved me and raised me instead, along with some other shells she'd rescued. She mostly just wanted us for some sort of experiments they're always running, but Mistress never really explained it to me. We used to live in some of the lava tubes that had been converted into dormitories, and we were always being monitored by these cameras that were connected to Luna's communication system. It was sort of cramped, but not too bad, and we had ports and netscreens, so we weren't entirely cut off from the outside world. After a while I got really good at hacking into the communication system, which I mostly just used for silly stuff. We were all curious about school, so I used to hack into the Lunar school system and download the study guides, things like that."

Cress squinted up at the moon, now so far away. It was hard to believe it's where she came from. "Then one day, one of the older boys—Julian—asked me if I thought I could find out who his parents were. It took a couple days, but I did, and we learned that his parents lived in one of the lumber domes, and that they were both alive, and that he had two younger siblings. And then we figured out how to send them a message and tell them that he was alive. He thought that if they knew he hadn't been killed after all, they would come find him. We got so excited, thinking we could all contact our families. That we would all be rescued." She gulped. "It was really naïve, of course. The next day, Mistress came and took Julian away, and then some technicians removed all of the monitoring equipment so we couldn't access the net anymore. I never saw Julian again. I think . . . I think his parents must have contacted the authorities when they got his comm, and I think he may have been killed, to prove that the infanticide laws were being taken seriously."

She ran her fingers absently through her hair, surprised when they slipped through it so quickly. "After that, Mistress Sybil started to pay more attention to me. She sometimes took me out of the caverns and up into the domes and gave me different tasks. Altering the coding of the broadcast system. Tapping into net-links. Programming intelligence software to pick up on specific verbal cues and divert information to separate comm accounts. At first I loved it. Mistress was nice to me then, and it meant I got to leave the lava tubes and see some of the city. I felt like I was becoming her favorite, and that if I did what she asked me to do, eventually it wouldn't matter that I was a shell anymore, and I would be allowed to go to school and be just like any normal Lunar.

"Well, one day Sybil asked me to hack a communication between a couple of European diplomats and I told her that the signal was too weak. I needed to be closer to Earth, and I required better net connectivity, and advanced software . . ."

Cress shook her head, remembering how she had told Sybil exactly what Sybil would need to craft the satellite for her young prodigy. Cress had practically designed her own prison.

"A few months later, Mistress came to get me, and told me we were going on a trip. We boarded a podship, and I was so, so excited. I thought she was taking me to Artemisia, to be presented to the queen herself, to be forgiven for being born a shell. It feels so stupid now. Even when we started flying away from Luna, and I saw that we were heading toward Earth, I thought that's where we were going. I figured, all right, maybe Lunars really can't accept me this way, but Mistress knows that Earthens will. So she's letting me go to Earth, instead. The trip took hours and hours and by the end of it I was shaking with excitement, and I'd worked up this whole story in my head, how Mistress was going to give me to some nice Earthen couple, and they would raise me as their own, and they lived in an enormous tree house—I don't know why I thought they would live in a tree house, but for some reason that's what I was hoping for. I mean, I'd never seen real trees." She frowned. "Still haven't, actually."

There was a short silence, before Thorne said, "And that's when she took you to the satellite, and you became the queen's programmer."

"Programmer, hacker, spy...somehow, I never stopped believing that if I did everything she asked, someday they would let me go."

"And how long before you decided that you'd rather be trying to save Earthen royalty than spy on them?"

"I don't know. I was always fascinated by Earth. I spent a lot of time reading Earthen news and watching their dramas. I started to feel connected to the people down there...down here. More than I ever did to Lunars." She wrung her hands. "After a while, I started to pretend that I was a secret guardian, and it was my job to protect Earth and its people from Levana."

To her relief, Thorne didn't laugh. He didn't say anything for a long time and Cress couldn't determine if the silence was comforting or awkward. Maybe he thought her fantasies were childish.

A long while later, Thorne finally spoke. "If I'd been in your position, and I had only one D-COMM chip that I could use to communicate with Earth, I would have found some dirt on a hotshot spaceship pilot and blackmailed him into coming to get me out of that satellite, rather than trying to rescue the emperor."

Though he looked serious, Cress couldn't help but smile. "No, you wouldn't have. You would have done the same thing I did, because you know that the threat Levana poses to Earth is much bigger than you or me . . . much bigger than any of us."

But the captain just shook his head. "That's very good of you to say, Cress. But trust me. I would have blackmailed someone."

Nineteen

KAI SCOOPED HIS HAIR OFF HIS BROW, STARING AT THE holograph that floated above the conference table with a mixture of horror and awe. Part of him wanted to laugh. Not at all because it was funny, but because there didn't seem to be any better reaction.

The holograph showed the planet Earth. And all around it were hundreds of small yellow lights, many clumped above Earth's most-populated cities.

Hundreds of tiny spaceships.

They were surrounded.

"And they're all Lunar?" he said. "We're sure?"

"Without a doubt," said European Prime Minister Bromstad, his face grouped with the other Earthen Union leaders on the massive netscreen. "What's most disconcerting is that we were given zero indication of their approach. It's as if they all just... *flickered* into existence, ten thousand kilometers over our heads."

"Or," said Queen Camilla of the United Kingdom, "as if they were there all along, but we were unable to detect them. Haven't we been hearing for years about these Lunar ships sneaking into our atmosphere, bypassing all of our security measures?"

"Does it matter how long they've been there, or how they got there in the first place?" asked American Republic President Vargas. "They're obviously there now, and this is obviously a threat."

Kai squeezed his eyes shut. "But *why*? She's getting exactly what she wants. Why threaten us now? Why show us her hand?"

"Perhaps to ensure the Commonwealth doesn't back out of the marriage alliance at the last minute?" Bromstad suggested.

"But she has absolutely no reason—" Kai huffed and dropped his hand to the back of his chair…what had once been his father's chair. He was far too restless to sit down as he glanced around at his cabinet members and advisers, his country's highly educated experts, who were looking as baffled as he felt. "What do you all make of this?"

His experts traded looks among themselves, before Chairman Deshal Huy started to drum his fingers against the table. "It does seem to indicate that they're sending us a message of some sort."

"Perhaps this is their way of RSVPing for the wedding," muttered Governor-General Williams from Australia.

"Perhaps we should ask them," said Konn Torin, tapping a finger against his brow. "If Luna is to become a peaceful ally of the Earthen Union, we might as well start opening the lines of communication."

"Naturally," said Africa's Prime Minister Kamin. Kai could all but hear her rolling her eyes. "As they've been so open with us in the past."

"And you have a better idea?"

"*I* certainly do," said Williams. "This could be our best chance to reciprocate the recent invasion. We should coordinate a full-scale attack—take out as many of these ships as we can. Show Luna that they can't keep threatening us every time Levana throws another fit. If they want a fight, we'll fight."

"War," said Prime Minister Kamin. "You're suggesting we start a war."

"*They* started the war. I'm suggesting we end it."

Kamin sniffed. "And you think our militaries are prepared to launch an attack against an entire fleet of Lunar ships? We don't have the faintest idea what type of weaponry they have, and I think the recent attacks illustrated that they're not going to fight by any strategies we're familiar with. They're unpredictable, and as much as it pains me to admit, our military expertise has suffered from generations of peace. Our numbers are down, few of our men have been trained for space combat—"

"I agree with Australia," interrupted Queen Camilla. "This could be the only time we ever have the element of surprise on our side."

"*Surprise?*" barked President Vargas. "They're surrounding *us.* What if they're hoping that we attack them? What if all this drivel about the marriage alliance has been a ruse, just to keep us distracted while they move into position?"

Kai's knuckles whitened on the back of the chair. "The alliance isn't a ruse, and nobody is starting a war!"

Camilla smirked. "Oh, yes. I'd forgotten that the young emperor is so very knowledgeable in these matters."

His blood began to simmer. "This holograph indicates that while these ships may have Earth surrounded, they are still outside the territorial designations of the Earthen Union. Correct?"

"For now," said Governor-General Williams.

"Right. Which means that *for now,* these ships aren't violating any terms that we've established with Luna. I'm not saying Levana isn't taunting us or threatening us, but it would be foolish of us to react to it without first coming up with some sort of strategy."

Williams shook his head. "By the time we've finished strategizing, we very well may have been obliterated."

"Fine," said Kai, squaring his shoulders. "The Treaty of Bremen states we need a majority rule to execute an act of war against any political entity. All in favor to attack these Lunar ships, say aye."

"Aye," said Williams and Camilla in unison. The other three leaders remained silent, but Kai could tell from their pinched expressions that no one was happy about it.

"Measure fails."

"Then what do *you* propose we do?" asked Queen Camilla.

"There is a Lunar delegate staying in the palace right now," said Kai, cringing to himself. "I'll speak with him. See if I can figure out what's going on. The alliance negotiations are between Luna and the Commonwealth, so just let me handle it."

He canceled the communication link before the other leaders could argue, or see how frustrated he was becoming. Frustrated that he never knew what Levana was thinking or what she was going to do next. Frustrated that he was bowing to her every whim and yet she still decided to pull a stunt like this, for no apparent reason other than to get the rest of the Union all riled up. Frustrated that, if he were honest with himself, a large part of him agreed that attacking those ships might be the best course of action.

But if war broke out, they had no chance of completing the peace alliance, which meant no hope for getting their hands on the letumosis antidote.

He glanced around at the other men and women sitting around the holograph. "Thank you," he said, his voice sounding almost calm. "That will be all."

"Your Majesty," said Nainsi, rolling into the boardroom as the experts filed out, "you have a meeting scheduled with Tashmi-jiĕ in six minutes."

He stifled a groan. "Let me guess. We must be discussing table linens today?"

"I believe catering staff, Your Majesty."

"Ah, right, that sounds like an excellent use of my time." He clipped his portscreen to his belt. "Let her know I'm on my way."

"THANK YOU FOR AGREEING TO MEET ME OUT HERE," SAID Tashmi Priya, bowing. "I thought the fresh air might help you focus on some of the final decisions to be made in regards to the ceremony."

Kai smiled wryly. "That's a very diplomatic way of pointing out that I haven't been taking this wedding planning very seriously. Which is probably true." He tucked his hands into his pockets, amazed at how good the crisp breeze felt on his face. He was still flushed with irritation after the meeting with the Union leaders. "Although, it is nice to be out here. I feel like I haven't left my office all month."

"I suspect there is security footage somewhere to prove that."

They passed by a koi pond, shadowed by the drooping branches of a weeping willow and surrounded by a patch of the gardens that had been recently dug up and tilled, prepared to replant for the coming autumn season. Smelling the fresh earth, Kai was momentarily baffled at how the life of the palace continued—how the life of the city and the Commonwealth and all of Earth had gone on, even while he'd locked himself in that office and racked his brain for some way to protect it all.

"Your Majesty?"

He started. "Yes, I'm sorry." He gestured at a simple stone bench. "Shall we?"

Priya adjusted the fabric of her sari as she sat down. The gold and orange fish swarmed to the rocky barrier of the pond, hoping for food.

"I wanted to speak with you about an idea I've had regarding the hired vendors that will be assisting with the wedding ceremony, but it's one that I don't think Her Lunar Majesty would approve. Nevertheless, I thought the decision should be yours."

"Hired vendors?"

"Caterers, footmen, ushers, florists, and the like."

Kai adjusted the cuff of his shirt. "Oh, right. Go on."

"I thought it might be prudent to staff the event with a mix of humans *and* androids."

He shook his head. "Levana would never stand for it."

"Yes. That's why I would suggest we use escort-droids that she would not recognize as such."

He stiffened. "Escorts?"

"We would use only the most realistic models. We could even place special orders for those with more humanoid characteristics. Complexion flaws, natural hair and eye colors, varying body types and bone structures. I would be sure to find androids that wouldn't draw attention to themselves."

Kai opened his mouth to refute, again, but paused. Escort-droids were designed mostly for companionship. It would be an insult of the highest order if Levana became aware that they were at her wedding ceremony.

But . . .

"They can't be brainwashed."

Priya was silent for a moment, before continuing, "We could

also use them to record the proceedings, in case Her Majesty or her guests attempt anything . . . untoward."

"Has Levana insisted on having no cameras again?" The queen hated being recorded, and she'd demanded there be no recording devices at the annual ball when she was his special guest.

"No, Your Majesty, the queen recognizes the importance of this event being broadcast on an international scope. She's put up no resistance on that front."

He released a breath.

"However, with androids we could ensure that we'll have eyes everywhere, so to speak." She shrugged. "Hopefully this would be a precaution that is unnecessary."

Kai fidgeted with his cuff. It was a smart idea. The most powerful men and women on Earth would be at this ceremony, making it awfully easy for Levana to abuse her powers of manipulation. Having loyal staff who couldn't be affected could be an insurance policy against a worldwide political catastrophe.

But Levana hated androids. If she found out, she would be livid, and he'd like to avoid any more outbursts from the queen if he could.

"Thank you for the recommendation," he said. "When do you need a decision?"

"The end of this week, if we're to place the order in time."

"I'll let you know."

"Thank you, Your Majesty. Also, I wanted to tell you of a small realization I had this morning that amounts to one more benefit in broadcasting the nuptials."

"What's that?"

"Her Majesty refuses to remove her veil while in the presence of any recording devices, and so she will wear it throughout the wedding and coronation." Reaching forward, she patted Kai's wrist. "Which means you won't have to kiss her."

He couldn't help a sharp laugh. The knowledge did relieve a bit of his terror, but it was also a painful reminder. He figured he would still have to kiss her eventually. The thought made him sick.

"Thank you, Tashmi-jiĕ. That does make it slightly less horrific."

Her whole face softened. "May I speak openly, Your Majesty?"

"Of course."

She withdrew her hand and knotted her fingers on her lap. "I don't mean to overstep any professional boundaries, but I have a son, you see. He's about a year older than you are."

Kai gulped, surprised at a tinge of guilt. He had never imagined who this woman might be when she left the palace every day. He had never bothered to picture her with a family.

"Lately, I've tried to imagine what this would be like on him," Priya continued, gazing up at the drooping tree branches. The leaves were changing to gold, and every now and then a breeze would shake some loose and send them pinwheeling down to the pond. "What kind of toll would be paid for a young man with these responsibilities, forced to make these decisions." She took in a deep breath, as if she regretted her words before she said them. "As a mother, I'm worried about you."

He met her gaze, and his heart lurched.

"Thank you," he said, "but you needn't worry. I'm doing my best."

She smiled gently. "Oh, I know you are. But, Your Majesty, I've been planning this wedding for twelve days, and I've seen you age years in that time. It pains me to think how much harder everything will become after the wedding."

"I'll have Torin still. And the cabinet, and the province reps... I'm not alone."

Even as he said it, he felt the jolt of a lie.

He wasn't alone. Was he?

Anxiety crawled up his throat. Of course he wasn't. He had an entire country behind him, and all the people in the palace, and . . .

No one.

No one could truly understand what he was risking, what sacrifices he may be making. Torin was smart enough to realize it, of course, but at the end of the day he still had his own home to return to.

And Kai hadn't confided in him that he and Nainsi were searching for Princess Selene again. He would never tell Torin that a part of him hoped Cinder would be safe. And he would never tell a single living soul how terrified he was, every moment of every day. How afraid he was that he was making an enormous mistake.

"I'm sorry, Your Majesty," Priya said. "I'd hoped, if it wasn't too forward of me, that I might offer some motherly advice."

He pressed his fingertips onto the cool stone of the bench. "Perhaps I could use some of that."

Priya adjusted her sari on her shoulder, the gold embroidery catching in the sunlight. "Try to find something that makes you happy. Your life is not going to get easier once Queen Levana is your wife. If you had even one small thing that brought you happiness, or hope that things could someday be better, then maybe that would be enough to sustain you. Otherwise, I fear it will be too easy for the queen to win."

"And what would you suggest?"

Priya shrugged. "Perhaps this garden is a good place to start?"

Following her gesture, Kai took in the stalks of bamboo bowing over the stone walls, the myriad lilies beginning to fade after summer's long showing, the bright fish that clustered and pressed against each other, ignorant of the turmoil in the world above their small pond. It was beautiful, but . . .

"You aren't convinced," said Priya.

He forced a smile. "It's good advice. I just don't know if I have the energy to be happy right now, about anything."

Priya seemed sad at his response, though not surprised. "Please, think about it. You deserve a respite every now and then. We all do, but you more than anyone."

He shrugged, but it had no enthusiasm. "I'll keep it in mind."

"That's all I can ask." Priya stood, and Kai rose to join her. "Thank you for your time. Let me know your decision on the escort-droids."

Kai waited until she'd returned to the palace before settling onto the bench again. A slender golden leaf fluttered into his lap and he picked it up, twirling it between his fingers.

Priya's advice had merit. One bit of happiness, of hope, could make the difference in preserving his sanity, but it was a request easier made than fulfilled.

He did have *some* happiness to look forward to. Seeing Levana's signature on the Treaty of Bremen. Distributing her antidote and eradicating his planet of this awful plague.

But those victories would come hand-in-hand with a lifetime of attending celebratory balls with Levana at his side, and next time, Cinder wouldn't be there to distract him. Though admittedly, that lifetime might be cut shorter than expected. It was a morbid thought, that his premature death would at least keep him from too many painful dances.

He sighed, his thoughts circling back to Cinder. He couldn't avoid thinking about her these days, maybe because her name was at the top of every report, every newsfeed. The girl he'd invited to the ball. The girl he'd *wanted* to dance with.

He thought of that moment, spotting her at the top of the staircase, her hair and dress drenched from the rain. Noticing that she wore the gloves he'd given her. A smile tugged at him. It probably wasn't what Priya had in mind—the most hopeless situation of all. His relationship with Cinder, if it could even be called that, had been fleeting and bittersweet.

Maybe if things were different. Maybe if he wasn't marrying Levana. Maybe if he had a chance to ask Cinder the questions that plagued him: Had it all been a deception? Had she ever considered telling him the truth?

Maybe then he could imagine a future in which they could start again.

But the engagement was very real, and Cinder was . . .

Cinder was . . .

He jerked forward, nearly crushing the leaf in his fist.

Cinder was searching for Princess Selene. Had maybe even found her.

That knowledge was fraught with its own questions. What were Cinder's motives and what was she doing now? How would the people of Luna react when Princess Selene returned? What kind of person had she become? Would she even want her throne back?

Despite the lingering doubts, he did believe that Selene was alive. He believed she was the true heir to the Lunar throne, and that she could end Levana's reign. He believed that Cinder, who had proven to be the most resilient and resourceful person he'd ever known, actually stood a chance of finding her, and keeping her safe, and revealing her identity to the world.

It may have been a fragile hope, but right now, it was the best hope he had.

Twenty

CRESS AWOKE TO A DIZZYING ASSORTMENT OF SENSATIONS. Her legs throbbed and the bottoms of her feet ached. The weight of the sand that they'd buried themselves in to keep warm pressed down on her from neck to toes. Her scalp was still tingling from its strange new lightness. Her skin felt dry and scratchy, her lips brittle.

Thorne stirred beside her, moving slowly so as not to disturb the square of parachute material they'd draped over themselves to keep windblown sand out of their faces, though the grains in Cress's ears and nose proved that it hadn't been entirely effective. Every inch of her body was covered in the stuff. Sand under her fingernails. Sand at the corners of her lips. Sand in her hair and in the folds of her earlobes. Attempting to rub the dry sleep from her eyelashes proved a difficult, painstaking operation.

"Hold still," said Thorne, settling a palm on her arm. "The tarp may have gathered some dew. We shouldn't let it go to waste."

"Dew?"

"Water that comes up from the ground in the morning."

She knew what dew was, but it seemed silly to expect it in

this landscape. Still, the air did seem almost damp around her, and she didn't argue when Thorne instructed her to find the tarp's corners and lift them up, sending whatever moisture there was down to its middle.

What they found when they had shimmied out from beneath it was a little less than a single gulp of water, muddied from the sand that had blown up onto the fabric overnight. She described their underwhelming success to Thorne and watched disappointment crease his brow, though it soon faded with a shrug. "At least we still have plenty of water from the satellite."

Plenty being their last two bottles full.

Cress looked out at the brightening horizon. After walking nearly the entire night, Cress doubted they could have slept for more than a couple of hours, and her feet felt like they would fall off with the next step. She was disheartened when she looked up at the mountains and discovered that they didn't seem any closer now than they had the evening before.

"How are your eyes?" she asked.

"Well, I've been told they're dreamy, but I'll let you decide for yourself."

Flushing, she turned back to him. Thorne had his arms crossed over his chest and a devil-may-care grin, but there was something strained beneath it. She realized that the lightness in his tone had also rung false, covering up whatever frustrations were simmering just beneath his cavalier attitude.

"I couldn't disagree," she murmured. Though she immediately wanted to crawl back beneath the parachute and hide from embarrassment, it was worth it to see Thorne's grin become a little less forced.

They packed up their camp, drank some water, and retied the

towels around Cress's ankles, all while the taunting morning dew steamed and disappeared around them. The temperature was already climbing. Before closing up their pack, Thorne shook out the sheets and made Cress wrap one around herself like a robe, then adjusted his own sheet to make a hooded cloak that came over his brow.

"Is your head covered?" he asked, brushing his foot along the ground until he found the metal bar he'd been using as a cane. Cress tried her best to mimic the way he'd covered himself before confirming that it was. "Good. Your skin is going to crisp up like bacon soon enough. This will help for a little while at least."

She fidgeted with the cumbersome sheet while trying to guide Thorne up the slope they'd camped on. She was still exhausted and half numb from walking. Every limb throbbed.

They hadn't traversed four dunes before Cress stumbled, landing on her knees. Thorne dug his heels into the ground for purchase. "Cress?"

"I'm fine," she said, pulling herself up and rubbing the sand from her shins. "Just a little drained. I'm not used to all this exercise."

Thorne's hands were hanging in midair, like he'd meant to help pull her to her feet, but she noticed it too late. Slowly, they sank to his sides. "Can you keep going?"

"Yes. I just need to get into a rhythm again." She hoped it was true and that her legs wouldn't be loose cables all day long.

"We'll walk until it gets too hot, then rest. We don't want to exert ourselves too much, especially under full sun."

Cress started down the dune again, counting their steps to bide the time.

Ten steps.

Twenty-five.

Fifty.

The sand grew hot, singeing the soles of her feet through the towels. The sun climbed.

Her imagination circled through her favorite fantasies, anything to keep herself distracted. She was a shipwrecked pirate from the second era. She was an athlete training for a cross-country journey. She was an android, who had no sense of exhaustion, who could march on and on and on. . . .

But the dreams became more and more fleeting, reality pushing them aside with pain and discomfort and thirst.

She began to hope that Thorne would let them stop and relax, but he didn't. They trudged on. Thorne was right about the sheets, which kept the merciless sun from scorching her, and she became grateful for the dampness of her own sweat keeping her cool. She began counting again as sweat dripped down the backs of her knees, and though she felt awful for thinking it, part of her was glad Thorne couldn't see her in this state.

Not that he was immune to the trials of the desert. His face was red, his hair messed from rubbing against his makeshift hood, and dirt streaked down his cheeks where there was a shadow of facial hair.

As it grew hotter, Thorne encouraged Cress to finish off the water they'd opened in the morning, which she drank with relish, only afterward realizing that Thorne hadn't taken any for himself. She was still thirsty, but the day was stretching on in front of them and they had only one more bottle. Though Thorne had told her they shouldn't ration it, she couldn't bring herself to ask for more if he wasn't drinking also.

She began to sing to herself to pass the time, humming all the pretty songs she could recall from her music collection on the satellite. She let the familiar melodies distract her. Walking became easier for a time.

"That one's pretty."

She paused, and it took a moment for her to realize Thorne was talking about the song she was singing, and it took another moment for her to remember which one it had been. "Thank you," she said uncertainly. She'd never sang in front of anyone—never been complimented on it. "It's a popular lullaby on Luna. I used to think that I'd been named for it, before I realized what a common name 'Crescent' is." She sang through the first verse again. "*Sweet crescent moon, up in the sky. You sing your song so sweetly after sunshine passes by. . . .*"

When she glanced back at Thorne, he had a faint smile on his lips. "Your mom sang you a lot of lullabies?"

"Oh, no. They can tell you're a shell right when you're born, so I was only a few days when my parents gave me up to be killed. I don't remember them at all."

His smile disappeared, and after a long silence, he said, "You probably shouldn't be singing, now that I think of it. You'll lose moisture through your mouth."

"Oh." Pressing her lips tight together, Cress placed her fingertips against Thorne's arm, the signal that had come to mean they were starting down a slope, and slogged on. Her skin had been scraped raw by the heat, despite the shelter of her makeshift robe, but she was propelled on by the thought that it was nearly midday. And while midday would bring about the highest temperatures yet, Thorne had also promised a respite from walking.

"All right," Thorne finally said, as if the words were being dragged up from his throat. "That's enough. Let's rest until the temperature goes down again."

Cress groaned with relief. She would have kept walking all day if he had asked it of her, but how glad she was that he hadn't.

"Do you see any shade at all? Or someplace that looks like it might be shaded when the sun starts going down?"

Cress squinted across the dunes. Though there was some shade over the occasional hillock, at high noon it was almost nonexistent. Still, they were coming up on a big hill that would soon cast some shadows—it was the best they could do.

"This way," she said, spurred on by the promise of rest.

But as they crested one more dune, her eye caught on something in the distance. She gasped, grabbing Thorne's arm.

"What is it?"

She gaped at the glorious sight, struggling to find words to describe it. Blue and green, a stark contrast against the orange desert sand. "Water. And . . . and trees!"

"An oasis?"

"Yes! It must be!"

Relief spilled over her. She began to tremble with the promise of shade, water, *rest*.

"Come on—it isn't far," she said, plowing through the sand with renewed energy.

"Cress. Cress, wait! Reserve your energy."

"But we're almost there."

"Cress!"

She barely heard him. Already she could imagine the cool water slipping down her throat. The breeze beneath a palm's canopy. Maybe there would be food, some strange tropical Earthen food she'd never tasted, that would be juicy and crisp and refreshing...

But mostly she thought of collapsing into a nice patch of shade, cooled and protected from the sun, and sleeping until nighttime brought the return of cooler temperatures and endless stars.

Thorne trooped after her, having given up trying to make her stop, and soon she realized she was being cruel to make him go so fast. She slowed a little, but kept her eyes on the lake that shimmered at the base of a dune.

"Cress, are you *sure*?" he asked when he'd caught his breath.

"Of course I'm sure. It's right there."

"But...Cress."

Her pace slowed. "What's wrong? Are you hurt?"

He shook his head. "No, just...all right. All right, I can keep up. Let's get to this oasis."

She beamed and grabbed his free hand, leading him over the desert's ripples and tides. Her fantasies took over, eclipsing her fatigue. The towels had nearly rubbed the soles of her feet raw and her calves were sunburned where her sheet didn't protect them and her brain was swirling with thirst, but they were close. So close.

And yet, as she slipped along the powdery sand, it seemed that the oasis never came any closer. It always lingered at the horizon, as if the shimmering trees were receding with each step she took.

She plowed on, desperate. The distances were deceptive, but soon they would reach it. If only they kept moving. One step at a time, one foot in front of the other.

"Cress?"

"Captain," she panted, "it's...it isn't far."

"Cress, is it getting any closer?"

She stumbled, her pace slowing drastically until she stopped, gasping for breath. "Captain?"

"Do you see it getting closer? Do the trees look bigger than they were before?"

She squinted at the water, the trees, the most gorgeous sight, and swiped her sleeve over her face. She was so hot, but no sweat was left behind on the cloth.

The truth was so painful, she almost didn't have the strength to say it. "N-no. But that's . . . how could . . ."

Thorne sighed, but it was not a disappointed sigh, merely resigned. "It's a mirage, Cress. It's the light playing tricks on your eyes."

"But . . . I can *see* it. There are even islands in the lake, and trees . . ."

"I know. Mirages always seem real, but you're only seeing what you want to see. It's a trick, Cress. It's not there."

She was mesmerized by how the water rippled in little waves, how the trees trembled like a breeze was teasing their branches. It looked so real, so tangible. She could almost smell it, almost taste the cool wind blowing toward her.

Cress barely managed to stay standing, her fear of being scorched by the hot sand alone giving her the strength.

"It's all right. Lots of people see mirages in the desert."

"But . . . I didn't know. I should have known. I've heard stories, but I didn't . . . I didn't think it could look so real."

Thorne's fingers brushed against the sheet, finding her hand. "You're not going to cry, are you?" he said, his tone a mixture of gentle and stern. Crying was not allowed, not with water so precious.

"No," she whispered, and she meant it. Not that she didn't

want to cry, but because she wasn't sure her body could make enough tears.

"Good, come on. Find us a sand dune to sit down for a while."

Cress peeled her attention away from the fleeting, bitter illusion. Scanning the nearest dunes, she led him toward a southward-facing slope. The moment she was over the crest, it was as if a thin string that had been holding her up snapped. Cress let out a pained groan and collapsed into the sand.

Thorne brought the blanket and parachute square out of the pack and laid it out for them to sit on, to keep them off the hot sand, then pulled the corners over their heads like a canopy that blocked out the sun's brightness.

He put an arm around Cress's shoulders and tugged her against him. She felt so dumb, so betrayed—by the desert, by the sun, by her own eyes. And now the truth was settling upon her.

There was no water.

There were no trees.

Nothing but endless sand, endless sun, endless walking.

And they may never make it out. They couldn't go on forever. She doubted she could go on for another day like this, and who knew how long it would take to reach the end of the desert. Not when every sand dune multiplied into three more, when every step toward the mountains seemed to send them even farther into the distance, and they didn't even know that the mountains would offer any protection when they got there.

"We are not going to die here," Thorne said, his voice soft and reassuring, like he'd known exactly where her thoughts had been taking her. "I've been through much worse than this and I've survived just fine."

"You have?"

He opened his mouth, but paused. "Well...I was in jail for a long time, which wasn't exactly a picnic."

She adjusted the towels on her feet. The hair-ropes had begun to cut into her skin.

"The military wasn't much fun either, come to think of it."

"You were only in it for five months," she murmured, "and most of that was spent in flight training."

Thorne tilted his head. "How'd you know that?"

"Research." She didn't tell him just how much she'd researched into his past, and he didn't ask.

"Well—so maybe this is the worst I've been through. But it doesn't change the fact that we're going to survive. We'll find civilization, we'll comm the Rampion, and they'll come get us. Then we'll overthrow Levana and I'll get loads of reward money and the Commonwealth will pardon my crimes or whatever and we'll all live happily ever after."

Cress nestled against Thorne's side, trying to believe him.

"But first, we have to get out of this desert." He rubbed her shoulder. It was the kind of touch that would have filled her with giddiness and yearning if she hadn't been too tired to feel anything. "You have to trust me, Cress. I'm going to get us out of this."

Twenty-One

"THERE," SAID DR. ERLAND, SNIPPING OFF THE ENDS OF THE surgery thread. "That's all I can do for him."

Cinder wet her lips and found that they had begun to split from dryness. "And? Will he . . . is he going to . . .?"

"We have to wait and see. He's lucky the bullets didn't puncture a lung, or he wouldn't have made it this far, but he did lose a lot of blood. I'll monitor the anesthetics closely for the next day or two. We want to keep him sedated. Levana's soldiers are designed as disposable weapons—they are very effective when they're in good health, but their genetic alterations make it difficult for them to rest, even when their bodies need time to recover from injury."

She stared down at Wolf's wounds, now sewed together with dark blue thread that formed ugly bumps and ridges where open flesh had been before. Numerous other scars littered his bare chest, long since healed. It was obvious that he had been through a lot. Surely this wouldn't be the end of him, after everything?

A table beside her held a tray with the two small bullets the doctor had removed—they seemed too small to have done so much damage.

"I can't let anyone else die," she whispered.

The doctor looked up from cleaning the surgical tools. "They may be treated as disposable assets to the queen, but they are also resilient." He dropped the scalpel and tweezers into a blue liquid. "With proper rest, it's possible that he'll make a full recovery."

"Possible," she repeated dumbly. It wasn't enough.

She slumped down onto the wooden chair beside Wolf's bed and slipped a hand into his, hoping he would appreciate the touch, even though she wasn't Scarlet.

She crushed her eyes shut, the wave of remorse flooding over her. *Scarlet.* Wolf would be furious when he woke up. Furious and devastated.

"Now perhaps you might deign to tell me how you managed to be in the company of both a Lunar soldier and a Lunar royal guard, of all the possible allies in this galaxy."

She sighed. It took a while to gather her thoughts and find the beginning of such a story. Ultimately she decided to tell him about tracking down Michelle Benoit, and how she'd been hoping to find out more about the woman who had protected her secret to the death. How she'd been searching for clues about her past, who had brought her to Earth, and why anyone would put so much faith into a child who, at the time, was a mere three years old and on the brink of death after the queen's attempted murder.

She explained how they'd followed the path of clues to Paris, where she learned that Michelle Benoit was dead, but she found her granddaughter instead. Scarlet...and Wolf. How they became allies. How Wolf was training her to use her mental abilities and to fight.

She told him about the attack aboard the Rampion and how Sybil Mira had taken Scarlet, and now it was only her and Wolf...

and this guard, who she wanted to trust, felt she *needed* to trust, and yet she didn't even know his name.

"He said that he serves his princess," Cinder said, the words wispy and thin. "Somehow, he knew about me."

Erland rubbed at his frizzy hair. "Perhaps he overheard Thaumaturge Mira, or the queen herself talking about you. We're lucky that his fealty is to the true crown. Many of Levana's minions would just as soon kill you and claim a reward than see you recognized as queen."

"I figured as much."

He sneered, like he wasn't happy to have to acknowledge the guard could be an ally after all. "And speaking of recognizing you as the true queen . . ."

She shriveled into her seat, squeezing Wolf's hand.

"Miss Linh, I have spent years planning for the time when I would find you again. You should have come to me straightaway."

Cinder wrinkled her nose. "That's precisely why I *didn't*."

"And what does that mean?"

"When you came to my jail cell and dropped this whole princess thing on me . . . how was I supposed to react? All of a sudden I went from being nobody to being long-lost royalty, and you expected me to jump up and accept this *destiny* that you'd worked out in your head, but did you ever consider that maybe that's not the destiny I want? I wasn't raised to be a princess or a leader. I just needed some time to figure out who I was . . . am. Where I came from. I thought maybe those answers were in France."

"And were they?"

She shrugged, remembering the underground lab they'd found on the Benoit farm, with the suspended-animation tank where she had slept, half alive, for eight years. Where some nameless, faceless person had given her a new name, a new history, and new robotic limbs.

"Some of them were."

"And how about now? Are you ready to accept your destiny, or are you still *searching*?"

She frowned. "I know that I am who you say I am. And someone has to stop Levana. If that someone has to be me, well . . . yes. I accept that. I'm ready." She glanced down at Wolf and bit back her next words. *At least, I thought I was ready, before I ruined everything.*

"Good," said the doctor. "Because it's time we developed a plan. Queen Levana cannot be allowed to rule any longer, and she certainly cannot be allowed to rule *Earth*."

"I know. I agree. I had a plan, actually. *We* had a plan."

He raised an eyebrow at her.

"We were going to use the wedding to our advantage, especially with all the media that's going to be there. We were going to get past palace security, and I was going to sneak into the ceremony and . . . stop it."

"Stop the wedding?" Erland said, sounding unimpressed.

"Yes. I was going to tell everyone who I am. With all the cameras and the media and the whole world watching, I was going to insist that Kai couldn't marry her. I was going to tell the world about Levana's plans to invade all the Earthen countries, so that the other leaders would refuse to accept her as a world leader. And then I would demand that Levana relinquish her crown . . . to me." She pulled away from Wolf, finding that her palm had grown too warm. She rubbed it nervously on her pant leg.

Dr. Erland's expression had gone dark. He reached forward and pinched Cinder hard above her elbow.

"Ow, hey!"

"Hmph. For a moment I thought you must be another one of my hallucinations, as surely your plan couldn't be *that* stupid."

"It's not stupid. The news would go viral in minutes. There's nothing Levana could do to stop it."

"It certainly would go viral. Everyone would be clamoring to witness the tirade of the crazy cyborg who fancies herself a princess."

"They could test my blood, like you did. I can prove it."

"No doubt Her Majesty would stand by patiently while you did so." He huffed, as if he were talking to a small child. "Queen Levana has her talons so deep into the Commonwealth that you would be dead before you finished the word *princess*. Your Emperor Kai would do anything to appease her right now. To ensure that war doesn't break out again and to get his hands on that letumosis antidote. He wouldn't risk angering her just to validate the claim of a sixteen-year-old girl who is already a wanted criminal."

She crossed her arms. "He *might*."

He raised an eyebrow at her, and she sulked in her chair.

"Fine," Cinder said. "What do you suggest? You clearly know all about this political revolution stuff, so please enlighten me, O wrinkled one."

Dr. Erland grabbed his hat off a small writing desk and pulled it onto his head. "You can begin by learning some manners, or no one will ever believe *you* could be royalty."

"Right. I'm sure that poor etiquette is the number one reason for most failed revolutions."

"Are you quite finished?"

"Not hardly."

He pinned her with a glare and she glared right back.

Finally, Cinder rolled her eyes. "Yes, I'm finished."

"Good. Because we have a lot to discuss, beginning with how we are going to get you to Luna."

"*Luna?*"

"Yes. Luna. The rock in the sky that you are destined to rule. I trust you're familiar with it?"

"You expect me to go to Luna?"

"Not *today*, but eventually, yes. You're wasting your time with this wedding business and viral media. The people of Luna don't care what the people of Earth think. Proclaiming your identity here won't persuade them to rebel against their monarch, or crown you as their queen."

"Of course it will. I'm the rightful heir!"

She drew back, stunned by her own words. She didn't think she'd ever felt so invested in her identity, and determined to claim her place. It was a strange feeling, bordering on pride.

"You *are* the rightful heir," said the doctor. "But you have to convince the people of Luna, not the people of Earth. The Lunar people must be informed that you are alive. Only with them on your side can you expect to have any success in claiming your birthright. Of course, Levana will not give up easily."

She massaged her neck, waiting for the adrenaline warnings to dissipate. "Fine. Let's say you're right and this is the only way. How are we supposed to get on Luna? Aren't all the entry ports underground? And, I might guess, heavily monitored?"

"Precisely my point. We must find a way to sneak you through the ports. Obviously we can't use your ship . . ." He trailed off, rubbing his cheek. "It will require careful strategizing."

"Oh, good, more strategizing. My favorite."

"In the meantime, I suggest you not venture too far outside the heart of this town, and stay inside your ship as much as possible. It isn't entirely safe here."

Cinder glowered. "In case you didn't notice, everyone already saw me. There's no hiding me now."

"That isn't what I mean. This area has suffered more cases of letumosis than any other on Earth. Although there haven't been any severe breakouts in over a year, we can't let our guard down. Not with you."

"Um . . . I'm immune. Remember? That little discovery that kicked off this whole mess?"

He sighed, long and slow. The defeat in his expression shot a dart of worry down her spine.

"Doctor?"

"I have seen evidence that the disease is mutating," said Dr. Erland, "and that Lunars may no longer be immune. At least, not all of us."

Her skin began to crawl. It was amazing how fast the old fears returned. After weeks of being invincible in the face of one of Earth's most merciless killers, the threat was back. Her immunity could be compromised.

And she was in Africa, where it had all started.

A knock startled them both. The guard stood in the hall, damp from a recent shower and wearing some Earthen military clothes found aboard the Rampion. Though his wounds were no longer visible, Cinder noticed that he was carrying himself stiffly, favoring his unwounded side.

In his hands was a tray of flatbread that smelled thickly of garlic.

"Heard you talking. I thought your surgery might be finished," he said. "How's your friend?"

Cinder glanced at Wolf. He, too, would be vulnerable.

Everyone in this room was Lunar, she realized with a jolt. If Dr. Erland was right, then they were all vulnerable now.

Cinder had to swallow to unclog her voice. "He's still alive." Leaving Wolf's side, she held a hand toward the guard. "I'm Cinder, by the way."

He squinted. "I know who you are."

"Yeah, but I figured a formal introduction would be nice, now that we're on the same side."

"Is that what you've decided?"

Cinder frowned, but before she could respond, he'd shifted the flatbread to his other hand and grasped hers.

"Jacin Clay. Honored."

Not knowing how to read his tone, which sounded almost mocking, Cinder pulled away and glanced at the doctor, who had his fingers pressed against Wolf's wrist. Evidently, he had no intention of joining the introductions.

Cinder wiped her palms on her pants and eyed the tray. "So, what? You can shoot a gun, fly a spaceship, *and* bake?"

"This was brought by some kids." He pushed the tray toward Cinder. "They said it was for you, but I told them you couldn't be bothered."

She took it awkwardly. "For me?"

" 'The cyborg,' to be specific. Seemed unlikely there would be two of you around."

"Huh. I wonder why."

"I suspect it will not be the first gift you receive from the citizens of Farafrah," said Dr. Erland.

"What for? These people don't know me."

"Of course they do—or at least, they know of you. We are not so cut off from the world here as you might think. Even I had a reputation when I first arrived."

She set the tray down on the desk. "And they haven't turned you in? What about the reward money? And the fact that you're Lunar? Don't they care?"

Instead of answering, Dr. Erland slid his gaze toward Jacin, who was now leaning statue-like beside the door. It was easy to forget his presence in a room when he stood so still and said so little. No doubt his training as a guard had taught him that. No doubt he was used to going unnoticed.

But while Cinder had made the choice to trust him, it was obvious from the doctor's expression that she was so far alone in that decision.

"Right," said Jacin, pushing himself off the wall. "I'll go check on your ship. Make sure no one's backing out screws and calling them souvenirs." He left the hotel room without looking back, his limp almost passing for a swagger.

"I know, he seems a little...abrasive," Cinder said once he was gone. "But he knows who I am, and he saved my life, and Wolf's. We should treat him as an ally."

"You may choose to reveal all your secrets, Miss Linh, but it does not mean I must reveal mine, or those of the people in this town."

"What do you mean?"

"The people here do not care that we are Lunar, because we are not the only ones. I estimate fifteen percent of the population of Farafrah, and other neighboring oases, is made up of Lunars, or those of Lunar descent. This is where many of our people choose to come after they escape, and they have been immigrating here since the time of Queen Channary. Perhaps even earlier."

"Fifteen percent?" she asked. "And the Earthens know?"

"It is not widely discussed, but it seems to be common knowledge. They have come to live in harmony together. Once the plague struck, many Lunars took to nursing the sick and burying the dead, as they themselves did not catch the sickness. Of course, no one knew they were the original carriers. By the time that theory was posed, the two races had become too intermingled. They work together now, helping each other survive."

"But it's illegal to harbor Lunar fugitives. Levana would be furious."

"Yes, but who would tell her? No one cares about a poor, diseased town in the Sahara."

Thoughts swarming, she picked up a piece of the bread, glistening with golden oil and speckled with herbs. The soft inside was still steaming when she pulled it apart.

It was a gift . . . from Lunars. From her own people.

Her eyes widened and she gaped up at the doctor again. "Do they know? About . . . me?"

He sniffed. "They know that you stood up against the queen. They know that you continue to defy her." For the first time since she'd arrived, Cinder thought she detected a smile beneath the doctor's annoyed expression. "And I may have led them to believe that, one of these days, you intend to assassinate her."

"Wha—*assassinate* her?"

"It worked," he said with an unapologetic shrug. "These people will follow you anywhere."

Twenty-Two

"LUNAR THAUMATURGE AIMERY PARK, YOUR MAJESTY."

Kai and Torin stood as the thaumaturge glided past Nainsi into Kai's office. Although Aimery bowed respectfully to Kai as he came to stand on the opposite side of his desk, so low that the long sleeves of his maroon jacket nearly brushed the carpet, there was something supremely disrespectful in his air that always set Kai on edge. He had never quite been able to pinpoint what it was about this man—maybe it was the way he always wore a faint smile at the corners of his lips, or perhaps how that smile only reached his eyes when he was using his gift to manipulate someone.

"Thank you for joining us," said Kai, gesturing to the chair across from him. "Please make yourself comfortable."

"My pleasure," said Aimery, settling gracefully into the offered chair. "Anything for Luna's future king."

The designation made Kai squirm. It was easy to forget that he would be taking on a new title as much as Levana was, but the difference was that Luna had very strict laws governing who could be put into positions of power, and Earthens certainly did not make the cut. He would be crowned King Consort, meaning he would be a pretty figurehead with virtually no power whatsoever.

Unfortunately, the Commonwealth did not have the same fail-safes put in place. Kai's great-great-great-grandfather, the country's first emperor, must have trusted his descendants to make sound decisions on their spouses.

"I wanted to discuss with you a discovery recently made by the Earthen Union," Kai said, nodding at Torin.

His adviser stepped closer to the desk and set a portscreen in its center. With a click, the holograph of Earth with 327 Lunar spaceships surrounding it flickered to life above the desk.

Kai watched the thaumaturge closely, but the man did not show an iota of a reaction to the holograph, even with hundreds of yellow dots reflected like fireflies in his dark eyes.

"This is real-time imagery of Earth and its surrounding space," said Kai. "The markers have all been confirmed to be Lunar spacecrafts."

Aimery's cheek seemed to twitch, as though he was on the verge of laughing, yet his voice remained as smooth as caramel when he spoke. "It is a very striking picture indeed, Your Majesty. Thank you for sharing it with me."

Clenching his teeth, Kai lowered himself into his own chair. He was tempted to keep standing, as a show of power, but he'd been around Lunars enough to know that such mind games rarely had any effect, and at least when he was sitting he could pretend to be comfortable. Pretend that he hadn't been dreading this conversation all day.

"You're very welcome," Kai deadpanned. "Now perhaps you can explain to me what they're all doing up there."

"Recreation." Aimery leaned back, leisurely crossing his legs.

"We have many wealthy families on Luna who enjoy the occasional holiday cruise through our galaxy. I'm told it can be very relaxing."

Kai narrowed his eyes. "And these holiday cruises routinely bring them to within ten thousand kilometers of Earth? Where they remain anchored for days?"

"I am sure the view afforded them by such a location must be quite lovely." One side of Aimery's mouth quirked. "Breathtaking sunrises, I'm told."

"Interesting. Because all three hundred twenty-seven of these ships bear the insignia of the Lunar Crown. It seems to me that these are actually crown-sanctioned ships either conducting some sort of surveillance on the Earthen Union, or preparing an attack should war be declared."

Aimery's expression remained neutral. "My mistake. Perhaps I should have said that we have many wealthy, *crown-sanctioned* families who enjoy the occasional holiday."

They held each other's gazes for a long moment, while the holographic oceans sparkled beneath the sun, while the white clouds swirled through the atmosphere.

"I don't know why Queen Levana has chosen to threaten us at this time and in this manner," Kai finally said, "but it is an unnecessary show of force, and one that trivializes all that we are attempting to accomplish with our peaceful negotiations. I want these ships to return to Luna within the next twenty-four hours."

"And if Her Majesty refuses?"

Kai's fingers twitched, but he forced them to relax. "Then I cannot take responsibility for the actions of the rest of the Union. After the Lunar attacks that occurred on the soil of all six Earthen countries, it would be within the jurisdiction of any one of my peers to meet this blatant threat of war with their own show of force."

"Forgive me, Your Majesty. You did not say before that these Lunar ships had entered into the territorial boundaries of the Earthen Union. Surely, if Her Majesty was aware that we have intruded into your legal atmospheric space, she would have them removed at once." He leaned forward, showing a flash of white teeth. "You *are* insinuating that Luna has trespassed into your legal boundaries, aren't you?"

This time, Kai couldn't keep his hands from curling into fists beneath the desk. "At this time, they are outside the territorial boundaries. But that does not—"

"So you're saying Luna has committed no crime as laid out by the Union's own laws? Then how, exactly, would a show of force against these ships be warranted?"

"We will not be bullied into accepting any more of your demands," said Kai. "Her Majesty must know that she is already walking a *very* narrow tightrope. My patience is wearing thin and the Union is tired of bowing to Levana's every whim, only to have her gratuitous displays of power thrown into our faces again and again."

"*Queen* Levana has no more demands to make of you," said the thaumaturge. "The Commonwealth has been exceedingly accommodating to our requests, and I find it unfortunate that you see the presence of these thus-far peaceful Lunar ships as threatening."

"If they aren't there to send us a message, then *why* are they there?"

Aimery shrugged. "Perhaps they are waiting for the finalization of the peace alliance between Luna and the Commonwealth.

After all, once Her Majesty has signed your Treaty of Bremen, peaceful travel between our two nations will be made possible—even encouraged." He smirked. "And the Commonwealth really is so beautiful this time of year."

Kai's stomach writhed as the thaumaturge uncrossed his legs and stood. "I trust that will be all, Your Majesty," he said, tucking his hands into his wide red sleeves. "Unless you also wanted to discuss the approved symphony numbers to be played during the wedding feast?"

Flushing, Kai pushed himself off his chair and turned off the holograph. "This is not the end of this discussion."

Aimery politely listed his head. "If you insist, Your Majesty. I will inform my queen that you wish to discuss this matter with her in due course—though perhaps it would be prudent to wait until after the ceremony? As it is, she is quite distracted." He bowed, and when he stood tall again, his face had taken on a taunting grin. "I will be sure to give my queen your love next I speak with her."

Kai was shaking with rage by the time Aimery strode out of his office. How was it that Lunars didn't even have to use their mind powers, and they *still* drove him mad every time he talked to them?

He had the sudden urge to throw something, but the portscreen he was holding belonged to Torin, so he kindly passed it back to his adviser instead. "Thanks for all your help," he muttered.

Torin, who hadn't said a word during the meeting, loosened his necktie. "You did not need my help, Your Majesty. I could not have argued your points any better than you did." He sighed and clipped the port to his belt. "Unfortunately, Thaumaturge Park made all very sound points himself. In the eyes of intergalactic law, Luna has not yet committed a crime. At least, not in the case of *these* ships."

"Maybe the intergalactic laws need to be revisited."

"Perhaps, Your Majesty."

Kai collapsed back into his chair. "Do you think he was just trying to get a rise out of me, or are all those ships really going to invade the Commonwealth once the alliance is forged? Somehow, I'd just assumed Levana would be content to call herself empress. I didn't think she'd want to bring her whole army here and let them make themselves right at home." Saying the words out loud made him flinch with how naïve he sounded. Kai cursed beneath his breath. "You know, I'm beginning to think I entered into this marriage thing a bit hastily."

"You made the best decision you could at the time."

Kai rubbed his hands together, attempting to dispel the feeling of vulnerability the thaumaturge's presence had given him. "Torin," he said, sliding his eyes toward his adviser, "if there was a way to avoid this marriage *and* keep us from going to war *and* get that antidote...you would agree that that would be the best course of action, wouldn't you?"

Torin lowered himself slowly into the chair that the thaumaturge had vacated. "I'm almost afraid to ask, Your Majesty."

Clearing his throat, Kai called for Nainsi. A second later, her short, glossy-white body appeared in the doorway. "Nainsi, have you found anything new?"

As she approached the desk, her sensor flashed, once at him, and once at Torin. "Permission clearance for Adviser Konn Torin requested."

Torin's eyebrow jutted up, but Kai ignored it. "Clearance granted."

Nainsi came to a stop beside the desk. "I've run a full report on Michelle Benoit, including a detailed timeline of her activities, occupations, achievements, and military service, and biographical information on eleven persons who seemed close enough to warrant attention. My data retrieval system is broadening the search to neighbors and potential acquaintances beginning in the year 85 T.E."

"Who is Michelle Benoit?" Torin asked, in a tone that suggested he didn't really want to know the answer.

"Michelle Benoit was born in 56 T.E.," said Nainsi, "and is noted most for her twenty-eight years of service in the European Federation armed forces, twenty of which were served as wing commander. She received a Distinguished Service Medal for piloting the diplomatic mission to Luna in the year 85 T.E. The mission included—"

"We think she might have something to do with Princess Selene," Kai interrupted, tapping some fast instructions into the built-in netscreen on his desk. A moment later, a satellite photo of farmlands in southern France appeared across the screen. "She owns this farm"—he pointed to a dark spot, where the ground had been recently scorched—"and this field is where Cinder landed the first time she returned to Earth, right before the attack. So, we assume that Cinder believes that Michelle Benoit is attached to the princess as well."

Torin's face darkened, but he seemed to be withholding judgment until Kai finished. "I see."

"Nainsi, have you found anything useful?"

"*Useful* is a subjective term relative to the actions that are taken prior to receiving information and the resulting—"

"Nainsi. Have you found anything *relevant*?"

"Relevant to what?" said Torin. "What are you hoping to find?"

"Princess Selene."

Torin sighed. "Again?"

"Yes. Again," said Kai. He gestured toward the sky. "Aren't you the one who told me we had to try to stand up against Levana?"

"I didn't mean by chasing ghosts."

"But think about it. She's the true heir to the Lunar throne. You honestly don't think finding her would give us an advantage?"

Torin's mouth pressed into a thin line, but to Kai's relief, he seemed to be considering the question. "I don't want you to be distracted from the things that are truly important."

Kai snorted. "The important things, like jade centerpieces and whether my wedding sash should have flying bats or a pair of cranes embroidered on it?"

"This isn't a joke."

"*Clearly.*"

Rubbing his forehead, Torin eyed Nainsi for a long moment, before casting his gaze toward the ceiling. "Your Majesty. According to Linh Cinder's own warnings, Queen Levana already means to murder you because you were attempting to find the princess before. What will her retaliation be when she realizes you haven't stopped?"

"It doesn't matter—she already intends to kill me, so what else can she do? And Princess Selene would be the true heir. Her existence would negate any claim Levana has to her throne."

Torin dropped his shoulders. "And you think that by finding a girl who's, what? Fifteen years old?"

"Sixteen."

"A sixteen-year-old girl. You believe that finding her is what the Commonwealth needs right now, more than anything else?"

Kai gulped, but his answer was solid. "I do."

Torin settled back in his seat, resigned. "All right. Fine. I won't try to dissuade you." He eyed Nainsi again, this time with distrust, as if this were all the android's fault. "Please, continue."

Nainsi launched back into her report. "Michelle Benoit disappeared from her farm on 11 August; her identity chip was left in her home, having been removed from her wrist. Evidence did not indicate whether or not there had been a struggle. Two weeks later, her granddaughter, Scarlet, who had lived with Benoit for eleven years, traveled from their home in Rieux, France, to Paris. Tracking records indicate she was in Paris for two days before her identity chip went off the grid. Presumably, the chip was removed and destroyed. Timeline cross-examination indicates that her ID chip was last seen near an abandoned Paris opera house, at the same time that a nearby scan-bank machine recorded what appears to be the landing and takeoff of a 214 Rampion. Satellite feeds, however, picked up no such spaceship at that location. Deductive reasoning leads me to believe that this was the ship on which Linh Cinder is hiding and that Scarlet Benoit may have boarded the ship at that time."

Kai frowned and was glad when even Torin looked intrigued by this information.

"Cinder made a special trip to Paris for this girl?"

"My logic aptitude suggests this is a possibility."

"What else do we know about this . . . Scarlet?"

"According to her ID records, she came to live with Michelle Benoit in 115 T.E., two years after the recorded death of Princess Selene. Her birth date indicates that she is eighteen years old.

However, there is no hospital record of Scarlet Benoit's birth, and her data was not input until she was four years old, so we cannot confirm the validity of any of her records."

"You lost me."

"Scarlet Benoit was not born in a hospital. Neither was her father, Luc Raoul Benoit. Without official records, we must treat any information about their births as circumspect. It is possible that everything we know about Scarlet Benoit is false information."

Kai pressed his hands onto the desk. "Are you saying there's a chance this girl, this Scarlet Benoit . . . is really Princess Selene?"

"It is a possibility that cannot be proved or disproved at this time, but I have found no evidence to warrant a dismissal of this hypothesis."

Kai filled his lungs, feeling that he hadn't taken a full breath in weeks. "And Cinder knows it. Cinder figured it out . . . and now . . . she has her. Cinder's found the princess."

"Your Majesty," said Torin, "you are jumping to some large conclusions."

"But it makes sense, doesn't it?"

Torin scowled. "I will withhold my opinion on the matter until we have some information that is based on more than speculation."

"Android speculation," Kai said, pointing at Nainsi. "It's better than regular speculation."

He pushed himself out of his chair and began to pace in front of the grand picture window. Princess Selene was alive. He just knew it.

And Cinder had found her.

He almost laughed.

"I'm surprised to see you taking this all with such good humor, Your Majesty," said Torin. "I would think you would be horrified with this turn of events."

"Why? She's alive!"

"If this girl *is* the missing princess, then she is currently being held captive by a dangerous felon, Your Majesty."

"Wha—Cinder's not dangerous!"

Torin seemed unexpectedly furious as he, too, launched himself to his feet. "Have you forgotten that she's *Lunar*? She is a Lunar who had contacts working within this very palace. She coerced you—the most protected person in the country—into giving her a personal invitation to our annual ball, then infiltrated it with, I can only assume, the intention of provoking Queen Levana. She escaped from a high-security prison and has managed to evade capture by our entire military, which ultimately led to an attack that killed thousands of Earthens. How can you possibly say she isn't dangerous?"

Kai straightened his spine. "Levana attacked us—not Cinder."

Groaning, Torin rubbed his fingers over his temples. It had been a long time since Kai had seen that expression on his adviser. The expression that indicated he thought Kai was a moron.

Indignation flared inside him. "And for the record, she declined my invitation to the ball. She only came to *warn* me. And Dr. Erland . . ." He hesitated. He still didn't know what to think about her relationship with Dr. Erland. "Levana wants her killed. I don't see that we've given her much choice other than to run."

"Your Majesty, I worry that your . . . your feelings for this girl are causing a bias that could jeopardize your ability to make logical decisions where she's concerned."

Kai's face grew warm. Was he so transparent?

"I'm still trying to find her, aren't I? I still have half the military out searching for her."

"But are you trying to find her, or this princess?"

He gestured at Nainsi. "If they're together, what does it matter? We can find them both!"

"And then you will give Luna a new queen, and Linh Cinder will be pardoned?"

"I don't know. Maybe. Is that such a horrible thing to hope for?"

"She's still one of them. You've said yourself that she lied to you about everything. What do you know about her? She stole an ID chip out of a dead girl's wrist. She helped a known thief escape from prison. Do I need to go on?"

Cringing, Kai spun back to face the window, crossing his arms stubbornly over his chest. He hated that every word Torin had said was indisputable—while every hope Nainsi had given him was based on vague observations and hazy guesses.

"I understand that you feel partially responsible for condemning her to execution," Torin said, his tone growing gentler. "But you have to stop idolizing her."

"Idolize—" Kai faced him again. "I don't idolize her."

Torin gave him a speculative look, until Kai began to grow uncomfortable.

"I might *admire* her sometimes, but even you have to admit that it's pretty impressive what she's done. Plus, she stood up to Levana at the ball. You weren't impressed by that? Just a little?"

Torin buttoned his suit jacket. "My point, Your Majesty, is that you seem to be putting an awful lot of faith in a girl you know virtually nothing about, and who has caused us all a great deal of trouble."

Kai scowled. Torin was right, of course. He didn't know anything about Cinder, no matter how much he felt that he did.

But he was the emperor. He had resources. He may not know much about Cinder, but if she could find out about the lost Lunar princess, then he could find out more about *her*. And he knew just where to start looking.

Twenty-Three

THIS TIME WHEN CRESS AWOKE, IT WAS NOT SAND ENGULFING her—although there was plenty of that—but arms. Thorne had pulled her against him so close that she could feel the rise and fall of his chest and his breath on the back of her neck. She groggily peeled her eyelids open.

Night had fallen. The moon had returned, larger than the night before and surrounded by a sea of stars that winked and glittered at them.

She was deathly thirsty and couldn't find any saliva to wet her parched tongue. She started to shiver, despite the layers of sheets and blankets and the parachute and the heat rising off her scorched skin. Despite Thorne's protective warmth.

Teeth rattling, she nestled against him as much as she could. His embrace tightened around her.

She looked up. The stars were moving, swirling over her head like a whirlpool trying to suck the whole planet into its depths. The stars were taunting her. Laughing.

She shut her eyes tight, and was met with visions of Sybil's cruel smile. News headlines echoed in her head, spoken in a child's nasally voice. *14 CITIES ATTACKED . . . LARGEST MASSACRE IN THIRD ERA . . . 16,000 DEATHS . . .*

"Cress. Cress, wake up."

She jolted, still shaking. Thorne was hovering above her, his eyes bright with moonlight.

He found her face, pressed his palm to her forehead, and cursed. "You're running a fever."

"I'm cold."

He rubbed her arms. "I'm sorry. I know you're not going to like this, but we need to get up. We need to keep moving."

They were the cruelest words he could have said. She felt impossibly weak. Her whole body seemed to be made of sand that would blow apart with the slightest breeze.

"Cress, are you still with me?" He cupped her cheeks in both hands. His skin was cool, soothing.

"I can't." Her tongue stuck to the roof of her mouth when she spoke.

"Yes, you can. It will be better to walk at night when it's cool than to try and move during the day. You understand that, right?"

"My feet hurt . . . and I'm so dizzy . . ."

Thorne grimaced. She thought of stroking her fingers through his hair. In all the pictures she'd seen of him, even his jail pictures, he'd been so polished, so neat. But now he was a wreck, with whiskers on his chin and dirt in his hair. It did not make him any less handsome.

"I know you don't want to keep going," he said. "I know you deserve a rest. But if we just lie here, you might never get up."

She didn't think that sounded so awful. As the sand began to rock beneath her, she pressed her hand against his chest, seeking out the steadying heartbeat. She sighed happily when she found it. Her body began to dissolve, little grains of sand scattering. . . .

"Captain," she murmured. "I think I'm in love with you."

An eyebrow shot up. She counted six beats of his heart before, suddenly, he laughed. "Don't tell me it took you two whole days to realize that. I must be losing my touch."

Her fingertips curled against him. "You knew?"

"That you're lonely, and I'm irresistible? Yeah. I knew. Come on, Cress, you're getting up."

Her head dropped into the sand, sleep threatening to take over. If he would just lie down beside her and take her into his arms, she would never have to get up again.

"Cress—hey, no more sleeping. I need you. Remember the vultures, Cress. *Vultures.*"

"You don't need me. You wouldn't be here at all if it weren't for me."

"Not true. Well... only kind of true. We've already been over this."

She shuddered. "Do you hate me?"

"Of course not. And you should stop wasting your energy talking about stupid things." Scooping an arm beneath her shoulders, he forced her to sit up.

She gripped his wrist. "Do you think you could ever love me back?"

"Cress, this is sweet, but aren't I the first guy you've ever *met?* Come on, up you go."

She turned her head away, dread pressing down on her. He didn't believe her. He didn't understand how intensely she felt.

"Oh, spades and aces and stars." He groaned. "You're not crying again, are you?"

"N-no." She bit her lip. It wasn't a lie. She certainly *wanted* to cry, but her eyes were all dried up.

Thorne pulled a hand through his hair, knocking away a cloud of sand. "Yes," he said firmly. "We are obviously soul mates. Now *please*, stand up."

"You've probably told lots of girls you loved them."

"Well, yeah, but I would have reconsidered if I'd known you were going to hold it against me."

Misery washing over her, she crumpled against his side. Her head spun. "I'm dying," she murmured, struck by the certainty of it. "I'm going to die. And I've never even been kissed."

"Cress. *Cress.* You're not going to die."

"We were going to have such a passionate romance, too, like in the dramas. But, no—I'll die alone, never kissed, not once."

He groaned, but it was out of frustration, not heartbreak. "Listen, Cress, I hate to break this to you, but I am sweaty and itchy and haven't brushed my teeth in two days. This just isn't a good time for romance."

She squeaked and tucked her head between her knees, trying to get the world to stop turning so fast. The hopelessness of their situation was crushing her. The desert would never end. They would never get out. Thorne would never love her back.

"*Cress.* Look at me. Are you looking at me?"

"Mm-hmm," she mumbled.

Thorne hesitated. "I don't believe you."

Sighing, she pried her head up so she could peer at him through the curtain of chopped hair. "I'm looking at you."

He crouched close to her and felt for her face. "I promise, I will not let you die without being kissed."

"I'm dying now."

"You are not dying."

"But—"

"I will be the judge of when you are dying, and when that

happens, I guarantee you will get a kiss worth waiting for. But right now, you have to get up."

She stared at him for a long moment. His eyes were surprisingly clear, almost like he could see her back, and he didn't flinch before her skeptical silence. He didn't grin nonchalantly or offer a teasing follow-up. He just waited.

She couldn't help it when her attention drifted down to his mouth, and she felt something stir inside her. Resolve.

"Do you promise?"

He nodded. "I promise."

Shuddering at the pain that awaited her, she braced herself and held her hands out to him. The world tilted as he hoisted her up and she stumbled, but Thorne held her until she was steady. Hunger gnawed at her empty stomach. Pain bit into her raw feet, shooting up through her legs and into her spine. Her whole face contorted, but she ignored it the best she could. With Thorne's help, she retied the sheet around her head.

"Are your feet bleeding?"

She could barely see them in the darkness, and they were still wrapped in the towels. "I don't know. They hurt. A lot."

"Your fever might be from an infection." He handed her the last bottle of water, now half full. "Or you're dehydrated. Drink all of that."

She paused with the water bottle already tipped against her mouth, carefully, so as not to lose a single drop. It was a tempting offer. She could drink it all and still be thirsty, but . . .

"*All* of it," said Thorne.

She drank until she could stop without her throat crying for more. "But what about you?"

"I've had my fill."

She knew it wasn't true, but her tolerance for selflessness lessened with every gulp and soon she'd done as he asked and drank it all. She stood wavering on her feet with the bottle turned up to the sky, hoping to capture another drop, until she was sure there was nothing left.

She swooned, longingly placing the empty bottle into the blanket-sack on Thorne's shoulder. Peering at the horizon, she spotted the mountainous shadows, still so far away.

Thorne picked up his cane and she forced herself to take in three solid breaths before she started, hoping they would give her courage. She estimated the amount of steps it would take to reach the next sand dune, and then began counting. One foot in front of the other. Warm air in, warm air out. The fantasy of being a brave explorer had long since dissipated, but she still clung to the knowledge that Thorne was relying on her.

She plodded up the dune as her teeth began to chatter again. She stumbled twice. She tried to call up comforting daydreams. A soft bed, a worn blanket. Sleeping in well past the sunrise, in a softly lit room where flowers grew outside the windowsill. Waking up in Thorne's arms. His fingers stroking the hair off her brow, his lips pressing a good-morning kiss against her temple...

But she couldn't hold on to them. She had never known a room like that, and the hard-earned visions were too quickly overshadowed by pain.

One dune came and went. She was already panting.

Two dunes. The mountains lingered tauntingly in the distance.

Each time they topped one, she would focus on the next. *We'll just crest that hill, and then I'll sit for a minute. Just one more...*

But instead of letting herself rest when the goal was reached, she chose another and kept going.

Thorne didn't comment when she slipped and landed on her knees. He just picked her up and set her back on her feet. He said nothing when her pace slowed to a mere crawl, so long as they didn't stop. His presence was reassuring—never impatient, never harsh.

After ages of delirious, mind-numbing progress through the sand, when she felt as though every limb were about to fall off, the sky to the east began to brighten, and Cress realized that the landscape was changing. The sand dunes were becoming shorter and shallower and, not far in the distance, they seemed to end in a long, flat plain of rocky red soil, dotted with scarce, prickly shrubs. Beyond that began the foothills of the mountains.

She glanced at Thorne and was surprised to catch the evidence of exhaustion etched into his features, though he replaced it with steadfast determination as they came to a stop.

She described the sight as well as she could.

"Can you guess how long it will take to reach those shrubs?"

She estimated, unable to bury the panic that it would turn out to be another illusion and that the respite of sand and swells would flee farther away with every step they took. "No."

He nodded. "That's all right. We'll try to get to them before it gets too hot. We might be able to get some dew off their branches."

Dew. Water. Even just a lick, just a taste . . . never again would she snub a single muddy gulp.

She started again, her legs screaming with the first few steps, until they began to numb again to the endless walking.

Then her eye snagged on something big and white, and she froze.

Thorne crashed into her, and Cress would have collapsed if he hadn't wrapped his arms around her shoulders, steadying her.

"What's wrong?"

"There's...an animal," she whispered, afraid to startle the creature that stood at the top of the dune.

It had already seen them and was staring serenely at Cress. She tried to place it with what she knew of Earthen wildlife. A goat of some sort? A gazelle? It had slender white legs atop enormous hoofs and a rounded belly that showed the edges of ribs. Its calm face was tan with swaths of black and white, like a mask around its eyes. Two towering spiral horns twisted up from its head, doubling its height.

It was the first Earthen animal she had ever seen, and it was beautiful and regal and mysterious, watching her with dark, unblinking eyes.

For a moment, she imagined that she could speak to it with her mind, ask it to lead them to safety. It would recognize the goodness inside her and take pity, like an ancient animal goddess sent to guide her to her destiny.

"An animal?" Thorne said, and she realized he'd been waiting for her to further explain what she was seeing.

"It has long legs and horns and ... and it's *beautiful*."

"Oh, good, we're back to this, then." She could hear the smile in his tone, but she dared not take her gaze from the creature, lest it dissolve into the air like a phantom.

"Could mean there's a water source nearby," Thorne mused. "We should keep going."

Cress took a tentative step forward. She felt the slip of sand more keenly than she had before, and recognized just how clumsy she and Thorne were, stumbling and scrambling over the dunes, while this creature stood so elegant and calm.

The creature tilted its head, not moving as Cress inched closer.

She didn't realize she was holding her breath until the beast's eyelids flickered and it turned its head toward something on the other side of the dune.

The crack of a gunshot rang out across the desert.

Twenty-Four

THE CREATURE BALKED AND TUMBLED DOWN THE DUNE, blood dribbling from the wound in its side. Cress cried out and fell backward. Thorne pulled her down into the sand. "Cress! Are you all right?"

She was shaking, watching as the animal fell and rolled the rest of the way, gathering clumps of sand on its hide. She wanted to scream, but any noise was paralyzed inside her, and she could think of nothing but that the animal had wanted to say something to her and now the world was tilting and fading and she was going to be sick and there was blood in the sand and she didn't know what had happened and—

"Cress! *Cress!*"

Thorne's hands were on her, searching, and she realized dully that he thought she had been shot. She grabbed his wrists, holding them tight and trying to convey the truth through her grip when words wouldn't come to her.

"I'm—I'm all—"

She paused. They both heard it. Panting, along with the slip and scramble of footsteps.

Cress cowered, pressing into Thorne's embrace as terror

washed over her. A man appeared at the top of the dune, carrying a shotgun.

He saw the animal first, dying or dead, but then spotted Cress and Thorne from the corner of his eye. He yelped, barely keeping his balance, and gaped at them. His eyebrows disappeared beneath a gauzy headdress. His brown eyes and the bridge of his nose were all she could see of his face, the rest of him covered in a robe that draped nearly to his ankles, protecting him from the harsh desert elements. Beneath the robe peeked a pair of denim pants and boots that had long been sun bleached and caked with sand.

He finished his own inspection of Cress and Thorne and lowered the gun. He began to speak and for a moment Cress thought that the sun and exhaustion had driven her mad after all—she didn't understand a word he said.

Thorne's grip tightened on her arms.

For a moment, the man stared at them in silence. Then he shifted, his eyebrows lowering and revealing flecks of gray in them.

"Universal, then?" he said, in a thick accent that still made it a struggle to capture the words. He scanned their ragged clothes and sheets. "You are not from here."

"Yes—sir," said Thorne, his voice rusty. "We need help. My... my wife and I were attacked and robbed two days ago. We have no more water. Please, can you help us?"

The man squinted. "Your eyes?"

Thorne's lips puckered. He'd been trying to hide his new disability, but his eyes still looked unfocused. "The thieves gave me a good blow to the head," he said, "and my sight's been gone ever since. And my wife has a fever."

The man nodded. "Of course. My—" He stumbled over the

language. "My friends are not far. There is an oasis near here. We have a . . . a camp."

Cress swooned. *An oasis. A camp.*

"I must bring the animal," the man said, tilting his head toward the fallen creature. "Can you walk? Maybe . . . ten minutes?"

Thorne rubbed Cress's arms. "We can walk."

The ten minutes seemed like an hour to Cress as they followed the man through the desert, treading in the wake carved out by the animal's carcass. Cress tried not to look at the poor beast, keeping her thoughts instead on the promise of safety.

When she spotted the oasis, like paradise before them, a sudden burst of joy clawed up and out of her throat.

They'd made it.

"Describe," Thorne murmured, gripping her elbow.

"There's a lake," she said, knowing that this one was real and not sure how she ever could have confused that vague mirage with something so stark and vibrant. "Blue as the sky, and surrounded by grasses and maybe a few dozen trees . . . palm trees, I think. They're tall and skinny and—"

"The people, Cress. Describe the people."

"Oh." She counted. "I can see seven people . . . I can't tell their genders from here. Everyone is wearing pale-colored robes over their heads. And there are—I think, camels? Tied up near the water. And there's a fire, and some people are setting out mats and tents. And there's so much shade!"

The man with his kill stopped at the bottom of the slope.

"The man is waiting for us," Cress said.

Thorne bent near to her and placed a kiss against her cheek. Cress froze. "Looks like we made it, *Mrs. Smith.*"

As they got closer to the camp, the people stood. Two members of the group walked out into the sand to greet them. Though they wore their cloaks over their heads, they'd pulled the covers down around their chins and Cress could see that one of them was a woman. The hunter spoke to them in his other language, and a mixture of sympathy and curiosity entered the faces of these strangers, but not without a touch of suspicion.

Though the woman's eyes were the sharpest of the group, she was the first to smile. "What a trial you've been through," she said, with an accent not quite as heavy as the hunter's. "My name is Jina, and this is my husband, Niels. Welcome to our caravan. Come, we have plenty of food and water. Niels, assist the man with his bag."

Her husband came forward to take the makeshift sack off Thorne's shoulder. Though it had become lighter as their water had disappeared, Thorne's face was one of relief to have the weight gone. "We have some food in there," he said. "Preserved nutrition packs, mostly. It's not much, but it's yours, if you'll help us."

"Thank you for the offer," said Jina, "but this is not a negotiation, young man. We will help you."

Cress was grateful that no questions were asked as she and Thorne were led to the fire. The people shifted, eyeing them curiously as they made room on thickly woven mats. The hunter left them, dragging the animal's carcass to some other corner of the camp.

"What kind of animal was that?" Cress asked, eyes stuck to the path left by its body.

"Desert addax," said Niels, handing her and Thorne each a canteen full of water.

"It was beautiful."

"It will also be delicious. Now drink."

She wanted to mourn the animal, but the water was a

blessed distraction. She dragged her attention to the canteen and did as she was told, drinking until her stomach ached from fullness.

The people remained largely silent, and Cress felt the presence of their curiosity and stares closing in around her. She avoided meeting their eyes, and unconsciously crept closer and closer against Thorne, until he had no choice but to put an arm around her.

"We're deeply grateful to you," he said, offering an easy smile to no one in particular.

"It was very lucky that you found us, or that Kwende found you," said Jina. "The desert is not a kind place. You must have a very lucky star."

Cress's lips tugged into a smile.

"You're very young." The words sounded accusatory to Cress's ears, but the woman's face was kind. "How long have you been married?"

"Newlyweds," said Thorne, giving Cress a squeeze. "This was supposed to be our honeymoon. So much for that lucky star, I guess."

"And I'm not as young as I look," Cress added, feeling like she had to offer something to the act—but her voice squeaked and she quickly regretted speaking.

Jina winked. "You'll be grateful for that youthfulness someday."

Cress lowered her gaze again, and was glad when a wide spoon and a bowl of steaming food was set before her, smelling exotic and spicy and rich.

She hesitated, and risked a sideways glance at the woman who had handed it to her, not sure if she was supposed to share or pass it to the next person or eat very slow and delicately or—

But within moments, everyone around the fire was enjoying their own food with relish. Flushing with hunger, Cress pulled the bowl onto her lap. She nibbled slowly at first, trying to identify the Earthen foods. Peas she easily recognized—they had those on Luna too—but there were some other sorts of vegetables that she didn't know, mixed with rice and covered in a thick, aromatic sauce.

She scooped out a chunk of something yellowish and firm. She bit into it, and discovered it was tender and steaming on the inside.

"Don't they have potatoes where you come from?"

Cress jerked her head up, and saw Jina watching her curiously. She gulped. "This sauce," she said quietly, hoping Jina wouldn't notice her evading the question. *Potatoes, of course!* Luna's potatoes were a darker color, with a flakier texture. "What is it?"

"Just a simple curry. Do you like it?"

She nodded enthusiastically. "Very much. Thank you."

Realizing that all eyes had turned to her again, she hastily shoveled the rest of the potato into her mouth, though the spices were making her cheeks flush. As she ate, a plate of dried meats was passed to her—she did not ask from what animal—and then a bowl filled with a juicy orange fruit and sweet, green-tinted nuts that were full of so many more flavors than the protein-nuts Sybil had often brought for her.

"Are you traders?" Thorne asked, accepting the handful of shelled nuts that Cress pressed into his palm.

"We are," said Jina. "We make this trek four times a year. I am upset by the threat of thieves. We haven't had such trouble in ages."

"Desperate times," said Thorne with a shrug. "If you don't

mind my asking, why camels? It makes your way of life seem very...second era."

"Not at all. We make our living serving many of the smaller communities in the Sahara, many of which don't even have magnets on their own streets, much less on the trade routes between them."

Cress noticed Thorne's hand tightening around his bowl. *The Sahara.* So her stargazing had been correct. But his expression remained impassive and she forced hers to do the same.

"Why not use wheeled vehicles then?"

"We do occasionally," said one of the men, "for special circumstances. But the desert does harsh things to machinery. They're not as reliable as the camels."

Jina took a few slices of the sticky sweet fruit and added it to the top of her curry. "This may not be a luxurious life, but we stay busy. Our towns rely on us."

Cress listened attentively, but kept her attention on the food. Now that they were safe, sheltered, and fed, she was developing a new fear: that at any moment, one of these men or women might look at her and see something different, something not quite... Earthen.

Or that they would recognize Thorne, one of the most-wanted fugitives on the planet.

Whenever she dared to look up, she found their focus pinned on her and Thorne. She hunkered over her bowl of food, trying to fend off their prying eyes, and hoped that no one spoke to her. She became certain that any word she said would mark her as *different*, that simply by meeting their gazes she would give herself away.

"Not many tourists come through here," said Jina's husband,

Niels. "Any foreigners are usually just here for mining, or archeology. This side of the desert's been almost forgotten since the outbreaks started."

"We heard the outbreaks aren't half as bad as rumored," said Thorne, lying with an ease that astonished Cress.

"You heard wrong. The plague outbreak is as bad as they think. Worse."

"Which town were you traveling to?" asked Jina.

"Oh—whichever one you're going to," Thorne said, not missing a beat. "We don't want to burden you. We'll take our leave in any town with a netscreen. Er...you wouldn't happen to have any portscreens on hand, would you?"

"We do," said the oldest woman, perhaps in her fifties. "But net access is fickle here. We won't have a good connection until we get to Kufra."

"Kufra?"

"The next trading town," said Niels. "It will take us another day to get there, but you should be able to find whatever you need."

"We'll rest today and tonight and set out tomorrow," said Jina. "You need to replenish yourself, and we want to avoid the high sun."

Thorne flashed a most grateful smile. "We can't thank you enough."

A bout of dizziness spun through Cress's head, forcing her to set down the bowl.

"You don't look well," someone said, she wasn't sure who.

"My wife was feeling ill earlier."

"You should have said. She could have heat sickness." Jina stood, setting aside her food. "Come, you should not be so near the fire. You can use Kwende's tent tonight, but you should drink more before you sleep. Jamal, bring me some damp blankets."

Cress accepted the hand that pulled her to her feet. She turned to Thorne and gathered her courage to give him a small, non-theatrical kiss on the cheek, but as soon as she bent toward him, blood rushed to her head. The world flipped over. White spots pricked at her eyesight, and she collapsed into the sand.

Twenty-Five

CINDER PULLED BACK THE DRAPES AND STEPPED INTO THE shop, holding the curtain for Jacin as she surveyed the shelves around her. Jars were filled with assorted herbs and liquids, many of them labeled in a language she didn't know, although if she stared at them for too long her netlink would begin searching for a translation. These exotic ingredients were scattered among boxes of drugs and bottles of pills that she recognized from pharmacies in the Commonwealth, along with bundles of gauze and bandages, pasty ointments, portscreen accessories designed for taking various vital stats, massage oils, candles, and anatomical models. Flecks of dust caught on a few streams of light that filtered in from dirty windows, and a fan spun lazily in the corner, doing little to dispel the dry heat. In the corner, a holograph displayed the progression of internal bleeding due to a side injury, occasionally flickering.

Jacin meandered toward the back of the shop, still walking with a slight limp.

"Hello?" Cinder called. Another curtain hung over a doorway on the far wall, alongside an old mirror and a standing sink that was overgrown with a potted plant.

The curtain swished and a woman ducked through, pulling an apron on over plain jeans and a brightly patterned top. "Coming, com—" She spotted Cinder. Her eyes widened, followed by an enormous smile as she yanked the apron strings behind her. "Welcome!" she said in the thick accent that Cinder was becoming familiar with.

"Hi, thank you." Cinder set a portscreen down on the counter between them, pulling up the list that Dr. Erland had recorded for her. "I'm here for some supplies. I was told you would have these things?"

"Cinder Linh."

She raised her head. The woman was still beaming. "Yes?"

"You are brave and beautiful."

She tensed, feeling more like the woman had threatened her than complimented her. In the moments following the unexpected statement, she waited for her lie detector to come on, but it never did. Brave, maybe. At least, she could comprehend why someone would say that after they'd heard the stories about the ball.

But beautiful?

The woman kept smiling.

"Um. Thank you?" She nudged the portscreen toward her. "My friend gave me this list—"

The woman grabbed her hands and squeezed. Cinder gulped, surprised not only by the sudden touch, but at how the woman didn't flinch when she took her metal hand.

Jacin leaned over the counter and slid the portscreen toward the woman so suddenly that she had to release Cinder's hand in order to catch it. "We need these things," he said, pointing at the screen.

The woman's smile vanished as her gaze swept over Jacin, who was wearing the shirt from his guard uniform, freshly cleaned and patched so that the bloodstains hardly showed on the maroon fabric. "My son was also conscripted to become a guard for Levana." Her eyes narrowed. "But he was not so rude."

Jacin shrugged. "Some of us have things to do."

"Wait," said Cinder. "You're Lunar?"

Her expression softened when she focused on Cinder again. "Yes. Like you."

She buried the discomfort that came with such an open admission. "And your son is a royal guard?"

"No, no. He chose to kill himself, rather than become one of her puppets." She flashed a glare at Jacin, and stood a little taller.

"Oh. I'm so sorry," said Cinder.

Jacin rolled his eyes. "I guess he must not have cared about you very much."

Cinder gasped. "Jacin!"

Shaking his head, he snatched the portscreen back from the woman. "I'll start looking," he said, shouldering past Cinder. "Why don't you ask her what happened next?"

Cinder glared at his back until he had disappeared down one of the rows. "Sorry about that," she said, searching for some excuse. "He's . . . you know. Also Lunar."

"He is one of hers."

Cinder turned back to the woman, who looked offended at Jacin's words. "Not anymore."

Grunting, the woman turned to reposition the fan so Cinder could catch most of the gentle breeze. "Courage comes in many forms. You know about that." Pride flickered over the woman's face.

"I guess so."

"Perhaps your friend was brave enough to join her guard. My son was brave enough not to."

Rubbing absently at her wrist, Cinder leaned against the counter. "Did something happen? Afterward?"

"Of course." There was still pride on her face, but also anger, and also sadness. "Three days after my son died, two men came to our house. They took my husband out into the street and forced him to beg the queen's forgiveness for raising such a disloyal child. And then they killed him anyway, as punishment. And as a warning to any other conscripts who were thinking of disobeying the crown." Her eyes were beginning to water, but she held on to a pained smile. "It took me almost four years to find a ship that was coming to Earth and willing to accept me as a stowaway. Four years of pretending that I didn't hate her. Of pretending to be one more loyal citizen."

Cinder gulped. "I'm so sorry."

Reaching forward, the woman cupped Cinder's cheek. "Thank you for defying her in a way that I never could." Her voice turned to steel. "I hope you kill her."

"Do you carry fentanyl-ten?" asked Jacin, returning to the counter and dropping three small boxes onto it.

Pressing her lips, the woman took the portscreen out of his hand. "I will do this," she said, slipping around the counter and heading toward the front corner of the store.

"That's what I thought," he muttered.

Cinder propped her chin on her metal fist, eyeing him. "I never realized royal guard was a mandatory position."

"Not for everyone. A lot of people want to be chosen. It's a big honor on Luna."

"Did you?"

He slid his gaze to her. "Naw. I always wanted to be a doctor."

His tone was thick with sarcasm, and yet Cinder's optobionics didn't peg it as a lie. She crossed her arms. "So. Who were you protecting?"

"What do you mean?"

Something scraped against the floor—the shopkeeper shoving around dusty bins.

"When you were conscripted to be a royal guard. Who would Levana have murdered if you'd refused?"

His pale eyes frosted over. Reaching past the counter, he angled the fan toward himself. "Doesn't matter. They're probably going to end up dead anyway."

Cinder looked away. Because he'd chosen to join her side, his loved ones could suffer. "Maybe not," she said. "Levana doesn't know that you betrayed her yet. She could think I glamoured you. That I'm forcing you to help us."

"And you think that will make a difference?"

"It might." She watched as the shopkeeper dug through a bin. A fly buzzed near her head and Cinder batted it away. "So how does one get chosen to be a royal guard anyway?"

"There are certain traits they look for."

"And loyalty isn't one of them?"

"Why would it be? She can fake loyalty. It's like with your special-op friend. He would have shown fast reflexes, good instincts, and some amount of common sense. Match him up with a thaumaturge who can turn him into a wild animal, and it no longer matters what he thinks or wants. He just does what he's told."

"I've seen Wolf fight it," Cinder said, feeling compelled to defend him now that Scarlet wasn't here to do it. The first time Cinder had seen Wolf, he'd been covered in blood and crouched threateningly over Scarlet, although Scarlet had always insisted that he wouldn't have hurt her. That he was different from the others—stronger.

Of course, that was before Wolf had gotten himself shot taking a bullet for a thaumaturge, moments before Scarlet was kidnapped.

"It's obviously not easy to do," she amended. "But it is possible for them to fight against the mind control."

"Lots of good that seems to have done him."

Locking her jaw, Cinder pressed her metal hand against the back of her neck, letting it cool her down. "He'd rather fight, and lose, than become another one of her pawns. We all would."

"Good for you. Not everyone's given that option."

She noticed that his hand had settled comfortably on the knife sheathed against his thigh. "Clearly Levana didn't want you for your chattiness. So what were the traits you possessed, that made her think you'd be a good guard?"

That look of smug amusement returned, like he was letting her in on a private joke. "My pretty face," he said. "Can't you tell?"

She snorted. "You're starting to sound like Tho-Thorne." She stumbled over his name. Thorne, who would never make jokes about his own charisma again.

Jacin didn't seem to notice. "It's sad, but true."

Cinder swallowed her sudden remorse. "Levana chooses her personal guards based on who makes the best wall decorations? I'm suddenly feeling better about our chances."

"That, and our very weak minds."

"You're kidding."

"Nope. If I'd been good with my gift, I might have made thaumaturge. But the queen wants her guards to be easily controlled. We're like puppets for her to shuffle around. After all, if we show the slightest resistance to being controlled, it could mean the difference between life and death for Her Majesty."

Cinder thought of the ball, when she'd had the gun and had tried to shoot Levana. The red-haired guard had jumped in front of the bullet without hesitation. She'd always assumed he'd been doing his duty to protect the queen, that he'd done it willingly, but now she recognized how his movements were too jerky, too unnatural. And how the queen hadn't even flinched.

She'd been controlling him. Jacin was right. He'd acted just like a puppet.

"But you were able to resist control on the ship."

"Because Thaumaturge Mira was preoccupied with your operative. Otherwise, I would have been the same brainless mannequin that I usually am." His tone was self-deprecating, but Cinder could detect bitterness beneath it. Nobody liked to be controlled, and she didn't think anyone ever got used to it.

"And you don't think they suspect that you're..."

"A traitor?"

"If that's what you are."

His thumb traced around the knife handle. "My gift is pretty much worthless. I couldn't even control an Earthen, much less a skilled Lunar. I could never do what you do. But I've gotten pretty good at keeping my thoughts empty when the queen or a thaumaturge is around. To them, I have about as much brains and willpower as a tree stump. Not exactly threatening."

Near the front of the store, the woman started humming to herself as she scavenged for Cinder's supplies.

"You're doing it right now, aren't you?" said Cinder, crossing her arms. "Keeping your thoughts empty."

"It's habit."

Closing her eyes, Cinder felt around for him with her thoughts. His presence was there, but just barely. She knew that she could have controlled him without any effort at all, but the energy rolling off his body didn't give anything away. No emotions. No opinions. He simply melted into the background. "Huh. I always thought your training must have taught you that."

"Just healthy self-preservation."

Furrowing her brow, she opened her eyes again. The man before her was an emotional black hole, according to her Lunar gift. But if he could fool Levana . . .

She narrowed her eyes. "Lie to me."

"What?"

"Tell me a lie. It doesn't have to be a big one."

He was silent for a long time and she imagined she could hear him sifting through all the lies and truths, weighing them against each other.

Finally, he said, "Levana's not so bad, once you get to know her."

An orange light blinked on in the corner of her vision.

At Jacin's mocking grin, Cinder started to laugh, the tension rising off her shoulders like heat waves off the desert sand. At least her cyborg programming could still tell whether or not he was lying to her. Which meant he hadn't been lying when he'd said he was loyal to his princess, and his princess alone.

The shopkeeper returned and dumped an armful of different drugs on the counter, scanned the portscreen, whistled, then drifted away again.

"Now that you know all about me," said Jacin, as if it were anywhere close to true, "I have a question for you."

"Go for it," she said, organizing the bottles into neat rows. "My secrets are mostly public knowledge these days."

"I may be able to hide my emotions from the queen, but I can't hide the fact that I'm Lunar, and that I can be controlled by her. But when you first came to that ball, your gift seemed nonexistent. Honestly, I thought you were Earthen at first. And I know that's why the queen and Thaumaturge Mira were taunting you … treating you like a shell, which you might as well have been for how powerless you were." He stared at Cinder, as if trying to see into the mess of wires and chips in her head. "Then, suddenly, you weren't powerless anymore. Your gift was practically blinding. Maybe even worse than Levana's."

"Gee, thanks," Cinder muttered.

"So, how did you do it? How could you hide that much power? Levana should have known immediately…we all should have known. Now when I look at you, it's practically all I see."

Biting her lip, Cinder glanced toward the mirror over the shop's small sink. She caught her reflection and wasn't surprised to find a smudge of dirt on her jaw—how long had it been there?—and strands of hair falling messily out of her ponytail. True to form, the mirror showed her just as she had always been. Plain. Dirty. A cyborg.

She tried to imagine what it would be like to see herself as she saw Levana: frighteningly gorgeous and powerful. But it was impossible with that reflection staring back at her.

That was why Levana despised mirrors so much, but Cinder found her reflection almost comforting. The shopkeeper called her brave and beautiful. Jacin called her blinding. It was kind of nice to know that they were both wrong.

She was still just Cinder.

Tucking a strand of hair behind her ear, she tried her best to explain to Jacin the "bioelectrical security system" her adoptive father had invented and installed on her spinal cord. For years it had prevented her from using her gift, which was why, until recently, she hadn't known she was Lunar at all. The device was meant to protect her, not only by preventing her from using her gift so that Earthens wouldn't know what she was, but also to prevent the side effects that most Lunars experienced when they didn't use their gift for long periods of time—side effects of delusions and depression and madness.

"That's why you might overhear Dr. Erland babbling to himself sometimes," she said. "He didn't use the gift for years after coming to Earth, and now his sanity is—"

"Wait."

She paused, not only because Jacin had spoken, but because something had changed in the air around him. A sudden spike of emotion, catching Cinder off guard.

"This device kept you from losing your mental stability? Even though you weren't using your gift for . . . for years?"

"Well, it *kept* me from using my gift in the first place, and also protected me from those side effects."

He turned his face away from her and took a minute to school his features back into nonchalance, but it was too late. There was a new intensity behind his eyes as he grasped the implications.

A device that could take away a person's Lunar gift would make them all equal.

"Anyway," said Cinder, rubbing the back of her neck where the device was still installed, though now broken. "Dr. Erland disabled it. My gift had been coming and going for a couple weeks before the ball, but then all the emotional stress overwhelmed my system, and the device, and—there I was. Fully Lunar. Not a moment too soon." She cringed, recalling the sensation of a gun pressed against her temple.

"Do any more of these devices exist?" he said, his eyes strangely bright.

"I don't think so. My stepfather died before it was fully tested, and as far as I know he didn't manufacture any others. Although he may have left behind some plans or blueprints that explain how it works."

"Doesn't seem possible. An invention like that...it could change everything." He shook his head, staring into space as the shopkeeper returned and set a basket full of supplies on the counter. She grabbed the bottles from before and threw them on top, along with Cinder's portscreen.

"This is perfect," said Cinder, pulling the basket toward her. "Thank you so much. The doctor said you could put it on his tab?"

"No payment from Cinder Linh," said the woman, waving one hand, while she pulled a portscreen out of her apron pocket. "But— may I take your picture for my net profile? My first celebrity!"

Cinder flinched away from her. "Er...I'm sorry. I'm not really doing the picture thing these days."

The woman wilted in disappointment, tucking her port back into her pocket.

"Sorry, really. I'll talk to the doctor about paying you, all right?" She hauled the basket off the counter without waiting to hear another argument.

"Not doing pictures these days?" Jacin muttered as they hurried through the shop. "How very Lunar of you."

Cinder glared against the sudden, burning sunlight. "Very wanted criminal of me too."

Twenty-Six

ALTHOUGH SCARLET'S THOUGHTS WERE AS THICK AS MUD, her fingers were nimble and fast, dancing through the familiar motions of powering down the podship. Just like all those nights she returned to the farm after finishing her deliveries. She could almost smell the musty tang of her grandmother's hangar, combined with the fresh, earthy breeze coming off the fields. She lowered the landing gear and eased down the brakes. The ship settled, humming idly for a moment before she shut down the engine, and it fell silent.

Something thumped behind her. A woman began to yell shrilly, her anger made sticky and confusing in Scarlet's cobwebbed brain.

A headache began to throb in the front of her skull, gradually taking over her entire head. Scarlet flinched and leaned back in the pilot's seat, pressing her palms over her eyes to block out the pain, the swamp of confusion, the sudden piercing light that burst through her vision.

She groaned, slumping forward. No harness caught her like she'd expected and soon she was hunched over her knees, taking full, gasping breaths as if she'd nearly drowned.

Her mouth was dry, her jaw aching as if she'd been grinding her teeth for hours. But as she held very still, and choked on very deep breaths, the throbbing in her head began to subside. Her thoughts cleared. The muffled yelling sharpened and spiked.

Scarlet opened her eyes. A surge of nausea passed over her, but she swallowed hard and let it pass.

She knew instantly that this was not her delivery ship, and she was not in her grandmother's hangar. The smell was all wrong, the floorboards too clean....

"...want Lieutenant Hensla sent down immediately, along with a full team for scouting and ship identification ..."

The woman's voice shot like electricity through Scarlet's nerves, and she remembered. The ship, the attack, the gun in her hand, the bullet hitting Wolf in the chest, the sense of hollowness as the thaumaturge burrowed into her brain, took over her thoughts, took away all sense of identity and will.

"...use the shuttle's history to track the last location, and see if it has any lingering connectivity to the main ship. They may have gone to Earth. Figure it out. *Find her.*"

Scarlet raised her head enough that she could peer out of the podship's side window. Luna. She was on Luna, docked in an enclosed space that was nothing at all like the hangars she had known or the podship dock of the Rampion. It was large enough to house a dozen shuttles, and a few were already lined up alongside hers, their sleek shapes ornamented with the royal Lunar insignia. The walls were jagged and black, but speckled with small glowing lights, to mimic a nonexistent sky. A faint light was glowing up from the ground, so that the shadows of the podships stretched like birds of prey along the cavernous walls.

At the end of the row of ships was an enormous arched

doorway, embedded with glittering stones that depicted a crescent moon rising above planet Earth.

"...took this D-COMM from the programmer who betrayed us. See if the software techs can use it to trace the companion chip..."

The podship door behind her was still open, and the thaumaturge was standing just outside the ship, yelling at the people who had gathered around her—two guards in red and gray uniforms and a middle-aged man who wore a simple belted robe and was hastily plugging information into a portscreen. The thaumaturge's long white coat was smeared with blood, and soaked through where it draped over her thigh. She stood slightly hunched, her hands pressed over the wound.

The arched door began to open, cutting a slit through the center of the glittering Earth as the doors peeled back. Scarlet ducked back down. She heard the subtle click and hum of magnets, the clatter of footsteps.

"Finally," the thaumaturge seethed. "The uniform is ruined— cut away the material and be quick. The bullet didn't pass through, and the wound hasn't—" She cut off with a hiss.

Daring to glance up, Scarlet saw that three new people had arrived, dressed in white lab coats. They brought a hovering gurney with them, stocked with a full lab's worth of medical supplies, and were all crowded around the thaumaturge, one unbuttoning her coat while another tried to cut a square of fabric away from her pants, though the material seemed to have cemented itself to the wound.

The thaumaturge recovered and rearranged her features to disguise how much pain she was in, though her olive skin had taken on a yellowish pallor. One of the doctors managed to peel the material away from the wound.

"Have Sierra send for a new uniform, and contact Thaumaturge Park to inform him that there will soon be changes to our procedures for gathering intelligence in relation to the Earthen leaders."

"Yes, Thaumaturge Mira," said the middle-aged man. "Speaking of Park, you should know that he already had a meeting with Emperor Kaito regarding our fleet of operatives that appears to no longer be in disguise."

She cursed. "I forgot about the ships. I hope he was smart enough not to tell them anything before we've established an official statement." She paused to take in a warbling breath. "Also, inform Her Majesty of my return."

Scarlet slid down in the seat. Her eyes darted to the door on the other side of the podship. She considered starting the engine, but she had no chance of escaping in the Rampion's shuttle. They had to be underground, and the port's exit probably required special authorization to open.

But if she could reach one of those other ships...

Trying to take calming breaths, she inched herself over the central console, into the copilot's seat.

She braced herself, her heart pummeling against her collarbone. She counted down from three in her head, before unlatching the door. Prying it open at glacial speeds, so the movement wouldn't be noticed by the Lunars behind her. Slipping out and settling her sneakers onto the floor. Now she could tell where the peculiar light was coming from—the entire floor was set in glowing white tiles, making it feel as if she were walking on . . .

Well, the moon.

She paused to listen. The doctors were discussing entrance wounds, the assistant was listing times for a meeting with the queen. For once, the thaumaturge had gone silent.

Breathe, breathe…

Scarlet stepped away from the podship. Her hair was clinging to her damp neck and she was trembling with fear and building adrenaline and the encroaching knowledge of how this would never work. She wouldn't be able to get into the Lunar ship. They would shoot her in the back at any moment. Or she would get in the ship but not know how to fly it. Or the port's exit wouldn't open.

But the Lunars were still carrying on behind her and she was so close and this could work, this had to work …

Crouching against the Lunar ship's shimmering white body, she licked her lips and inched her fingers toward the door panel—

Her hand froze.

Her heart plummeted.

The air around her fell silent, charged with an energy that made every hair stand up on Scarlet's arms. Her mind stayed sharp this time, fully aware of how close she had come to getting inside that ship and making a mad dash for her safety, and at the same time fully aware that she'd never had a chance.

With a snap, her hand unfroze and she dropped it to her side.

Scarlet forced her chin up and, using the side of the podship for balance, she stood and turned to face the thaumaturge. Sitting on the hovering gurney, Sybil Mira had been stripped down to a light undershirt and was leaning to one side so the doctors could have access to the bullet wound. There was blood speckled on her cheek and brow and her hair was tangled and clumped haphazardly with yet more blood, but she still managed to look intimidating as her gray eyes held Scarlet pinned against the ship.

The doctors were hunkered over her thigh, working intently, as if they were afraid she would notice they were there as they cleaned and inspected and stitched. The two guards had their guns in hand, though their stances were relaxed as they awaited orders.

The assistant, who had been middle-aged and plain in every way before, had changed. Though he still wore the belted robe, he himself had become unearthly handsome. Early twenties, strong jawed, with pitch-black hair slicked neatly back from a widow's peak on his brow.

Scarlet clenched her jaw and forced her brain to remember what he looked like before. To not give any weight to his imposed glamour. It was only a small rebellion, but she embraced it with all the mental strength she had left.

"This must be the hostage taken from the cyborg's ship," the assistant said. "What shall I have done with her?"

The thaumaturge's gaze narrowed on Scarlet, with a hatred that could have melted skin off bones.

The feeling was mutual. Scarlet glared right back.

"I need time to brief Her Majesty about her," said Sybil. "I suspect she will want to be present when the girl is questioned." She twitched as pain flickered across her face. Scarlet could see the moment when the thaumaturge lost interest in Scarlet's fate, when her shoulders slumped and she drew on whatever energy she had left to lower herself fully onto the gurney. "I don't care what you do with her in the meantime. Give her to one of the families if you want."

The assistant nodded and gestured to the guards.

Within seconds, they had stepped forward and pulled Scarlet away from the podship, locking her hands behind her with some sort of binding that dug into her forearms. By the time they began marching her toward the enormous arched doors, the doctors and the thaumaturge were already gone.

Twenty-Seven

TIME PASSED IN A HAZE, DREAMS AND REALITY BLURRING together. Being pulled from her sleep, forced to sit up and drink some water. Snips of muddled conversations. Shivering. Hot and sweating and kicking off the thin blankets. Thorne beside her, tying a blindfold around his head. Hands holding the water bottle to her lips. Drink. Drink. *Drink.* Eat this soup. Drink some more. Unfamiliar laughter making her curl up into a ball and burrow beneath the blankets. Thorne's silhouette in the moonlight, rubbing his eyes and cursing. Gasping for breath in the hot air, sure that she was going to suffocate beneath the blankets and that all the oxygen would be sucked up into the dark night sky. Desperate for water. Itchy from the sand still in her clothes and hair.

Light. Darkness. Light again.

Finally Cress awoke, groggy but lucid. Saliva was thick and sticky in her mouth and she was lying on a mat inside a small tent, alone. It was dark beyond the thin fabric walls and the moonlight spilled over the pile of clothing at her feet. She felt for her hair, meaning to strangle her wrists with it, but found it chopped beneath her ears.

The memories returned, lazy at first. Thorne in the satellite,

Sybil and her guard, the fall and the knife and the cruel desert stretching to the ends of the earth.

She could hear voices outside. She wondered whether the night had just begun or was already ending. She wondered how long she'd slept. She seemed to recall arms around her, soft knuckles brushing sand off her face. Had it been a dream?

The tent's flap opened and a woman appeared with a tray, the older woman from the fire. She beamed and set down the food—some sort of soup and a canteen of water.

"Finally," she said in that thick, unfamiliar accent, crawling over the mounds of disheveled blankets. "How do you feel?" She pressed a palm to Cress's forehead. "Better. Good."

"How long was I . . . ?"

"Two days. We're behind schedule now, but no matter. It's good to see you awake."

She sat down beside Cress. It was a snug fit in the tent, but not uncomfortable.

"You will have a camel to ride when we leave. We need to keep your wounds clean. You were lucky we got you before the infection."

"Wounds?"

The woman gestured to her feet and Cress bent over. It was too dark to see, but she could feel bandages. Even two days later they were sore to the touch and her leg muscles tingled from exertion.

"Where's—" She hesitated, unable to remember if Thorne had given himself a fake name. "My husband?"

"By the fire. He's been entertaining us with talk of your whirlwind romance. Lucky girl." She gave a sly wink that made Cress withdraw, then patted Cress's knee. She handed the bowl of soup

to her. "Eat first. If you're strong enough, you can come join us."
She scooted back toward the entrance.

"Wait. I have to—um." She blushed, and the woman gave her
an understanding look.

"I'm sure you do. Come along, I'll show you where to do your
business."

There was a pair of boots by the tent's opening that were far
too big for her. The woman helped Cress stuff them with cloth
until they bordered on comfortable, though the bottoms of her
feet still stung, and then she led her away from the fire, to a hole
they'd dug into the sand at the edge of the oasis. Two sheets had
been hung up for privacy and there was a young palm tree to balance on while Cress relieved herself.

When she was done, the woman guided her back to the tent
and then left her alone to savor the soup. Her appetite had returned tenfold since her first meal in the oasis. Her gut felt hollow, but the broth soothed her as she listened to the chatter of
strangers. She tried to pick out Thorne's voice, but couldn't.

When Cress crawled out of the tent again, she saw eight forms
seated around the fire. Jina was stirring a pot half buried in the
sand, and Thorne sat relaxed and cross-legged on one of the mats.
He had a bandanna around his eyes.

"She rises!" yelled the hunter, Kwende.

Thorne raised his head, and his surprise broke into a toothy
grin. "My wife?" he said, louder than necessary.

Cress's nerves crawled to find so many strangers staring at
her. Her breathing became erratic and she considered feigning a
dizzy spell to seek solace back in the tent.

But then Thorne was standing, or trying to, wobbling on one
knee like he might tip right over into the fire. "Uh-oh."

Cress darted to his side. With her help, he heaved himself up to his feet and grasped her hands, still shaky.

"Cress?"

"Yes, Cap—um—"

"You're awake, finally! How do you feel?" He sought out her forehead, his palm landing first on her nose before sliding up to her forehead. "Oh, good, your fever's gone down. I was so worried." He pulled her into an embrace, dwarfing her in his arms.

Cress squeaked, but the sound was muffled in the cotton of his shirt. He released her just as quickly and cupped her face in both hands. "My dear Mrs. Smith, *never* scare me like that again."

Although his act was overdone, Cress felt a jolt behind her sternum at seeing his mouth set just so, feeling his hands so tender against her cheeks.

"I'm sorry," she whispered. "I feel much better now."

"You *look* much better." His lips quirked. "At least, I'm assuming you do." Thorne dug his toes into the sand and flicked up one end of a long stick, catching it easily. "Come on, let's go for a walk. Try to get some real alone time on this honeymoon of ours." He twisted his face into a wink that was obvious even beneath the blindfold.

The crowd around the fire hollered as Thorne took Cress's hand. She guided him away from the taunts, glad that the night's darkness hid her burning cheeks.

"You seem to be getting around well," she said when they'd gone some distance from the fire, though she was glad when Thorne didn't release her hand.

"I've been practicing walking with the new cane. One of the guys made it for me, and it's a lot nicer than that metal one. The camp setup still confuses me, though. I swear they keep moving stuff around every time I think I've got it figured out."

"I should have been there to help you," she said as they neared the small lake. "I'm sorry I slept so long."

He shrugged. "I'm just glad you're all right. I really was worried."

Her attention caught on their entwined fingers like a beacon. Every twitch, every heartbeat, every step was broadcast through her entire body.

It wasn't long before her imagination had them lying together in the warm sand, his fingers stroking through her hair, his lips working their way along her jaw.

"So listen," said Thorne, snapping her away from the dream. "I told everyone that once we get to town, we're going to call up my uncle in America and have him send transportation, so we won't be continuing on with them."

Cress tucked her hair behind her ears, still shaking off the tendrils of the fantasy. The touch of night air on her neck was unexpectedly pleasant. "And you think we'll be able to contact your crew?"

"That's my hope. The ship doesn't have any tracking equipment, but given that you were able to find our location before, I thought maybe you could think of some way to at least get a message to them."

They made a full circle around the camels, who eyed them with blatant disinterest, while Cress's brain started rummaging through a dozen possible means of communicating with an untraceable ship, and what she would need to accomplish it. She hadn't been able to do it from the satellite, but with the right net access...

She was grateful when they arrived at their little tent. Though the walk had been short, the large boots had already begun to burn. She sank down on the mat and pulled one off, inspecting the bandages as well as she could in the dark. Thorne settled down beside her.

"Everything all right?"

"I hope we can find some shoes when we get to this town." She sighed dreamily. "My first pair of real shoes."

He smirked. "Now you're sounding like a true Earthen lady."

She glanced toward the fire to make sure no one overheard them. "Can I ask why you're wearing a blindfold?"

His fingers skimmed the material. "I think it was making people uncomfortable—my staring into space all the time, or looking right through them."

She dipped her head, pulling off the second boot. "It didn't make me uncomfortable. I think your eyes are . . . well, dreamy."

His lips quirked. "So you *have* noticed." Pulling off the bandanna, he tucked it into a pocket, before stretching his legs out in front of him.

Cress fidgeted with the blunt ends of her hair, staring at his profile with a longing that made her entire body ache. Finally, after an agonizing minute of gathering her courage, she shifted closer to him and leaned her head against his shoulder.

"Good idea," he said, wrapping an arm around her waist. "How could they not think that we're in love?"

"How couldn't they?" she murmured. She squeezed her eyes shut and tried to memorize the exact feel of him.

"Cress?"

"Mm?"

"We're good, right?"

She peeled her eyes open. A crop of palm trees in front of her glowed orange in the fluttering firelight and she heard the burst and crackle of sparks, but the noise seemed far away.

"What do you mean?"

"I was just thinking about, you know, what you said out in the desert. I figured it was mostly the fever speaking, but even still, I have this habit of saying things without really thinking about them, and with you being new to this whole socializing thing . . ." He trailed off, his arm tightening around her waist. "You're awfully sweet, Cress. I don't want to hurt you."

She gulped, her mouth feeling suddenly chalky. Never had she thought that such kind words could sting, but she couldn't help feeling that his compliment didn't mean what she wanted it to mean.

She peeled her head off his shoulder. "You think I'm naïve."

"Sure, a little," he said, so matter-of-factly that it seemed less of an insult than being called sweet. "But mostly I just think I'm not the best person to demonstrate all the goodness humanity has to offer. I don't want you to be too disappointed when you realize that."

Cress knotted her fingers in her lap. "I know you better than you think, Captain Thorne. I know that you're smart. And brave. And thoughtful and kind and—"

"Charming."

"—charming and—"

"Charismatic."

"—charismatic and—"

"Handsome."

She pressed her lips and glared at him, but his mocking grin had swept away any hints of sincerity.

"Sorry," he said. "Please, continue."

"Perhaps more vain than I'd realized."

He threw his head back and laughed. Then, to her surprise, he reached over and took her hand, his other arm still around her waist. "For having such limited social experience, you, my dear, are an excellent judge of character."

"I don't need experience. You can try to hide it behind your bad reputation and criminal escapades, but I can see the truth."

Still beaming, he nudged her with his shoulder. "That on the inside, I'm really just a sappy, lovelorn romantic?"

She dug her toes into the sand. "No . . . that you're a hero."

"A *hero*? That's even better."

"And it's true."

He hid his face behind his hand, dragging Cress's hand along with it. It occurred to her that this entire conversation was a joke to him. But how could he not see it?

"You're killing me, Cress. When have you ever seen me do *anything* that would be considered heroic? Rescuing you from the satellite was all Cinder's idea, you're the one who kept us from crashing and got us through the desert—"

"I'm not talking about any of that." She yanked her hand out of his grip. "What about when you tried to raise money to help pay for android assistance for the elderly? *That* was heroic, and you were only eleven!"

His smile slipped away. "How did you know about that?"

"I did my research," she said, crossing her arms.

Thorne scratched his jaw, his confidence momentarily thrown. "All right," he said slowly. "I stole a necklace from my mom and tried to sell it. When I got caught, I figured they wouldn't punish me if they thought I'd been trying to do a good thing, and since I had to give the money back either way it didn't really matter. So I made up the story about giving the money to charity."

She frowned. "But . . . if that's the case, what were you really going to do with it?"

He sighed dreamily. "Buy a hover-racer. The Neon Spark 8000. Man, I really wanted that."

Cress blinked. A hover-racer? A *toy*? "Fine," she said, smothering the twinge of disappointment. "What about when you released that tiger from the zoo?"

"Really? You think *that* was heroic?"

"He was a poor, sad animal, locked up his whole life! You must have felt bad for him."

"Not exactly. I grew up with robotic cats instead of real pets, so I thought that if I let him out he would bow to my every whim and I could take him to school and be ridiculously popular because I was the kid with the pet tiger." He waved his hand through the air, as if he could illustrate his story as he spoke. "Of course, the second he was out and everyone went running for their lives I realized how stupid that was." He rested his elbow on his knee, cupping his chin. "This is a fun game. What else do you have?"

Cress could feel her worldview crumbling. All those hours of scouring his records, justifying his mistakes, certain that she alone knew the *true* Carswell Thorne...

"What about Kate Fallow?" she said, almost dreading his response.

He cocked his head. "Kate Fallow... Kate Fallow..."

"When you were thirteen. Some classmates stole her portscreen and you stood up for her. You tried to get it back."

"Oh, that Kate Fallow! Wow, when you research, you really research, don't you?"

She chewed on her lip, watching him for a reaction, something to say that in this one instance, at least, she had been right. He'd rescued that poor girl. He'd been her hero.

"Actually, I did have a little bit of a crush on Kate Fallow," he said distractedly. "I wonder what she's up to these days."

Her heart fluttered, grasping at the slim strings of hope. "She's studying to be an architect."

"Ah. That makes sense. She was really good at math."

"So? Don't you see how heroic that was? How selfless, how *valiant*?"

The corner of his lips twitched, but it was halfhearted and quickly faded as he turned his face away from her. He opened his mouth to speak, but hesitated, before, finally, he sought out her hand again.

"Yeah, I guess you're right," he said, squeezing. "Maybe there's a little bit of a hero in me after all. But...really, Cress. Only a little."

Twenty-Eight

THEY DECIDED TO SPEND AN EXTRA DAY IN THE CAMP, TO make sure Cress was fully recovered, but set out early the following morning, packing up their tents and mats beneath a still-dark sky. Jina told Cress that they should arrive in Kufra by late afternoon, and that by getting such an early start, they would cover a lot of ground before the scorching heat claimed the sand. They ate a quick meal of dried meats, gathered some wild dates from the trees, and left the sanctuary of the oasis.

Though it required a lot of careful repacking of trade goods and equipment, Cress was given a camel to ride. She was grateful—the mere thought of walking made her want to break down in sobs—and yet she soon found that the beast was not the epitome of comfort either. Within hours, her hands ached from clenching the reins and her calves were red and irritated. The cloak that the caravaners loaned her kept her better protected from the sun, but as the day stretched on, there was no respite from the heat.

They traveled east, parallel with the mountains. Thorne stayed at her side, a steadying hand on one of the saddlebags and the tip of his new, lighter cane skimming the sand. Still wearing the blindfold, he walked with deceptive ease. Cress offered to let him ride the camel numerous times, but he always declined. She sensed that it was becoming a matter of pride. He was proving, perhaps to himself, that he could walk without assistance, that he could be independent, that he could keep a confident smile on his face as he did so.

They spent most of the morning in silence, and Cress couldn't help losing herself in daydreams that mostly revolved around his fingertips tracing patterns on the inside of her wrist.

By midday, they were under attack by the relentless heat and windblown sand that pummeled them, trying its best to seep into the folds of their clothes. But the sun was no longer on their faces, and gradually the dunes gave way to a hard, rocky plateau.

In the afternoon, when the sun was at its worst, they came across a dried-up riverbed and stopped to rest. They found a shaded spot in the overhang of a squat cliff, and two of the men wandered off and returned a while later with all their water canteens full to the brim. Jina explained that there was a water hole hidden in a nearby cope of rocks that was fed from the same underground spring Kufra was situated on—the trading city where they were headed.

Climbing back onto the camel after the break was torture, but Cress reminded herself that anything was better than walking.

The afternoon brought more rocky lowlands, followed by a few hours of dunes. They passed a snake and Cress found that she was the only one who was afraid of it, despite Kwende confirming that it was poisonous. The snake curled up on itself and watched them pass by with lazy eyes, not even bothering to hiss or bare its fangs like the snakes on the net dramas always did. Still, from her vantage point, Cress carefully monitored where Thorne stepped and her heartbeat didn't slow until the snake could no longer be seen behind them.

Then, when Cress was sure the insides of her thighs had been rubbed raw, Thorne reached up and fumbled around until his palm landed on her knee.

"Do you hear that?"

She listened, but all she heard was the familiar soft clopping of the camels. "What?"

"Civilization."

She squeezed the camel's reins, but it wasn't until they crested the next dune that the noise separated itself from the dead desert silence, and she saw it.

A city sprouted up in front of them, unfolding in the desert among sheltering rocky cliffs. The buildings were all compacted together, but even from this distance Cress could see the blur of green trees sprouting between them. It did not seem possible—that a city could exist in the middle of such a harsh, unforgiving desert, and yet there it was, without any preamble. One step—desert. The next—paradise.

"You're right," Cress breathed, eyes wide. "We're almost there. We made it."

"What does it look like?"

"I don't know where to start. It looks crowded. There are people and buildings and streets and *trees*...."

Thorne laughed. "You just described every town on the planet."

She couldn't help giggling along with him, suddenly overcome with elation. "I'm sorry. Let me think. Most of the buildings are made out of stone, or maybe clay, and they're kind of a tan, peachy color, and the whole city is surrounded by a tall stone wall, and there are a lot of palms on all the streets. There's a lake that looks like it stretches right down the middle of the city, almost from end to end, and I see little boats in it, and so many trees and plants, and I think ... to the north, beyond the houses, I think they're growing crops of some sort. Oh!"

"What? Oh what?"

"*Animals!* At least a few dozen ... goats, maybe? And—that one over there has sheep! They look just like they do on the net!"

"Tell me about the people."

She tore her focus away from the creatures that were lazing in what shade they could find and tried to pick out the people wandering the streets. Though it was moving into evening, what appeared to be the main road was still teeming with small open-air shops, vibrantly patterned fabric walls fluttering in the breeze. "There's a lot of them. Mostly dressed in robes like we are, but there's a lot more color."

"And how big is the city?"

"*Hundreds* of buildings!"

Thorne smirked. "Try to temper that enthusiasm, city girl. I told everyone that we met in Los Angeles."

"Right. Sorry. It's just ... we made it, Captain."

His hand slipped down her leg, wrapping loosely around her ankle. "I'll be glad to get off these sand dunes, but there will be a lot more things to trip over here than in the desert. Try not to go too far, all right?"

She stared down at his profile and recognized the strained look of concern in the tilt of his lips, the crease between his eyebrows. She hadn't seen that look since they'd stumbled across the caravaners, and she'd thought he was growing more comfortable with his blindness. But maybe he'd only been trying to hide his weakness from the others.

"I wouldn't leave you," she said.

It was clear from the moment they rolled into town that the caravan was well-known and expected and late. The caravaners wasted no time in setting up a spot amid the shops and unloading their goods, while Cress tried to drink in the architecture and details and beauty that surrounded her. Though the city had appeared bleached and sandy from afar, up close she could pick out vibrant swatches of orange and pink decorating the sides of buildings, and cobalt-blue tiles lining doorways and steps. Almost every surface was bedecked in some decoration, from gold trim to intricately carved archways to an enormous fountain that stood in the middle of the main square. Cress peered into the burbling water as they passed, mesmerized by the starburst pattern laid out on the fountain's base.

"What do you think?" asked Jina.

Cress beamed. "It's breathtaking."

Jina scanned the surrounding market stalls and building fronts as if she'd never really looked at them before. "This has always been one of my favorite stops along our route, but you would hardly recognize it from a couple decades ago. When I was first learning the trade, Kufra was one of the most beautiful cities in the Sahara . . . but then the plague struck. Nearly two-thirds of the population was annihilated in only a few years, and many more fled to other towns, or left Africa altogether. Homes and businesses were abandoned, crops left to burn beneath the sun. They've been trying to recover ever since."

Cress blinked, and looked again, past the beautiful ornamentation and vibrantly painted walls, trying to see the town that Jina described, but she couldn't. "It doesn't seem abandoned."

"Not here, on the main square. But if you head out to the

northern or eastern neighborhoods, it's practically a ghost town. Very sad."

"It was very wealthy, then?" said Thorne, cocking his head. "Before the plague?"

"Oh, yes. Kufra was on many of the trade routes between the uranium mines in central Africa and the Mediterranean. One of Earth's most valuable resources, and we nearly have a monopoly on it. Excepting Australia, but there's plenty of demand to share."

"Uranium," Thorne said. "For nuclear power."

"It also powers most of today's spaceship engines."

Thorne whistled, sounding impressed, though Cress thought he had probably already known that.

"Follow me," said Jina. "There's a hotel around the corner."

Jina led them through the cramped maze of market stalls, passing everything from crates overflowing with dark sugar dates to tables lined with fresh goat cheeses to a med-droid clinic offering free blood scans.

Leaving the market lanes behind, they passed through a worn gate into a courtyard garden, filled with more palms and a tree with big yellow fruits hanging from its branches. Cress beamed when she recognized them and ached to tell Thorne about the lemons, but managed to smother her excitement.

They stepped into a small lobby, with an arched doorway that led into a dining area where some people were crowded around a table playing cards. The room smelled sweetly perfumed and heady, almost intoxicating.

Jina approached a girl who sat behind the desk and they spoke in their other language, before she turned back to them. "They're going to keep your room on our tab. They have a small kitchen here—order whatever you need. I have work to do, but I will ask about some shoes for you when I have a chance."

Cress thanked her repeatedly until Jina trotted off to complete her business.

"Room eight, upstairs," said the clerk, handing Cress a small tag embedded with a sensor key. "And please do join us for our nightly Royals competition in the lobby restaurant to your left. The first three hands are complimentary to guests."

Thorne cocked his head toward the dining area. "You don't say."

Cress eyed the players gathered around the table. "Do you want to go see?"

"No, not right now. Let's find our room."

On the second floor, Cress found the door marked with a black-painted 8. As she swiped the tag and opened the door, her attention landed first on a bed set against the wall, draped with cream-colored netting that hung from four tall posts. Pillows and blankets with gold embroidery and tassels were more elaborate by far than the linens she'd had on the satellite, and infinitely more inviting.

"Describe," said Thorne, shutting the door behind them.

She gulped. "Um. Well. There's . . . a bed."

Thorne gasped. "What? This hotel room comes with a *bed*?"

She scowled. "I mean, there's only one."

"We are married, darling." He wandered around the room until his cane struck the writing desk.

"That's a little desk," she said. "There's a netscreen above it. And over here's a window." She pulled back the curtains. The angled sunlight cut across the floor. "We can see the whole main street from here."

She heard a thud and spun around. Thorne had kicked off his

shoes and collapsed spread-eagle on the mattress. She smiled, wanting little more than to crawl up beside him and rest her head on his shoulder and sleep for a long, long time.

But there was *one* thing she wanted even more.

Through the room's only other door, she could make out a tiny porcelain sink and an old-fashioned claw-foot tub. "I'm going to take a bath."

"Good idea. I'll be right behind you."

Her eyes widened, but Thorne was already laughing. He propped himself up on his elbows. "I mean," he said, flicking his fingers through the air, "I'll take one when you're done."

"Right," she murmured, and slipped into the washroom.

Cress may not have ever been in an Earthen washroom before, but she knew enough to realize that this was not the top of latrine-technological advancement. The small overhead light functioned via an actual switch on the wall, rather than computer, and the sink faucet had two water-spotted handles for warm and cold. The shower was a giant metal disk positioned over the free-standing tub and a lot of the white porcelain had been damaged with time, revealing black cast iron underneath. A bar was hung with plush white towels, in far better shape than the towel Cress had used on the satellite.

She pulled her clothes off with more than one sigh of contentment. Her bottom layers clung to her with a layer of sweat and grime. The bandages on her feet were filled with sand and dried blood, but the blisters had been reduced to raw pinkish skin. She threw everything into a pile on the floor and turned on the water. It came on hard and cold. She got in as soon as she could stand it and found that it felt shockingly good against the sunburns on her face and legs.

The water heated fast and soon a cloud of steam was wafting up around her. She found a bar of soap, packaged in waxy paper. With a moan of ecstasy, Cress sat down in the water and lathered up her hair, amazed at how short and light and easy to clean it was.

As she soaked, she started to hum, imagining her favorite opera music blaring through the satellite speakers. Surrounding and uplifting her. Her quiet humming turned into singing, the words whimsical and foreign. She sang one of her slow Italian favorites, humming the melody when she forgot the words. By the time she reached the end of the song, she was beaming beneath the fall of water.

Cress opened her eyes. Thorne was leaning against the washroom's doorway.

She pushed herself to the back of the tub and wrapped her arms over her chest. A cascade of water splashed onto the floor. "Captain!"

His grin widened. "Where did you learn to sing like that?"

Her face flamed. "I—I don't—I'm not wearing any clothes!"

He raised an eyebrow. "Yes. I'm aware of that." He pointed to his eyes. "No need to rub it in."

Cress curled her toes against the bottom of the tub. "You shouldn't have been . . . you shouldn't . . ."

He held up his hands. "All right, fine, I'm sorry. But that was beautiful, Cress. Really. What language was it?"

She shivered, despite the steam. "Old Italian. I don't know what all the words mean."

"Huh." He turned toward the sink. "Well . . . I liked it."

Her mortification began slipping away as she watched him fumble around for the faucet.

"Do you see any washcloths?"

She told him where to find them and after knocking a second bar of soap onto the floor, he had found a clean cloth and was soaking it in the sink.

"I think I might go down to the lobby for a bit," he said, swiping the cloth over his face and leaving streaks of clean amid the dirt.

"Why?"

"See if I can get more information on this place. If we can find one of those abandoned neighborhoods, that would be the best place for Cinder and the others to come get us... after we contact them."

"If you give me a minute, I can..." She trailed off, gaping at Thorne as he peeled off his shirt. Her heart stuck in her throat as she watched him wring out the cloth, before washing off his arms and neck, chest and underarms. Setting the cloth aside, he cupped his hands beneath the faucet and slicked water through his hair.

Her fingers twitched with the sudden irrepressible desire to touch him.

"That's all right," he said, as if she hadn't just lost the ability to form coherent sentences. "I'll bring us back some food."

Cress splashed herself with the water, willing her brain to focus. "But—you said there are things to trip over and that I shouldn't leave you and... don't you want me to come?"

His hand searched around the walls until it stumbled across one of the hanging towels. He pulled it off the rack and briskly rubbed it over his face and through his hair, making it stand on end. "No need. I won't be long."

"But how will you—"

"Really, Cress. I'll be fine. Maybe you can take a look at that netscreen, see if you can figure out some way to contact the crew." He grabbed his shirt from the counter and shook it out, sending dust and sand flying, before pulling it over his head. He retied the bandanna over his eyes. "Be honest. Do I look like a famous wanted criminal right now?"

He struck a pose, complete with dazzling smile. With the messy hair, filthy clothes, and bandanna, she had to admit that he was almost unrecognizable from his prison photo. Yet somehow still heart-throbbingly gorgeous.

She sighed. "No. You don't."

"Good. I'll see about getting us some clean clothes while I'm down there too."

"Are you sure you don't need me?"

"I was overreacting before. We're in civilization now. I've got this."

He was all charisma as he blew her a kiss and left.

Twenty-Nine

STEPPING BACK FROM THE RAMPION'S HULKING SIDE, CINDER shaded her eyes with one arm and peered up at their slipshod work. Jacin was still up on one of the squeaky metal ladders the townspeople had brought them, painting over all that remained of the ship's signature decoration—the lounging naked lady, the mascot that Thorne had painted himself before Cinder had ever met him. Cinder had hated the painting from the moment she laid eyes on it, but now she was sad to see it covered up. Like she was erasing a part of Thorne, a part of his memory.

But word had gotten out through the media that the wanted ship had this very specific marking, and that was unacceptable.

Swiping a bead of sweat from her brow, Cinder surveyed the rest of their work. They didn't have enough paint to cover the entire ship, so they'd opted to focus on the main ramp's enormous side panel, so that it would at least look like that exterior piece had been fully replaced, which wasn't uncommon, rather than looking like they had tried to cover something up, which would defeat the purpose.

Unfortunately, it seemed that as much black paint had ended up on the dusty ground and the townspeople, who had come out in droves to help them, than had actually ended up on the ship. Cinder herself had paint dried on her collarbone, her temple, clumped in her hair, and stuck in the joints of her metal hand, but she was relatively unscathed compared with some of their assistants. The children in particular, eager to be helpful at first, had soon made a game of seeing who could paint up their bodies to look the most cyborg.

It was a strange sort of honor. Since Cinder had arrived, she'd been seeing this mimicry more and more. The backs of T-shirts illustrated with bionic spines. Shoes decorated with bits of assorted metal. Necklaces hung with washers and vintage lug nuts.

One girl had even been proud to show Cinder her new, real tattoo—wires and robotic joints overtaking the skin of her left foot. Cinder had smiled awkwardly and resisted the urge to tell her that the tattoo wasn't cybernetically accurate.

The attention made Cinder uncomfortable. Not because she wasn't flattered, but because she wasn't used to it. She wasn't used to being accepted by strangers, even appreciated. She wasn't used to being admired.

"Hey, mongrels, try to stay in the lines!"

Cinder looked up, just as Jacin flicked his paintbrush, sending a splatter of black paint at the three children beneath him. They all shrieked with laughter and ran for cover beneath the ship's underside.

Wiping her hands on her cargo pants, Cinder went to look at the finger painting the kids had been doodling on the other side of the ramp's plating. Simple stick figures depicted a family holding hands. Two adults. Three children of various heights. And at the end—Cinder. She knew it was her by the ponytail jutting out from the side of her head and how one of the stick figure's legs was twice as wide as the other.

She shook her head, baffled.

The ladder shook beside her as Jacin clambered down. "You should wipe it off," he said, unhooking a damp rag from his belt.

"It's not hurting anything."

Scoffing, Jacin draped the rag over her shoulder. "The whole point of this is to get rid of obvious markings."

"But it's so small. . . ."

"Since when are you so sentimental?"

She blew a strand of hair out of her face. "Fine." Pulling the rag off her shoulder, she set to scrubbing the paint off before it could dry. "I thought I was the one giving the orders around here."

"I hope you don't really think I'm here just to be bossed around some more." Jacin dropped his paintbrush into a bucket at the ladder's base. "I've taken enough orders in my life."

Cinder refolded the rag, searching for a spot that wasn't already soaked through with paint. "You have a funny way of showing loyalty."

Chuckling to himself, though Cinder wasn't sure what he found so amusing, Jacin stepped back and peered up at the enormous black square that now made up the ship's main ramp. "Good enough."

Scrubbing away the last bit of the painting—her own amateur portrait—Cinder stepped back to join him. The ship no longer looked like the Rampion she'd come to think of as home. It no longer looked like the stolen ship of Captain Carswell Thorne.

She swallowed the lump in her throat.

All around her, strangers were helping to gather up the painting supplies, scrubbing paint off one another's faces, pausing to take enormous drinks of water, and smiling. Smiling because they'd spent the morning together, accomplishing something.

Somehow, though Cinder knew she was at the center of it all, she couldn't help feel disconnected from the camaraderie, the friendships that had been forged over years of being part of one community. And soon, she would be leaving. Maybe, someday, even returning to Luna.

"So. When do we start your flying lessons?"

Cinder started. "Excuse me?"

"Ship needs a pilot," said Jacin, nodding toward the front of the ship, where the cockpit windows were glinting almost blindingly bright in the sun. "It's time you learned how to fly it yourself."

"But...aren't you my new pilot?"

He smirked. "In case you haven't noticed, people tend to get killed around you. I don't think that's a trend that's bound to stop any time soon."

A boy a few years younger than Cinder ran up to offer her a bottle of water, but Jacin took it out of his hand before Cinder could and took a few long drafts. Cinder would have been annoyed, if his words—at once so practical and so painful—weren't keeping her from feeling anything other than shock.

"I'll start teaching you the basics after we eat," he said, passing the bottle to her. Cinder took it numbly. "Don't worry. It's not as hard as it looks."

"Fine." Cinder finished off the water. "It's not like I'm busy trying to prevent a full-scale war or anything."

"Is that what you're doing?" He eyed her suspiciously. "Here I thought we were painting a spaceship."

A comm pinged in the corner of Cinder's vision. From Dr. Erland. She tensed, but the comm was only two tiny words that made her entire world start spinning again. "He's awake," she said, mostly to herself. "Wolf is awake."

Turning away from the ship and lingering townsfolk, Cinder thrust the empty water bottle into Jacin's stomach and took off running toward the hotel.

Wolf was sitting up when Cinder burst into the hotel room. His feet were bare, his torso still covered in bandages. He didn't look at all surprised to see Cinder, but then, he would have heard her pounding up the old wooden stairs. Probably smelled her too.

"Wolf! Thank the stars. We were so worried. How do you feel?"

His eyes, duller than usual, flickered past her toward the hallway. He frowned, like he was confused.

A second later, Cinder heard footsteps and turned just as Dr. Erland brushed past her, carrying a medical kit.

"He is still under heavy painkillers," said the doctor. "Try not to ask too many confusing questions, if you would."

Gulping, Cinder followed the doctor to Wolf's side.

"What happened?" said Wolf, his words barely slurred. He sounded exhausted.

"We were attacked by a thaumaturge," said Cinder. Part of her felt like she should take Wolf's hand, but the most intimate contact she'd ever had with him before was the occasional friendly punch to the jaw. It wouldn't have felt natural, so instead she stood just within arm's reach, her hands fisted in her pockets. "You were shot. We didn't know…but you're all right. He's all right, isn't he, doctor?"

Erland flashed a light past Wolf's eyes. Wolf flinched back.

"He is better than I would have expected," he said. "It seems you're on target to make a full recovery, so long as you can avoid re-opening your wounds in the meantime."

"We're on Earth," said Cinder, not sure if that was obvious to Wolf or not. "In Africa. We're safe here, for now."

But Wolf seemed distracted and upset as he tilted his head back and sniffed. His frown deepened. "Where's Scarlet?"

Cinder grimaced. She had known the question would be coming. She had known that she wouldn't know how to answer when it did.

His expression darkened. "I can't smell her. Like she hasn't been here in . . . like she isn't here."

Dr. Erland pressed a thermometer against Wolf's brow, but Wolf snatched it away before it could gauge his temperature. "*Where is she?*"

Miffed, the doctor fisted his hand on his waist. "Now that is precisely the type of jerky movement you should be avoiding."

Wolf snarled, showing his sharp teeth.

"She's not here," said Cinder, forcing herself not to shrink away when Wolf turned his glare on her. She struggled to form an explanation. "The thaumaturge took her. During the fight on the ship. She was alive—I don't think she was even injured. But the thaumaturge took her aboard the podship. Jacin thinks she needed Scarlet to pilot it."

Wolf's jaw went slack. With terror, with denial. He jerked his head, no.

"Wolf . . ."

"How long? How long ago . . . ?"

She scrunched her shoulders against her neck. "Five days."

He grimaced and turned away, his face contorting with pain that had nothing to do with his wounds.

Cinder took half a step toward him, but paused. There were no words that would mean anything to him. No explanation, no apology.

So she braced herself for Wolf's anger instead. She expected fury and destruction. His pupils had narrowed to pinpricks and his fists started to flex. Though Cinder had practiced her mind control sporadically on Jacin and the doctor since they'd arrived in Farafrah, it would be a true test of her abilities if Wolf lost control.

And she could sense it brimming inside him. Fear burning and roiling. Panic writhing inside his chest. The animal straining to be unleashed inside the man.

But then Wolf's breath hitched and all the fury drained out of him with a shudder. Like a man shot fatally through the heart, he collapsed over his knees, covering his head with his good arm like he wanted to block out the world.

Cinder stood, staring. All her senses were attuned to Wolf, focused on the energy and emotions that clouded around him. It was like watching a candle extinguish.

It was like watching him die.

Gulping, Cinder sank into a crouch in front of him. She considered reaching out and placing a hand on his arm, but she couldn't bring herself to do it. It was too much like an invasion, especially when her gift was attuned to him like this. When she was watching him break and crumble in front of her. She longed to put him back together. To take away the vulnerability that didn't fit him. But it was his right to mourn. It was his right to be terrified for Scarlet, as she was.

"I'm sorry," she whispered. "But we will find her. We're trying to come up with some way to get to Luna, and we'll find her. We'll rescue—"

His head jolted up so fast that Cinder nearly fell over from surprise. His eyes had brightened again.

"Rescue her?" he seethed, his knuckles turning white. "You don't know what they'll do to her—what they've already done to her!"

It happened fast. One moment he was a broken man, crumpled over his own knees. The next he was on his feet, grabbing the frame of the bed and upending it against the wall. The medical kit crashed to the floor. The room shook. Crying out, Cinder scurried backward.

Then the chaos quieted, just as suddenly. Wolf froze, teetered on his feet, and fell so hard onto the floor that the hotel trembled from the impact.

Dr. Erland stood above his prone body, empty syringe in hand, glaring at Cinder over his thin-framed spectacles.

She gulped.

"Wouldn't it be handy," said the doctor, "if we had someone here with the mental faculties capable of controlling one of his kind when he goes on just that sort of a tirade?"

Hands shaking, Cinder pushed her mess of hair out of her face. "I was—getting around to it."

"Well. Faster next time, if I might make a suggestion." Sighing, he tossed the syringe onto the room's small desk and glowered down at the unconscious man. Blood was beginning to seep through the bandages beneath Wolf's shoulder blade. "Perhaps it will be best to keep him sedated, for the time being."

"Perhaps."

The doctor's lips puckered, wrinkles creasing down his cheeks. "Do you still have those tranquilizer darts I gave you?"

"Oh, please." Cinder forced herself to stand, though her legs still shook. "Do you have any idea how many times I've nearly died since you gave me those? They're long gone."

Dr. Erland harrumphed. "I'll make you some more. I have a feeling you're going to need them."

Thirty

CRESS HUMMED TO HERSELF AS SHE RUBBED A TOWEL THROUGH her hair, amazed at how the weight of it no longer pulled on her. She emerged from the washroom rejuvenated—her skin was bright pink from scrubbing and she'd managed to get almost all the dirt out from beneath her fingernails. The bottoms of her feet and the insides of her legs were still sore, but all those complaints were petty compared to the sensation of unexpected luxury. A soft towel. Short, clean hair. More water than she could drink in a year. Or at least, her long bath had made it seem endless.

Cress eyed her pile of clothes and couldn't bear to put them back on. As Thorne hadn't returned yet, she pulled a blanket off the bed and wrapped it around herself instead, then struggled to kick the corners out of her way as she crossed to the netscreen on the wall.

"Screen, on."

It was set to an animated netfeed that showed orange octopuses and blue children bopping around to tech-beats. Cress changed it to the local newsfeed, then opened a new box in the corner to check their GPS coordinates.

Kufra, a trading city at the eastern edge of the Sahara. She zoomed out on the map and tried to pinpoint where the satellite would have landed, though it was impossible to gauge how far they'd walked. Probably not half as far as it had seemed. Regardless, there was nothing, *nothing*, in the vast open sands to the north and west.

She shuddered, realizing how close they'd come to being food for the vultures.

She sent the map away, beginning to concoct a strategy for contacting the Rampion. Though they didn't have the D-COMM chip anymore, that didn't mean the Rampion was completely out of touch. After all, with or without tracking equipment, it would still have communication capabilities and a net protocol address. She could have hacked into the military database and tracked down the original NPA for the ship, but it would be a waste of time. If it was that easy, the Commonwealth would have been able to contact the Rampion as soon as they had determined which ship they were after.

Which meant the address had been changed, probably not long after Thorne's desertion.

Which most likely meant the auto-control system had been replaced. Hopefully Thorne would have some information on where and when the new system had been purchased, or what programming it had been replaced with.

If he didn't know anything, well . . . she was going to have to get creative.

That was not worth worrying about just yet. First things first.

She had to make sure there was someone aboard that ship to contact.

She began by checking the newsfeeds. A simple search made

it clear that, at this time, the Earthen media had no more information on the whereabouts of Linh Cinder than they'd had five days ago.

" . . . *Lunar satellite. . .*"

She snapped her attention to the news anchor who was rambling in a foreign language, most likely the language that the caravan hunter had first spoken to them. Cress frowned, thinking she was only hearing things. But then, as she squinted at the man's lips, she thought she heard *Sahara* and, again, *Lunar.*

"Set translation overdub to universal language."

The language switched as the news anchor was replaced with video footage from a vast desert, a horrendously familiar desert. And there in the middle of it was the wreckage that she and Thorne had abandoned. Her satellite, still attached to the obliterated Lunar podship and the parachute strung out behind it. A large square was cut from the fabric.

She gulped.

It wasn't long before the gist of the story had come through. Multiple witnesses had seen something drop out of the sky—the blaze could be seen as far north as the Mediterranean—and the satellite had been discovered two days later. There was no question that it was Lunar built. There was no question that someone had survived and abandoned the wreckage, taking what supplies they could carry.

Authorities were still scouring the desert. They did not know whether they were looking for one survivor or many, but they could be sure they were looking for Lunars, and in the state of tension between Luna and Earth, they were not willing to risk the queen's wrath if these fugitives were not found.

Cress buried her hands in her damp, tangled hair.

The implications hit her in fast succession.

If any of the caravaners learned about the crash, they would no doubt suspect that Cress and Thorne were the survivors. They would turn them in, and when the authorities found Thorne, they would recognize him immediately.

And not just the caravaners. Everyone would be suspicious about strangers right now.

But then—a light amid the panic.

If Linh Cinder learned about this wreckage, then she too, would know what had happened. She would know that Thorne and Cress were alive.

The crew would come for them.

It was all a question of who found them first.

Cress ripped herself out of the chair and threw on her dirty clothes, ignoring how they scratched against her skin.

She had to tell Thorne.

She was cautious creeping down the hallway, trying to act natural but not knowing what natural looked like. She was already aware of how much her fair complexion and hair made her stand out here, and she didn't want to draw any more attention than she had to.

The noise from the hotel lounge roared up the staircase. Laughter and bellowing and the clinking of glasses. Cress peeked over the banister. The crowd had quadrupled since they'd left the lobby—this must be a popular hour. Men and women loitered around the bar and card tables, snacking on bowls of dried fruits.

The crowd around a corner table hollered in delight, and Cress was relieved to spot Thorne in their midst, still blindfolded, and holding a hand of cards. She crept through the crowd toward him, her mouth watering from unfamiliar, spicy aromas.

The crowd shifted, and she froze.

There was a woman on Thorne's lap. She was net-drama beautiful, with warm brown skin and full lips and hair that hung in dozens of long, thin braids dyed various shades of blue. She wore simple khaki shorts and a blousy top, but somehow she made them look elegant.

And she had the longest legs Cress had ever seen.

The woman leaned forward and pushed a pile of plastic chips toward one of the other players. Thorne tilted his head in laughter. He took one of the few chips still in front of him and flipped it over his knuckles a few times before tucking it into the woman's palm. In response, she trailed her fingernails down his neck.

The air burned around Cress, clinging to her skin and pressing against her, tightening around her throat until she couldn't breathe. Suffocating, she turned and dashed from the lounge.

Her knees were shaking as she ratcheted up the stairs. She found door number 8, and dumbly shook the knob—seeing those fingernails teasing his skin again, and again—before she realized that the door was locked. The key was inside, beside the washroom sink.

She sobbed and slumped against the wall, beating her forehead against the frame. "Stupid. Stupid. Stupid."

"Cress?"

She spun around, swiping at the hot tears. Jina stood before her, having just emerged from her own room down the hall. "What's wrong?"

Cress ducked her head away. "I-I'm locked out. And Carswell…Carswell is…" She dissolved, crying into her palms as Jina rushed forward to embrace her.

"Oh, there, there, it's not worth getting so worked up about."

This only made Cress cry harder. How twisted their story had become. Thorne was not her husband, despite their made-up romance, despite the nights spent in his arms. He had every right to flirt with whomever he chose, and yet . . .

And yet . . .

How wrong she'd been. How stupid.

"You're safe now," Jina said, rubbing her back. "Everything is going to be fine. Here, I brought you some shoes."

Sniffing, Cress looked down at the simple canvas shoes in Jina's hand. She took them with shaking hands, stammering out her gratitude, though it was buried beneath hiccups.

"Listen, I was just going to meet Niels for a late meal. Would you like to join us?"

Cress shook her head. "I don't want to go back down there."

Jina petted Cress's hair. "You can't stay up here without your key. We'll slip right past the lobby. There's a restaurant on the corner. Does that sound nice?"

Cress tried to calm herself. All she wanted was to get into her room and hide under the bed, but she would need to go talk to the girl at the desk again to get another key. She would bring even more attention to herself, especially now that her eyes were red and her face flushed. People would talk, and she suddenly remembered how bad it was that people would talk.

And she didn't want to still be standing in the hallway, sniffling and miserable, when Thorne came back. If she could have some time to calm down, then she could speak to him rationally. She would go on like her heart wasn't shattered.

"All right," she said. "Yes, thank you."

Jina kept her securely tucked beneath her arm and hurried them both down the stairs and through the lobby. She guided her along the walkway that lined the main road. The crowd had dwindled, many of the shops now covered up for the night. "It isn't right to see such a pretty girl crying like that, especially after all you've been through."

Cress sobbed again.

"Don't tell me you and Carswell had a fight, after surviving the great Sahara together?"

"He's not—" She ducked her head, watching sand slip down the cracks of the clay pavers.

Jina took her elbow. "He's not what?"

Cress sniffled into her sleeve. "Nothing. Never mind."

There was a pause, before Jina spoke, slowly, "You're not really married, are you?"

Clenching her teeth, Cress shook her head.

Jina lightly stroked her arm. "We all have our secrets, and I can venture to guess your reasons. If I'm right, I don't blame you for the lies." She leaned close, so that her forehead touched Cress's frizzing hair. "You're Lunar, aren't you?"

Her feet stumbled and froze. She ripped herself away from Jina's gentle touch, instincts telling her to run, to hide. But Jina's expression was full of sympathy, and the panic quickly fizzled.

"I caught word of the fallen satellite. I figured it must have been you. But it's all right." She tugged Cress forward again. "Lunars aren't so rare around here. Some of us have even come to appreciate having you around."

Cress stumbled along beside her. "Really?"

The woman tilted her head, squinting at Cress. "Mostly we've found that your people just want to keep to themselves. After going through all the trouble of making it to Earth, why risk getting caught and sent back, after all?"

Cress let herself be led on as she listened, surprised at how rationally Jina was speaking about it all. All the Earthen media had led her to believe there was such a hatred toward Lunars, that she could never be accepted. But what if that wasn't true at all?

"I hope you won't be offended by my asking," Jina continued, "but are you . . . ungifted?"

She nodded dumbly, and was surprised at the smug grin that passed over Jina's face, like she'd guessed it all along. "There's Niels."

Cress's thoughts were swimming. To think that she and Thorne could have told them the truth from the start . . . but, no, he was still a wanted criminal. She would have to think of a new story as to why she and Thorne were together. Did they think he was Lunar too?

Niels and Kwende were standing outside a big dusty vehicle with enormous traction wheels. Its hood was up, a cord plugged into a generator attached to a building, and a wide door was open in the back. They were loading things into it—many sacks of goods that Cress thought she recognized from the camels.

"Making room for the new cargo?" said Jina, coming up to stand with the men.

If Niels was surprised to see Cress there without her husband, he didn't show it. "About done," he said, dusting his hands. "The engine's near a complete charge. Should have no problem getting us to Farafrah and back without having to break into the petroleum reserves."

"Fara . . . ?" Cress glanced at Jina. "You're not staying?"

Jina clicked her tongue. "Oh, Jamal and a few others are, but we've had a new order, so we need to make a special trip. There's always more business to attend to."

"But you just got here. What about the camels?"

Niels laughed. "They'll stay in the town stables and be happy for the break. Sometimes they suit our needs, and sometimes we need something a bit faster." He thumped a palm down on the side of the truck. "Have you been crying?"

"It's nothing," she said, dipping her head.

"Jina?"

Jina's hand tightened on Cress's arm, and she responded to his unspoken query in their other language. Cress flushed, wishing she knew what Jina was saying.

Then he smiled cryptically, and nodded.

Cress was grabbed suddenly from behind. A hand clamped over her mouth, muffling her startled cry as she was shoved past Jina, past Niels. Her head was forced down as she was thrust into the back of the vehicle, banging her shins on the bumper. The hatch slammed shut. Pitch blackness surrounded her.

Niels barked something she didn't understand, and then the engine rumbled beneath her. She heard two more doors slam near the front of the vehicle.

"No!" She threw herself at the hatch, pounding her fists against the metal. She screamed until her throat went hoarse, until the rumble and sway of the vehicle grew rough and the bumps threw her against a pile of bolted fabrics.

Her mind was still spinning when, not minutes later, she felt the vibrations change. They'd already left the paved streets of Kufra behind.

BOOK

Three

"The cat has caught the bird, and she will

scratch out your eyes as well.

You will never see your Rapunzel again."

Thirty-One

THE GIRL RETURNED FROM HER TRIP TO THE BAR, SETTING A
drink against Thorne's wrist so he would know where it was.

He tilted his head toward her and lifted the cards. "What do you think?"

Her braids brushed his shoulder. "I think . . ." She tugged at two cards in his hand. "These two."

"Precisely the two I was thinking," he said, taking hold of the two cards. "Our luck is changing, right about . . . now."

"Two to the blind man," said the dealer, and Thorne heard the cards slapping down on the table. He slid them up into his hand.

The woman clicked her tongue. "That's not what we wanted," she said, and he could hear the pout in her voice.

"Ah, well," said Thorne. "We can't win them all. Or, apparently, any of them." He waited until the bidding came around before folding. The woman leaned closer from behind him and nuzzled his neck. "The next hand will be yours."

Thorne grinned. "I am feeling lucky."

He listened as the bidding went twice around the table and the winner claimed the pot with jesters and sevens. From the man's gruff voice, Thorne pictured a scraggly beard and an excessive belly. He'd drawn up detailed mental images of all the players at the table. The dealer was a tall and skinny man with a fine mustache. The lady beside him was elderly and something kept jangling when she took her cards, so Thorne pictured an abundance of gaudy jewelry. He judged the man to his right to be scrawny with bad skin, but that was probably because he was winning the most.

Of course, the woman who had draped herself over Thorne was viciously hot.

And not at all lucky, it turned out.

The dealer dealt out another hand and Thorne raised his cards. Behind him, the girl let out a sad whistle. "So sorry, love," she whispered.

He pouted. "No hope? What a shame."

The bidding opened, moving around the table. Check. Bet. Raise.

Thorne tapped his fingers against his cards and sighed. They were useless, judging from the woman's sad inflection.

Naturally, he put his palm against his chips and slid the entire stack toward the center of the table, listening to the happy clatter of chips falling against one another. Not that he had a lot of them. "All in," he said.

The woman behind him was silent. The hand on his shoulder didn't even twitch. Nothing to acknowledge that he'd gone against her suggestion.

Poker face, indeed.

"You're a fool," said the scrawny player, but he folded.

Then the bearded man snorted with a sound that made Thorne's spine tingle—not from concern, but expectation. This was his man.

"I'd raise if I thought you had anything left to bet," he said, followed by the clicking and clacking of chips.

The last two players folded. The dealer passed out cards to replace the throwaways—two to Thorne's opponent.

He kept all his cards. If his lady disapproved, her statuesque hands hinted at nothing.

They didn't bother to bid for the second round, knowing that Thorne was maxed out. Thorne fanned his cards out on the table. The dealer called them out, his finger thumping against his opponent's hand. "Doubles." Then—"Royal triplets win!"

Thorne arched an eyebrow as the old lady with the jewelry let out a delighted giggle. "To the blind man!"

"I trust the royal triplets were mine?"

"Indeed. Nice hand," said the dealer, pushing the chips in Thorne's direction.

He heard a chair crash to the ground. "You outdated piece of junk! You should have told him to fold that hand!"

"I did," said the girl behind Thorne, in an even tone that failed to acknowledge the insult. "He chose to ignore my recommendation."

Thorne tipped back in his chair. "It's your own fault for teaching her the game so well. If I'd won even a couple hands I wouldn't have been suspicious, but even my luck isn't this bad." He twirled his fingers through the air, enjoying the explanation. "I just had to wait until there was a hand she claimed wasn't salvageable—and then I'd know I had a winner." Beaming, he leaned forward and scooped the chips toward him, enjoying the way they filled up his arms. He heard a couple drop to the floor, but left them, unable to suffer the indignity of rummaging around with his fingers.

"But," he said, beginning to stack up his earnings, chip by

chip, having no idea what color or value any of them were, "I'm willing to make you a deal, if you aren't too sore a loser."

"What deal? That was almost everything I had."

"Your own fault, of course. For cheating."

The man gargled something incoherent.

"But I'm nothing if not a businessman. I'd like to buy your escort-droid from you." He waved his fingers over the stacks of chips. "Would you say she's worth about . . . this much?"

The man spluttered. "You can't even see her!"

Smirking, Thorne reached up and patted the hand that still rested on his shoulder. "She's very believable," he said. "But I'm a man of keen observation and, what can I say? She seems to be missing a pulse." He gestured at the chips again. "Fair trade?"

He heard the screech of chair legs on tiles and the clomping of the man's boots as he rounded the table. "Uh-oh."

Thorne grabbed his cane from where he'd propped it against the table, just as he was pulled out of his seat by his shirt collar.

"Now, let's be gentleme—"

A crunching pain rattled through his skull, snapping his head back. He fell onto the floor, his cheekbone throbbing and the taste of iron on his tongue. Testing that his jaw worked, he pressed a hand against his face, knowing the punch would leave one heck of a mark. "That," he muttered through his muddled thoughts, "was not politically correct."

A man roared, followed by more chairs screeching and furniture falling and something like dishes shattering and people yelling and then there was a mess of limbs crawling and tumbling as a full-scale brawl broke out in the bar.

Thorne curled up on himself, holding his cane above his head as a pathetic shield against the chaos, trying to make himself as small a target as he could. A wayward knee connected with his hip. A falling chair battered his forearms.

Two hands snaked beneath his armpits, hauling him backward. Thorne kicked at the floor, allowing himself to be pulled out of the cluster of elbows and knees.

"You all right?" said a man.

Thorne used his cane to level himself onto his feet and shoved his back against a wall, glad for its support and protection. "Yeah, thanks. If there's one thing I hate, it's a guy who goes berserk when he gets caught cheating. If you're going to do it, you have to be ready to take the fallout like a man."

"Good policy. But I think he was more upset over you insulting his woman."

Thorne cringed and wiped some blood from his mouth. He was glad that at least all of his teeth felt secure. "Don't tell me she's not an escort-droid. I could have sworn . . ."

"Oh, she's definitely an escort. Cute one too. It's just a lot of men don't like admitting that their arm accessory is bought and programmed."

Readjusting the bandanna, Thorne shook his head. "Again. If you're going to do it, own it like a man. Not to be rude, but do I know you?"

"Jamal, from the caravan."

"Jamal. Right. Thanks for the rescue."

"My pleasure. You probably want to get some ice on that eye. Come on, let's get out of this mess before anyone else takes a dislike to you."

Thirty-Two

"OOOOOOOWW," THORNE MOANED, PLACING A COOLING PACK against his throbbing cheekbone. "Why did he have to hit so *hard*?"

"You're lucky he didn't break your nose or knock out any teeth," said Jamal. Thorne could hear him shuffling around, followed by glasses clinking together.

"That's true. I am rather attached to my nose."

"There's a chair behind you."

Thorne tested the floor with his cane until it struck something hard, and eased himself onto the chair. He leaned the cane against the side and adjusted the pack on his cheekbone.

"Here."

He held out his free hand and was glad when a cold, condensation-slicked glass was put into it. He sniffed first. The drink smelled faintly of lemons. Taking a sip, he found that it was cold and frothy, tart and delicious. The absence of sudden warmth suggested there was no alcohol.

"*Tamr hindi,*" said Jamal. "Tamarind juice. My favorite thing in the trading cities."

"Thank you." Thorne took a bigger gulp, his cheeks puckering from the sourness.

"Have you always been such a gambler?" Jamal asked.

"I guess you could say I enjoy a challenge. No survival skills? Let's honeymoon in the desert. Can't see? Let's go play some cards. I would have won too, if that guy hadn't gotten so touchy."

He thought he heard a chuckle, but then Jamal slurped at his drink.

"Were you there the whole time? Watching that escort-droid bleed me dry and not saying anything?"

"If a blind man wants to lose his head in a suicide card game, why should I stop him?"

Thorne relaxed against the back of the chair. "I guess I can respect that."

"I am curious why you didn't bring your girl with you. I'd have thought she'd be a valuable asset."

"I thought she could use the rest." Thorne adjusted the cooling pack on his face. "Plus, I don't think she's ever played Royals before, and there are all those tricky rules to explain . . ."

"And she probably wouldn't have been pleased about you wanting an escort-droid?"

Thorne guffawed. "Oh, no, no, I didn't want the escort for *me*. I thought she'd make a nice gift." A silence followed and he was sure he could picture the skepticism on Jamal's face, despite having no idea what Jamal looked like. "She was for this android . . . spaceship . . . friend of mine. It's complicated."

"It always is." Jamal clinked their glasses together. "I get it, though. You get your hands on an escort-droid, all the while keeping everyone's attention away from the true prize upstairs. You do seem like the protective sort."

Thorne's instincts hummed at something in Jamal's tone. "Well. I am a lucky man."

"Yes, you are. A girl like that doesn't fall out of the sky every day."

Thorne kept his smile for a heartbeat, then downed the rest of the drink. His nose crinkled. "Speaking of Mrs. Smith, I should get back to her. Promised to bring up some food and then got carried away . . . you know how it is."

"I wouldn't be in any hurry," said Jamal. "I saw her with Jina a couple hours ago. I think the ladies were going out for some refreshments."

The grin froze on Thorne's face, and now he knew for sure something wasn't right. Cress, leave the hotel without telling him? Not likely.

But why would Jamal lie about something like that?

"Ah. Good," he said, hiding his uncertainty. He set the empty glass down on the floor, tucking it beneath the chair so he wouldn't trip on it later. "Cress could use some . . . girly . . . time. Did they happen to say where they were going?"

"No, but there are plenty of eateries on this street. Why? Afraid she might run off without you?"

Thorne snorted, but it sounded forced even to him. "Naw. This'll be good for her. Making friends . . . Eating stuff."

"Exploring all that Earth has to offer?"

His expression must have been hilarious, because Jamal's laugh was loud and abrupt.

"I knew you wouldn't be surprised," he said. "Kwende thought you didn't know she was Lunar, but I figured you would. You strike me as the type of man who has a keen sense of value. Especially when I saw you bargaining for that escort downstairs. Even blind, you do seem to have impeccable taste in female companionship."

"This is true," Thorne murmured, trying to recapture this

conversation. Sense of value? Impeccable taste? What was he *talking* about?

"So tell me how you came across her. It was a Lunar satellite, I've got that much, but how did you get tangled up with her to begin with? Did you find her still in space, or down here in the desert? Must have been in space, I guess. There was that podship in the wreckage."

"Um. It's kind of a long story."

"No matter. Not like I'm going to be up in space any time soon. But then to *crash*. That couldn't have been part of your original plan." Ice cubes crackled. "Tell me this, did you plan on bringing her to Africa the whole time, or are there more lucrative markets elsewhere in the Union?"

"Um. I thought...Africa..." Thorne scratched his jaw. "You said they've been gone for a couple hours?"

"Give or take." Chair legs squeaked across the floor. "So you must have known she was a shell when you found her? Couldn't find me trading in their kind otherwise, don't care how much they're worth."

Thorne spread his free hand out on his knee and pressed his sudden panic into it. So they knew about the crashed satellite, and they knew Cress was a shell, and they seemed to be under the impression there was a market for that. And that Thorne wanted to, what? Sell her? Trade her as stolen goods? Was there some strange black-market demand for shells that he wasn't aware of?

"Honestly, Lunars terrify me too," he said, trying to hide his ignorance. "But not Cress. She's harmless."

"Harmless, and not terrible to look at, either. So short, though." There were footsteps—Jamal walking to the other side of the room, something being poured. "Another drink?"

Thorne eased his tense knuckles off his own leg. "I'm fine, thank you."

Glass on wood.

"So do you know where you're taking her yet? Or are you still shopping around for a good price? I figured you were probably taking her to that old doctor in Farafrah, but I have to tell you, I think Jina's interested. Could save you a lot of trouble."

Thorne smothered his discomfort and tried to imagine they weren't talking about Cress at all. They were business associates, discussing merchandise. He just had to figure out what Jamal knew that he clearly didn't.

He slipped his finger beneath the blindfold, stretching the fabric away from his eyes. It was becoming too tight, and his cheek was throbbing more painfully than ever. "Interesting proposition," he said slowly. "But why deal with a middleman when I can go straight to the end buyer?"

"Convenience. We'll take her off your hands and you can be off on the next treasure hunt. Plus, we know this market better than anyone. We'll make sure she ends up in a nice place—if you care about that sort of thing." He paused. "What were you hoping to get for her, anyway?"

Merchandise. Business transactions. He attempted nonchalance, but his skin was crawling and he found it difficult to set aside the memory of Cress's hand in his.

"Make me an offer," he said.

There was a long hesitation. "I can't speak for Jina."

"Then why are we having this conversation? Sounds to me like you're wasting my time." Thorne reached for his cane.

"She did give me a number," said Jamal. Thorne paused, and after a long silence, Jamal continued, "But I'm not qualified to finalize anything."

"We could at least find out if we're all playing the same game."

More slurping, followed by a long sigh.

"We could offer you 20,000 for her."

This time, the shock was impossible to hide. Thorne felt like Jamal had just kicked him in the chest. "20,000 *univs*?"

A sharp laugh rang off the walls. "Too low? You'll have to discuss it with Jina. But if you don't mind me asking, what were you *hoping* to get for her?"

Thorne snapped his mouth shut. If their starting offer was 20,000 univs, what did they think she was really worth? He felt like a fool. What was this—Lunar trafficking? Some sort of weird fetishism?

She was a girl. A living girl, smart and sweet and awkward and unusual, and she was worth far more than they could ever realize.

"Don't be shy, Mr. Smith. You must have had some number in mind."

His thoughts started to clear, and it occurred to him that in many ways, he was just like these people. A businessman out to make a quick profit, who had been lucky enough to stumble onto a naïve, overly trusting Lunar shell.

Except, he had a bad habit of just taking the things that he wanted.

He dug his fingernails into his thighs. If she was worth that much, why wouldn't they simply take her?

Panic swept through him, like a lightning bolt arcing through every limb. This wasn't a negotiation—this was a *distraction*. He'd been right before. Jamal was wasting his time. Intentionally.

Thorne dropped the cooling pack and launched himself out of the chair, grabbing the cane. He was at the door in two strides, his hand fumbling for the knob, yanking open the door.

"Cress!" he yelled, trying to remember how many doors

they'd passed to get to Jamal's room. He was turned around, unable to remember which side of the hall his and Cress's room had been on to begin with. "CRESS!" He stormed down the hall, pounding aimlessly on the walls and doors he passed.

"Can I help you, Master?"

He spun toward the female voice, his optimism thinking for a second that it was her, but no. The sound was too airy and fake, and Cress called him Captain.

Who would call him *Master*?

"Who's that?"

"My previous master called me Darling," said the voice. "I'm your new escort-droid. The house rules gave my former master a choice of returning your earnings to you, or accepting your offered trade. He chose the trade, which means that I am now your personal property. You seem stressed. Would you like me to sing a relaxing song while I rub your shoulders?"

Realizing that he was gripping his cane like a weapon, Thorne shook his head. "Room eight. Where is it?"

He heard a couple doors open down the hallway.

"Cress?"

"What's all the noise about?" said a man.

Someone else started talking in that language Thorne didn't recognize.

"Here's room eight," said the escort. "Shall I knock?"

"Yes!" He followed the sound of her knocking and tested the knob. Locked. He cursed. "CRESS!"

"Can we keep it down out here?"

"I'm afraid I'm programmed to avoid destruction of property, so I am unable to break down this door for you, Master. Shall I go to the front desk and retrieve a key?"

Thorne pounded at the door again.

"She's not in there," said Jamal from down the hall.

That other language again, fast and annoyed.

"Shall I translate, Master?"

Growling, Thorne marched back toward Jamal, his cane whipping against the corridor walls. He heard yelps of surprise as people ducked back into their rooms to avoid being hit. "Where is she? And don't try to tell me she's out enjoying a pleasant meal in town."

"And what will you do if I won't tell you? Propose a staring contest?"

He despised that his alarm was showing, but every word raised his temperature, degree by boiling degree. It seemed like hours since he'd so flippantly said good-bye to Cress, when she was still in the bath, when her singing was still echoing in his ears. And he'd left her. He'd just *left* her—and why? To show off his gambling skills? To prove that he was still self-sufficient? To prove that he didn't need anyone, not even her?

Every moment that stretched on was agony. They could have taken her anywhere, done anything to her. She could be alone and frightened, wondering why he hadn't come for her. Wondering why he'd abandoned her.

He lashed out, his hand thwapping Jamal in the ear. Surprised, Jamal tried to duck away, but Thorne had already grabbed the front of his shirt and hauled him closer. "Where is she?"

"She's no longer your concern. If you were so attached, I guess you should have kept a better eye on her, rather than running off and flirting with the first steel-boned escort that passed by." He placed a hand over Thorne's. "She saw that, you know. Saw that escort hanging all over you downstairs. Looked pretty shaken up by the sight. Didn't even hesitate when Jina offered to take her away."

Thorne gritted his teeth as blood rushed to his face. He couldn't tell whether Jamal was lying, but the thought of Cress seeing him gambling with that escort-droid, and having no idea what he was really doing . . .

"See, it's all just business," continued Jamal. "You lost her, we took her. At least you got a pretty new toy out of the deal, so try not to feel too upset."

Grimacing, Thorne tightened his grip around the cane and brought it up as hard as he could, right between Jamal's legs.

Jamal roared. Backing up, Thorne swung the cane toward his head. It cracked hard, but was quickly jerked out of his hand as Jamal let off a stream of curses.

Thorne reached for the gun that had been nearly forgotten since he and Cress had left the satellite. He pulled it from his waistband and took aim. Screams from the other people in the hall bounced down the corridors, followed by the slamming of doors and the pounding of feet on the stairway.

"From this distance," he said, "I'm pretty sure I can hit you a few times. I wonder how many shots I can get in before I get a fatal one." He listed his head. "Then I guess I'll just take your portscreen, which probably has all your business contacts in it. You said something about a doctor in . . . Fara-whatta? I guess we'll try him first."

He released the safety.

"Wait, *wait*! You're right. They were taking her to Farafrah, just a tiny oasis, about three hundred kilometers northeast of here. There's some doctor there who has a thing for Lunar shells."

Thorne took a step back into the hallway, though he kept the gun up and ready. "Escort-droid, you still there?"

"Yes, Master. Can I be of assistance?"

"Get me the coordinates of a town called Farafrah, and the fastest way to get there."

"You're an idiot to go after her," said Jamal. "She'll already be sold, and that old man isn't going to pay for her twice. You should just cut your losses and move on. She's just a Lunar shell—she isn't worth it."

"If you honestly believe that," said Thorne, stowing the gun again, "then you really don't recognize true value when you see it."

Thirty-Three

CRESS CROUCHED IN THE CORNER OF THE VAN, GRIPPING HER knees against her chest. She was trembling, despite the sweltering heat. She was thirsty and hungry and her shins were bruised where they'd collided with the van's ledge. Though she'd pulled down the bolts of fabric to sit on, the constant jerking of the truck on the uneven ground made her backside ache.

The night was so dark she couldn't see her hand in front of her face, but sleep wouldn't come. Her thoughts were too erratic as she tried to discern what these people wanted with her. She'd played the moments before her capture over in her head a hundred times, and Jina's expression had definitely lit up when Cress had confirmed Jina's suspicions.

She was a shell. A worthless shell.

Why had Jina sensed value in that?

She racked her brain, but nothing made sense.

She tried her best to remain calm. Tried to be optimistic. Tried to tell herself that Thorne would come for her, but doubts kept crowding out the hope.

He couldn't see. He didn't know where she'd gone. He probably didn't even know she was missing yet, and when he found out . . . what if he thought she'd abandoned him?

What if he didn't care?

She couldn't forget the image of Thorne sitting at that card table with some strange girl draped over him. He hadn't been thinking about Cress then.

Perhaps Thorne wouldn't come for her.

Perhaps she'd been wrong about him all this time.

Perhaps he wasn't a hero at all, but just a selfish, arrogant, womanizing—

She sobbed, her head cluttered with too much fear and anger and jealousy and horror and confusion, all of it writhing and squirming in her thoughts until she couldn't keep her frustrated screams bottled up any longer.

She wailed, scrunching her hair in her fists until her scalp burned.

But her screams died out fast, replaced with clenched teeth as she attempted to calm herself again. She rubbed her fingers around her wrists as if she had long strands of hair to wrap around them. She swallowed hard in an attempt to gulp down the rising panic, to keep herself from hyperventilating.

Thorne would come for her. He was a hero. She was a damsel. That's how the stories went—that's how they *always went.*

With a groan, she settled into her corner and started to cry again, cried until no more tears would come.

Suddenly, she jolted awake.

There was salt dried on her cheeks and her back ached from being hunched over. Her butt and sides were bruised from the bumping of the van, which, she realized, had come to a stop.

She was instantly alert, the grogginess shaken off by a new wave of fear. There was a hint of light coming through the cracks around the doors, which meant they'd driven through the night. A door slammed and she could make out Jina's chatter, no longer friendly and comforting. The van shook as the driver got out.

"Making good time," Cress heard a man say. "Someone want to help me back here?"

Another man laughed. "Can't take the little waif yourself?"

Jina's voice cut through their boasting. "Try not to bruise her. I want top payment this time, and you know how he negotiates. Nitpicking every little thing."

Cress gulped as the boots came closer. She steeled herself. She would lunge. She would fight. She would be ferocious. Bite and scratch and kick if she had to. She would take him by surprise.

And then she would run. Fast as a cheetah, graceful as a gazelle.

It was still early. The sand would be cool on her bare feet. Her blisters were almost healed, and while her legs still ached horribly, she could ignore them. Hopefully they would deem her not worth coming after.

Or maybe they would shoot her.

She gulped down the thought. She had to take the risk.

The lock clanked. She took in a deep breath, waited for the door to open—and pounced. A guttural scream was ripped out of her, all her anger and vulnerability swelling up and unleashing in that one vicious moment as her clawed fingers scrabbled for his eyes.

The man caught her. Two hands snapped around her pale wrists. Her momentum kept her careening outside the truck and she would have tumbled to the sand if he hadn't held her half suspended. Her war cry was abruptly cut off.

The man started to laugh—laughing at her, at her pathetic attempts to overpower him.

"She is a tiger, I'll give you that," he said to the man who had teased him. He twisted Cress around so he could hold both of her wrists in one firm grip. Her body still dangled from his hold as he began marching her away from the van and into the dunes.

"Let me go!" she shrieked, kicking back at him, but he was undeterred by her flailing. "Where are you taking me? Let me go!"

"Calm down, little girl, I'm not going to hurt you. Wouldn't be worth it." He snorted and dropped her down the other side of the dune.

She stumbled and rolled a couple times in the sand before bolting into a crouch. She swiped hair and sand from her face. By the time she looked up at the man, he had a gun pinned on her.

Her heart sputtered.

"Try to run, I shoot. And I don't mean to kill. But you're smarter than that, aren't you? You've got nowhere to go anyway, right?"

Cress gulped. She could still hear the voices on the other side of the dune. She hadn't been able to tell how many caravaners were still along in the group.

"Wh-what do you want from me?"

"I suspect you have business to tend to?"

Standing, she stumbled a bit down the hill, the sand unstable beneath her. The man didn't flinch. He jerked the barrel of the gun toward her feet. "Go on. It'll be another few hours before we stop, so better get it out of the way now. Don't want you losing your water in the back of that nice van. We wouldn't get our security deposit back, and Jina hates that."

Her lower lip trembled and she cast another glance around the desert, the wide openness of this barren landscape. She shook her head. "No, I can't. Not with . . ."

"Ah, I won't watch." To prove his point, he spun around and scratched behind his ear with the gun. "Just make it quick."

She spotted another man over the dune, faced away from her, and suspected he was relieving himself. Cress turned away, ashamed and embarrassed. She wanted to cry, wanted to beg the man to let her be, to just leave her here. But she knew it wouldn't work. And she didn't want to beg this man for anything.

Thorne would come for her, she thought as she stumbled to the base of the dune in search of what privacy she could find.

Thorne had to come for her.

Thirty-Four

"FATEEN-JIĚ?"

The girl spun around, her long black braid swinging against her lab coat. "Your Majesty!"

A ghost smile flickered over Kai's face. "Do you have a moment to assist us with something?"

"Of course." Fateen tucked a portscreen into her coat pocket.

Kai moved toward the wall of the white corridor, allowing room for researchers and technicians to pass by. "We need access to some patient records. I realize they're probably confidential, but . . ." Kai trailed off. There was no "but," only a vague hope and a fair amount of confidence that his title was the only credential he needed.

But Fateen's gaze darkened as they flickered between him and Torin. "Patient records?"

"A few weeks ago," said Kai, "I came to check on Dr. Erland's progress and Linh Cinder was here. The Lunar cyborg from—"

"I know who Linh Cinder is," she said, her hardness fading as quickly as it had come.

"Right, of course." He cleared his throat. "Well, at the time, the doctor told me she was there fixing a med-droid, but I was thinking about it, and I thought maybe she had actually been a . . ."

"A draft subject?"

"Yes."

Fateen shrugged. "Actually, she was a volunteer. Come on, there should be a vacant lab you can use. I'm happy to pull up Linh Cinder's records for you."

He and Torin followed her, Kai wondering whether she would have been as accommodating had it been any other patient. Since the arrest, Linh Cinder had become a matter of public concern, and therefore her private records weren't so private anymore.

"She was a volunteer? Really?"

"Yes. I was here the day she was brought in. They'd had to override her system to get her in here. I guess she put up quite a fight when they came for her."

Kai frowned. "Why would a volunteer put up a fight?"

"I'm using *volunteer* in the official sense. I believe her legal guardian recommended her for the testing." She swiped her wrist over an ID scanner, then ushered them into Lab 6D. The room smelled of bleach and peroxide and every surface glistened to a perfect shine. A counter along the far wall was set before a window overlooking a quarantine room. Kai grimaced, reminded of his father's last days spent in a room not entirely unlike that one, although his had been equipped with blankets and pillows, his favorite music, a tranquil water fountain. The patients who came to these labs would not have received the same luxuries.

Fateen paced to the adjoining wall. "Screen, on," she said, tapping something into her portscreen. "I do believe these records were a part of the investigation following her jailbreak, Your Majesty. Do you think the detectives may have missed something?"

He threaded his fingers through his hair. "No. I'm just trying to answer some of my own questions."

The lab's log-in screen faded, replaced with a patient profile. *Her* profile.

LINH CINDER, LICENSED MECHANIC
ID #0097917305
BORN 29 NOV 109 T.E.
RESIDENT OF NEW BEIJING, EASTERN COMMON-
WEALTH. WARD OF LINH ADRI.
CYBORG RATIO: 36.28%

"Is there something specific you're looking for?" Fateen asked, sliding her fingers along the screen so that the profile trekked down into blood type (A), allergies (none), and medications (unknown).

Then the plague test. Kai stepped closer. "What's this?"

"The doctor's notes from when we injected her with the letumosis microbe solution. How much we gave her and, subsequently, how long it took her body to rid itself of the disease."

At the end of the study, the simple words.

CONCLUSION: LETUMOSIS IMMUNITY CONFIRMED

"Immunity," said Torin, coming to stand beside them. "Did we know about this?"

"Perhaps the detectives didn't think it was relevant to their search? But it's common knowledge here in the labs. Many of us have theorized it's a result of her Lunar immune system. There's a long-held theory that letumosis was brought here by migrating Lunars, who are unaffected carriers of the disease."

Kai fidgeted with his shirt's collar. How many Lunars would have had to come to Earth to create such a widespread epidemic?

If this theory was correct, they could have a lot more fugitives on the planet than he'd realized. He groaned at the thought—the mere idea of having to deal with more Lunars made him want to beat his head against a wall.

"What does this mean?" asked Torin, pointing to a box at the bottom of the profile.

ADDITIONAL NOTES: FINALLY. I'VE FOUND HER.

The words gave Kai a chill, but he wasn't sure why.

Fateen shook her head. "Nobody knows. Dr. Erland entered it, but he gave no indication of what it meant. Probably it refers to her immunity—he finally found what he was looking for when she was brought in." Her tone became bitter. "Though lots of good that did us when *both* of them decided to skip town."

Fateen's port pinged and she glanced down on it. "I'm so sorry, Your Majesty. It seems today's draft subject has just arrived."

Kai ripped his attention away from those haunting words. "The draft is still in effect?"

"Of course," Fateen said with a smile, and Kai realized what a stupid question it was. Here he was, the emperor, and he had no idea what was going on in his own country. In his own research labs.

"With Dr. Erland gone, I just thought maybe it was over," he explained.

"Dr. Erland may be a traitor, but there are still a lot of people here who believe in what we're doing. We won't quit until we've found a cure."

"You're doing great work here," said Torin. "The crown

appreciates all the advances that have been made already in these labs."

Fateen tucked her port back into her pocket. "We've all lost someone to this disease."

Kai's tongue grew heavy. "Fateen-jiě, did Dr. Erland ever inform you that Queen Levana has developed an antidote?"

She blinked at him, confused. "Queen Levana?"

He glanced at Cinder's chart, evidence of her immunity—and her Lunar biology. "A part of our marriage alliance will include the manufacturing and distribution of this antidote."

Torin's voice was terse. "Though His Majesty will require that this information remain confidential until the crown issues an official statement."

"I see," she said slowly, still watching Kai. "That would change everything."

"It would."

Her comm pinged again. Shaking off her surprise, Fateen bowed to Kai. "I'm sorry, Your Majesty. If you would excuse me?"

"Of course." Torin gestured toward the hall. "Thank you for your assistance."

"My pleasure. Take all the time you need."

She bowed and left the lab with her braid swinging. The moment the door closed behind her, Torin scowled at the emperor. "What reason did you have for giving her that information? Until the antidote is confirmed as both effective, harmless, and capable of reproduction, it's foolhardy to spread such rumors."

"I know," said Kai. "It just seemed like she should know. She mentioned the draft and I realized how many people are still dying. Not just being killed by the disease, but being killed by us while we try to find a cure, and all the while an antidote is out there, just out of . . ." His eyes widened. *Immunity confirmed.* "Stars. The queen's antidote!"

"Pardon me?"

"Cinder was here the day I gave the antidote to Dr. Erland. He must have given it to her, and she went straight to the quarantines, knowing that she was immune. She was taking it to her sister, trying to save her. But she must have been too late, so she gave the antidote to that little boy instead, Chang Sunto." He shook his head, surprised at how light this realization made him. He found himself smiling. "Her guardian is wrong. Cinder didn't take her sister's ID chip because she was jealous or she wanted to steal her identity or anything like that. She took it because she loved her."

"And you believe that cutting out a loved one's ID chip is a healthy response?"

"Maybe she'd somehow figured out that the androids were harvesting them and giving them to Lunars. Or maybe she was just in shock. But I don't think it was out of malice."

He collapsed against the wall, feeling as if he'd just discovered an important clue in the mystery that was Linh Cinder. "We should let Fateen-jiĕ and the others know that Chang Sunto wasn't a miraculous recovery. This confirms that the queen's antidote is real, and maybe they can use that information in their research. It might be useful, or—"

His elbow bumped the netscreen and an image shimmered beside him. Kai jumped away as the holograph projected out of the screen, rotating within arm's reach.

It was a girl, life-size, her different layers flickering and folding into one another. Skin and scar tissue melded with a steel hand and leg. Wires merged with her nervous system. Blue blood pumped through silicon heart chambers. All the inorganic tissue had a faint glow, as the holograph pinpointed what wasn't natural about her so that even the untrained eye could comprehend.

Cyborg.

Kai backed away, feeling disoriented as he gaped at her. Even her eyes had that faint glow to them, along with the optic nerves that stretched to the back of her brain, where there was a metal plate fitted with ports and cables and wires and an access hatch that opened in the back of her skull.

He remembered her guardian saying that Cinder was unable to cry, but he'd never thought...never expected this. Her eyes, her *brain* ...

He looked away and dragged a palm down his face. This was an invasion, a terrible kind of voyeurism, and the sudden guilt made him wish he could erase the sight from his mind forever. "Screen, off."

A silence engulfed them, and he wondered if Torin felt the same guilt he did, or if he'd even been caught by the same morbid curiosity.

"Are you all right, Your Majesty?"

"Fine." He gulped. "We knew she was cyborg. None of this should be a surprise. I just hadn't expected it to be so *much.*"

Torin slid his hands into his pockets. "I'm sorry. I know I haven't always been fair where Linh Cinder was concerned. From the moment I saw you talking to her at the ball, I've been worried she would be an unnecessary distraction to you, and you were already dealing with so much. But it's obvious that you did have legitimate feelings for her, and I'm sorry for all that's happened since then."

Kai shrugged uncomfortably. "The problem with that is that even *I* don't know if I had legitimate feelings for her, or if it was always just a trick."

"Your Majesty. The Lunar gift has limitations. If Linh Cinder had been forcing these feelings onto you, then you wouldn't still be feeling them."

Starting, Kai met Torin's gaze. "I don't..." He gulped, heat climbing up his neck. "It's that obvious?"

"Well, as Queen Levana likes to point out, you are still young and not yet adept at disguising your emotions like the rest of us." Torin smiled, a teasing look that crinkled the corners of his eyes. "To be frank, I feel that it is one of your better qualities."

Kai rolled his eyes. "Ironically, I think that might be why I liked Cinder so much in the first place."

"That she couldn't disguise her emotions?"

"That she didn't *try*. At least, that's how it seemed." Kai leaned back against the exam table, feeling the sterile paper crinkle beneath his fingers. "Sometimes it just seems like everyone around me is pretending. The Lunars are the worst. Levana and her entourage... Everything about them is so fake. I mean, I'm *engaged* to Levana, and I still don't even know what she really looks like. But it isn't just them. It's the other Union leaders, even my own cabinet members. Everyone is trying to impress everyone else. Trying to make themselves out to be smarter or more confident than they actually are."

He raked his hand through his hair. "And then there was Cinder. This completely normal girl, working this completely mundane job. She was always covered in dirt or grease and she was so *brilliant* when she was fixing things. And she joked about stuff with me, like she was talking to a normal guy, not a prince.

Everything about her seemed so genuine. At least, that's what I'd thought. But then it turned out she was just like everyone else."

Torin paced to the window overlooking the quarantine room. "And yet you're still trying to find reasons to believe in her."

It was true. This whole escapade had been sparked by Torin's accusations that Kai didn't know anything about Cinder. That even now, knowing that she was cyborg, knowing that she was Lunar, he still wanted to believe that not everything about her had been based on some complicated deception.

And in coming here, he *had* learned some things.

He'd learned that she was immune to letumosis, that maybe all Lunars were.

He'd learned that those brown eyes that kept infiltrating his dreams had been man-made, or had at least been tampered with.

He'd learned that her guardian had sold her body off for testing, and that she hadn't hated her sister, and that the cyborg draft was still in effect. Still ordering cyborgs to the labs every day. Still sacrificing them in order to find an antidote that Queen Levana already had.

"Why cyborgs?" he murmured. "Why do we only use cyborgs for the draft?"

Torin sighed. "All due respect, Your Majesty. Do you really think this is the best issue to be concerning yourself with right now? With the wedding, the alliance, the war . . ."

"Yes, I do. It's a valid question. How did our society decide that their lives are worth less? I'm responsible for everything that happens in this government—everything. And when something affects the citizens like this . . ."

The thought struck him like a bullet.

They weren't citizens. Or, they were, but it was more complicated than that, had been since the Cyborg Protection Act had been instated by his grandfather decades ago. The act came after a series of devastating cyborg crimes had caused widespread hatred and led to catastrophic riots in every major city in the Commonwealth. The protests may have been prompted by the violent spree, but they were a result of generations of growing disdain. For years people had been complaining about the rising population of cyborgs, many of whom received their surgeries at the hands of taxpayers.

Cyborgs were too smart, people had complained. They were cheating the average man out of his wages.

Cyborgs were too skilled. They were taking jobs away from hardworking, average citizens.

Cyborgs were too strong. They shouldn't be allowed to compete in sporting events with regular people. It gave them an unfair advantage.

And then one small group of cyborgs had gone on a spree of violence and theft and destruction, demonstrating just how dangerous they could be.

If doctors and scientists were going to continue to perform these operations, people argued, there needed to be restrictions placed on their kind. They needed to be controlled.

Kai had studied it all when he was fourteen years old. He had agreed with the laws. He'd been convinced, as his grandfather before him had been, that they were so obviously *right*. Cyborgs required special laws and provisions, for the safety of everyone.

Didn't they?

Until this moment, he didn't think he'd given the question a second thought.

Realizing that he'd been staring at an empty lab table with his knuckles pressed against his forehead, he turned around and stood a little straighter. Torin was watching him with that ever-present wise expression that so often drove him crazy, waiting patiently for Kai to form his thoughts.

"Is it possible the laws are wrong?" he said, peculiarly nervous, like he was speaking blasphemy against his family and his country's age-old traditions. "About cyborgs?"

Torin peered at him for a long time, giving no hint to what he thought of Kai's question, until finally he sighed. "The Cyborg Protection Act was written up with good intentions. The people saw a need to control the growing cyborg population, and the violence has never again reached the level it was at that time."

Kai's shoulders sloped. Torin was probably right. His grandfather had probably been right. And yet . . .

"And yet," said Torin, "I believe it is the mark of a great leader to question the decisions that came before him. Perhaps, once we've solved some of our more immediate problems, we can readdress this."

More immediate problems.

"I don't disagree with you, Torin. But there's a draft subject in this very research wing, at this very moment. I'm sure this seems like an immediate problem to him . . . or her."

"Your Majesty, you cannot solve every problem in a week. You need to give yourself time—"

"You agree that it's a problem then?"

Torin frowned. "Thousands of citizens are dying from this disease. Would you discontinue the draft and the research opportunities it provides on the basis that the Lunars are going to solve this for us?"

"No, of course not. But using cyborgs, and *only* cyborgs...it seems wrong. Doesn't it?"

"Because of Linh Cinder?"

"No! Because of *everyone*. Because whatever science has made them, they were once human too. And I don't believe—I can't believe that they're all monsters. Whose idea was the draft anyway? Where did it come from?"

Torin glanced toward the netscreen, looking strangely conflicted. "If I recall, it was Dmitri Erland's idea. We had many meetings about it. Your father wasn't sure at first, but Dr. Erland convinced us that it was for the best of the Commonwealth. Cyborgs are easy to register, easy to track, and with their legal restrictions—"

"Easy to take advantage of."

"No, Your Majesty. Easy to convince both them and the people that they are the best candidates for the testing."

"Because they aren't human?"

He could see that Torin was growing frustrated. "Because their bodies have already been aided by science. Because now it's their turn to give back—for the good of everyone."

"They should have a choice."

"They had a choice when they accepted the surgical alterations. Everyone is well aware what the laws are regarding cyborg rights."

Kai thrust his finger toward the blackened netscreen. "Cinder became a cyborg when she was eleven, after a freak hover accident. You think an eleven-year-old had a choice about anything?"

"Her parents—" Torin paused.

According to the file, Cinder's parents had died in that same hover accident. They didn't know who had approved her cyborg surgery.

Torin set his mouth into a straight, displeased line. "She is an unusual circumstance."

"Maybe so, but it still doesn't feel right." Kai paced to the quarantine window, rubbing a knot in his neck. "I'm putting an end to it. Today."

"Are you sure this is the message you want to send to the people? That we're giving up on an antidote?"

"We're not giving up. *I'm* not giving up. But we can't force people into this. We'll raise the grant money for volunteers. We'll increase our awareness programs, encourage people to volunteer themselves if they choose to. But as of now, the draft is over."

Thirty-Five

CINDER STUMBLED UP THE SHIP'S RAMP, PULLING HER SHIRT away from her hips in an effort to get some airflow against her skin. The desert heat was dry compared with the suffocating humidity of New Beijing, but it was also relentless. Then there was the sand, that annoying, hateful sand. She had spent what seemed like hours trying to clean it out from her cybernetic joints, discovering more nooks and crannies in her hand than she'd known existed.

"Iko, close ramp," she said, sinking onto a crate. She was exhausted. All her time was spent worrying over Wolf and trying to be gracious to the townsfolk who had brought her so many gifts of sugar dates and sweet rolls and spiced curries that she wasn't sure if they were trying to thank her, or fatten her up for a feast.

On top of that were the constant arguments with Dr. Erland. He wanted her to focus on finding a way to get onto Luna without being captured, and while she had conceded that that would have to happen eventually, she was still set on putting a stop to the royal wedding first. After all, what did it matter if she dethroned Levana on Luna *after* she was crowned empress of the Commonwealth? There had to be a way to do both.

But the royal wedding was only a week away, and Iko's clock seemed to tick faster with every hour.

"How is he?" asked Iko. Poor Iko, who was stuck alone inside the spaceship's system for hours at a time while Cinder was at the hotel.

"The doctor started weaning him off the sedatives this morning," said Cinder. "He's afraid that if Wolf wakes up again when no one is there, he'll have a mental breakdown and reinjure himself, but I told him we can't keep him unconscious forever."

The ship sighed around her—oxygen hissing out of the life support system.

Reaching down, Cinder pulled off her boots and dumped the sand out onto the metal floor. "Has there been any news?"

"Yes, two interesting developments, actually."

The netscreen on the wall brightened. On one side was a static order form with CONFIDENTIAL emblazoned across the top. Despite the spark of curiosity it caused, Cinder's attention was drawn immediately to the other article, and a picture of Kai.

EMPEROR DEMANDS IMMEDIATE DISCONTINUATION OF CYBORG DRAFT

Heart skipping, Cinder hopped off the crate to get a better look. The very mention of the draft brought memories flooding back to her. Being taken by androids, waking up in a sterile quarantine room, strapped to a table, having a ratio detector forced into her head and a needle plunged into her vein.

The article opened with a video of Kai at a press conference, standing behind a podium.

"Play video."

"This policy change in no way indicates a sense of hopelessness," Kai was saying on the screen. "We are not giving up on finding a cure for letumosis. Please be aware that our team has made stunning progress in the past months and I am confident that we are on the verge of a breakthrough. I want all those who are suffering from this sickness or have loved ones who are battling it right now to know that this is not a sign of defeat. We will never give up until letumosis has been eradicated from our society." He paused, his silence punctuated by flashes that bounced off the Commonwealth's flag behind him.

"However, it recently came to my attention that the use of the cyborg draft to further our research was an antiquated practice that was neither necessary nor justifiable. We are a society that values human life—*all* human life. The purpose of our research facilities is to stanch the loss of that life as quickly and humanely as possible. The draft went against that value and, I believe, belittled all that we have accomplished in the one hundred and twenty-six years since our country was formed. Our country was built on a foundation of equality and togetherness, not prejudice and hatred."

Cinder watched him with a weakness in her limbs. She yearned to reach into the screen and wrap her arms around him and say thank you—*thank you.* But, thousands of miles away, she found herself hugging herself instead.

"I anticipate the criticism and backlash that this decision will cause," Kai continued. "I am fully aware that letumosis is a problem that affects every one of us, and that my decision to end the cyborg draft without first conferencing with my cabinet and your representatives is both unexpected and unconventional. But I could not stand by while our citizens were being forced to sacrifice their lives under a mistaken belief that their lives are less valuable than those of their peers. The letumosis research team will be developing new strategies for the continuation of their research, and we at the palace are optimistic that this change will not hinder our ongoing search for an antidote. We will continue accepting test subjects on a volunteer basis. There is a comm link below for anyone wanting more information on the volunteer process. Thank you. I will not be taking questions today."

As Kai left the stage and was replaced with the press secretary, already trying to calm a boisterous crowd, Cinder sank to the floor.

She could hardly believe what she'd heard. Kai's speech was not only about letumosis and research and medical procedures. His speech had been about equality. Rights. Moving past the hatred.

With one speech—not three minutes spent behind the podium—Kai had begun to unravel decades of cyborg prejudice.

Had he done it for her?

She grimaced, wondering whether it was absurdly self-absorbed for her to even think that. After all, this declaration would save countless cyborg lives. It would set a new standard for cyborg rights and treatment.

It wouldn't solve everything, of course. There was still the Cyborg Protection Act that claimed cyborgs as property of their guardians and limited their freedoms. But it was something. It was a start.

And the question came back again and again. *Had he done it for her?*

"I know," said Iko with a dreaminess in her tone, though Cinder hadn't said anything. "He's fantastic."

When she could focus her thoughts enough to skim through the rest of the article, Cinder saw that Kai was right. The hostility had already begun. This particular journalist had written a scathing criticism piece, defending the cyborg draft and accusing Kai of unjust preferential treatment. Though he didn't mention Cinder directly, it would only be a matter of time before someone did. Kai had invited a cyborg to the annual ball, and they would use it against him. He would be attacked for this decision. Viciously.

But he had done it anyway.

"Cinder?" said Iko. "Have you moved on to the escort-droids yet?"

She blinked. "I'm sorry, what?"

The screen changed, pulling the first document to the forefront. Cinder shook her head to clear it. She'd forgotten all about the second item that Iko had wanted to tell her about—the order form labeled "Confidential."

"Oh, right." She pulled herself to her feet. She would think about Kai and his decision later. *After* she had found a way to keep him from marrying Levana. "What is this?"

"It's an order placed by the palace two days ago. I stumbled on it by accident when I was trying to figure out their florist order. Turns out the queen is having her bouquet made of lilies and hosta leaves. *Boring.* I would have gone with orchids myself."

"You found a confidential order form from the palace itself?"

"Yes, I did, thank you for noticing. I'm turning into quite the savvy hacker. Not that I have anything better to do."

Cinder scanned the form. It was a rental agreement placed with the world's largest escort-droid manufacturer, which was headquartered just outside New Beijing. The palace wanted sixty escorts for the day of the wedding, but only those from the

"Reality" line, which included models with average eye colors and varying body types. The idea was that such imperfections (as the company called them) gave a more life-like experience with your escort.

It took her about four seconds to grasp the order's purpose.

"They're going to use them as staff during the wedding," she said, "because Lunars can't manipulate them. Smart."

"That's what I thought too," said Iko. "The agreement states that they'll be delivered to the florist and catering companies the morning of the wedding and that they'll be smuggled into the palace along with the human staff. Well, it doesn't use the word *smuggle*."

It didn't exactly make Cinder feel better about the wedding, but she was glad that the palace was taking some precautions against their Lunar guests.

Then, as she read through the order form and the delivery instructions, she gasped.

"What is it?" said Iko.

"I just had an idea." She took a step back, running it through in her head. The idea was too raw and messy for her to be certain, but on the surface . . . "Iko, that's it. That's how we're going to get onto Luna."

The lights flickered. "I don't compute."

"What if we hid on a ship that was already going to Luna? We could be smuggled in, just like these androids are being sneaked into the palace."

"Except all the ships that go to Luna are Lunar ships. How will you get aboard one of them?"

"*Right now* they're all Lunar ships. But I might know how we can change that."

The feeds on the netscreen shifted, bringing the ticking clock front and center. "Does it still involve stopping the wedding?"

"Yes. Sort of." Cinder held up a finger. "If we can *delay* the wedding, and persuade Queen Levana to host the ceremony on Luna instead of Earth, then all the Earthen guests will have to go there, just like all those Lunar aristocrats are coming here."

"And then you'll be on one of *their* ships?"

"If we can make it work." She started to pace back and forth through the cargo bay, her thoughts burning with the start of a new plan. "But I have to get Kai to trust me first. If *he* can persuade Levana to change the location . . ." Chewing the inside of her cheek, Cinder glanced at the video of the press conference, the headline confirming that he really had ended the draft. "We still need to get into the palace, but no more big distractions or hijacking the media. We need to be subtle. Sneaky."

"Oh! Oh! You should pose as a guest! Then you would have an excuse to buy a fancy dress too."

Cinder tried to protest, but hesitated. The idea had potential, *if* she could keep her glamour up long enough so that no one would recognize her. "I would have to be wary of those escorts. Plus, we would need invitations."

"I'm on it." The order form disappeared, replaced with a streaming list of names. "A gossip newsfeed posted a list of all the guests a few days ago. Did you know they're sending actual paper invitations? Very classy."

"Sounds wasteful," Cinder murmured.

"Maybe so," said Iko. "But also easy to steal. How many do we need? Two? Three?"

Cinder ticked her fingers. One for her. One for Wolf . . . hopefully. If not, would it be better for her to go alone or to bring the doctor? Or even Jacin? Levana and her entourage would recognize any one of them, and she didn't trust that they were capable of creating strong enough glamours for themselves.

She would just have to hope that Wolf was better by then.

"Two," she said. "Hopefully."

Names and titles dragged down the screen. Diplomats and political representatives, celebrities and media commentators, entrepreneurs and the very, very rich. She couldn't help thinking that it sounded like a really dull party.

Then Iko shrieked. An ear-splitting, metal-on-metal, over-heated-processor and wires-on-fire shriek.

Cinder covered her ears. "What? What's wrong?"

The list of names stopped and Iko highlighted a line.

LINH ADRI AND DAUGHTER LINH PEARL, OF NEW BEIJING, EC, EARTH

Gaping, Cinder pulled her hands away from her ears.

Linh Adri? And *Pearl*?

She heard footsteps thumping from the crew quarters and Jacin appeared in the cargo bay, eyes wide. "What happened? Why is the ship screaming?"

"Nothing. Everything's fine," Cinder stammered.

"No, everything is *not* fine," said Iko. "How can they be invited? I've never seen a bigger injustice in all my programmed life, and believe me, I have seen some big injustices."

Jacin raised an eyebrow at Cinder.

"We just learned that my former guardian received an invitation to the wedding." She opened the tab beside her stepmother's name, thinking maybe it was a mistake.

But of course not.

Linh Adri had been awarded 80,000 univs and an official invitation to the royal wedding as an act of gratitude for her assistance in the ongoing manhunt for her adopted and estranged daughter, Linh Cinder.

"Because she sold me out," she said, sneering. "Figures."

"See? *Injustice.* Here we are, risking our lives to rescue Kai and this whole planet, and Adri and Pearl get to go to the royal wedding. I'm disgusted. I hope they spill soy sauce on their fancy dresses."

Jacin's concern turned fast to annoyance. "Your ship has some messed-up priorities, you know that?"

"*Iko.* My name is Iko. If you don't stop calling me the 'ship,' I am going to make sure you never have hot water during your showers again, do you understand me?"

"Yeah, hold that thought while I go disable the speaker system."

"*What?* You can't *mute* me. Cinder!"

Cinder held up her hands. "Nobody is disabling anything!" She glared at Jacin, but his only response was a one-shouldered shrug. She rolled her eyes. "You're both giving me a headache, and I'm trying to think."

Jacin leaned against the wall, crossing his arms over his chest. "Did you know that I was there that night, at the Commonwealth ball?"

Her eyelid twitched. "How could I forget?" She didn't think of it often, not since he'd joined their side, but sometimes when she looked at him she couldn't help remembering how he had been the one to grab and hold her while Levana taunted Kai, trying to bargain with Cinder's life.

"Flattered. Thing is, you were pretty memorable that night,

too, what with being publicly humiliated, almost shot in the head, and ultimately arrested. So it strikes me as odd that you seem to be doing everything you can to figure out a way to go back there."

She threw her hands in the air. "And you can't think of a single reason why I would want to be at that wedding?"

"One more fling with your toy before he becomes Levana's property? You were swooning over him an awful lot at the—"

Cinder punched him.

Jacin stumbled against the wall, already chuckling as his hand came up to his cheekbone. "Did I hit a nerve, or was it a wire that time? You have plenty of both, right?"

"He's not a toy, and he's not her property," she said. "Insult either of us again and next time I'll hit you with the metal fist."

"You tell him, Cinder!" Iko cheered.

Jacin lowered his hand, revealing a red mark. "Why do you care? This wedding isn't your problem."

"Of course it's my problem! In case you haven't noticed, your queen is a tyrant. Maybe the Commonwealth doesn't want me anymore, but that doesn't mean I'm going to let Levana come down here and dig her claws into my country and ruin it like she ruined yours."

"Ours," he reminded her.

"*Ours.*"

He shook a strand of hair out of his face. "So that's it? Some overzealous sense of patriotism for a country that's trying to hunt you down as we speak? You *do* have some fried wires. In case you didn't realize it, the second you step foot on Commonwealth soil, you're dead."

"Thanks for that *stellar* vote of confidence."

"And you don't really seem like the type of girl to sacrifice herself over some hyped-up delusions of true love. So what aren't you telling me?"

Cinder turned away.

"Oh, come on. Please don't tell me you're obsessing over this wedding because you actually think you're in love with him?"

"I am," said Iko. "*Madly.*"

Cinder massaged her temple.

After an awkward silence, Iko said, "We are still talking about Kai, right?"

"Where did you even *find* her?" said Jacin, gesturing at the ceiling speakers.

"I'm not just doing this for Kai." Cinder dropped her hand to her side. "I'm doing this because I'm the only one who can. I'm going to overthrow Levana. I'm going to make sure she can't hurt anyone else."

Jacin gaped at her like she'd just sprouted an android arm from the top of her head. "You think that *you* are capable of over-throwing Levana?"

Screaming, Cinder threw her arms into the air. "That's kind of the whole idea! Don't *you*? Isn't that the entire reason you're helping us?"

"Stars, no. I'm not crazy. I'm here because I saw an opportunity to get away from that thaumaturge without getting killed, and—" He cut himself off.

"And what?"

His jaw flexed.

"*And what?*"

"And it's what Her Highness would have wanted me to do, although now she's probably going to die for it."

Cinder furrowed her brow. "What?"

"And now I'm stuck with you and some backward plan you have that's going to get us all back to square one—right in the hands of Queen Levana."

"Wha—but—Her *Highness*? What are you even talking about?"

"Princess Winter. Who do you think?"

"Princess..." Cinder drew a step away from him. "You mean, the queen's *stepdaughter*?"

"Oooooooooooohhh," said Iko.

"Yeah, the only princess we've got, if you haven't noticed. Who did you think I was talking about?"

Cinder gulped. Her gaze flickered to the netscreen, where their original plan had long since been hidden beneath newsfeeds and that blasted clock. Jacin had never been told about their intentions of interrupting the wedding and announcing her identity to the world.

"Um. Nobody," she stammered, scratching her wrist. "So, um...when you say you're loyal to 'your princess'...you're talking about *her*. Right?"

Jacin peered at her like he couldn't figure out why he was wasting his time with such an idiot.

Cinder cleared her throat. "Right."

"I should have let Sybil have you," he muttered, shaking his head. "I thought maybe the princess would be proud if she heard about me turning against Sybil. That she would approve of my decision. But who am I kidding? She'll never even know."

"Do you...do you love her?"

He glared at her, disgusted. "Don't try to push your swoony psychodrama on me. I'm sworn to protect her. Can't very well do that from down here, can I?"

"Protect her from what? Levana?"

"Among other things."

Cinder collapsed onto one of the storage crates, feeling like she'd just sprinted halfway across the desert. Her body was drained, her brain frazzled. Jacin didn't care about her at all—he was loyal to the queen's stepdaughter. She hadn't even known the queen's stepdaughter *had* people who were loyal to her.

"Help me," she said, not hiding the pleading in her tone as she met Jacin's gaze again. "I swear to you, I can stop Levana. I can get you back to Luna, where you can protect your princess, or do whatever you need to do. But I need help."

"That much is pretty obvious. Are you going to let me in on this miracle plan of yours?"

She gulped. "Maybe. Eventually."

He shook his head, looking like he wanted to laugh as he gestured out toward the streets of Farafrah. "You're just desperate because the strongest ally you have right now is lying in a drug-induced coma."

"Wolf is going to be fine," Cinder said, with more conviction than she expected. Then she sighed. "I'm desperate because I need as many allies as I can get."

Thirty-Six

THEY STOPPED AGAIN THAT NIGHT AND CRESS WAS GIVEN some bread, dried fruit, and water. She listened to the sounds of camp outside the van and tried to sleep, but it came only in fits.

They started early again the next morning.

She became less and less sure that Thorne would come for her. She kept seeing him embracing that other woman, and imagined that he was glad he no longer had to bother himself with the weak, naïve Lunar shell.

Even the fantasies that had consoled and comforted her for so many years aboard the satellite were growing feeble. She was not a warrior, brave and strong and ready to defend justice. She was not the most beautiful girl in the land, able to evoke empathy and respect from even the most hard-hearted villain. She was not even a damsel knowing that a hero would someday rescue her.

Instead, she spent the agonizing hours wondering whether she was to become a slave, a servant, a feast for cannibals, a human sacrifice, or whether she would be returned to Queen Levana and tortured for her betrayal.

Eventually, late in the second day of her entrapment, the

vans stopped and the doors were thrown open. Cress cringed at the brightness and tried to scuffle away, but she was grabbed and hauled outside. She landed on her knees. Pain shot up her spine, but her captor ignored her whimpering as he tugged her to her feet and bound her wrists.

The pain soon faded, trounced by adrenaline and curiosity. They'd arrived at a new town, but even she could tell this one had never been as wealthy or populated as Kufra. Modest buildings the color of the desert stretched down a sand-spotted road. Walls of red clay, painted indigo and pink, had long been bleached in the sun, their roofs covered with broken tiles. A fenced area not far away held half a dozen camels and there were a few more wheeled, dirty vehicles stationed along the street, and—

She blinked the sun and sand from her eyes.

A spaceship sat in the center of town. A Rampion.

Her heart skipped with frenzied hope, but it was quickly smothered. Even from this distance she could see that the Rampion's main hatch was painted black, not adorned with a lounging lady as had been reported when Thorne's ship landed in France.

She whimpered, tearing her eyes away as her captors herded her into the nearest building. They entered a dark hallway. Only a small window in the front let in any light, and it had been caked with windblown sand over the years. There was a tiny desk set into a corner with a board of old-fashioned keys hanging on the wall. Cress was shuffled past it and taken to the end of the corridor.

The walls reeked with something pungent—not a bad scent, but too overpowering to be pleasant. Cress's nose tickled.

She was pushed up a staircase, so thin that she had to follow behind Jina, with Niels behind her. An eerie silence haunted the sand-colored walls. The stench was stronger up here and a shiver raced down her spine, making goose bumps bloom across her arms. Her fear had bundled itself up in a cluster of nerves at the base of her spine.

By the time they reached the last door in the hallway and Jina raised her fist to knock, Cress was shaking so hard she almost couldn't stand. She was surprised to find herself longing for the security of the van.

Jina had to knock twice before they heard footsteps and the creak of the door. Niels kept Cress tucked securely behind Jina, and all she could see were the cuffs of a man's brown trousers and worn white shoes with fraying laces.

"Jina," said a man—sounding like he'd just woken from a nap. "I heard a rumor out of Kufra that you were on your way."

"I've brought you another subject. Found her wandering in the desert."

A hesitation. Then the man said, without question, "A shell."

His certainty made Cress squirm. If he had not had to ask, that meant he could sense her. Or, rather, *couldn't* sense her. She remembered Sybil complaining that she could not sense Cress's thoughts—how much more difficult it was to train and command a person like her, as if it were all Cress's doing.

This man was Lunar.

She flinched away, wanting to curl up until she was no larger than a grain of sand, until she blew away into the desert and disappeared.

But she could not disappear. Instead, as Jina stepped aside, she found herself face-to-face with a man well into his years.

She started. They *were* face-to-face—he was barely taller than her.

Behind a pair of thin wired spectacles, his blue eyes widened, looking remarkably lively despite the wrinkles that folded and creased around them. He was balding, with tufts of untamed gray hair that stuck out above his ears. A bizarre déjà vu struck her, as if she'd seen him before, but that was impossible.

He whipped off his spectacles and rubbed at his eyes. When he replaced them, his lips were puckered and he was examining Cress like a bug for dissection. She pressed back against the wall, until Niels grabbed her elbow and yanked her forward.

"Definitely a shell," the old man murmured, "and a phantom, it seems."

Cress's heart pounded a rough, erratic rhythm against her rib cage.

"I'm asking 32,000 univs for her."

The man blinked at Jina like he'd forgotten she was there. He stood a bit straighter and made a great fuss about removing his spectacles again, to clean them this time.

Cress dug her fingernails into her palm to distract herself from her panic. She stared past the man. A single window was covered in blinds, and there was dust swirling in and out of a beam of sunlight that knifed through them. There was a closed door, presumably a closet, a desk, a bed, and a pile of rumpled blankets in the corner. The blankets were clotted with blood.

A chill raced across her skin.

Then she spotted the netscreen.

A netscreen. She could comm for help. She could contact the last hotel, in Kufra. She could tell Thorne—

"I will give you 25,000." The man's tone had solidified while he cleaned his glasses, and was now all business.

Jina snorted. "I will not hesitate to take this girl to the police and have her deported. I'll collect my citizen's reward from them."

"A mere 1,500 univs? You would sacrifice so much on your pride, Jina?"

"My pride, and to know that one less Lunar is walking around on my planet." She said this with a sneer, and for the first time it occurred to Cress that Jina might truly hate her—for no other reason than her ancestry. "I'll let her go for 30,000, Doctor. I know you're paying as much for shells these days."

Doctor? Cress gulped. This man in no way resembled the finely polished men and women in the net dramas, with their crisp white coats and advanced technology. Somehow, the title served to make her more wary, as visions of scalpels and syringes flashed through her mind.

He sighed. "Ah, 27,000."

Jina tilted her head back, peering down her nose. "Deal."

The doctor took her hand, but he seemed to have drawn back into himself. He couldn't look at Cress full-on, as if he were ashamed that she had witnessed the transaction.

Defiance jolted down Cress's spine.

He should be ashamed. They should all be ashamed.

And she would not let herself become mere baggage to be bartered for. Mistress Sybil had taken advantage of her for too long. She wouldn't let it happen again.

Before these thoughts could become anything more than rebellious anger, she was shoved into the room. Jina shut the door, enclosing them all in the hot, dusty space that smelled of stale chemicals. "Make the transfer quick," she said, folding her arms. "I have other business to tend to in Kufra."

The doctor grunted and opened the closet. There were no

clothes inside, but rather a miniature science lab, with mystery machines and scanners and a stand of metal drawers that clanked when he opened them. He pulled out a needle and syringe and made quick work of removing its packaging.

Cress backed away, arms pulling against her bindings, but Niels stopped her.

"Yes, yes, let me get a blood sample from her, then I'll make the transfer."

"Why?" Jina said, stepping between them. "So you can determine something's wrong with her and compromise our deal?"

The doctor harrumphed. "I have no intention of compromising anything, Jina. I merely thought she would be more complicit while you're here, allowing me to more safely extract a sample."

Cress's gaze darted around the room. A weapon. An escape. A hint of mercy in the eyes of her captor.

Nothing. There was nothing.

"Fine," Jina said. "Niels, hold her so the doctor can do what he needs to do."

"No!" The word was ripped out of Cress as she stumbled away. Her shoulder collided with Niels and she started to fall backward, but then he was gripping her by the elbow and hauling her against him. Her legs had become soggy and useless beneath her. "No—please. Leave me alone!" She pleaded at the doctor and saw such a mixture of emotion on his lined face that she fell silent.

His eyebrows were bunched together, and his mouth tightly pursed. He kept rapidly blinking behind his glasses, like trying to clear away an eyelash, until his gaze fell away from her altogether. There was pity in him. She knew it—she knew this was sympathy he was trying to disguise.

"Please," she sobbed. "Please let me go. I'm just a shell, and I'm stranded here on Earth, and I haven't done anything to anyone, and I'm nobody. I'm nobody. Please, just let me go."

He did not meet her eyes again, even as he stepped forward. She tensed, trying to back away, but Niels held her firm. The doctor's touch felt papery, but his grip was strong as he took her wrist in one hand.

"Try to relax," he murmured.

She flinched as the needle dug into her flesh, the same spot where Sybil had taken blood a hundred times. She bit hard on the inside of her cheek, refusing to so much as whimper.

"That was all. Not so awful, was it?" His tone was eerily soft, like he was trying to comfort her.

She felt like a bird who'd had her wings clipped and been thrown into a cage—another filthy, rotting cage.

She'd been in a cage all her life. Somehow, she'd never expected to find one just as awful on Earth.

Earth, she reminded herself as the doctor plodded back across the groaning floorboards. She was on Earth. Not trapped in a satellite in space. There was a way out of this. Freedom was just out that window, or just down those stairs. She would not be a prisoner again.

The doctor fit the syringe full of her blood into a machine and flipped on a portscreen.

"There now, I will transfer over the funds, and you can be on your way."

"You're using a secure connection?" Jina asked, taking a step forward as the doctor tapped in some sort of code word. Cress squinted, watching where his fingers landed, in case she would later need it. It could save time not having to hack it.

"Trust me, Jina, I have more reason than you to keep my

transactions hidden from prying eyes." He studied something on the screen, before saying, more solemnly, "Thank you for bringing her."

Jina scowled at his balding head. "I hope you're killing all these Lunars when you're done with them. We have enough problems with the plague. We don't need them too."

His blue eyes flashed and Cress detected a hint of disdain for Jina, but he covered it over with another benign look. "The payment has been transferred. If you would untie the girl before you go."

Cress kept still as the bindings were taken off her wrists. She whipped her hands away as soon as they were gone and scurried against the nearest wall.

"Lovely doing business with you again," Jina said. The doctor merely grunted. He was watching Cress from the corner of his eye, trying to stare at her without being obvious.

And then the door closed and Jina and Niels were gone. Cress listened to their feet clopping down the hallway, the only noise in the building.

The doctor rubbed his palms down the front of his shirt, like cleansing them of Jina's presence. Cress didn't think he could feel half as filthy as she did, but she stayed as still as the wall, glaring.

"Yes, well," he said. "It is more awkward with shells, you know. Not so easy to explain."

She snarled. "You mean, not so easy to brainwash."

He tilted his head, and the odd look had returned. The one that made her feel like a science experiment under a microscope. "You know that I'm Lunar."

She didn't answer.

"I understand you're frightened. I can't imagine what sort of mistreatment Jina and her hooligans put you through. But I am not going to hurt you. In fact, I'm doing great things here, things that will change the world, and you can help me." He paused. "What is your name, child?"

She didn't answer.

When he moved closer, his hands extended in a show of peace, Cress shoved all her fear down into her gut and used the wall to launch herself at him.

A roar clawed up from her throat and she swung her elbow, as hard as she could, landing a solid hit against his jaw. She heard the snap of his teeth, felt the shock in her bones, and then he was falling backward and landing so hard on the wooden floor that the entire building shook around them.

She didn't check to see if he was unconscious, or if she'd given him a heart attack, or if he was in any shape to get up and follow her.

She wrenched open the door and ran.

Thirty-Seven

DR. ERLAND WOKE UP ON THE FLOOR OF A HOT, DUSTY HOTEL room, unable for a moment to remember where he was.

This was not the laboratories beside New Beijing Palace, where he'd watched cyborg after cyborg break into red and purple rashes. Where he'd seen the life drain out of their eyes, and cursed the sacrifice of another life, while plotting the next step in his hunt for the only cyborg that mattered.

This was not the labs of Luna, where he'd studied and researched with a singular drive for recognition. Where he'd seen monsters born at the end of his surgical tools. Where he'd watched the brainwaves of young men take on the chaotic, savage patterns of wild animals.

He was not Dr. Dmitri Erland, as he'd been in New Beijing.

He was not Dr. Sage Darnel, as he'd been on Luna.

Or perhaps he was—he couldn't think, couldn't remember . . . didn't care.

His thoughts kept turning away from himself and his two hateful identities, and swarming back to his wife's heart-shaped face and honey-blonde hair that became frizzy whenever the ecology department was injecting new humidity into Luna's controlled atmosphere.

His thoughts were on a screaming baby, four days old and confirmed a shell, as his wife dropped her into the hands of Thaumaturge Mira, with all the coldness and disgust she would have shown a rodent.

The last time he'd seen his little Crescent Moon.

He watched the whirling ceiling fan that did nothing to dispel the desert heat and wondered why, after all these years, his hallucinations had chosen this time to torture him.

This shell girl did not *really* have his wife's freckles or blonde hair. This shell girl did not have his unfortunate height or his own blue eyes. This shell girl was not his daughter, returned from the dead to haunt him. The illusion was all in his mind.

Perhaps it was fitting. He'd done so many horrible things. The recent attack against Earth was only the culmination of years of his own efforts. It was through his own research that Queen Channary had begun developing her army of wolf hybrids, and through his experiments that Levana was able to see it to its bloody finale.

And then there were all those he'd hurt to find Selene and end Levana's reign. All those he'd murdered to find Linh Cinder.

He'd been too optimistic to think he could repay those debts now. He'd tried hard to duplicate the antidote Levana had given to Emperor Kaito. He'd had to try, and for his pains—more sacrifices. More blood samples. More experiments, though now he was forced to find true volunteers, when the traffickers couldn't bring him new blood on their own.

He had discovered, back in New Beijing when he'd studied the antidote brought by Queen Levana, that Lunar shells held the secret. The same genetic mutation that made them immune to the Lunar tampering of bioelectricity could be used to create antibodies that would fight off and defeat the disease.

And so he'd begun gathering shells and their blood and their DNA. Using them, just as he'd used the young men who would become mindless soldiers for the queen. Just as he'd used the cyborgs who were too often unwilling candidates of the letumosis experimentation.

Of course his brain would do this to him. Of course his insanity would reach such a depth that the hallucinations would return to him the only thing he had ever cared for, and they would twist reality so that she became just another one of his victims.

Just another person bought and discarded.

Just another blood sample.

Just another lab rat who hated him.

His little Crescent Moon.

Over his head, his portscreen dinged on his laboratory shelf.

It took more energy than he thought he had to pull himself to his feet, groaning as he used the age-polished bedpost for leverage.

He took his time, avoiding the truth, partly because he didn't know what he wanted the truth to be. A hallucination he could deal with. He could write it off and continue with his work.

But if it was her ...

He could not lose her one more time.

He passed the open closet and pushed aside the window blinds, glancing out onto the street. He could see the curve of the ship two streets away, reflecting the sunlight as dusk set in. He should get this over with before Cinder came to check on her Wolf friend. He had not had any subjects sold to him since she'd been here, and he did not think she would understand. She had such a tough time understanding the sacrifices that had to be made for the good of all. She, who should understand better than anyone.

Sighing, he paced back to the small lab setup and the girl's blood sample. He picked up the portscreen and clicked on the report generated from the test. He felt woozy as he scanned the data culled from her DNA.

Lunar.

Shell.

HEIGHT, FULLY GROWN: 153.48 CENTIMETERS

MARTIN-SCHULTZ SCALE IRIS PIGMENTATION: 3

MELANIN PRODUCTION: 28/100, WITH LOCALIZED

CONCENTRATED MELANIN TO FACE / EPHELIS

Her physical statistics were followed by a list of potential diseases and genetic weaknesses, with suggestions for treatments and preventions.

It did not tell him what he needed to know until he steeled himself and linked her chart to his own, a chart that he had practically memorized for as many times as he had taken his own blood for experimentation.

He sat down on the edge of the bed while the computer ran through the charts, comparing and contrasting more than 40,000 genes.

He found himself hoping that the hallucination was true and she was not his daughter. That his daughter had been killed by Sybil Mira, as he'd been led to believe so many years ago.

Because if it *was* her, she would despise him.

And he would agree with her.

She was gone already, he was sure. He didn't know how long he'd been unconscious, but he doubted she would stay close. He had already lost that little ghost. Twice, now.

The portscreen finished running the comparison.

Match found.

Paternity confirmed.

He took off his spectacles and set them on the desk and exhaled a long, trembling breath.

His Crescent Moon was alive.

Thirty-Eight

CRESS HELD HER BREATH AND LISTENED—LISTENED SO HARD IT was giving her a headache—but all she heard was silence. Her left leg was beginning to cramp from being curled into such an awkward position, but she dared not move for fear she would bump something and alert the old man to her location.

She hadn't run from the hotel. Though she'd been tempted, she'd known that Jina and the others could still be out there, and running into them would put her right back where she'd started. Instead, she'd ducked into the third room down the long, slender corridor, surprised to find the door unlocked and the room abandoned. It had the same setup as the doctor's room: bed, closet, desk, but to her chagrin it was missing a netscreen. If she hadn't been so desperate to find a hiding spot, she would have wept.

She'd ended up in the closet. It was empty, with a bar for hanging clothes situated below a single shelf. Cress had used all her strength to clamber up onto that shelf, propelling up the closet's side walls with both feet, before squeezing her way into the tiny alcove. She'd used her toes to pull the door shut. For once, she was glad of her small size, and she figured that if he found her she'd at least have the leverage from being so high up. She wished she would have thought to grab some sort of weapon.

But her hope was that there would be no need for it. She suspected that when he woke up, he would think she'd run out into the town and he would go searching for her, which should give her ample time to get back to that netscreen and contact Thorne at their last hotel.

She had lain there for hours, waiting and listening. Though it was uncomfortable, it kind of reminded her of sleeping beneath the bed in the satellite during those long hours when Luna could be seen through her windows. She'd always felt safe then, and the memory brought a strange sense of protection, even now.

After a while, she began to wonder whether she'd killed the man. The guilt that sparked in her chest made her angry. She had nothing to feel guilty about. She'd been defending herself, and he was a Lunar-trafficking monster.

Not long after she'd had this thought, she heard shuffling, so quiet it could have been a mouse in the walls. It was followed by a couple of thumps and a groan. Her body seized up again, her right shoulder aching from the way she was lying on it.

This had been a mistake. She should have run when she'd had the chance. Or she should have used the time that he was unconscious to tap into his netscreen. In hindsight, she'd had plenty of time, but now it was too late and he was awake and he would find her and—

She squeezed her eyes shut until white specks flickered in the darkness.

Her plan had not failed yet. He could still go outside in search of her. He could still leave the building.

She waited.

And waited.

Breathing in and breathing out. Filling herself with hot, stifling air. Her pulse skipped at every sound, every muffled scrape, every wooden thump, trying to create a picture in her mind of what was happening in the room at the end of the hall.

He never left his room. He didn't come to look for her at all.

She scowled into the darkness. A bead of sweat lobbed its way off her nose.

When solid darkness had crept into her closet and, despite the discomfort and stiff muscles, Cress found herself dozing off, she snapped herself awake and determined that she had hidden long enough. The old man wasn't searching for her, which seemed absurd, knowing how much he'd paid for her. Shouldn't he have been a little more concerned?

Or maybe all he'd really wanted was her blood. It was a peculiar coincidence, given how Mistress Sybil had saved so many non-gifted infants from death because she'd seen some value in their blood too.

She tried not to let her suspicions and paranoia dig any deeper. Whatever the old man wanted, she couldn't stay in this closet forever.

Tilting one foot off the shelf, she nudged open the closet door. It squeaked, a sound that was drum-shatteringly loud, and she froze with one leg extended.

Waiting. Listening.

When nothing happened, she prodded the door open a bit more and shimmied to the edge of the shelf. She lowered herself as gently as she could down to the floor.

The floorboards groaned. She halted again, heartbeat thundering.

Waited. Listened.

Dizzy and parched, Cress made her way to the corridor. It

was empty. She crept to the next door. Again, it was unlocked, but the room looked exactly like the one she'd just left. Abandoned and empty.

Her skin was crawling, every sense heightened as she shut the door and moved on to the next.

In the third room, the blinds were closed, but the light from the corridor fell on a netscreen hanging in the darkness. She barely stifled a gasp. Trembling with anticipation, she shut the door behind her.

Then her attention landed on the bed and she pressed a hand over her mouth.

A man was lying there. Sleeping, she realized, as she waited for her heartbeat to stop thudding so painfully against her ribs. She dared not move until she could be certain that the rise-and-fall pattern of his chest was steady and deep. She hadn't woken him.

She glanced at the netscreen again, weighing the risks.

She could slip into the corridor again and keep searching. There were two doors on this floor she hadn't yet opened . . . but they were both back toward the old man's room. Or she could go downstairs and try her luck there.

But every step she took on the old floorboards could alert someone to her presence, and she had no guarantee that any of the other doors would be unlocked, or that they would have netscreens.

The minutes ticked by as she stood with one hand on the doorknob, the other over her mouth, trapped by indecision. The man never stirred, never so much as twitched.

Finally she forced herself to take a step toward the netscreen. Her gaze darted to the sleeping form again and again, making sure that his breathing didn't change.

"Netscreen," she whispered. "On."

The screen flickered and she began repeating, "Netscreen, mute, netscreen, mute, netscre—" But her command was unnecessary. As the netscreen brightened, she found herself staring at a map of Earth, not a net drama or newsfeed. Four locations had been marked. New Beijing. Paris. Rieux, France. A tiny oasis town in the northwest corner of Nile Province in the African Union.

A sense of coincidence stirred in her, but her brain was already skimming too far ahead to dwell on it. Within moments, she had sent the map away and called up a comm link. She hesitated. The only time she'd ever sent a comm was when she talked to Cinder, using a link that couldn't be traced or monitored. She knew intimately how much access Queen Levana had to Earth's net and all those comms that Earthens mistakenly believed were private.

But she couldn't dwell on that. What interest would Queen Levana have in a single comm link established between two small towns in north Africa? She was, no doubt, far too preoccupied with her plans for intergalactic dominance.

"Netscreen," she whispered, "show hotels in Kufra."

Her awkward pronunciation brought up a list of seven possible Kufras. She selected the one with the least distance from her current location and was then faced with the names of a dozen lodging options, their ads and contact information flashing on the sidebar. She scowled, reading each carefully. None of their names sounded familiar. "Show in map." The city of Kufra spilled out across the screen, a satellite-taken photograph that, after a moment of squinting at the brown-tinted roads, began to breach the gaps in her memory. Then she spotted a courtyard outside one of the hotels and, after zooming into the photo, recognized a lemon tree standing against one wall. She dared to smile and tapped on the hotel's contact information.

"Establish comm link."

Within seconds she found herself staring at the same clerk who had checked in her and Thorne, with Jina's help. She nearly collapsed with relief.

"Thank you for comming—"

"Shh!" Cress waved her arms, silencing the woman, and glanced at the man on the bed. He twitched, but only briefly.

"Sorry," she whispered. The woman leaned closer toward the screen to hear her. "My friend is sleeping. I need to speak with a guest at your hotel. His name is Carswell Tho—Smith. I believe he's in room eight?"

She was glad when the woman's voice dropped low. "One moment." She tapped something offscreen.

Cress jumped at a ping, but the man slept on. An alert appeared in the corner of the netscreen.

[97] NEW ALERTS REGARDING SEARCH "LINH CINDER."

She blinked. *Linh Cinder?*

"I'm sorry," said the receptionist, snapping Cress's attention back to her. "Mr. Smith left the hotel yesterday evening after causing a commotion with some of our other guests." Her eyes had become suspicious and she scanned the dark room with increased curiosity. "In fact, we're currently undergoing an investigation, as some witnesses believe he may have been a wanted—"

Cress canceled the link. Her nerves were writhing beneath her skin and her lungs felt too small to take in all the air they needed.

Thorne wasn't there. He'd had to run and now she had no

idea how to find him and he was being hunted and he would be captured and she would never see him again.

The screen pinged again. The alerts on Linh Cinder had increased by two.

Linh Cinder. New Beijing. Paris. Rieux, France.

The sequence began to click.

Baffled, Cress pulled up the alerts. They were the same news stories she'd been wading through for weeks aboard the satellite. Criticisms and speculations and conspiracy theories and very little evidence. Still no confirmed sightings. Still no arrests made and not even a mention of Captain Thorne, despite what the hotel clerk had said.

And then her attention caught on a headline and her legs nearly buckled. She splayed her fingers on top of the desk to keep standing.

LUNAR ACCOMPLICE DMITRI ERLAND STILL EVADING AUTHORITIES

Dmitri Erland.

The Lunar doctor who had been on the letumosis research team. The doctor who had helped Cinder escape from prison. The doctor who was, perhaps, the second most-wanted fugitive on Earth, even more so than Thorne.

She knew it was him even before she'd pulled up his picture. This was why the old man had struck her as familiar. She *had* seen him before.

But . . . wasn't he supposed to be on their side?

She was so engrossed with her unanswered questions that she didn't hear the subtle creaking of the bed until a hand grabbed her.

Thirty-Nine

CRESS SQUEAKED AS SHE WAS SPUN AROUND. SHE FOUND herself staring into a face that was both handsome and murderous, his eyes glowing in the light of the netscreen.

"Who are you?"

Her instinct was to scream, but she smothered it, choking off the noise until it was little more than a whimper. "I-I'm sorry for intruding," she said. "I needed a netscreen. M-my friend is in danger and I needed to send a comm and—I'm so sorry, I promise I didn't steal anything. P-please don't call for the doctor. Please."

He seemed to have stopped listening to her, instead sending his steely gaze around the room. He released her arm, but remained tense and defensive. He wasn't wearing a shirt, but he had bandages around his torso that covered him almost as much as a shirt would have. "Where are we? What happened?" His words were staggered and slurred.

He grimaced, squeezing his eyes shut, and when he opened them again it seemed that he couldn't quite focus on anything.

That's when Cress's attention caught on something more terrifying than his faded scars and intimidating muscles.

He had a tattoo on his arm. It was too dark to read it, but Cress knew instantly what it was. She'd seen them in countless videos and photographs and documentaries hastily cobbled together. He was a Lunar special operative. One of the queen's mutants.

Visions of men digging their claws into their victims' chests, locking their jaws around exposed throats, howling at the moon, curled and crawled through her head.

This time, she couldn't temper the instinct. She screamed.

He grabbed her and forced her jaw shut with his enormous hands. She sobbed, trembling. She was about to die. Her body would pose no more resistance to him than a twig.

He snarled and she could make out the sharp points of his teeth.

"You should have killed me when you had the chance," he said, his breath hot on her face. "You turned me into this, and I will kill you before I become another experiment. Do you understand me?"

Tears began to work their way out of her lashes. Her jaw was aching where he held her, but she was more afraid of what would happen when he let go. Did he think she worked for the doctor? Could it be that he was just one more victim sold off to the old man? He was Lunar, so they had that much in common. If she could convince him that they were allies, maybe she could get away long enough to run. But could these monsters even be reasoned with?

"*Do you understand me?*"

Her lashes fluttered, and the door behind him opened.

His moves were fast and fluid and Cress's head spun as the man turned and pulled her in front of him, plastering her against his chest. He stumbled, as if the sudden movement had made him dizzy, but caught himself as light spilled into the room. A silhouette stood in the doorway—not the old man, but a guard. A Lunar guard.

Cress's eyes widened with recognition. *Sybil's* guard. The pilot in Sybil's podship, who could have saved her but didn't.

The wolf operative hissed. Cress would have collapsed if his grip hadn't been so firm.

Sybil had found her. Sybil was here.

Her tears began to spill over. She was trapped. She was dead.

"Take one step and I'll snap her neck!"

The guard said nothing. Cress wasn't sure he'd even heard the threat. His eyebrows were raised as he surveyed the scene, and he seemed to recognize her. But rather than look victorious, he seemed merely stunned.

"What have—Scarlet?" The words were almost incomprehensible beneath a growl. "Where's Scarlet?"

"Aren't you that hacker?" said the guard, still staring at Cress.

The operative's grip tightened. "You have five seconds to tell me where she is, or this girl is dead, and you're next."

"I'm not with them," Cress choked. "He-he doesn't care about me."

The guard raised his hands in a placating gesture. Cress wondered where Mistress Sybil was.

When the operative's hold didn't loosen, it occurred to her that both of these men worked for the Lunar queen. Why would they be threatening each other?

"Just relax," said the guard. "Let me get Cinder or the doctor. They can explain."

The operative flinched. "Cinder?"

"She's out in the ship." His gaze dipped again to Cress. "Where did you come from?"

She gulped, her head ringing with the same question the operative had posed.

Cinder?

"What is going on here?"

She shuddered at the doctor's voice, stronger than it had been during his negotiations with Jina. Then footsteps. The guard stepped aside to let the doctor into the room, still dark but for the corridor light. Cress couldn't help but feel a sting of pride to see that she'd left a mark on his jaw.

Though lots of good her newfound courage had done her in the end.

The doctor froze and took in the scene. "Oh, stars," he muttered. "Of all the bad timings..."

Though the sight of him reignited Cress's hatred, she also remembered that this was not just some cruel old man who traded for Lunar slaves. This was the man who had helped Cinder escape.

Her head spun.

"Let her go," said the doctor, speaking gently. "We are not your enemies. That girl is not your enemy. Please, allow me to explain."

Wolf pulled an arm away from her, dragging a hand down his face. He swayed for a moment before recovering his balance. "I've been here before," he muttered. "Cinder... Africa?"

Loud thumping on the distant staircase intruded on his confusion. Then there was yelling and Cress thought she heard her name, and the voice—

"Cress!"

She cried out, forgetting about the vise-like grip around her, except that it kept her from launching herself toward him. "Captain!"

"CRESS!"

The doctor and the guard both spun around as the footsteps barreled down the hall and they all watched as Captain Thorne, blindfolded, ran right past the door.

"*Captain!* I'm in here!"

The footsteps stopped and reversed and he ran back until his cane smacked the door frame. He froze, panting, one hand braced on the jamb. He had a furious bruise across one side of his face, though it was largely hidden by the bandanna. "Cress? Are you all right?"

Her relief didn't last. "Captain! To your left there's a Lunar guard and on your right is a doctor who's running tests on Lunars and I'm being held by one of Levana's wolf hybrids and *please be careful!*"

Thorne took a step back into the hallway and pulled a gun from his waistband. He spent a moment swiveling the barrel of the gun in each direction, but nobody moved to attack him.

With some surprise, Cress realized that the operative's grip had weakened.

"Er . . ." Thorne furrowed his brow, aiming the gun somewhere near the window. "Could you describe all those threats again because I feel like I missed something."

"Thorne?"

He pointed the gun toward Wolf, and Cress between them. "Who said that? Who are you? Have you hurt her? Because I swear if you hurt her—"

The Lunar guard reached forward and plucked the gun out of his hand.

"Hey!" Furious, Thorne raised his cane, but the guard easily blocked the blow with his forearm, then took the cane away too. Thorne raised his fists.

"That's enough!" yelled the doctor. "No one is hurt and no one is going to get hurt!"

Snarling, Thorne turned to face him. "That's what you think, wolf man . . . doctor . . . wait, Cress, which one is this?"

"I am Dr. Dmitri Erland and I am a friend of Linh Cinder's. You might know me as the man who helped her escape from New Beijing Prison."

Thorne snorted. "Nice story, except I'm pretty sure *I'm* the one who helped Cinder escape from prison."

"Hardly. The man you just hit is also an ally of Cinder's, as is the lupine soldier who is still on heavy painkillers and probably delirious and who will no doubt pull out some stitches if he doesn't lie down right away."

"Thorne," the operative said again, ignoring the doctor's warnings. "What's going on? Where are we? What happened to your eyes?"

Thorne cocked his head. "Wait . . . *Wolf?*"

"Yes."

There was a long, long pause, before understanding filled Thorne's expression and he laughed. "Aces, Cress, you nearly gave me a heart attack with that wolf hybrid comment. Why didn't you tell me it was just him?"

"I . . . um . . ."

"Where's Cinder?" asked Thorne.

"I don't know," said Wolf. "And where—I thought Cinder said something about Scarlet? Before?" With one arm still loosely tied around Cress's neck, he dragged his free hand down his face, moaning. "Just a nightmare . . . ?"

"Cinder is here. She's safe," said the doctor.

Thorne grinned, the biggest, most enigmatic grin Cress had seen since the satellite.

Cress gaped around the room, nearly hyperventilating as her worldview flip-flopped before her.

Sybil's guard, who she had last seen on his way to board the Rampion. Could he have betrayed Sybil and joined them?

The doctor who had helped Cinder escape from prison.

The wolf operative. Only now, with Thorne's recognition, did she realize this was the man she'd seen on the video feed when they'd first contacted her.

And somewhere . . . Cinder.

Safe. They were *safe*.

Thorne held out his hand, and the guard put the cane back into it. "Cress, are you all right?" He crossed the room and bent down as if he could inspect her—or kiss her, though he didn't. "Are you hurt?"

"No, I'm . . . I'm all right." The words were so foreign, so impossible. So liberating. "How did you find me?"

"One of Jina's men told me the name of this place, and all I had to do was mention 'crazy doctor' to the folks outside and they all knew just who I was talking about."

Knees suddenly weak, she reached for his forearms to stabilize herself. "You came for me."

He beamed, looking for all the world like a selfless, daring hero.

"Don't sound so surprised." Dropping the cane, he pulled her into a crushing embrace that tore her away from Wolf and lifted her clean off the floor. "It turns out you are worth *a lot* of money on the black market."

Forty

CINDER STOOD WITH HER HAIR PINCHED BACK IN BOTH HANDS and the palace blueprint blurring on the netscreen before her. She'd been staring at it all day, but her brain kept running in circles.

"All right. What if—if the doctor and I could get some invitations and sneak in as guests . . . and then Jacin could create a diversion . . . or, no, if *you* created a diversion and Jacin came as one of the staff . . . but, the doctor is so well-known. Maybe Jacin and I could enter as guests and the doctor . . . but then how would we . . . *ugh.*" She threw her head back and glowered at the ship's metal ceiling with its crossed wires and air ducts. "Maybe I'm overcomplicating this. Maybe I should go in alone."

"Yes, because you aren't recognizable *at all*," said Iko, punctuating her statement by pulling up Cinder's prison photo in the blueprint's corner.

Cinder groaned. This was never going to work.

"*Oh!* Cinder!"

She jolted. "What?"

"This just came across the local newsfeed." Iko wiped away the blueprint and replaced it with a map of the Sahara Desert. A journalist was speaking in the background, and as they watched, a circle was drawn around some nearby cities, with lines and arrows connecting them. A ticker read: WANTED-CRIMINAL CARS-WELL THORNE SPOTTED IN SAHARA TRADING CITY. EVADES CAP-TURE. As the journalist jabbered on, Thorne's prison photo flashed on the screen, followed by the words, bright and bold. ARMED AND DANGEROUS. COMM AUTHORITIES IMMEDIATELY WITH ANY INFORMATION.

Cinder's stomach twisted, first with remorse, then with panic.

It was a false alarm. Thorne . . . Thorne was dead. Someone must have seen a look-alike and jumped to conclusions. It wasn't the first time. According to the media, Cinder had been spotted multiple times in every Earthen country, sometimes in multiple locations at once.

But that didn't matter. If people believed they'd seen the real thing, then they would come. Law enforcement. The military. Bounty hunters.

The desert was about to be flooded with people searching for them, and the Rampion was still sitting, obvious and enormous, in the middle of a tiny oasis town.

"We can't stay here," she said, pulling on her boots. "I'll go get the others. Iko, run the system diagnostics. Make sure we're set for space travel again."

She was down the ramp before Iko could respond, jogging toward the hotel. She hoped it wouldn't take long for the doctor to pack up his things, and Wolf—

She hoped his wounds had healed enough that it would be all right to move him. The doctor had started reducing his dosages. Would it be safe to wake him?

As she rounded the corner to the hotel, she spotted a girl leaning against an electric vehicle—the car was just old enough to be beat-up and grungy, but not old enough to have gained any vintage appeal. On the other hand, the girl was perhaps in her late teens and gorgeous, with light brown skin and braids dyed in shades of blue.

Cinder slowed, preparing for a fight. She didn't recognize the girl as one of the townspeople, and something felt wrong about her, though she couldn't place it. Was she a bounty hunter? An undercover detective?

The girl's expression stayed blank and bored as Cinder approached.

No outward recognition. That was good.

But then she smiled and twirled one of her silky braids around a finger. "Linh Cinder. Such a pleasure. My master has spoken so highly of you."

Cinder paused and studied her again. "Who are you?"

"I'm called Darla. I am Captain Thorne's mistress."

Cinder blinked. "Excuse me?"

"He asked me to stay and keep watch over the vehicle," she said. "He's just gone inside to be heroic. I'm sure he'll be glad to know you're here. I believe he's under the impression that you're out in space somewhere."

Cinder glanced from the girl to the hotel. When it seemed that the girl had no intention of reaching for a weapon or handcuffs or leaving her post against the car, Cinder pushed open the door. She rushed up the stairs, her mind spinning with the girl's words. It was a joke or a trap or a trick. It could not be possible that she was...that Thorne was...

Her foot slammed into the landing so hard she was almost

surprised it didn't crash through the floorboards. As she turned down the corridor she saw Jacin standing outside Wolf's room, arms crossed.

"Jacin—there's a girl down there—she said—she—"

He shrugged and gestured toward the room. "See for yourself."

Using the wall for balance, Cinder joined him in the doorway.

Dr. Erland was there, with a sizable bruise on his jaw.

And Wolf was awake.

And . . . stars above.

He was filthy. His clothes ripped and covered in dirt and his hair as shaggy as it had been the day she'd met him in his prison cell. His face was bruised, stubble was claiming his jawline, and he wore, of all things, a red bandanna around his eyes.

But he was grinning, with his arm around the waist of a petite blonde girl, and it was undeniably him.

It was a few seconds before Cinder found her voice and she had to grip the door frame to keep standing.

"Thorne?"

His head jerked around. "Cinder?"

"Wh—what are you—how? Where have you *been*? What's going on? Why are you wearing that stupid bandanna?"

He laughed. Gripping a wooden cane, he stumbled toward her, waving one hand until it landed on her shoulder. Then he was hugging her, suffocating her against his chest. "I missed you too."

"You jerk," she hissed, even as she returned the hug. "We thought you were dead!"

"Oh, please. It'd take a lot more than a satellite plummeting to

Earth to kill me. Although, admittedly, Cress may have saved us that time."

Cinder pushed him away. "What's wrong with your eyes?"

"Blind. It's a long story."

Her tongue flailed around all the questions stammering to get out, and she finally landed on: "When did you have time to take a *mistress*?"

His smile faltered. "Don't talk about Cress like that."

"What?"

"Oh—wait! You mean *Darla*. I won her in a hand of cards."

Cinder gawked.

"I thought she'd make a nice gift for Iko."

"You . . . what?"

"For her replacement body?"

"Um."

"Because Darla's an escort-droid?"

Slow, gradual understanding. An escort-droid. That would explain the girl's perfect symmetry and ridiculously lush eyelashes. And the way her presence felt *off*—because there was no bioelectricity coming off her.

"Honestly, Cinder, to listen to you, people would think I'm a helpless flirt or something." Tipping back on his heels, Thorne gestured toward the blonde girl. "By the way, you remember Cress?"

The girl smiled uncomfortably. Only then did Cinder recognize her—now with flaking, sunburned cheeks and hair chopped short and uneven.

"Hello," said Cinder, although the girl was quick to duck behind Thorne and cast her eyes nervously around all the people in the room.

Cinder cleared her throat. "And, Wolf, you're awake. This is . . . I'm . . . er, listen, Thorne—you were spotted in a nearby city. They're already pulling together search parties. This whole area is about to be flooded with people searching for us." She faced the doctor. "We need to get out of here. Now."

"Cinder?"

She tensed. Wolf's voice was rough and desperate. She dared to meet his eyes. His brow was damp with sweat, his pupils dilated.

"I had a dream where you said . . . you told me that Scarlet . . ."

Cinder gulped, wishing she could avoid the inevitable.

"Wolf . . ."

He paled, seeing it in her face before she spoke.

"It wasn't a dream," she murmured. "She was taken."

"Wait, what?" Thorne listed his head. "What happened?"

"Scarlet was taken by the thaumaturge after we were attacked."

Thorne cursed. Wolf slumped against the wall, his expression hollow. Silence stole into the room, until Cinder forced herself to stand up straighter, to be optimistic, to not lose hope.

"We believe she was taken to Luna," she said, "and I have an idea. For how we can get onto Luna without being seen, and how we can find her and save her. And now that we're all together again, I believe it can work. You just have to trust me. And right now—we can't stay here. We have to leave."

"She's dead," Wolf whispered. "I failed her."

"Wolf. She's not dead. You don't know that."

"Neither do you." He hunched over, burying his face behind both hands. His shoulders began to shake, and it was just like before. The way all his energy darkened and thickened around him. The way he seemed empty, missing.

Cinder took a step toward him. *"She's not dead.* They'll want to keep her for . . . for bait. For information. They wouldn't just kill her. So there's still time, there's time to—"

His anger flared like an explosion—one moment, nothing. Then a spark, and then, suddenly, he was burning up, raging and white hot.

He reached for Cinder, turning and pinning her against the wall with such force that the netscreen shook and threatened to crash to the floor. Cinder gasped, clamping both hands over Wolf's wrist as he held her suspended by her throat, feet dangling off the ground. The warnings on her retina display were instantaneous—rising pulse and adrenaline and temperature and irregular breathing and—

"You think I want that?" he growled. "For them to keep her, *alive*? You don't know what they'll do to her—but *I do*." In another instant, the fury softened, buried beneath terror and misery. "Scarlet . . ."

He released her and Cinder collapsed to the ground, rubbing her neck. Over the tumult in her thoughts, she heard Wolf turn and run, his footsteps crashing across the floor, down the hall-way toward Dr. Erland's room.

When they stopped, there was a short silence that filled up the entire hotel. And then howling.

Horrible, painful, wretched howling that sank into Cinder's bones and made her stomach turn.

"Wonderful," Dr. Erland drawled. "I'm glad to see you were so much more prepared this time."

Hissing around the pain, Cinder used the wall to pull herself to her feet, and glanced around at her friends, her allies. Cress was still hiding behind Thorne, her eyes now wide with shock.

Jacin was fingering the handle of his knife. Dr. Erland, with his messy gray hair and glasses perched at the end of his nose, could not have looked any less impressed.

"You all go ahead," she said. Her throat stung. "Load up the ship. Make sure Iko is ready to go."

Another long, heartbreaking howl shook the hotel, and Cinder steadied herself as well as she could. "I'll get Wolf."

Forty-One

CRESS FOLLOWED THE GUARD DOWN THE HOTEL STEPS.
Thorne was behind her, one hand on her shoulder and the other gripping his cane. She warned him about the last step as she turned down the dark hallway. Dr. Erland was in the back, already wheezing with the exertion of carrying his prized lab equipment down the stairs.

It was difficult for Cress to focus. She wasn't even sure where they were going. The ship, did Cinder say? At the time, Cress had been filled with horror at seeing the Lunar operative snap. His howls were still bouncing off her eardrums.

The guard shoved open the hotel door and they all scrambled down onto the rough, sand-covered road. Two steps later, he froze, thrusting his arms out to catch Cress, Thorne, and the doc-tor as they crashed into him.

Whimpering, Cress shriveled against Thorne and scanned the road.

Dozens of men and women dressed in the official uniform of the Commonwealth military had them surrounded, with guns raised. They filled up the roads and the spaces between buildings, peered down from rooftops and around rust-covered podships.

"Cress?" Thorne whispered, as tension prickled on the stifling air.

"Military," she murmured. "A lot of them." Her gaze landed on a girl with blue hair, and instant hatred blossomed inside her chest. "What is *she* doing here?"

"What? Who?"

"That—that *girl* from the last town."

Thorne tilted his head. "That's Darla. The escort-droid? Why are you and Cinder so confused about this?"

Her eyes widened. *She* was an escort-droid?

The girl was watching them without emotion, sandwiched between two soldiers with her hands hanging limp at her sides. "I am sorry, Master," she said, her voice carrying through the silence. "I would have warned you, but that would be illegal, and my programming prevents me from breaking human laws."

"Yeah, that's going to be the first thing we fix," said Thorne, before whispering to Cress, "I had to find one heck of a legal loophole to get her to help me steal that car."

A voice boomed and it took Cress a moment to spot the man holding a portscreen and amplifier to his mouth. "You are all under arrest for the harboring and assisting of wanted fugitives. Get down on your stomachs and put your hands on your heads and no one will be hurt."

Trembling, Cress waited to see what the guard would do. The gun he'd taken from Thorne was still tucked into his belt, but his hands were full of the doctor's stuff.

"We have you surrounded," the man continued, when no one moved. "There is nowhere to run. Get down, now."

The guard moved first, lowering himself to his knees and setting down the bag of medical supplies and the strange machine, before settling into the dirt.

Gulping, Cress followed suit, sinking down to the hard ground. Thorne dropped down beside her.

"Stars above," she heard the doctor moan, grumbling as he joined them on the ground. "I'm too old for this."

Hot and uncomfortable, with rough pebbles pressing into her stomach, Cress set her palms on top of her head.

The officer waited until they were on the ground before speaking again. "Linh Cinder. We have you surrounded. Come to the front exit immediately with your hands on top of your head and no one will be hurt."

CINDER RELEASED A STRING OF THE MOST CREATIVE CURSES she could think of as the man's voice died away. She left Wolf in the hallway, where he'd been unresponsive to her reminders that having a mental breakdown now wouldn't do anything to help Scarlet. He had only sat curled in on himself with his head tucked against his knees, saying nothing.

Ducking into the doctor's hotel room, Cinder inched her way to the window and peeled open the blinds.

The rooftop directly opposite the alley had two armed military officers with guns pointed right at her.

She dropped the blinds and cursed again, plastering herself to the wall.

A comm from Iko appeared in her vision. She pulled it up, already fearing what it would say.

RADAR IS PICKING UP MILITARY SHIPS FROM THE COMMONWEALTH. I THINK WE'VE BEEN SPOTTED.

"Do you think?" she muttered. Shutting her eyes, she jotted back a fast message, words scrolling across her eyelids as she thought them.

AT THE HOTEL, SURROUNDED BY EC MILITARY. PREPARE FOR IMMEDIATE TAKEOFF. WE WON'T BE LONG—I HOPE.

Letting out a slow breath, she pried open her eyes again. How was she supposed to get a mid-crisis wolf operative, a blind man, and an elderly doctor past all those soldiers without getting anyone killed?

She doubted the girl would be much help. Cress didn't strike Cinder as the bold, risk-taking type, and Cinder doubted she'd had much experience fighting her way out of situations like this.

She could abandon her friends and make a run for it herself. She could try to control Wolf and use him as a weapon, but even he couldn't take on that many soldiers at once, and they wouldn't hesitate to kill him. She could try to brainwash the soldiers so they would let them pass, but she'd have to abandon Wolf if he didn't come willingly.

Outside, the officer repeated his commands again and again, like a robot.

Squaring her shoulders, she returned to Wolf in the hallway. "*Wolf*," she said, stooping beside him, "I need you to help me out here."

He shifted enough to peer at her over his arm. His green eyes looked dull and faded.

"Wolf, *please*. We need to get to the ship, and there are a lot of people with guns out there. Come on—what would Scarlet want you to do?"

His fingers curled, nails digging into his thighs. Still, he said nothing, made no move to get up.

The officer's voice boomed again. *You are under arrest. Come out with your hands on your head. We have you surrounded.*

"Fine. You leave me no choice." Standing, she forced her shoulders to relax. The world shifted around her as she flipped off the panic and desperation and reached out instead for the energy crackling around Wolf.

Except this time it wasn't crackling. Not like usual.

This time, it was like controlling a corpse.

THEY STEPPED INTO THE DOORWAY TOGETHER.

At least sixty guns pointed at them that she could see—no doubt more hidden behind buildings and vehicles.

Jacin, Thorne, Dr. Erland, and Cress were all lying on the ground.

Two streets separated them from the ship.

She kept feeding lies to Wolf like medicine from a drip. *Scarlet will be fine. We will find her. We will save her. But, first, we have to get out of this mess. We have to get to the ship.*

From the corner of her eye, she saw his fingers twitch, but she didn't know whether he was acknowledging that there was still hope out there, or whether he was just ticked at her for using him like this. Turning him into a puppet, just like the thaumaturge that had turned him into a monster.

Standing on the hotel step, with sixty guns trained on her, Cinder realized she was no better than that thaumaturge. This really was war, and she really was in the middle of it.

If she had to make sacrifices, she would.

What did that make her, anyway? A real criminal? A real threat?

A real Lunar?

"Put your hands on your head and walk away from the building. Do not make any sudden movements. We are authorized to kill if necessary."

Cinder coerced Wolf to stay beside her. They walked in unison. The dusty air clouded around them, sticking to her skin. A dull ache was spreading through her head, but it wasn't anywhere near as difficult to control Wolf as it used to be. In fact, how easy it was made her sick. He wasn't even trying to fight her.

"About time," Thorne muttered as she passed.

"Cinder—save yourself," hissed Dr. Erland.

She tried her best not to move her lips as she spoke. "Can you glamour them?"

"Stop right there!"

She obeyed.

"On your knees, now. Keep your hands up."

"Only a few," said Dr. Erland. "Maybe together . . ."

She shook her head. "I've got Wolf. On top of that . . . I can control one Earthen, maybe two."

She clenched her teeth. Despite what the doctor had said, she couldn't just save herself. It wasn't only loyalty and friendship that made every fiber of her body rebel against the notion that she could abandon them all.

It was the knowledge that without them, she was useless. She needed them to stop the wedding and rescue Kai. She needed them to get her to Luna. She needed them to help her save the world.

"Jacin? Can you control any of them?"

"Yeah, right." She could practically hear his eyes roll. "The only way through this is to fight."

Thorne grunted. "In that case, has anyone seen my gun?"

"I've got it," said Jacin.

"Can I have it back?"

"Nope."

"I order you to stop talking!" the man bellowed. "I see any more lips move and that person gets a bullet in their head, understand? Get down!"

Cinder made a point to glare at the man as she took another step forward.

Like dominoes pushed over, she heard the unlatching of sixty safety mechanisms around her.

Cress whimpered. Thorne's hand fumbled around until it was gripping hers.

"I have six tranquilizers," Cinder said. "Let's hope it's enough."

"It won't be," muttered Jacin.

"This is your last warning—"

Cinder tilted her chin up, fixing her gaze on the man. Beside her, Wolf lowered himself into a fighting position, his fingers curled and ready, all at Cinder's urging. For the first time, she felt a spike of new emotion from him. Hatred, she thought. For her.

She ignored it.

"This is your *first* warning," she said.

Holding Wolf at the ready, she pinpointed one of the Earthen soldiers who was standing at the front of the line and plucked out her willpower. The young woman swiveled and pointed her gun at the man who was evidently in charge. The woman's eyes widened in shock as they took in her own rebellious hands.

Around her, six more soldiers changed targets, aiming at their own comrades, and Cinder knew they were under Dr. Erland's control.

And that was all they had. Seven Earthen soldiers at their disposal. Jacin's gun. Wolf's fury.

It would be a bloodbath.

"Stand down and let us pass," Cinder said, "and no one will get hurt."

The man narrowed his eyes at her, making a point not to look at his own peer now holding him at gunpoint. "You can't win this."

"I didn't say we could," said Cinder. "But we can do a lot of damage trying."

She opened the tip of her finger, loading a tranquilizer from the cartridge in her palm, just as a wave of dizziness crashed over her. Her strength was waning. She couldn't hold on to Wolf much longer. If she dropped her control and he snapped again . . . she didn't know what he would do. Become comatose all over again, or go on a rampage, or turn his anger on her and the rest of their friends?

Beside her, Wolf growled.

"Actually, we *can* win," said a female voice.

Cinder tensed. There was a pulse in the air. A ripple of uncertainty. The man with the portscreen swiveled around as silhouettes began to emerge from around the buildings, creeping down alleyways, materializing in windows and doorways.

Men and women, young and old. Dressed in their tattered jeans and loose cotton shirts, their head scarves and cotton hats, their tennis shoes and boots.

Cinder gulped, recognizing almost all of them from her brief stay in Farafrah. Those who had brought her food. Those who had helped paint the ship. Those who had doodled cyborg designs on their bodies.

Her heart lifted for a moment, and then plummeted down into her gut.

This would not end well.

"This is a matter of international security," said the man. "You are all ordered to return to your homes. Anyone who defies this order will be held in contempt of justice by the laws of the Earthen Union."

"So hold us in contempt. *After* you let them pass."

Cinder squinted into the glare of the sun, looking for the source of the voice. She spotted the woman from the medical shop. The Lunar whose son had killed himself rather than join Levana's guard.

Some of the soldiers diverted their guns, pivoting away from Cinder and aiming into the crowd, but the man with the amplifier held up an arm. "These people are wanted criminals! We do not wish to use lethal force to apprehend them, but we will if necessary. I urge you to stand down and return to your homes."

His threat was followed by a standstill, though the few civilian faces Cinder could see didn't appear frightened. Only determined.

"These people are our friends," said the shopkeeper. "They came here seeking sanctuary, and we're not going to let you come in and take them."

What were they thinking? What could they possibly do? They may have outnumbered the soldiers, but they were unarmed and untrained. If they got in the way, they would be slaughtered.

"You're not giving me a choice," said the man, his knuckles

tightening around the portscreen. A bead of sweat dripped down the side of his face.

The shopkeeper's tone took on a new venom. "You have *no idea* what it's like to not be given a choice."

Her fingers twitched, a gesture virtually unnoticeable, but the effect passed like a shock wave through the crowd. Cinder flinched. Looking around, she saw that many of the townspeople looked suddenly strained, their brows furrowed, their limbs trembling.

And all around them, the soldiers began to shift. Redirecting their aim, as those controlled by Cinder and Dr. Erland had, until every soldier was targeting his own neighbor, until every soldier had a gun aimed at his own head.

Their stunned eyes filled first with disbelief, and then terror.

Only the leader was left standing in the middle, gaping at his own troop.

"That's what it's like," said the woman. "To have your own body used against you. To know that your brain has become a traitor. We came to Earth to get away from that, but we're all lost if Levana gets her way. Now, I don't know if this young lady can stop her, but it seems she's the only one worth putting any faith into right now, so that's what we're going to do."

Cinder cried out suddenly, pain splitting her skull. Her hold on Wolf and the female soldier snapped. Her knees buckled, but there was an arm suddenly around her waist, holding her up.

Panting from the mental exertion, she peered up into Wolf's face. His eyes were bright green again. Normal.

"Wolf . . ."

He peeled his gaze away, as a gun clattered to the ground. Cinder jumped. The woman she had been controlling was gaping around at her comrades, trembling. Not knowing where to look. Not knowing what to do. She nervously raised her hands in surrender.

Red with anger, the man with the portscreen lowered the amplifier. He faced Cinder again, his eyes filled with hatred. Then he tossed his portscreen to the ground.

Thorne swiveled his head from side to side. "Uh, could someone explain to me—"

"Later," said Cinder, letting her weight sink against Wolf. "Get up. It's time for us to go."

"No arguments here," said Thorne, as he and the others clambered to their feet. "But does someone think they could grab my escort-droid? I kind of went through a lot to get her, and—"

"*Thorne.*"

Cinder felt light-headed and weak as they weaved their way through the stalemate. It felt like walking through a maze of stone sculptures—stone sculptures who carried big guns and followed them with their eyes, writhing inside with fury and distrust. Cinder tried to meet the gazes of the townspeople, but many of them had their own eyes shut tight and were shaking from concentration. They couldn't hold the soldiers forever.

Only the obvious Earthens met her look and nodded with scared, fleeting smiles. Not a fear of their Lunar neighbors, she thought, but a fear of what would happen if Levana took control of Earth. What would happen if Lunars ruled everything. What would happen if Cinder failed.

Jacin grabbed the escort-droid's wrist and pulled her along after them.

"That woman was right," Wolf said when they'd broken away from the crowd, and the Rampion—their freedom—rose up from the streets in front of them. "There's nothing worse than your own body being used against you."

Cinder stumbled, but Wolf caught her and dragged her a few steps before she found her balance again. "I'm sorry, Wolf. But I had to. I couldn't leave you there."

"I know. I understand." Reaching out, he grabbed a sack out of the doctor's hand, lessening his load as they hurried toward the ship. "But it doesn't change the fact that no one should have that sort of power."

Forty-Two

THE LUNAR BOY COULDN'T HAVE BEEN MORE THAN EIGHT years old, and yet Scarlet was certain that she would wring his neck like a chicken if she ever got the chance. He was, without a doubt, the most horrible child that ever lived. She couldn't help thinking that if all Lunar children were like this, their whole society was doomed and Cinder would be better off letting them destroy themselves.

Scarlet didn't know how, exactly, she had ended up the property of Venerable Annotel and his wife and the little monster they'd raised. Maybe it was favoritism from the crown, or maybe they'd purchased her, like an Earthen family might purchase a new android. Either way, for seven days, she had been the new toy. The new pet. The new test subject.

Because at eight years old, young Master Charleson was learning how to control his Lunar gift. Evidently, Earthens were great fun to practice on, and Master Charleson had a very sick sense of humor.

Chained from a collar around her neck to a bolt in the floor, Scarlet was being kept in what she figured was the boy's playroom. An enormous netscreen took up one wall and countless virtual reality machines and sports-tech had been abandoned in the corners, out of her reach.

His practice sessions were agony. Since she'd come to the Annotel household, Scarlet had had long-legged spiders crawl up her nose. Snakes as long as her arm wriggle their way through her belly button and wind their bodies around her spine. Centipedes burrow into her ear canals and creep around the inside of her skull before emerging on her tongue.

Scarlet had screamed. She had thrashed. She had gouged her own fingernails into her stomach and blown her nose until it bled in an effort to get the trespassers out.

And all the while, Master Charleson had laughed and laughed and laughed.

It was all in her head, of course. She knew that. She even knew it when she was roughly banging her head on the floor to try to knock out the spiders and centipedes. But it didn't matter. Her body was convinced, her brain was convinced. Her rational mind was overcome.

She hated that little boy. *Hated* him.

She also hated that she was starting to be afraid of him.

"Charleson."

His mother appeared in the doorway, temporarily rescuing Scarlet from his most recent infatuation—squinty-eyed ground moles, with their fat bodies and enormous reptilian claws. One had been gnawing at her toes while its talons shredded the sole of her foot.

The illusion and the pain vanished, but the horror lingered. The rawness of her throat. The damp salt on her face. Scarlet rolled onto her side, sobbing in the middle of the playroom floor, grateful that the boy couldn't maintain the brainwashing while he was distracted.

Scarlet paid no heed to the conversation until Charleson began to yell, and she forced open her swollen eyes. The boy was throwing a tantrum. His mother was talking in a soothing voice, trying to appease him. Promising something. Charleson, it seemed, was not appeased. A minute later, he stomped out of the room and Scarlet heard a door slam.

She exhaled with shaky relief. Her muscles relaxed, as they never could when the little terror was around.

She pushed her red hood and a tangle of curls out of her face. His mother sent her a withering glance, as if Scarlet were as disgusting as a mole, as offensive as a swarm of maggots on the woman's pristine kitchen counters.

Without a word, she turned and left the room.

It wasn't long before a different shadow filled the doorway, a handsome man wearing a black, long-sleeved jacket.

A thaumaturge.

Scarlet was almost happy to see him.

"**SHE WAS CAPTURED DURING MY BATTLE WITH LINH CINDER.** This girl was one of her accomplices."

"The battle in which you failed to either eradicate or apprehend the cyborg?"

Sybil's nostrils flared as she paced in between Scarlet and the lavishly carved marble throne. She was wearing a pristine new coat, and moving with an awkward stiffness, no doubt a result of the gunshot wound. "That is correct, My Queen."

"As I thought. Go on."

Sybil clasped her hands behind her back, knuckles whitening. "Unfortunately, our software technicians have had no success in tracking the Rampion using either the podship or the D-COMM chip that I confiscated. Therefore, the primary purpose of this interrogation is to ascertain what information our prisoner might have that will be useful in our ongoing search for the cyborg."

Queen Levana nodded.

Scarlet, kneeling in the center of the stone-and-glass throne room, had a very good view of the queen, and though part of her wanted to look away, it was difficult. The Lunar queen was as beautiful as she'd always been told—more, even. Scarlet suspected there had been a time when men would have fought wars to possess a woman of such beauty.

These days, Emperor Kai was being forced to marry her in order to *stop* a war.

In her famished, delirious, mind-weary state, Scarlet almost laughed at the irony. She barely swallowed it back down.

The queen noticed the twitch of her lips, and frowned.

Pulse quickening, Scarlet cast her eyes around the throne room. Though she had been forced to kneel, they had not put her in any restraints. With the queen herself present, plus a handful of guards and a total of ten thaumaturges—Sybil Mira, plus three in red and six in black—she supposed they hadn't been too concerned that she might try to escape.

On top of that, the velvet-draped chairs to either side of the throne were filled with at least fifty...well, Scarlet didn't know *who* they were. Jurors? The Lunar media? Aristocrats?

All she knew was that they looked ridiculous. Clothing that twinkled and floated and glowed. Faces painted to look like solar systems and rainbow prisms and wild animals. Brightly colored hair that curled and wisped, defying gravity in order to create massive, elaborate structures. Some of the wigs even housed caged songbirds, though they were being remarkably quiet.

With that thought, it occurred to Scarlet that these were all probably glamours that she was looking at. These Lunars could be wearing potato sacks for all she knew.

Sybil Mira's heels tapped against the hard floor, drawing Scarlet's attention back to her.

"How long had you been a part of Linh Cinder's rebellion prior to your capture?"

She stared up at the thaumaturge, her throat sore from days of screaming. She considered saying nothing. Her gaze flicked to the queen.

"How long?" said Sybil, her tone already growing impatient.

But, no, Scarlet did not care to remain silent. They were going to kill her, that much was obvious. She was not so naïve that she couldn't see her own mortality closing in around her. After all, there were bloodstains on the throne room floor, streaking toward the wall opposite the queen's throne. Or, where a wall should have been, but it was instead an enormous open window, and a ledge that jutted out, leading to nowhere.

They were fairly high up—three or four stories, at least. Scarlet didn't know what was beyond that ledge, but she guessed it made for a convenient way to dispose of the bodies.

Sybil grabbed her by the chin. "I suggest you answer the question."

Scarlet clenched her teeth. Yes, she would answer. When would she ever be given such an audience again?

When Sybil released her, she turned her attention back to the queen.

"I joined Cinder on the night your special operatives

attacked," she said, her voice hoarse but strong. "It was also the night you killed my grandmother."

Queen Levana had no reaction.

"You probably have no idea who my grandmother was. Who I am."

"Is it relevant to these proceedings?" asked Sybil, sounding annoyed that Scarlet had already hijacked her interrogation.

"Oh, yes. Incredibly relevant."

Levana settled her cheek against her knuckles, looking bored.

"Her name was Michelle Benoit."

Nothing.

"She served twenty-eight years in the European military, as a pilot. She received a medal once, for piloting a mission here, to Luna, for diplomatic discussions."

A slight narrowing of the eyes.

"Many years later, a man that she had met on Luna showed up at her doorstep, with a very interesting parcel. A little girl... almost dead, but not quite."

A puckering around the lips.

"For years, my grandmother kept that little girl hidden, kept her alive, and she ultimately paid for that with her life. That was the night that I joined Linh Cinder. That was the night that I joined the side of the true queen of—"

Her tongue froze, her jaws and throat icing over.

But her lips still managed a smug smile. She'd already said more than she thought Levana would allow, and the fury in the queen's eyes made it worthwhile.

The onlookers were rustling softly, no one daring to talk, even as they cast confused glances at one another across the room.

Sybil Mira had gone pale as she looked from Scarlet to the queen. "I apologize for the prisoner's outburst, My Queen. Would you like me to continue questioning her in private?"

"That won't be necessary." Queen Levana's voice was lyrical and calm, as if Scarlet's words hadn't bothered her in the slightest, but Scarlet knew it was a ruse. She'd seen the flash of murder in the queen's eyes. "You may continue with your questions, Sybil. However, we are scheduled to depart for Earth tonight, and I would hate to be delayed. Perhaps your prisoner could use a bit more motivation to stay focused on the answers we're interested in."

"I agree, Your Majesty." Sybil nodded to one of the royal guards that flanked the doors.

Moments later, a platform was wheeled into the throne room, and the audience seemed to perk up.

Scarlet gulped.

On the platform was a large block of ebony wood, intricately carved on all sides with scores of people prostrating themselves before a man in long, flowing robes, who wore a crescent moon as if it were a crown. On top of the block, set amid hundreds of hatch marks, was a silver hatchet.

Scarlet was pulled to her feet by two guards and dragged onto the platform. Letting out a slow breath, she lifted her chin, trying to stifle her mounting fear.

"Tell me," said Sybil, passing behind her. "Where is Linh Cinder now?"

Scarlet held the queen's stare. "I don't know."

A beat, before her own hand betrayed her, reaching out and wrapping around the silver handle. Her throat tightened.

"Where is she?"

Scarlet gritted her teeth. "I. Don't. Know."

Her hand yanked the blade from the wood.

"You must have talked about the possibility of an emergency landing. A safe place to hide should you need to. Tell me. *Speculate* if you must. Where would she have gone?"

"I have no idea."

Scarlet's other hand slammed onto the top of the block, fingers splayed out against the dark wood. She gasped at her own sudden movements, finally tearing her gaze away from the queen to look at her traitorous limb.

"Perhaps an easier question, then."

Scarlet jumped. Sybil was right behind her now, whispering against her ear.

"Which finger do you value the least?"

Scarlet squeezed her eyes shut. She tried to clear her thoughts, to be logical. She tried to not be afraid.

"I was their only pilot," she said. "None of them had any clue how to fly a spaceship. If they tried to go back to Earth, they would have crashed."

Sybil's footsteps retreated, but Scarlet's hand remained stretched against the block, the hatchet still hovering in the air.

"My guard was an accomplished pilot, and he was quite alive when we abandoned the ship. Assume that Linh Cinder brainwashed him into piloting the ship for her." Sybil came to stand where Scarlet could see her again. "Where, then, would she have had him go?"

"*I don't know.* Maybe you should ask him."

A slow, pleased smile climbed over the thaumaturge's face. "We'll start with the smallest finger, then."

Scarlet's arm reared back, and she flinched, turning her

face away as if not looking would keep it from happening. Her knees gave out and she collapsed beside the block of wood, but her arms stayed strong, inflexible. The only parts of her that weren't trembling.

Her grip on the hatchet tightened, prepared to swing.

"My Queen?"

The entire room seemed to inhale at the words, so softly spoken that Scarlet wasn't sure she'd really heard them.

After a long, long moment, the queen snapped, "What?"

"May I have her?" The words were faint and slow, as if the question were a maze that needed to be traversed carefully. "She would make a lovely pet."

Pulse thundering in her ears, Scarlet dared to open her eyes. The hatchet glinted in the corner of her vision.

"You may have her when we are done with her," said the queen, sounding not at all pleased at the interruption.

"But then she'll be broken. They're never any fun when you give them to me broken."

The room began to titter mockingly.

A bead of sweat fell into Scarlet's eyes, stinging.

"If she were my pet," continued the lilting voice, "I could practice on her. She must be easy to control. Maybe I would start to get better if I had such a pretty Earthen to play with."

The tittering stopped.

The frail voice became even quieter, barely a murmur, that still carried like a gunshot in the otherwise silent room.

"Father would have given her to me."

Scarlet tried to blink the salt from her eyes. Her breaths were ragged from the strain of trying to take back control of her arms and failing.

"I said that you may have her, and you may," said the queen, speaking harshly, as if to an annoying child. "But what you don't seem to understand is that when a queen threatens repercussions against someone who has wronged her, she must follow through on those threats. If she does not, she is inviting anarchy to her doorstep. Do you want anarchy, *Princess*?"

Dizzy with fear, with nausea, with hunger, Scarlet managed to raise her head. The queen was looking at someone seated beside her, but the world was blurring and Scarlet couldn't see who it was.

She heard her, though. The lovely voice, cutting through her.

"No, My Queen."

"Precisely."

Levana turned back to Sybil and nodded.

Scarlet didn't have a moment to prepare herself before the hatchet dropped.

BOOK

Four

"When Rapunzel saw the prince,

she fell over him and began to weep,

and her tears dropped into his eyes."

Forty-Three

CRESS STOOD TO THE SIDE OF THE LAB TABLE, CLUTCHING A portscreen as Dr. Erland held a strange tool beside Thorne's face, sending a thin beam of light into his pupils.

The doctor grunted, and bobbed his head in comprehension. "Mm-hmmm," he drawled, changing the tool's setting so that a green light clicked on near the bottom. "Mm-hm," he said again, switching to the other eye. Cress leaned closer, but she couldn't see anything that would warrant such thoughtful humming.

The tool in the doctor's hand made a few clicking sounds and he took the portscreen out of Cress's hand. He nodded at it before handing it back to her. She looked down at the screen, where the strange tool was transferring a jumble of incomprehensible diagnoses.

"Mmmm-hmmm."

"Would you stop *mm-hming* and tell me what's wrong with them?" said Thorne.

"Patience," said the doctor. "The optic system is delicate, and an incorrect diagnosis could be catastrophic."

Thorne crossed his arms.

The doctor changed the settings on his tool again and

completed another scan of Thorne's eyes. "Indeed," he said. "Severe optic nerve damage, likely as a result of traumatic head injury. My hypothesis is that when you hit your head during the fall, internal bleeding in your skull caused a sudden pressure buildup against the optic nerve and—"

Thorne waved, bumping the doctor's tool away from him. "Can you fix them?"

Dr. Erland huffed and set the tool down on the counter that ran the length of the Rampion's medbay. "Of course I can," he said, sounding insulted. "The first step will be to collect some bone marrow from the iliac crest portion of your pelvic bone. From that, I can harvest your hematopoietic stem cells, which we can use to create a solution that can be externally applied to your optic system. Over time, the stem cells will replace your damaged retinal ganglion cells and provide cellular bridges among the disconnected—"

"A-la-la-la-la, fine, I get it," said Thorne, covering his ears. "Please, never say that word again."

Dr. Erland raised an eyebrow. "Cellular? Hematopoietic? Ganglion?"

"That last one." Thorne grimaced. "Bleh."

The doctor scowled. "Are you squeamish, Mr. Thorne?"

"Eye stuff weirds me out. As does any surgery regarding the pelvic bone. You can knock me out for that part, right?" He lay back on the exam table. "Do it fast."

"A localized numbing agent will suffice," said Dr. Erland. "I even happen to have something that should work in my kit. However, while we can harvest the bone marrow today, I don't have the instruments necessary to separate the stem cells or create the injection solution."

Thorne slowly sat up again. "So . . . you *can't* fix me?"

"Not without a proper lab."

Thorne scratched his jaw. "All right. What if we skipped the whole stem cells, injection solution thing, and just swapped my eyeballs out for some cyborg prostheses instead? I've been thinking how handy X-ray vision could be, and I have to admit, the idea has kind of grown on me."

"Hmm. You're right," said Dr. Erland, eyeing Thorne over the frames of his glasses. "That would be *much* simpler."

"Really?"

"No."

Thorne's mouth twisted into a frown.

"At least now we know what's wrong," said Cress, "and that it can be fixed. We'll figure something out."

The doctor glanced at her, then turned away and set about organizing the medbay cabinets with the equipment they'd taken from his hotel. He seemed to be making an attempt to hide any emotions aside from professional curiosity, but Cress got the impression that he didn't care much for Thorne.

His feelings toward *her,* on the other hand, were a mystery. She didn't think he'd met her eye once since they'd left the hotel, and she suspected he was ashamed about the whole purchasing-Lunar-shells-for-their-blood thing. Which he had every reason to be ashamed of. Although they were on the same side now, she hadn't yet forgiven him for how he'd treated her, and countless others. Like cattle at an auction.

Not that she'd ever seen a cattle auction.

If she were honest with herself, she had uncertain opinions about most of the crew of the Rampion. After seeing Wolf snap in the hotel, Cress had done her best to steer clear of him when she could. His temper, and the knowledge of what his kind were capable of, made the hair prickle on her neck every time his vivid green eyes met hers.

It didn't help that Wolf hadn't spoken a word since they'd left Africa. While they'd all discussed the danger of staying in orbit before Cress could reinstate her systems for keeping them unobserved, Wolf had crouched solitary in a corner of the cockpit, staring empty-eyed at the pilot's seat.

When Cinder had suggested they go somewhere that was in reach of New Beijing while they figured out the next phase of their plan, Wolf had paced back and forth in the galley, cradling a can of tomatoes.

When they had finally descended into the desolate wasteland of the Commonwealth's northern Siberian regions, Wolf had lain on his side on the lower bunk bed of one of the crew quarters, his face buried in a pillow. Cress had assumed it was his bed, until Thorne informed her it had been Scarlet's.

She pitied him, of course. Anyone could see that he was devastated at Scarlet's loss. But she feared him more. Wolf's presence was like a ticking bomb that could explode at any moment.

Then there was Jacin Clay, Sybil's one-time guard, who spent most of his time in smug silence. When he did talk, he tended to say something rude or prickly. Plus, while he may have joined their side now, Cress couldn't help but think of all the times he had brought Mistress Sybil to her satellite, how many years he'd known about her captivity and done nothing to help her.

And then there was the escort-droid, with her *Master* this, and *Master* that, and *Would you like me to wash your feet and give you a nice foot rub, Master?*

"Captain!"

Cress bristled at the girly squeal, followed by a blur of blue that fluttered into the medbay and slammed into Thorne, nearly knocking him off the lab table.

He grunted. "Wha—"

"I love it!" said the escort. "I absolutely love it! It's the best present anyone has ever given me and you're the best captain in the whole wide galaxy! Thank you thank you thank you!" The android took to smothering Thorne's face in kisses, ignoring his struggles to back away on the table.

Cress pressed her fingers into the portscreen until her arms began to shake.

"Iko, let him breathe," said Cinder, appearing in the doorway.

"Right, sorry!" The android grabbed Thorne's cheeks and planted one more adamant kiss on his mouth before pulling away.

Cress's jaw began to ache from grinding her teeth.

"Iko?" said Thorne.

"In the flesh! How do I look?" She struck a pose for Thorne, then immediately started to laugh. "Oops—I mean . . . well, you'll just have to take my word for it that I am *gorgeous*. Plus I checked the manufacturer's catalogue and I can upgrade to *forty* different eye colors! I kind of like the metallic gold ones, but we'll see. Trends are so fleeting, you know."

Beginning to relax, Thorne smiled. "I'm glad you like her. But if you're here, who's running the ship?"

"I just switched out the personality chips," said Cinder. "Darla didn't seem to care one way or the other. Something about 'Whatever would please my master.'" Cinder pretended to gag. "I also undid some of her programming. Hopefully she won't be feeling too concerned about law-breaking after this."

"Just how I like my ships," said Thorne. "Darla, are you up there?"

"Ready to serve, Captain Thorne," said a new voice in the

speakers overhead, strangely robotic compared with Iko's hyper-active tones. "I am pleased to act as your new auto-control system and will strive to ensure the safety and comfort of my crew."

Thorne beamed. "Oh. I'm going to like her."

"When you're done with your examination," said Cinder, listing her head toward the door, "come out to the cargo bay. We have a lot we need to discuss."

WITHIN MINUTES, THE CREW OF THE RAMPION HAD assembled in the cargo bay. Iko sat cross-legged in the middle of the floor, mesmerized by the sight of her own bare toes. Dr. Erland had wheeled out the small desk chair from the medbay to sit on—Cress didn't think his old age and short legs would have allowed him to get up on one of the storage crates unassisted. Wolf leaned against the door to the cockpit, shoulders hunched, hands tucked into his pockets, and dark circles beneath his eyes. Opposite him, Jacin stood against the wall beside the corridor that led to the crew quarters and the galley, turned sideways as if he could only be bothered to give Cinder half his attention.

Cress led Thorne to one of the large storage crates—hoping it wasn't obvious that she was putting as much distance between herself and Wolf as she could.

Clearing her throat, Cinder came to stand before them, in front of the large netscreen embedded into the cargo bay wall.

"The royal wedding is in four days," she started. "And I think—I hope—that we're all in agreement that we cannot allow Levana to become the Commonwealth's empress. Her coronation would be a legally binding position that couldn't be easily undone, and giving her that sort of power . . . well. You know." She scuffed her boots against the metal floor. "Our plan before had been to interrupt the wedding and attempt to publicly dethrone Levana while she was here, on Earth. But Dr. Erland has convinced me that it won't make a difference. It might keep her from being empress, for now, but as long as the people of Luna still call her their queen, she will continue to harass Earth however she can. So, I believe the only way for us to truly rid ourselves of Levana is to go to Luna and persuade the people to rebel against her . . . and crown a new monarch." She seemed to hesitate, her eyes flashing toward Jacin, before she continued, "And I think . . . if we can pull it off . . . I know of a way to get us up there, without being seen."

Thorne tapped his cane against the plastic crate. "All right, Miss Cryptic. What's the new plan, then?"

Glancing around the room, Cinder tipped up her chin. "It starts with kidnapping the groom."

Thorne stopped tapping his cane and the room fell quiet. Pressing her lips, Cress dared to scan the faces of the rest of the crew, but everyone seemed perplexed.

Iko's hand shot into the air.

"Yes, Iko?"

"That is the best idea ever. Count me in."

Some of the tension started to dissipate, and Cinder even chuckled. "I hope you all feel that way, because I need your help for this to work. We need supplies still, and wedding invitations, and costumes . . ." She shook her head, clearing the dazed look that had entered her eyes. "But right now, I think our biggest problem will be locating Kai once we're inside. I haven't been able to find out anything about a tracking ID for him. The royal guard seems to have done *too* good a job at keeping any stalkers or assassins at bay."

Cress leaned forward. "Why not use the Tan Kaoru number?"

They all swiveled their attentions toward her, and Cress immediately shrank back.

"What's that?" said Cinder.

"It's, um, Emperor Kaito's tracking number. 0089175004. The net profile shows up as a palace guard named Tan Kaoru, but he's just a foil. It's really the ID that the royal security team uses to track His Majesty. I've been using it to confirm his location for ages."

"Really? How did you ever figure that out?"

Face burning, Cress opened her mouth, realized it was going to be a really long, tedious explanation, and closed it again.

"Doesn't matter," said Cinder, rubbing her temple. "If you're sure it's him."

"I am."

"So . . . great. Number 008 . . . Iko, did you get that?"

"Got it."

"Thanks, Cress."

She exhaled.

Cinder rubbed her hands together. "So, here's what I had in mind. Cress, you're in charge of disabling the palace security system. Wolf, you'll cover her."

Cress's head flew up, gaze clashing with Wolf's. She shriveled against Thorne's side. The last thing she wanted was to be paired with *Wolf*. Sure, Cinder and Thorne seemed to trust him, but how much could they really know about a man who had nearly strangled Cinder in that hotel, who had howled like a wild animal, who had been created for the purpose of killing humans in the most horrific, senseless way?

But nobody seemed to notice her fear, or if they did, they ignored it.

"Meanwhile," Cinder continued, "Iko and I will track down

Kai and get him to come back with us. We meet on one of the rooftops and Jacin picks us up and flies us out before they realize what's going on. At least, that's the idea." She tucked a strand of hair behind an ear. "It does leave one more major problem though. I won't be able to sneak in as a guest, or even a member of the staff. I'm too recognizable. So, how do I get into the palace without being noticed?"

"I could go without you?" suggested Iko.

Cinder shook her head. "Kai doesn't know you. If we're going to get him to trust us, I think . . . I think it has to be me."

Jacin scoffed, the first sound he'd made, but Cinder ignored him.

Cress bit her lip as the others started making suggestions. She could disguise herself as a member of the media? Scale the back walls? Hide in an enormous bouquet of flowers?

Already red with embarrassment, Cress forced her mouth to open. "What about . . ." She trailed off as everyone turned to her. "Um."

"What?" said Cinder.

"What about . . . the escape tunnels?"

"Escape tunnels?"

She pulled on her hair, wishing there was more of it to toy with, to twist and knot and take out her fluttering nerves on. But it was short now. Short and light and freeing, and everyone was still staring at her. Goose bumps raced down her arms.

"The ones that run beneath the palace. When they built it after the war, they had the tunnels put in to connect with fallout shelters and safe houses. In case of another attack."

Cinder glanced at the netscreen. "None of the blueprints I've seen have said anything about escape tunnels."

"They wouldn't be very safe if everyone knew about them."

"But how did you—" Cinder paused. "Never mind. Are you sure they're still there?"

"Of course they are."

"I don't suppose you remember where any of them go?"

"Of course I do." She wiped her clammy palms on her sides.

"Excellent." Cinder looked on the verge of relaxing. "So, before we get into the details... are there any questio—"

"How long before we're on Luna?" said Wolf, his voice gruff from misuse.

Cress gulped. His eyes were bloodshot. He looked like he could tear them all to pieces without a second thought.

Then she realized that there was a subtext to his question, one that everyone else had probably picked up on immediately. *Scarlet.* He really wanted to know, how long before he could go after Scarlet?

"A couple weeks, at least," said Cinder. Her voice had gone quiet, apologetic. "Maybe as many as three..."

Jaw tightening, Wolf turned his head away. Otherwise, he remained motionless, a brooding shadow in the corner.

Thorne raised a finger and Cinder went rigid again. "Yes?"

"Doesn't New Beijing Palace have its own medical labs? Say, medical labs that might have magical blindness-curing machines in them?"

Cinder narrowed her eyes. "You're not coming. It's too risky, and you would just be in the way."

Thorne grinned, unperturbed. "Think about it, Cinder. When Cress takes out that security system, every guard in that palace is going to run to one of two places. To the security control center to see what's going on, or to wherever their precious emperor is, to make sure he's safe and sound. Unless there was another, even more *obvious* disturbance happening somewhere else in the palace." He cupped his chin. "A big disturbance. Far, far away from you guys. Like, say, in the medical labs."

Knotting her hands in her lap, Cress swiveled her attention between Thorne and Cinder, wondering what sort of disturbance he had in mind. For her part, Cinder looked torn. She kept opening her mouth, before slamming it shut again. She did not seem happy to be contemplating Thorne's idea.

"I have a question too."

Cress jumped and turned to peer over her shoulder at Jacin. He looked supremely bored, one elbow propped against the wall and his hand buried in his hair, as if he were about to fall asleep standing up. But his blue eyes were sharp as he stared at Cinder.

"Let's say you manage to pull this off, not that I really think you will."

Cinder folded her arms.

"You do understand that once Levana realizes what you've done, she's not going to sit around waiting to see what you do next, right? The cease-fire will be over."

"I do understand that," said Cinder, her tone heavy as she pulled her gaze away from Jacin, meeting each of the others' in turn. "If we succeed, we'll be starting a war."

Forty-Four

THE MORNING OF THE WEDDING ARRIVED. CINDER WAS A wreck of frazzled thoughts and skittish nerves, but at the center of it was a strange sense of calm. Before the sun set again, she would know the outcome of all their planning and preparations. Either they would succeed today, or they would all become prisoners of Queen Levana.

Or they'd be dead.

She tried not to think of that as she showered and dressed and ate a meager breakfast of stale crackers and almond butter. It was all her churning stomach could handle.

The sun had just showed itself over the frosted Siberian tundra when they piled into the remaining podship—seven people crammed into a space meant for five—to embark on the forty-minute low-elevation flight to New Beijing. No one complained. The Rampion was far too large to hide. At least the podship would be able to blend in with all the other podships in a city suddenly swarming with foreign spacecraft.

The ride was torturous and mostly silent, punctuated only by Iko's and Thorne's occasional chatter. Cinder spent the ride switching between newsfeeds covering the royal wedding and the ongoing coverage of the rebellion in Farafrah.

The townspeople had given up their control of the military personnel as soon as reinforcements arrived. Rather than attempt to arrest and transport hundreds of civilians, the Commonwealth military, with permission from the African government, put the entire city into armed lockdown until they could all be thoroughly questioned and charged. The citizens were being treated as traitors to the Earthen Union for helping Linh Cinder, Dmitri Erland, and Carswell Thorne, although the news kept reporting that the government was willing to be lenient with anyone who came forward with information about the fugitives, their allies, and their ship.

So far, not one of the citizens of Farafrah seemed to be cooperating.

Cinder wondered if the Lunar townspeople were being treated the same as the Earthens, or if they were just waiting to be sent back to Luna for their real trial. To date, no journalists had mentioned that many of the rebels were Lunar. Cinder suspected the government was trying to keep that little fact quiet, to avoid mass panic in neighboring towns—or even all over the world—which would surely come once Earthens realized how easy it was for Lunars to blend in with them. Cinder could still remember when she'd believed there weren't any Lunars on Earth and how horrified she'd been when Dr. Erland had told her she was wrong. Her reaction seemed ridiculously naïve now.

As New Beijing came into view, Cinder sent the newsfeeds away. The buildings at the city's center were grand and imposing, like willowy sculptures of chrome and glass reaching toward the sky. Cinder was caught off guard by the sudden ache that hit her—homesickness. A homesickness she'd been too busy to recognize until that moment.

The palace stood regally beneath the morning sun, high on

its watchful cliff, but they veered away from it. Jacin followed Cinder's directions toward downtown, eventually mixing with clusters of hovers and, she was glad to see, multiple podships as well. Cinder's stop was first, two blocks away from the Phoenix Tower Apartments.

She took in a deep breath as she disembarked. Though autumn would be sweeping in fast over the next few weeks, New Beijing was still in summer's grip, and the day was starting off cloudless and warm. The temperature was just a click above comfortable, but not stifling with humidity as it had been the last time Cinder was in the city.

"If you don't see me at the checkpoint in ten minutes," she said, "loop the block a few times and come back."

Jacin nodded without looking at her.

"If you get the chance," said Iko, "give Adri a big kick in the rump for me. With the *metal* foot."

Cinder laughed, though the sound was awkward. Then they were gone, leaving her alone on a street she'd walked a thousand times.

She'd already called up her glamour, but it was difficult to focus, so she kept her head down anyway as she made her way to the apartments she had once called home.

It was strange to be alone, after weeks of being surrounded by friends and allies, but she was glad that no one else was joining her for this stage of the plan. It seemed weirdly important to distance herself from the girl she'd been when she lived in this apartment, and the idea of her new friends meeting her ex-stepfamily made her cringe.

Her shirt was already sticking to her back as she approached the apartment's main entrance. She waited until another resident came through, unlocking the doors with their embedded ID chip, and slipped in behind them. A familiar dread settled over her as she crossed the small lobby, a feeling that had once seemed normal. But this time, she also felt a sense of purpose as she entered the elevator. She was no longer the unwanted cyborg orphan who did as she was told and skittered off to her basement workroom to avoid Adri's bitter glares.

She was free. She was in control. She didn't belong to Adri anymore.

For perhaps the first time, she stepped out of the elevator with her head high.

The hallway was empty except for a mangy gray cat cleaning himself.

Cinder came to apartment 1820, squared her shoulders, and knocked.

Footsteps padded on the other side of the door, and she focused on her glamour. Cinder had chosen to take on the appearance of one of the officials she'd seen standing behind Kai at the last press conference. Middle-aged, slightly pudgy, with gray-flecked black hair and a too-small-for-her-face nose. She mimicked her exactly, down to the blue-gray business suit and sensible tan shoes.

The door opened and a cloud of stale hot air swept into the hallway.

Adri stood before her, tying the belt around her silk bathrobe. She almost always wore her bathrobe when she was at home, but this was not the same one Cinder was familiar with. Her hair was pulled back, and she wasn't yet wearing any makeup. There was a fine sheen of sweat on her face.

Cinder expected her body to recoil under her stepmother's

inspection, but it didn't. Rather, as she looked at Adri, she felt only a detached coldness.

This was just a woman with an invitation to the royal wedding. This was just another task to cross off the list.

"Yes?" said Adri, skeptical gaze swooping over her.

Cinder-the-Palace-Official bowed. "Good morning. Is Linh Adri-jiě at home?"

"I am Linh Adri."

"A pleasure. I apologize for disturbing you at such an early hour," said Cinder, launching into her practiced speech. "I am a member of the royal wedding planning committee, and I understand you were promised two invitations to the nuptials between His Imperial Majesty, Emperor Kaito, and Her Lunar Majesty, Queen Levana. As you are one of our distinguished civilian guests, I am honored to personally deliver your invitations for tonight's ceremony."

She held out two pieces of paper—in reality, disposable napkin scraps, but to Adri's eye, two finely crafted, hand-pressed paper envelopes.

At least, she hoped that's what Adri was seeing. The closest Cinder had yet to come to changing the perception of an inanimate object was her own prosthetic hand, and she wasn't sure if that counted.

Adri frowned at the napkins, but it quickly turned into a patient smile. No doubt because she now believed she was talking to someone from the palace. "There must be some mistake," she said. "We received our invitations last week."

Cinder feigned surprise and withdrew the napkins. "How peculiar. Would you mind if I took a look at those invitations? So I can make sure some mishap hasn't occurred?"

Adri's grin tightened, but she stepped aside and ushered Cinder into the apartment. "Of course, please come in. Can I offer you some tea?"

"Thank you, no. We'll just clear up this confusion and I won't intrude anymore on your time." She followed Adri into the living room.

"I must apologize for the heat," said Adri, grabbing a fan off a small side table and flicking it before her face. "The air has been broken for a week now and the maintenance here is completely incompetent. I used to have a servant to assist with these things, a cyborg ward my husband took in, but—well. It doesn't matter now. Good riddance."

Cinder bristled. *Servant?* But she ignored the comment as her gaze traveled over the room. It hadn't changed much, with the exception of the items displayed on the mantel of the holographic fireplace. Belongings that had held such prominent position before—Linh Garan's award plaques and alternating digital photos of Pearl and Peony—had been crammed together at the mantel's far edge. Now, at its center, stood a beautiful porcelain jar, painted with pink and white peonies and set atop a carved mahogany base.

Cinder sucked in a breath.

Not a jar. An urn. A cremation urn.

Her mouth went dry. She heard Adri padding across the living room, but her focus was pinned to that urn, and what—*who*—would be inside it.

Of their own accord, her feet began to move toward the mantel and Peony's remains. Her funeral had come and gone and Cinder had not been there. Adri and Pearl had wept. Had no doubt invited every person from Peony's classes, every person from this apartment building, every distant relative who had barely known her, who had probably griped about having to send the expected sympathy card and flowers.

But Cinder hadn't been there.

"My daughter," said Adri.

Cinder gasped and pulled away. She hadn't realized that her fingers were brushing against a painted flower until Adri had spoken.

"Gone only recently, of letumosis," Adri continued, as if Cinder had asked. "She was only fourteen." There was sadness in her voice, true sadness. It was perhaps the one thing they had ever had in common.

"I'm sorry," Cinder whispered, grateful that in her distraction, some instinct had maintained her glamour. She forced herself to focus before her eyes started trying to make tears. They would fail—she was incapable of crying—but the effort sometimes gave her a headache that wouldn't go away for hours, and now was not the time for mourning. She had a wedding to stop.

"Do you have children?" Adri asked.

"Er . . . no. I don't," said Cinder, having no idea if the palace official she was impersonating did or not.

"I have one other daughter—seventeen years old. It was not very long ago that all I could think of was finding her a nice, wealthy husband. Daughters are expensive, you know, and a mother wants to give them everything. But now, I can't stand the thought of her leaving me too." She sighed and tore her gaze away from the urn. "But listen to me, carrying on, when you must have so many other places to be today. Here are the invitations we received."

Cinder took them carefully, glad to change the subject. Now that she was seeing a real invitation up close, she changed the glamour she'd made up for the napkins. The paper was a little stiffer, slightly more ivory, with gold, embossed letters in a flourishing script on one side and traditional second-era kanji on the other.

"Interesting," said Cinder, opening the top invitation. She faked a laugh, hoping it didn't sound as painful as it was. "Ah, these are the invitations for Linh Jung and his wife. Your addresses must have gotten switched in our database. How silly."

Adri cocked her head. "Are you sure? When they arrived, I was certain—"

"See for yourself." Cinder angled the paper so Adri could see what wasn't there. What Cinder told her to see. What Cinder told her to believe.

"Goodness, so it is," said Adri.

Cinder handed Adri the napkins and watched as her stepmother handled them as though they were the most precious items in the world.

"Well then," she said, her voice barely warbling. "I'll see myself out. I hope you'll enjoy the ceremony."

Adri dropped the napkins into her robe's pocket. "Thank you for taking the time to deliver these yourself. His Imperial Majesty certainly is a gracious host."

"We are lucky to have him." Cinder meandered into the hallway. As her hand landed on the door, she realized with a jolt that this could be the last time she ever saw her stepmother.

The very last time, if she could dare to hope.

She attempted to smother the temptation that roiled inside her at the thought, but she still found herself turning back to face Adri.

"I—"

... have nothing to say. I have nothing to say to you.

But all the common sense in the world could not convince her of those words.

"I don't mean to pry," she started again, clearing her throat, "but you mentioned a cyborg before. You wouldn't happen to be the guardian of Linh Cinder?"

Adri's kindness fell away. "I *was,* unfortunately. Thank the stars that's all behind us now."

Against all her reasoning, Cinder stepped back into the apartment, blocking the doorway. "But she grew up here. Didn't you ever feel that she could have been a part of your family? Didn't you ever think of her as a daughter?"

Adri huffed, fanning herself again. "You didn't know the girl. Always ungrateful, always thinking she was so much better than us because of her . . . *additions.* Cyborgs are like that, you know. So self-important. It was awful for us, living with her. A cyborg *and* a Lunar, although we didn't know it until her mortifying spectacle at the ball." She tightened her belt. "And now she's soiled our family name. I have to ask that you not judge us by her. I did all I could to help the girl, but she was unredeemable from the start."

Cinder's fingers twitched, a familiar taste of rebellion. She ached to toss off her glamour, to yell and scream, to force Adri to *see* her, the real her, just once. Not the ungrateful, self-important little girl that Adri thought she was, but the orphan who had always just wanted a family, who had only wanted to belong somewhere.

But even as she thought this, a darker yearning climbed up her spine. She wanted Adri to be sorry. For how she had treated Cinder like a piece of property. For how she had taken Cinder's prosthetic foot and forced her to hobble around like a broken doll. For how she had taunted Cinder again and again for her inability to cry, her inability to love, her inability to ever be *human.*

She found herself reaching out with her mind, detecting the waves of bioelectricity that shimmered off the surface of Adri's skin. Before she could rein in the anger that roiled through her, Cinder pressed every ounce of guilt and remorse and shame into her stepmother's thick skull—twisting her emotions so rashly that Adri gasped and stumbled, her side slamming into the wall.

"But didn't you ever wonder how hard it must have been?" Cinder said through her teeth. A headache was coming on fast, throbbing against her dry eyes. "Didn't you ever feel guilty over the way she was treated? Didn't you ever think that maybe you could have loved her, if only you'd taken the time to talk to her, to *understand* her?"

Adri groaned and pressed one hand to her stomach, like the years of guilt had been eating away at her, slowly making her sick.

Cinder grimaced and began to ease up on the attack of emotions. When Adri met her gaze again, there were tears watering her eyes. Her breath was ragged.

"Sometimes . . . ," Adri said, her tone weak. "Sometimes I do think that maybe she was misunderstood. She was so young when we adopted her. She must have been afraid. And my darling Peony always seemed so fond of her and sometimes I think, if things had been different, with Garan, and our finances . . . perhaps she could have belonged here. You understand . . . if only she had been normal."

The last word struck Cinder between her ribs and she flinched, releasing the small strands of guilt.

Adri shuddered, swiping her robe's sleeve across her eyes.

It made no difference. Adri could be filled with all the guilt in the world, but in her own mind the blame would always be with Cinder. Because Cinder couldn't have just been *normal*.

"I-I'm so sorry," said Adri, pinching the bridge of her nose. She'd gone pale. The tears were gone. "I don't know what came over me. I—ever since I lost my daughter, sometimes my mind just—" She turned her focus back up to Cinder. "Please, don't misunderstand me. Linh Cinder—she's a lying, manipulative girl. I hope they catch her. I would do anything to make sure she can't ruin anyone else the way she ruined me and my family."

Cinder nodded. "I understand, Linh-jiě," she whispered. "I completely understand."

Curling her fingers around the invitations she'd come for, Cinder ducked back out of the apartment. The headache was splitting against her skull now, making it hard to focus on anything other than putting each foot in front of the other. She managed to maintain a flimsy grip on the glamour, not sure if Adri was still watching her, until she'd stepped into the elevator at the end of the corridor.

She froze.

On the back wall of the elevator was a mirror.

She stared back at her own reflection as the doors slipped shut behind her. Her heart started to pound. Thankfully no one else was in the elevator to witness her, because she lost her hold on the glamour immediately, gaping into her own brown eyes and, for the first time, felt horrified of who she saw in that reflection.

Because what she'd done to Adri, twisting her emotions against her, forcing her to feel guilt and shame, for no other reason than Cinder's own terrible curiosity, her own burning desire for retaliation . . .

It was something Levana would have done.

Forty-Five

IKO BLEW KISSES AND WAVED—A FLUTTERY, FIVE-FINGERED wave—as the podship coasted off the road and merged with the morning traffic. It was not a far walk to the warehouse, but she could feel her internal processor humming with excitement the whole way.

By her calculation, she would be arriving at the warehouse by 07:25. The delivery hover filled with the palace's order of sixty escorts was set to depart from the warehouse at 07:32. Half of the escorts would be dropped off at the catering office by 07:58. The rest would be delivered to the florist at 08:43, to be taken to the palace along with the human staff.

Iko expected that she would be inside the palace by no later than 09:50.

The industrial district was mostly deserted. Much of the city, and perhaps the whole world, had taken this as a holiday in order to watch the royal wedding. No one was around to notice Iko as she strutted down the alley toward the warehouse or hopped blithely over the chain-link fence into the yard where five delivery ships were backed up to the warehouse loading docks.

She was dressed simply in black slacks and a white blouse. She was still a little disappointed that she couldn't wear a fancy ball gown, but she felt stunning in her own way.

She couldn't wait for Emperor Kai to see her. The thought put an extra bounce in her step as she rounded the front of the first ship and darted up the stairs into the loading dock.

The sight before her made her pause and almost crash face-first onto her perfectly shaped nose.

The warehouse was filled with escort-droids, mostly girls, of all different skin tones and hair colors. Most were unclothed, sitting on the ground with their arms wrapped compactly around their knees and their heads tucked down. There were well over two hundred androids lined up in neat rows. Some had packing tape and protective tissue wrapped around their limbs to protect them during shipping. Some had been loaded onto pallets and settled onto plastic crates. Packing foam and cardboard littered the floor around them.

On the wall to Iko's left there were three stories of metal shelving filled with the packing crates, all labeled with the escort's makes and models and special features.

"Is this all of them?" said a man.

Iko ducked behind the wall of the warehouse, before inching forward and peering around the doorjamb. She spotted sixty androids—forty-five female and fifteen male, all standing in neat rows. They were all dressed in identical black pants and blush-toned silk tops, simple mandarin-collared dress shirts for the men, and elegant wraps for the women that tied at the waists and draped kimono-style on their arms. Each girl had her hair pulled into a tight bun with an orchid tucked into the side.

"Checking off the order now," said a woman, who was

marching between the rows and making notations on a portscreen. "The order form specified a petite model of make 618, not the medium."

"I know, but our last petite got shipped out last week. I cleared the change with the palace on Thursday."

The woman tapped something into the port. "Fifty-nine... sixty. That's all of them."

"Great. Let's load them up. Can't let them be late for their royal mission." The man pulled up the massive rolling door, opening the bay to one of the delivery ships, as the woman began making her way through the androids again, opening a panel in each of their necks. Their postures softened.

"Enter single file," ordered the man. "Squeeze in tight. It'll be a close fit."

The androids marched one by one into the ship.

There was no way Iko could get all the way over there without being noticed, and her different clothes would make it clear that she didn't belong.

The idea that they could mistake her for a rogue android and send her out for reprogramming made her wiring quiver.

Keeping low, she slinked along the wall, away from the two employees, and ducked beneath the first tower of industrial shelving. Hidden behind the crates, she made her way toward the rows of escort-droids that were waiting to be packaged up. Reaching the last row, she crouched down behind an android and felt for the latch on her neck. Iko glanced up to see that half of the rental escort-droids had already settled into the ship.

Humming to herself, she turned the android on. The processor whirred and her head raised. This one had white-blonde hair tipped with florescent green that hung to her waist. Iko brushed her hair off her shoulder and whispered, "I command you to stand up, scream, and run for the exit."

The girl launched to her feet almost before Iko finished speaking. She started to scream, a spine-chilling, ear-bleeding sound.

Iko threw herself to the ground behind the row of still-seated and oblivious androids and adjusted the volume on her audio processor, but it was too late. The android had already stopped screaming and was now running full speed for the exit, knocking her statue-like brethren over as she passed.

Iko heard the two employees' cries of shock, and then their footsteps pounding as they chased after the android. As soon as they jumped down into the loading yard, Iko bounced up and scurried through the rows of androids. The rental escorts said nothing, only blinked at her lazily as she pushed her way into their midst.

"Sorry, sorry, don't mind me, coming through, oh why *hello* there—" This to a particularly handsome Kai look-alike droid, which had no more reaction than any of the others. "Or not," she muttered, brushing past him. "Pardon me, a little space, please?"

By the time the two workers had returned, winded and ranting about faulty personality chips and those imbeciles up in programming, Iko had settled comfortably in the back of the ship, squeezed between two of her distant cousins and finding it difficult not to grin like a lunatic.

As it turned out, being human was every bit as much fun as she'd always thought it would be.

IT WAS EASY TO GRASP WHY THE GOVERNMENT OF 126 YEARS ago had chosen this spot for the royal family's safe house. It was less than ten miles from the city of New Beijing, but they were separated by such jagged cliffs that it seemed as though they had entered another country entirely. The house itself was built in a valley carved out with overgrown rice terraces, though Cinder doubted any rice had been cultivated there in generations, giving the house a sense of abandonment.

Jacin settled the podship beside the farmhouse and they stepped out onto a patch of land still soggy from heavy summer rains. The world was silent around them and the air perfumed with fall grasses and wildflowers.

"I hope the girl was right," said Jacin, moving toward the house. Despite its boarded-up windows, it appeared well maintained. Cinder suspected that a crew was responsible for checking on it a couple times a year, to patch roof tiles and ensure that the power generator wasn't malfunctioning, so that if a catastrophe ever did occur, it would still be a safe place for the emperor to retire to.

It was probably monitored, too, but she hoped that today, of all days, the country's security team would have their hands full elsewhere.

"One way to find out," she said, walking around to the side of the house, where iron doors rested over a cellar entryway. If Cress was right, these doors didn't lead to a dank storage cellar at all, but to a tunnel that would run beneath the cliffs and lead them straight into the palace sublevels.

Cinder pried open the doors and whipped her built-in flashlight around the stairs. The light caught on cobwebs and concrete and an old-fashioned switch that would light up the tunnel beneath, at least for a little distance.

"This seems to be it," she said, glancing back at the group. Thorne, blindfolded, was resting his elbow on a scowling Dr. Erland.

It was going to be a long walk.

"All right," she said. "Jacin, come back with the Rampion and circle the city until you get my comm."

"I know."

"And keep an eye out for anything suspicious. If you detect anything at all, keep flying and wait for us to contact you again."

"I know."

"If everything goes as planned, we'll be at the palace landing pad by 18:00 but if something goes wrong, we might have to come back here, or through one of the escape tunnels to the other safe—"

"Cinder," said Thorne. "*He knows.*"

She glared at him and wanted to argue, but going over their escape plan one more time wasn't going to do anything but remind her of all the things that could go wrong. Jacin *did* know—they'd discussed the matter into the ground, and everyone was all too aware of how easily this plan could fall apart without him. Without *any* of them.

"Fine. Let's go."

Forty-Six

CRESS STUDIED HERSELF IN THE FULL-LENGTH DRESSING ROOM mirror and almost began to cry.

She had somehow, someway, become a character in an opera.

Her skin had sloughed off the last of the sunburn, leaving the tiniest kiss of sun on her complexion.

Iko had cropped her hair so that it framed her face in pretty, golden waves, and though they'd had no makeup aboard the ship, Iko had also taught her to pinch her cheeks and nibble on her lips until they flushed a nice pinkish color.

She was, against her better judgment, beginning to warm to Iko. At least she wasn't as bad as that Darla had been.

And though Cress herself had been the one to place the rush purchase at the designer boutique, using a hacked financial account, she hadn't entirely believed this was all happening before this moment.

She was going to a royal wedding, in a gown of raw silk and chiffon, dyed deep royal blue to match her eyes (Iko's suggestion). The bodice was snug and the skirt so full she wasn't entirely sure she could walk without tripping. The shoes were simple form-fitting flats. Though she and Iko had discussed an array of fancy heels at length, Cinder had reminded them that Cress may have to run for her life at some point during the day's events, and practicality had won out.

"Bristol-mèi, what do you think?" asked the attendant as she finished with the last button on Cress's back.

"It's perfect. Thank you."

The girl preened. "We are thrilled that you chose us for your royal wedding debut. We could not be more honored." She scooped Cress's hair away from her ears. "Do you have your jewelry with you, to see how it looks all put together?"

Cress tugged awkwardly at her earlobe. "Oh, no, that's all right. I—uh—have to pick it up on the way. To the palace."

Though a flicker of confusion crossed the girl's face, she merely bowed her head and shuffled out of the dressing room. "Are you ready for your husband to see you?"

Cress flinched. "I suppose."

She followed the attendant out of the dressing room and into a luxuriously furnished sitting area, where she spotted her new "husband."

Wolf was scowling at a mirror and trying to pat down his unkempt hair. He wore an impeccably fitted tuxedo with a classic white bow tie and pressed lapels.

He caught Cress's eye in the reflection, and she couldn't help but stand a little straighter, but though his gaze skimmed over her, he had no reaction whatsoever.

Deflated, Cress clasped her hands. "You look great... sweetheart."

He did, in fact, look like a romance hero, all muscles and edges and chiseled bone structure. He also looked miserable.

Suddenly nervous, Cress gave a little twirl, displaying her full regalia.

Wolf only gave her a crisp nod. "The hover is waiting."

She let her hands drop to her sides, resigned to the fact that Wolf would dress for his role, but he would not play it. "Right. You have the invitations?"

He patted his breast pocket. "Let's get this over with."

IN THE DELIVERY SHIP, TRAVELING FROM THE WAREHOUSE TO the caterer, Iko had found it all too easy to command another android to switch clothes so that she could fit in with the rest of them in their staff uniforms—as long as no one was too put off by her blue hair braids, which had now been pulled into a neat bun.

She had departed the ship with the first group of rental androids at the catering office, so that when her body double was later discovered wearing the wrong clothes at the florist, Iko would be long gone.

And who would ever suspect her? She was just another brainless, obedient android.

But *that* was the hard part.

Standing in perfect unison with the others. Blinking precisely ten times a minute. Keeping quiet while the human catering staff chatted excitedly about maybe seeing the emperor himself and ruminated over how terrifying it would be if Queen Levana wasn't pleased with the food. Iko was forced to bite her tongue, allowing her programmed instincts, the instincts she'd spent her life trying to keep buried while she learned about humor and sarcasm and affection, to keep her expressionless.

From there, they had been herded into a large hover. Though it wasn't a far distance, the trip was made longer as the hover rounded to the back of the palace, near the research and laboratory facilities and, of course, the staff entrance.

Iko sensed the chatter of the catering staff grow more nervous as the hover began to slow.

She heard some gates being opened and then the hover came to a gradual stop and the staff began to file into a commercial loading dock. It was not the fancy entryway that Iko had always envisioned entering the palace through, but she tried not to let her disappointment show as she fell into line behind her stiff cohorts.

Two women were standing by the delivery entrance. One, wearing a jewel-toned sari, was notating something on her portscreen, while the other scanned ID chips, ensuring that the staff had been preapproved to work at this crucial event. When she'd finished with the humans, she ordered the escort-droids into two single-file lines. Iko slipped into the back as they were ushered inside.

They were marched through to the drab service halls, their shoes clicking in perfect synchronization. Iko kept careful track of their progress, counting doors and comparing it with the blueprint that had been downloaded to her memory. The kitchen was precisely where she expected it and even more massive in person than it had appeared on-screen, with eight industrial-size ovens, countless burners, and three counters that ran the length of the room where dozens of chefs were chopping, kneading, whisking, and measuring as they prepared to feed twelve hundred of the galaxy's most-honored guests.

The woman in the sari pulled a man in a chef's coat aside. "The androids," she yelled over the din, gesturing to Iko and the others. "Where do you want them?"

He scanned the line, his attention briefly snagging on Iko's blue hair. Evidently he determined that it wasn't in his job description to care, and he let his gaze slide past her. "Leave them there for now. We'll send them out with the regular staff during the first course. All they have to do is carry a tray and, smile. Think they can handle it?"

"We've been ensured that their programming is immaculate. It would be best if they could focus on our Lunar guests. I want them alert in case anything . . . untoward happens."

He shrugged. "No one on my staff wants anything to do with the Lunars."

The man returned to his work, organizing gold trays at different workstations, and the woman left without another look at the androids.

Iko stood very, very still, and she was very, very well behaved, and she waited. And waited. And tried to imagine what was happening with Cinder and Cress and the others. None of the kitchen staff paid them any attention other than to shoot them the occasional glare for taking up too much space in the overcrowded kitchens.

Iko waited until she was confident no one was looking, before she inched her hand behind the escort beside her. The android didn't even twitch as Iko sought out the latch on her neck, opened it, and ran her fingers over the control panel. She pushed up a switch.

"Now accepting input commands," said the android in a voice that was not quite human, not quite robot.

Iko dropped her hand to the side, and scanned the nearby chefs.

The kitchen was too loud. No one had heard.

"Follow me."

Then, when she was again sure no one was watching, she ducked into the nearest corridor.

The android followed like a trained pet. Iko took them down two hallways, listening for voices or footsteps but finding these lesser-used areas abandoned. As expected, all available staff was preparing for the ceremony and the reception, no doubt measuring the distance between plates and soup spoons at that very moment.

When they reached a maintenance closet, Iko ushered the escort-droid inside.

"I want you to know that I hold nothing against you," she said, by way of introduction. "I understand that it isn't your fault your programmer had so little imagination."

The escort-droid held her gaze with empty eyes.

"In another life, we could have been sisters, and I feel it's important to acknowledge that."

A blank stare. A blink, every six seconds.

"But as it stands, I'm a part of an important mission right now, and I cannot be swayed from my goal by my sympathy for androids who are less advanced than myself."

Nothing.

"All right then." Iko held out her hands. "I need your clothes."

Forty-Seven

CRESS DUG HER FINGERS INTO THE HOVER'S SEAT, LEANING into the window until her breath fogged against the glass. She couldn't open her eyes wide enough, not when there was so much to see, not when she could barely take it all in. The city of New Beijing was endless. To the east, a cluster of skyscrapers rose up out of the earth, silver and glass and sparkling orange under the late afternoon sun. Beyond the city center were warehouses and arenas, parks and suburbs, rolling on and on. Cress was glad for the distraction of all the new sights, the buildings, the people… Otherwise she thought she would be sick.

She gasped as the palace came into view atop its cliff, recognizing it from countless pictures and vids. Still, it was so different in real life. Even more magnificent and imposing. She splayed her fingers on the window, framing it in her vision. She could make out a line of vehicles and a mass of people outside the gates, winding down the cliff side and into the city below.

Wolf also had his fierce eyes focused on the approaching palace, but she could sense no amount of awe from him, only impatience. His knee wouldn't stop bouncing and his fingers kept flexing and tightening. Watching him was making her nervous.

He'd been so subdued back at the Rampion, so impossibly motionless. She wondered if this burst of energy was the first sign that the bomb inside him had started to tick.

Or maybe he was just anxious, like she was. Maybe he was tracing over their plan in his mind. Or maybe he was thinking about that girl. *Scarlet.*

Cress was sad that she hadn't met her. It was as if the crew of the Rampion were missing a vital piece, and Cress didn't understand how she fit. She tried to think of the things she knew about Scarlet Benoit. She'd researched her a little when Cinder and Thorne had landed the ship on her grandmother's farm, but not very much. At the time, she'd had no idea that Scarlet had joined them.

And Cress had only spoken with her once, when the whole crew had contacted her and asked for her help. She'd seemed nice enough, but Cress had been so focused on Thorne she could hardly remember anything other than curly red hair.

Fidgeting with the straps of her dress, she glanced at Wolf again, catching him in an attempt to loosen his bow tie.

"Can I ask you a question?"

His eyes swept over to her. "It's not about hacking security systems, is it?"

She blinked. "Of course not."

"Then fine."

She smoothed her skirt around her knees. "This Scarlet... you're in love with her, aren't you?"

He froze, becoming stone still. As the hover climbed the hill to the palace, his shoulders sank, and he returned his gaze to the window. "She's my alpha," he murmured, with a haunting sadness in his voice.

Alpha.

Cress leaned forward, propping her elbows on her knees. "Like the star?"

"What star?"

She stiffened, instantly embarrassed, and scooted back from him again. "Oh. Um. In a constellation, the brightest star is called the alpha. I thought maybe you meant that she's . . . like . . . your brightest star." Looking away, she knotted her hands in her lap, aware that she was blushing furiously now and this beast of a man was about to realize what an over-romantic sap she was.

But instead of sneering or laughing, Wolf sighed. "Yes," he said, his gaze climbing up to the full moon that had emerged over the city. "Exactly like that."

With a quick twist to her heart, Cress's fear of him began to subside. She'd been right back at the boutique. He *was* like the hero of a romance story, and he was trying to rescue his beloved. His alpha.

Cress had to bite the inside of her cheek to keep her imagination from skittering away with her. This wasn't some silly story. Scarlet Benoit was a prisoner on Luna. It was very likely that she was already dead.

It was a thought that settled heavy in Cress's gut as the hover pulled in front of the palace gates.

A greeter opened the door, and thousands of voices crowded in around them. With a shudder, Cress gave the greeter her hand as she'd seen girls do on the net dramas. Her heel hit the tiled drive and she was suddenly surrounded. Crowds of journalists and onlookers—both peaceful and angry—flocked around the courtyard, snapping photos, calling out questions, holding up signs that urged the emperor not to go through with this.

Cress ducked her head, wanting to crawl back into the hover and hide from the piercing lights and throbbing chatter. The world began to spin.

Oh, spades. She was going to faint.

"Miss? Miss, are you well?"

Her throat went dry. Blood rushed through her ears and she was drowning. Suffocating.

Then a firm grip was on her elbow, drawing her away from the courtier. She stumbled, but Wolf put his iron-solid arm around her waist and squeezed her against him, forcing her to match his strides. Beside him, she felt as small and frail as a bird, but there was also a sense of protection. She focused on that, and within moments, a comforting dream slipped around her.

She was a famous net-drama actress making a big debut, and Wolf was her bodyguard. He wouldn't let anything happen to her. She simply had to hold her head high and be brave and be graceful and be confident. Her fine ball gown became a costume. The media became her adoring fans. Her spine straightened, millimeter by trembling millimeter, as the tingling darkness began to recede from her vision.

"All right?" Wolf murmured.

"I am a famous actress," she whispered back.

She dared not look up at him, afraid it would ruin the spell her imagination had cast.

After a moment, his grip loosened.

The noise of the crowd behind them faded away, replaced with the calm serenity of bubbling streams and the whisper of bamboo in the palace gardens. Cress stared straight ahead at the looming entrance, flanked by crimson pergolas. Two more courtiers waited at the top of the steps.

Wolf produced the two embossed invitations. Cress was perfectly still as the scanner light flickered over the tiny chip that was embedded in the paper. She and Wolf wouldn't have fit the roles of Linh Adri and her daughter, but it had been child's play to change the ID profiles coded on each chip. According to the portscreen, Wolf was now Mr. Samhain Bristol, parliament representative from Toronto, East Canada Province, UK, and she was his young wife. The actual Mr. Bristol was, to Cress's knowledge, still safe at home and unaware that he had a body double negating the political point he was trying to make by *not* attending the royal wedding. Cress hoped it would stay that way.

She released a breath as the courtier returned the invitations to Wolf without a hint of hesitation. "We are so pleased you could join us after all, Bristol-dàren," he said. "Please proceed to the ballroom, where you will be escorted to your seats." By the time he finished, he was already reaching for the invitations of the couple behind them.

Wolf guided her forward, and if he was sharing any of her anxiety, he didn't show it.

The main corridor was lined with palace guards in fine red coats and tasseled epaulets. Cress recognized a painted screen on one wall—mountains standing over misty clouds and a crane-filled lake. Her gaze instinctively flitted up to one of the ornate chandeliers that lined the corridor, and though it was too small for her to see, she knew that one of the queen's cameras was there, watching them even now.

Though she doubted the queen or Sybil or anyone who could possibly have recognized Cress was bothering to watch the surveillance feeds at that moment, she nevertheless turned her head away and started laughing as if Wolf had made a joke.

He frowned at her.

"These chandeliers are *extraordinary*, aren't they?" she said, putting as much lightness into her tone as she could.

Wolf's expression remained unfazed, and after a blank moment, he shook his head and resumed his steady pace toward the ballroom.

They found themselves on a landing that swooped down a grand staircase and opened up into an enormous, beautiful room. The mere size of it reminded her of the desert's expansiveness and she was overwhelmed by the same awe and dizziness she'd had before. She was glad they weren't the only ones lingering at the top of the stairs and watching as the crowd drifted in and filled up rows of plush seats beneath them. There was at least an hour before the ceremony would officially begin, and many of the guests were using the time to mingle and take in the beauty of it all.

Many pillars throughout the room were carved with gold-tinted dragons, and the walls were filled with so many bouquets of flowers, some as tall as Cress, that it was like the gardens had begun to grow wild inside. Half a dozen birdcages stood beside the floor-to-ceiling windows, displaying doves and mockingbirds and sparrows, which sang a chaotic melody that rivaled the beauty of the orchestra.

Cress turned to face Wolf so that, should anyone look at them, it would seem as though they were in deep conversation. He bent his head toward her to complete the masquerade, though his focus was on the nearest guard.

"You don't suppose we should . . . mingle, do you?"

He screwed up his nose. "I think we'd better not." Glancing around, he held his elbow toward her. "But perhaps we could go sympathize with some caged birds."

Forty-Eight

AFTER PASSING THROUGH THE DANK CELLAR, CINDER WAS glad to discover that the escape tunnel was, well, fit for an emperor. The floor was tiled and the walls were smooth concrete with dim lightbulbs set every twenty steps. They could walk without fear of Thorne tripping on jagged rocks.

Nevertheless, they were making painfully slow progress, and more than once Cinder considered leaving them behind. Thorne did a decent job of keeping up, but Dr. Erland's age combined with his short legs made his pace feel like an agonizing crawl. If she didn't think it would offend him, she would have offered him a piggyback ride.

She kept reminding herself that they had planned for this. They were right on schedule.

It would all be fine.

She told herself again and again.

Eventually she began to notice signs that they were approaching the palace. Stockrooms filled with nonperishable goods and jugs of water and rice wine. Power generators that sat silent and unused. Large rooms, empty but for enormous round tables and uncomfortable-looking chairs, black netscreens and switch panels and processors—not state of the art, but new enough that it was clear these escape tunnels would be ready for use if they were ever needed. Should the royal family ever need to go into hiding, they would be able to stay down here for a long time.

And not just the royal family, Cinder realized as they trudged on, passing more stockrooms and hallways that branched in every direction. This was a labyrinth. It seemed that there was enough space for the entire government to come live down here, or at least everyone who worked in the palace.

"We're almost there," she said, tracking their position through satellite navigation and the map on her retina display.

"Wait, where are we going again? It's been so long since we left the ship, I can't remember."

"Very funny, Thorne." She glanced back. Thorne was walking with one palm on the wall, and Dr. Erland was using his cane. She wondered how long it had been since Thorne had given it to him, and how long it had been since the doctor's breathless wheezing had begun in earnest. She'd hardly noticed it, too preoccupied with the plan that filled up her head.

Now, seeing beads of sweat on the doctor's brow, dripping down from the brim of his hat, she paused. "Are you all right?"

"Dreamy," he breathed, his head lowered. "Just holding on . . . to a comet's tail. Stardust and sand dunes and . . . why is it so . . . blasted hot in here?"

Cinder rubbed the back of her neck. "Right. Um. We made good time," she lied. "Maybe we should rest for a minute?"

The doctor shook his head. "No—my Crescent Moon is up there. We stick to the plan."

Thorne inched toward them, looking equally perplexed. "Isn't it a full moon tonight?"

"Doctor, you're not having hallucinations, are you?"

Dr. Erland narrowed his blue eyes at her. "*Go.* I'm right behind. I'm . . . I'm better already."

Part of her wanted to argue, but she couldn't deny that there wasn't a whole lot of time to waste even if he wanted to. "Fine. Thorne?"

He shrugged and swung his hand toward her. "Lead the way."

Cinder double-checked the map and moved forward, waiting for one of the corridor offshoots to line up with the instructions Cress had given her. When she spotted a stairwell curling up out of view, she slowed down, and checked their location with the palace blueprint. "I think this is it. Thorne, watch your step. Doctor?"

"Hearty good, thank you," he said, gripping his side.

Bracing herself, Cinder started to climb. The stairs wrapped upward, the lights from below fading into shadows and, eventually, so much darkness that she turned on her flashlight again. The wall was smooth and undecorated but for a metal handrail. Cinder estimated that she'd trekked up three stories' worth of steps before she came to a door. It was big enough for four people to walk through side by side, made of thick, reinforced steel. As expected, there were no hinges and no handle on this side—a fail-safe in case anyone discovered the entrance into the safety tunnel and tried to sneak into the palace.

This door was only meant to be opened from the inside.

Gripping the handrail, Cinder raised her other fist and tapped out a melody.

Then she waited, wondering if she'd been loud enough, wondering if they were too soon, wondering if they were too late and the plan had already fallen apart.

But then she heard a noise. A thunking deadbolt, a grinding lock mechanism, the squeak of unused hinges.

Iko stood before her, beaming and holding a pile of neatly folded clothes. "Welcome to New Beijing Palace."

THOUGH HE DIDN'T WANT TO ADMIT IT OUT LOUD, THORNE was sad to be splitting up from Cinder and going forth with only the grumpy, wheezing doctor to act as his guide. So far, he hadn't sensed a whole lot of warmth coming off the old man, who didn't seem to think that fixing Thorne's blindness was a big priority, not to mention the crazy babble he'd been spouting down in the tunnels. Nevertheless, here they were. In the palace. Heading toward the labs where they would find the equipment necessary to do all that weird pseudo-science optical-repair stuff the doctor had talked about.

Alone.

Just the two of them.

"This way," said the doctor, and Thorne adjusted his direction, keeping one hand on the wall. He missed the cane, but he could hear it clacking up ahead of him, and the doctor seemed to need it more.

Thorne really, really hoped the doctor wasn't about to keel over. That would ruin oh so many things about this day.

"See anybody?" Thorne asked.

"Don't ask stupid questions."

Thorne scowled, but kept his mouth shut. It was as they'd hoped. No one would expect a palace break-in from the top-secret escape tunnels, so while all the guard power was being kept at the palace gates and around the ballroom, he and the doctor should have the lab wing all to themselves.

At least, until it was time to draw some attention away from Cinder and Cress.

The surface of the wall changed beneath his fingers, from a warm, papery texture, to something cool and smooth. He heard a door open.

"Here," said the doctor. "More stairs."

"Why not take the elevator?"

"It's android operated. Would require an authorized ID chip."

Thorne gripped the handrail and followed the doctor up, and up. The doctor had to stop twice to catch his breath, and Thorne waited, trying to be patient, all the while wondering what Cress was doing. If she would be ready when the time came.

He didn't dwell on it. She was with Wolf. She would be fine.

Finally, the doctor pushed open another door. A short distance across hard, slick floors. The new hum of lights overhead.

"Cozy Lab 6D. This is where I met the princess, you know."

"Lab 6D. Right. I've had good success meeting princesses in research labs myself." His nose wrinkled. The room smelled of hospitals, sterile and cold and medicinal.

"There's a lab table about four steps ahead of you. Lie down."

"Really? You don't want to take a break, catch your breath . . . ?"

"We don't have *time*."

Gulping, Thorne inched forward until his hand smacked a padded table. He sought out the edge before lifting himself onto it. Tissue paper crinkled beneath him. "But isn't this the part where you shove sharp objects into my pelvic bone? Maybe we don't want to rush."

"Are you nervous?"

"Yes. Terribly so, yes."

The doctor snorted. "Just like you. To finally show a bit of humanity beneath the arrogance, and of course it's only a concern for yourself. I'm hardly surprised."

"Wouldn't *you* be a little concerned in this situation? My eyesight. My pelvis."

"My country. My princess. My daughter."

"What *daughter*? What are you even talking about?"

The doctor harrumphed and Thorne could hear him banging through drawers. "I suppose your eyesight *was* lost while attempting to rescue Crescent from that satellite. For that alone, I suppose I do owe you."

Thorne scratched his cheek. "I suppose you do?"

"Did she tell you, by chance, how long she'd been imprisoned?"

"Cress? Seven years, in the satellite."

"Seven years!"

"Yeah. Before that I guess she was kept with a bunch of other shells in some volcanic dormitories or something. I don't remember. That thaumaturge had been collecting blood samples from them, but Cress didn't seem to know why."

A cabinet door slammed shut, followed by silence.

"Doctor?"

"Collecting blood samples? From shells?"

"Weird, right? But at least she wasn't subjected to any bizarre genetic tampering like Wolf." Thorne shook his head. "I'm not sure about those Lunar scientists. They seem to be doing a lot of crazy stuff up there."

Another silence, before more rustling. Thorne heard a chair or a table being wheeled toward him.

"They must have been using shell blood to develop the antidote," the doctor mused. "But the timing doesn't make sense. She was taken before letumosis even broke out, here on Earth. Before it was known to exist."

Thorne tilted his ear toward the doctor as his rambling faded off. "What now?"

"Unless... *Unless*."

"Unless... what now?"

"Oh, stars. That's why they wanted them. The poor children. My poor, sweet Crescent Moon..."

Thorne settled his chin on his palm. "Never mind. You finish your nonsensical ramblings and let me know when you're ready to proceed."

Another rumble of wheels on the hard floor. "You do not deserve her, you know," the doctor said, with a new edge to his tone.

"I'm sure I—wait, what?"

"I hope she comes to her senses soon, because I see how she looks at you and I do not care for it, not one bit."

"Who are we talking about?"

Something clattered as the doctor dropped what Thorne assumed were medical tools onto a metal tray. "It doesn't matter now. Lie down."

"Pause one second. And be honest." Thorne held up a finger. "Are you having a mental breakdown right now?"

The doctor huffed. "Carswell Thorne. I may have just made a very important discovery that must be shared with Emperor Kaito and the other Earthen leaders immediately. But that cannot happen until we have finished with this whole charade. Now, by my estimation, we have fewer than five minutes to extract the needed stem cells and divide them for the regenerating solution. I may not like you, but I am aware that we are on the same side, and we are both invested in seeing Cress and Cinder leave this palace today, alive. Now, are you going to trust me or not?"

Thorne considered the question for probably longer than the

doctor wanted him to, before he sighed and lay back on the table. "Ready when you are. But first, don't forget to—"

"I haven't forgotten. Activating letumosis outbreak alarm—now."

Thorne heard the soft pad of fingertips on a netscreen, and then a blaring siren screamed through the halls.

Forty-Nine

CRESS WAS GETTING ANTSY. THE ROYAL NUPTIALS WERE SLATED
to begin in a mere twenty-seven minutes, and as far as she could
tell, all guards and security personnel were still very much at
their stations. On top of that, she and Wolf were running out of
ways to make themselves inconspicuous without having to
relocate to their seats. So far they'd each nibbled at the prawn
hors d'oeuvres being waiter-passed (Cress: one, Wolf: six), taken
turns excusing themselves to pretend to use the washroom while
really trying to discern if any of the guards appeared concerned
about a potential security breach, and three times Cress had had
to laugh dreamily and hold Wolf's hand in order to get some loi-
tering female admirer to mosey on. It was the most impressive
acting she'd ever done, because touching Wolf made her uneasy
and it was difficult to imagine him making any jokes.

"Maybe we should start thinking of a Plan B," Cress murmured when she noticed that the symphony had begun replaying
their set.

"Already done," said Wolf.

She peered up at him. "Really? What is it?"

"We continue on to the security center as planned. I just have
to knock out a lot more guards between here and there."

She chewed on her lip, not terribly enthusiastic with Plan B. Then—"There. Look."

She followed his gesture. Two guards were speaking with their heads lowered. One had badges indicating a significantly higher rank. He pointed down a corridor, in the direction of the research wing.

Well, it was really in the direction of just about anything, but Cress hoped he was talking about a disturbance in the research wing. That would mean that the others had made it inside and raised the alarms.

A second later, the two guards left the ballroom.

"Do you think they've done it?" Cress said.

"Time to find out."

Wolf offered her his elbow and together they meandered out into the main corridor. The remaining guards paid them no attention as they turned down a connecting hallway. Cress kept repeating the instructions that she'd memorized—take the fourth hallway on the right, past the courtyard with the tortoise fountain, then the second left. Her heart began to pound fervently in her chest.

Twice they were stopped by palace staff, and twice they asked for directions like confused, slightly drunk wedding guests and had to backtrack to a safe hiding place before Wolf deemed it safe to move again. But no alarm was raised and no guards came for them. Cress knew they had already been captured on countless cameras set throughout the palace, but she and Wolf wouldn't be recognizable like Cinder or Thorne or Dr. Erland, and even if they did raise suspicions, she hoped everyone would be too distracted by the emergency in the research labs to care. Still, the farther they got from the ballroom, the less likely it was that anyone would buy their innocence act.

She was grateful when Wolf's pace picked up. Cinder and Iko would be waiting on them now, and they were running out of time.

They reached a skybridge that locked together two of the palace's towers. The glass floor showed a peaceful stream bubbling underneath, amid lush grasses and heavy-headed chrysanthemums. Past the bridge, they found themselves in a circular lobby, with empty seating arrangements carved from dark wood, statues of mythical creatures circling the perimeter, and a jungle of potted bamboos and orchids giving the room a heady scent.

Recognizing the space, Cress marched to a three-foot carving of a luck dragon and spun it around on its pedestal to face the wall. "Lunar camera in the left eye," she explained, then hurried toward the elevators.

A white android stood in the center of the elevator bank with its pronged grippers folded in front of its abdomen. It flashed a blue sensor over them.

"I apologize for the inconvenience," it said, in a perfect monotone meant to convey a diplomatic lack of bias. "We are experiencing a level-one security breach and all elevators have been temporarily shut down. Please enjoy a hot cup of tea while we wait for clearance." One of its prongs gestured to an alcove where a machine held a fine porcelain teapot, steaming at its spout, and an assortment of leaves and spices.

"Do you have security override capabilities?" Cress asked the android.

"I do, but only an official code or—"

Cress crouched down and swiveled the android away from her. "Don't suppose you have a screwdriver or something we can use to open the control panel?"

"—a palace official with sufficient clearance—"

Wolf stooped over her, dug his fingernails into the groove, and snapped the whole panel off in his fist.

"—could override a level-one security breach. I apologize for the continued inconvenience, but I have to ask that you—"

Wolf pulled the portscreen that the doctor had given him out of his pocket and passed it to Cress. She yanked out a connector cable and plugged it into the android, stopping the automatic diagnostics scan before it could begin. She began a manual search for the security override settings.

"—stop tampering with official government property. Tampering with a royal android could result in a fine of up to 5,000 univs and six months of— Identity confirmed: Royal Adviser Konn Torin. Security override complete. Awaiting instructions."

"Elevator to main floor," said Cress.

"Proceed to Elevator A."

Cress ejected the cable. Wolf pulled her to her feet as the nearest doors opened and tugged her inside.

Her heart was thumping as the elevator descended. She imagined those doors opening again onto an army of guards, their guns aimed and ready. She figured that by now they were no doubt being watched. Thorne's distraction could only count for so much, and there were two cameras in each elevator in the palace. The only question was how long it would take any guards to reach them once they figured out where they were heading.

The elevator came to a stop. The doors hesitated for too long, and her pulse fluttered wildly, until they opened onto an empty hallway. She released a long-held breath.

This floor of the palace was mostly business space, used for diplomatic meetings and the offices of a multitude of government officials. She recognized bits and pieces of it. The name plaque on that desk. The painting on that wall. In her head, Cress was back in her satellite, even as she and Wolf jogged through the carpeted corridor. She was seeing Wolf and herself through the cameras along the ceilings. She was picturing how the two of them would have looked to her from up there, always disconnected and uninvolved and watching, watching. As they rounded a corner, she imagined herself clicking to another feed. As they passed one camera, she pictured it changing from their front view to their backs.

They reached the next elevator bank without issue, though this one had no watchful android.

She tapped the elevator key, but it remained blank. The words ELEVATORS TEMPORARILY DOWN DUE TO LV. 1 BREACH were scrolled across its screen in red text. Cress scowled and dug her fingernails around the frame. Surely there was a way to get clearance in the event that someone important enough needed to get past, but without a designated android—

She was grabbed by the elbow and hauled back. She yelped, thinking for a moment a guard had captured her, but it was only Wolf pulling her toward an alcove.

"Stairs," he said, yanking open a door. As it shut behind them, Cress heard the sounds of boots clomping in the distance.

Her heart leaped into her throat and she glanced at Wolf to see if he'd heard, but before she could speak, he swept her over one shoulder and was jumping over the stairs, leaping down to the landing in a single bound. She squealed, but then clamped her hand over her mouth to rein in her sudden terror.

Down, down, down. Finally they passed a plaque labeled SUB-LEVEL D: MAINTENANCE / SECURITY.

This time, when Wolf set her down and pushed open the door, it felt as if they were no longer inside the palace at all. The walls were plain white, the floors dull concrete gray. The stairwell had spilled them into a small lobby, with the elevator off to their left and a cluttered desk in front of them. Behind the desk was a room fully enclosed in tinted glass, where an empty chair sat before a bank of three dozen screens showing security footage within the palace and the surrounding property. Four of the screens were flashing security-breach warnings.

And then there was the guard, aiming a gun at them.

"Stay where you are! Put your hands where I can see them!"

Cress shakily moved to follow his command, but before her fingertips could even brush her hair, Wolf had shoved her out of the way. She cried out and fell to the ground. Her dress ripped somewhere in the lining and a gunshot echoed off the concrete. She screamed and covered her head.

"Cress, get up. Now."

Pulling her arms away, she saw that the guard was unconscious and slumped against his desk. Bending down, Wolf kicked the gun away, then slid the guard toward the glass door and held his wrist over the ID scanner. A light flickered green.

"Come on. There were more guards right behind us."

Trembling, Cress pushed herself off the floor and followed Wolf into the security control room.

Fifty

"AM I WEARING THIS RIGHT?" CINDER SAID, FIDGETING WITH
the belted wraparound blouse that had three different ties that
were supposed to lace together in some mysterious fashion.

"Yes, it's fine," said Iko. "Would you stop moving your head?"
She slapped her hands on Cinder's ears to hold her head still.

Cinder shifted from foot to foot, trying to calm her racing
thoughts while Iko twisted her hair into a pinching bun that made
her scalp throb. It seemed as if it had been hours since Thorne
and Dr. Erland had left them, though the clock counting the seconds in her head claimed it had been less than seventeen minutes.

In one corner of her vision was a newsfeed hosting its own
countdown. The countdown to the start of the royal wedding.

Cinder shut her eyes and tried to will away another bout of
nausea. She'd never been so nervous in her entire life, and it wasn't
just the waiting or the knowledge that so many things could go
wrong or the terror that she could be caught and returned to
prison at any minute.

What really terrified her, what really made her nerves hum,
was knowing that she was going to see Kai again. Face to face.
Looking into his eyes for the first time since she'd fallen in the
palace gardens.

At the time, his expression was so filled with shock and betrayal her heart had split in two, especially when not an hour before she had stood dripping wet at the top of the ballroom stairs and Kai had looked up at her and smiled.

Smiled.

The two expressions could not have been more different, and they'd both been directed at her.

She didn't know what to expect when he saw her now, and the uncertainty was terrifying.

"Cinder—are you watching the news?"

She refocused on the news broadcaster who was reporting word of a temporary delay to the ceremony. They were being told that all was well and the ceremony would begin shortly, but that the security team was taking extra precautions—

"That's it. Let's go."

Only once they peered down the service corridor in each direction, confirming both that no one was around and that the pale lights on the nearest ceiling cameras were off, did Cinder begin to appreciate the extent of her vulnerability.

She was the most-wanted criminal in the world, returning to the scene of her crime.

But there was no changing her mind now.

She sent the news broadcast away, pulling the palace blueprint over her vision instead. "Locating now," she said, using her internal positioning system to mark where she and Iko stood, before inputting the tracker code for Emperor Kai that Cress had given them.

She held her breath while it searched, and searched.

And then—there he was. A green dot in the north tower. Fourteenth floor. The sitting room connected to his personal chambers. He was pacing.

She shivered. She was so close to him, after being a galaxy apart.

"Got him."

They kept to hallways that she expected to be unoccupied. She found herself continuously glancing at the cameras on the ceilings, but not one of them moved or flashed or indicated that it was turned on, and slowly Cinder's paranoia began to fade.

Cress had done it. She'd shut down the security system.

Then they rounded a corner into the elevator bank of the north tower and Cinder crashed into a woman.

She stumbled back. "Oh—sorry!"

The woman eyed Cinder. She was a member of the staff, dressed in the same blush-toned top and black pants that they were.

Cinder called up her glamour, turning her cyborg hand into a human one and giving her complexion the same flawless tone as an escort's. She flashed a smile that she hoped hid her surprise and bowed.

It took a few heartbeats more to realize why she was so startled. Not because they'd run into someone here in the hall-way, but because she hadn't sensed this woman around the corner.

It was a feeling so subtle she'd hardly known she was doing it before—reaching out with her consciousness and lightly touching on the bioelectricity that shimmered off every human being. She'd gotten used to feeling Thorne and Wolf and Jacin and Dr. Erland when they were nearby, their presence like a shadow in her subconscious. It was instinctual, no more difficult than breathing.

But this woman was a blank slate to her. Like Cress, a shell. Like Iko.

"My apologies," said the woman, returning Cinder's bow.

"This wing of the palace is off-limits to anyone without a crown-issued pass. I must ask you to leave."

"We have a pass," said Iko, smiling brightly. "We've been asked to check with His Imperial Majesty and see if he requires any refreshments while we wait for the ceremony to begin." She made to step around the woman, but a palm shot out and pressed against her sternum.

The woman's serene gaze, though, remained on Cinder.

"You are Linh Cinder," she said. "You are a wanted fugitive. I am required to alert authorities."

"Er, sorry, but this is a bad time for me." Stepping back, Cinder raised her prosthetic hand and fired a tranquilizer dart at the woman's thigh. It clanged, the tip catching briefly in the fabric of her pants, before it fell to the floor.

That was all the confirmation she needed.

Cinder clenched her jaw and swung for the side of the woman's head, but the woman ducked and whipped a leg up, her foot catching Cinder in the side.

She grunted and stumbled away, her back crashing into a wall.

With an impassive expression, the woman leaped after her, aiming an elbow for Cinder's nose. Cinder barely blocked, using the momentum to spin around, locking her elbow around the woman's neck.

The woman bucked her hips, sending Cinder tumbling over her head. She landed on her back, her vision spotty.

"Iko—she's a—"

She heard a click and the fighting stalled around her.

Cinder moaned. "An android."

"I noticed," said Iko, holding up a control panel studded with snapped wires. "Are you all right?" Iko crouched beside Cinder, her expression a perfect model of concern.

Though she was still panting, Cinder found herself smiling. "You're the most human android I've ever known."

"I know." Iko scooped a hand beneath Cinder and helped her sit up. "Your hair is a mess, by the way. Honestly, Cinder, can't you look presentable for more than five minutes?"

Cinder braced herself on Iko and climbed to her feet. "I'm a mechanic," she said, an automatic response. She glanced at the woman, whose arms had fallen limp at her sides and whose eyes were staring emptily toward the elevators.

Shaking her head to clear it, Cinder tapped the elevator call button. The screen flashed twice with a warning about a level-one security breach, before turning green. The nearest elevator opened.

Somewhere, many floors underneath the palace, Cress had just given her clearance.

Together, she and Iko dragged the android into the elevator and left her in a corner. Cinder's hands were shaking so hard with adrenaline she almost pushed the button for the wrong floor. As the doors shut, she pulled the last few bobby pins out of her hair and instead whipped it into a quick, messy ponytail. Five minutes of being presentable had been plenty enough.

In her head, she narrowed her focus down to those two separate dots, merging ever closer.

Herself—gliding up between the tower floors.

And Kai.

SOMETHING WAS WRONG. THAUMATURGE SYBIL MIRA COULD sense it in the way the Earthen guards were acting, in how there were too many whispers and hands resting on gun hilts. As she followed behind Queen Levana, Sybil found herself growing tense.

Her queen would not be happy should anything go wrong.

She glanced sideways at Thaumaturge Aimery. His eyes met hers. He'd noticed it too.

She looked ahead to her queen, who was wearing red and gold, traditional Commonwealth wedding colors. Her head was draped in a sheer veil and the long train of her gown had been embroidered with the ornate tails of the dragon and phoenix motif that converged in the front. The fabric billowed like a sail as she walked. Her posture suggested poise and confidence, as it always did. Had she noticed anything yet? Even if she had, she may only attribute it to her presence, and how the weak Earthens would simultaneously ogle and cower from her. But Sybil knew it was more than that.

The hair prickled on her neck.

They were nearly to the main corridor when a guard stepped in front of their escorts. Her Majesty came to a stop, her skirt settling at her feet. Aimery stopped as well, but Sybil continued forward to place herself at Her Majesty's side, taking care not to favor her uninjured leg. She may have been forced to tell the queen about her failure in capturing Linh Cinder, but she'd so far managed to avoid the embarrassing fact that she was shot during the fight. By her *own guard*, no less.

"My sincerest apologies, Your Majesty," the Earthen guard began with a quick bow.

Sybil glowered, and with a twitch of her fingers, the guard dropped to one knee. He grunted.

"You will show my queen proper respect when addressing her," Sybil said, slipping her hands into her sleeves.

It took a moment for the guard to recover from his shock. She did not allow him to stand or even raise his head from its lowered, respectful position, and finally he cleared his throat and proceeded, his voice more strained than before. "Your Majesty, we are experiencing an unanticipated malfunction of our security systems. We've determined that for your safety, and the safety of Emperor Kaito, we must delay the ceremony." He paused to inhale. "We're optimistic that the delay will be short. However, I'm afraid I must ask you to return to your quarters. We will inform you immediately once this matter is cleared and we can proceed with the ceremony." A drop of sweat traced down his neck. "Your escorts will happily return you to—"

"What sort of malfunction?" asked the queen.

"I'm afraid I can't divulge any details at this point, but we are working to correct the—"

"That is not an acceptable answer to my queen's reasonable question," said Sybil. "You have suggested that my queen may be in danger. I demand to know what details you have of the situation, so that I may personally see to her safety. We will not be kept ignorant on these matters. Now, what sort of malfunction are you experiencing?"

She could see his jaw flexing, his eyes fixed on the ground before the queen's feet. Sybil doubted he was high ranking enough to answer the question, but his fear was working against his resolve. The two lower-ranked guards that had accompanied him didn't move or fidget, and yet their rigid posture hinted at their own discomfort. Perhaps she should prostrate them all.

"A manual one," the guard said finally. "Our security system has been shut down, which can only be done at the central control room."

"And that is within the palace?"

"Yes, Thaumaturge Mira."

"You're telling me that your malfunction is truly a security *breach*."

"It is a possibility we are considering. Our number one priority is the safety of our guests. Again, I must ask that you return to your quarters, Your Majesty."

Sybil laughed. "The palace may have been infiltrated. You can't keep someone away from your own security mainframe, and yet you think we'll be safe in the *guest* quarters?"

"That's enough, Sybil."

Sybil froze and glanced at her queen. Her long, pale fingers were interlaced over her skirt, but Sybil guessed that beneath the veil, her eyes would be sharp as needles.

"My Queen?"

"I am sure these men are well aware of the importance of this wedding ceremony, and the global repercussions that could follow should anything prevent this marriage from taking place. Aren't you, gentlemen?"

The guards said nothing. The kneeling man was beginning to tremble. Sybil could guess that his neck was aching from holding his head at such an awkward position.

Two steps clicked on the floor to Her Majesty's other side. "My queen asked you a question," said Aimery, his voice both calm and menacing, like the roll of distant thunder.

The guard cleared his throat. "We have no desire to delay or prevent this wedding, Your Majesty. We only wish to resolve the problems swiftly so that the ceremony can continue as soon as possible."

"See that you do," said the queen. "Sybil, Aimery, let us return to our chambers and allow these men to fulfill their responsibilities without toiling over us." She began to turn, before pausing. Her veil swished past her elbows. "Please, do send word immediately as to the safety of my groom. I will be in fits until I know he is well."

"Yes, Your Majesty," said the guard. "We will be instating extra protection outside your chambers, as well as His Majesty's, until this is resolved."

Sybil waited until they were pacing away, following behind their escorts and guards, before she released her hold on the man. She wondered if those guards had any imagination for the wrath they would incur if this interruption wasn't resolved.

The delay itself, though, was not what made Sybil anxious. It was what—or who—could have caused such a delay.

Though Levana refused to even speak about the escaped cyborg, other than to rail about the inadequacy of the Earthen military, Sybil had deduced what her queen would not say outright.

It had been easy to extract her hostage's implications during the interrogation, and the redheaded girl had not been lying. Linh Cinder, the cyborg, was truly Princess Selene.

Sybil had seen the girl's glamour at the ball. More telling, she had seen Her Majesty's reaction to it. Her lost niece was the only person in the galaxy who could have caused such an uproar, and the idea that Princess Selene was out there, evading her, taunting her, would be driving the queen mad.

So far, the girl had proven herself to be remarkably resourceful. Escaping from New Beijing. Evading authorities in both Paris and that little African village. Even managing to get away from *her*.

Could it be that she was behind this? Would she be so reckless as to try to stop the queen's wedding?

If so, perhaps Sybil had not been giving her enough credit. A palace breach. A security malfunction. A disabled syst—

She almost missed a step. She was not one for clumsiness, and Aimery noticed. She didn't return his stare. Her thoughts were already racing.

It was not possible. She was jumping to conclusions.

She reached into her sleeve for the miniature portscreen that lived in its own small pocket and pulled up the surveillance feed for New Beijing Palace. All the cameras and trackers she'd painstakingly installed throughout the palace over countless dreary diplomatic meetings and discussions...

UNABLE TO ESTABLISH LINK

She gnashed her teeth.

Not only had the palace's security been tampered with. Their own surveillance system was down.

The entire system.

It didn't seem possible, but she knew Crescent's work when she saw it.

She tucked the port away. "My Queen."

The group halted.

"I would like to request permission to investigate this security breach myself."

One of the guards fidgeted. "I do apologize, but we've been ordered to return all of you to—"

Sybil twisted the bioelectricity around his head and the guard fell silent with a strangled gasp. "I was not asking *your* permission."

After a moment, Levana gave a single nod, the curtain of material barely shifting. "Granted."

She bowed.

"And, Sybil, should you find these perpetrators, I order their immediate deaths. I cannot be bothered with trivial arrests and trials on my wedding day."

"Of course, My Queen."

Fifty-One

KAI LAUGHED, A ROUGH SOUND THAT BORDERED ON HYPER-
ventilating. He couldn't tell if this unexpected turn of events was
terrible, or very, very funny. "The palace security has been *compromised*? What exactly does that mean?"

"The royal guard hasn't had time to document an official report, Your Majesty," said Torin, "but we do know that all security
cameras and scanners, including weapon scanners, have mal-
functioned. Or at least that your guards are unable to access
their feeds at this time."

"How long have they been down?"

"Almost eleven minutes."

Kai paced to the window. He caught sight of a groom in his
reflection—a white silk shirt split by a red sash that hung from
his shoulder. It made him think of blood every time he saw it.
He'd spent the past hour pacing around his private chambers and
avoiding his reflection as much as possible.

"Do you think Levana has anything to do with it?"

"It seems out of character for her to do anything that could
upset today's ceremony."

Kai strung his fingers through his hair. Priya would have a fit when she saw him, after those specialty stylists had spent forty minutes adjusting every last hair on his head.

"Your Majesty, I might ask that you move away from the window."

He turned around, surprised at the concern in Torin's voice. "Why?"

"We have to assume that this breach constitutes a threat to your safety, but we can't guess where that threat might come from."

"You think someone's going to try and assassinate me through a window? On the fourteenth floor?"

"We don't know what to think, but I don't want to take unnecessary risks until we have more information. The captain of the guard should be here shortly. I'm sure he has a plan in place for such circumstances. We may be forced to evacuate, or go into lockdown mode."

Kai drew away from the window. Lockdown mode? He hadn't known such a thing existed.

"Are we canceling the ceremony?" he asked, hardly daring to hope.

Torin sighed. "Not officially. Not yet. That course of action is a last resort. Queen Levana and her court have been confined to their quarters and, if necessary, will be escorted to a remote location. The ceremony is temporarily delayed, until we can ensure your safety and the safety of the queen."

Kai briefly perched on the edge of one of the carved-wood chairs but, too anxious to sit, bounced back to his feet and resumed pacing. "She's going to be furious. You might want to warn whoever has to break this news to her."

"I suspect everyone is well aware."

Kai shook his head, baffled. For weeks he'd lived in a mental fog, caught between misery and apprehension, fear and nerves and the constant desperate hopes that lingered in his head. Hope that there was a way out. Hope that the wedding day would never come. Hope that Princess Selene had been found and that, somehow, she would change everything.

And now—this.

There was no way it was a coincidence. Someone had purposefully hacked the palace security system. Who was capable of that? And what did they want to do, simply stop the wedding? There were plenty of people in the world who didn't want this wedding to take place, after all.

Or were their motivations more dangerous, maybe even sinister?

He peered up at Torin. "I know you don't like it when I talk about conspiracies, but *come on*."

Torin exhaled a long, painful sounding breath. "Your Majesty, this time, we may be in agreement."

Someone knocked, startling them both. Normally a speaker in the wall would have announced the arrival of whoever was on the other side, but that must have been a part of the failed system.

Which made Kai question—shouldn't there have been a backup system? Or had that, too, been compromised?

Torin moved toward the door first. "Announce yourself."

"Tashmi Priya, requesting to speak with His Majesty."

Kai massaged his neck as Torin unbolted and opened the door. Priya stood stiffly before them, even more put together than usual in an emerald and silver sari.

"Any news?" asked Kai.

Priya's expression was dazed, bordering on fearful. Kai braced himself for the worst, although he didn't know what the worst could be.

But instead of speaking, Priya shut her eyes and collapsed, crumpling onto the carpet.

Kai gasped and dropped down beside her. On her other side, Torin lifted her wrist, checking for a pulse.

"What's wrong with her?" Kai asked, before his eyes snagged on a small dart jutting from Priya's back. "What—"

"She'll be fine."

Kai froze.

Looked up. At black pants and a silk top and—

Cinder. His heart lurched into his throat.

She wore the same uniform as the wedding staff. Her hair was a mess, as it always was. She wasn't wearing gloves. She looked flustered.

Another girl entered behind her and shut the door. She was a little taller, with light brown skin and blue hair, though Kai couldn't spare her more than a cursory glance.

Because Cinder was there.

Cinder.

Unable to lift his jaw, Kai pushed himself to his feet. Torin stood too and stepped around Priya, trying to inch his way in between them like a shield, but Kai hardly noticed.

Cinder held his gaze. It seemed as if maybe she was waiting for something. Bracing herself. Despite the fact that her metal hand had some sort of dangerous-looking appendage jutting from one of the fingers, she looked almost bashful.

The silence was unbearable, but Kai couldn't think of a single thing to say.

Finally, Cinder gulped. "I'm sorry I had to—" She gestured at the unconscious wedding coordinator, then waved her hand like shaking it off. "But she'll be fine, I swear. Maybe a little nauseous when she comes to, but otherwise... And your android... Nainsi, right? I had to disable her. And her backup processor. But any mechanic can return her to defaults in about six seconds, so..." She rubbed anxiously at her wrist. "Oh, and we ran into your captain of the guard in the hallway, and a few other guards, and I may have scared him and he's, um, unconscious. Also. But, really, they'll all be just fine. I swear." Her lips twitched into a brief, nervous smile. "Um... hello, again. By the way."

"Ugh," said the other girl, rolling her eyes. "That was painful."

Cinder shot her a glare, but then the girl took a single step toward Kai and dipped into a graceful bow. "Your Imperial Majesty. It is *such* a pleasure to see you again."

He said nothing.

Cinder said nothing.

Torin, half positioned between Kai and Cinder, said nothing.

Finally the girl lifted her head. "Anytime now, Cinder."

Cinder jumped. "Right. Sorry."

She took a tentative step forward and looked about to speak again, but Kai finally found his voice.

"Are you *insane*?"

Cinder paused.

"Do you—are you—Queen Levana is *in this palace*. She'll kill you!"

She blinked. "Yes. I know."

"Which is why we need to stop wasting time," the girl muttered under her breath.

Kai frowned at her. "Who are you?"

She brightened. "Oh, I'm Iko! You may not remember me, but we met at the market that day you brought in the android, only I was about this tall"—she held her hand at hip height—"and shaped kind of like an enormous pear, and significantly more pale." She batted her eyelashes.

Kai returned his attention to Cinder.

"She's right," said Cinder. "We need to leave, now. And you're coming with us."

"I'm what?"

"He will do no such thing," said Torin. He started to move toward Cinder, but then his foot stalled midair and reversed. Suddenly he was stepping over Priya, walking backward until the backs of his knees hit a settee and he sank down onto the cushion.

Kai gaped at him, beginning to think this was all some bizarre anxiety dream.

"I'm sorry," said Cinder, holding up her cyborg hand. "But I have one more tranquilizer and, if you try to interfere, I'm afraid I'll have to use it on you."

Torin glared at her, putting as much seething hatred into the look as Kai had ever seen.

"Kai, I need to remove your ID chip."

He faced her again and felt—for the first time—a twinge of fear. Something clicked and he glanced down to see her ejecting a short knife from one of her fingers.

She was cyborg. This he'd almost gotten used to.

But she was also Lunar, and while he'd known that for just as long, he'd never before seen her act Lunar. Not so blatantly. Not until now.

Cinder took a step toward him.

He took a step back.

She paused, hurt flickering in her eyes. "Kai?"

"You shouldn't have come back here."

She licked her lips. "I know how this must look, but I'm asking you to trust me. I can't let you marry her."

He let out an abrupt laugh. The wedding. He'd almost forgotten about it, and he was the one in groom's clothes. "It's not your decision to make."

"I'm making it anyway." She moved forward again, and with another step back, Kai found himself pressed against a small table. Cinder's gaze dipped down and her eyes widened.

Kai followed the look.

Her foot was on the table. The child-size foot that had fallen off on the garden steps, its plating dented and the joints packed with dirt. He'd taken it out of his office when the security team had done the sweep for Levana's spy equipment.

His ears grew hot, and he felt as if he'd just been caught hoarding something strange and overtly intimate. Something that didn't belong to him.

"You, uh . . ." He gestured halfheartedly. "You dropped that."

Cinder peeled her attention away from the foot and met his gaze, speechless. He couldn't begin to guess what she was thinking. *He* didn't even know what it meant that he'd kept it.

The other girl, Iko, cupped her chin with both hands. "This is so much better than a net drama."

Cinder briefly lowered her gaze to compose herself, then held her hand toward him. "Please, Kai. We don't have much time. I need your wrist." Her voice was gentle and kind, and somehow that gave him greater pause than anything. Lunars—always so convincingly gentle, so deviously kind.

Shaking his head, he pressed his vulnerable wrist against his side. "Cinder, look. I don't know what you're doing here. I want to believe you have good intentions, but . . . I don't know anything about you. You lied to me about everything."

"I never lied to you." Cinder stole another look at the foot. "I maybe didn't tell you the *whole truth,* but can you blame me?"

He frowned. "Of course I can blame you. You had plenty of opportunities to tell me the truth."

The words seemed to surprise her, until she fisted her hands on her hips. "Right. And what if I'd said, oh, sure, Your Highness, I'd *love* to go to the ball with you, but first you should probably know that I'm cyborg. And then what?"

Kai looked away.

"You never would have talked to me again," she answered for him. "You would have been mortified."

"So you were just going to keep it hidden forever?"

"*Forever?*" Cinder waved her arm toward the window. "You are the emperor of an entire country. There was never going to be a *forever.*"

He was surprised how much the words stung. She was right. There wasn't room for such absurdity between them—an emperor. A cyborg. Her words shouldn't have hurt at all.

"What about being Lunar?" he said. "When was that going to come up?"

Cinder huffed, and he could tell she was growing exasperated. "We don't have time for this."

"How many times did you manipulate me? How much of it was just brainwashing?"

Her jaw fell open, as if she were appalled he could even suggest it. Then a fire stoked behind her eyes. "Why? Are you worried that you may have had actual feelings for a lowly cyborg?"

"I'm just trying to figure out what was real, and who *this* person is." He gestured from her head to her toes. "One day you're fixing portscreens at the market, the next you're breaking out of a high-security prison. And now—you've disabled my palace security, you're waving a knife at me, and you're threatening to tranquilize my chief adviser if you don't get what you want. What am I supposed to think? I don't even know whose side you're on!"

Cinder clenched her fists, but as his angry words settled, her eyes caught on something over his shoulder. The enormous picture window overlooking the Eastern Commonwealth. Her expression became distant. Calculating.

She took another step toward him. Kai flinched.

"I'm on *my* side," she said. "And if you want what's best for the Commonwealth, and this entire planet, you'd better be on my side too." She held out her hand, palm up. "Now give me your wrist."

He curled his fingers. "My responsibility is here. I have a country to protect. I'm not running away from that, and I'm certainly not running away with you." He tried to lift his chin, though it was difficult when Cinder's glare was making him feel about as important as a grain of salt.

"Really?" she drawled. "You'd rather take your chances with *her*?"

"At least I know when she's manipulating me."

"News flash: I have *never* manipulated you. And I hope I never have to. But you aren't the only one with responsibilities and an entire country of people who are relying on you. So I'm sorry, *Your Majesty*, but you are coming with me, and you're just going to have to figure out whether or not you can trust me when we're not so pressed for time."

Then she raised her hand and shot him.

Fifty-Two

WITHIN SECONDS OF THE DART HITTING KAI'S CHEST, HIS eyelids fluttered closed and he collapsed into Cinder. The adviser yelped and stood, but Iko intercepted him, pressing the man back as Cinder eased Kai's unconscious body onto the floor.

For a moment, she was paralyzed, her mind reeling from the things she'd just said—at what she'd just done.

"Cinder? Are you all right?" said Iko.

"Fine," she muttered, trembling as she propped Kai against the table and pulled out the dart. "He's going to hate me when he wakes up, but I'm fine." She couldn't help glancing up again, at the big picture window hung with heavy silk drapes. At her own reflection looking back at her. At the girl with one metal hand and messy hair, wearing the uniform of a servant.

She let out a slow, head-clearing breath, and pulled Kai's hand toward her.

"What are you going to do to him?"

Cinder paused long enough to look over at the adviser. His face was red with fury.

"We're taking him somewhere safe," she said. "Somewhere Levana can't get to him."

"And you think there won't be repercussions for that? Not only for you, but for everyone on this planet. Don't you realize that we are in the middle of a *war*?"

"We're not in the *middle* of a war, we're at the very beginning." She fixed her gaze on him. "And I'm going to put an end to it."

"She *can* put an end to it," said Iko. "We have a plan. And His Majesty will be safe with us."

Strangely embarrassed by Iko's confidence, Cinder refocused on Kai's wrist. She'd cut out so many ID chips in the past weeks she was almost used to it, though the first incision still reminded her of Peony's limp hand and blue fingertips. Every time.

A thick drop of blood welled up on his skin and Cinder instinctively tilted his arm so that it would roll down his fingers without soiling his white shirt.

"He believes that you've found the lost Princess Selene."

She paused and, after a beat, glanced up at Iko, then at the adviser. "He . . . what?"

"Is it true? Have you found her?"

Gulping, she refocused on Kai's wrist. Waited until her hands stopped trembling before she removed the small chip from his flesh.

"Yes," she said, her voice wary as she fished some clean bandages from her calf compartment and wrapped them around the wound. "She's with us."

"Then you also believe she can make a difference."

Her teeth clenched, but she forced herself to relax as she secured the bandages. "She *will* make a difference. The people of Luna are going to rally around her. She's going to reclaim her throne." Retracting the knife blade, she met the adviser's glare again. "But if this wedding goes through, it won't matter. No revolution on Luna is going to nullify a marriage and a coronation. If you give her this power, there's nothing I or anyone can do to take it from her. And I know that you're smart enough to see the repercussions of *that*." With a sigh, Cinder rolled down her pant leg again and stood up. "I understand that you have no reason to trust me, but I'm going to ask you to anyway. I promise, no harm will come to Kai while he's with us."

She was met with silence and a simmering glare.

She nodded. "Fair enough. Iko?"

Iko stooped and grabbed Kai's elbow. Together, they hauled him up, an arm over each of their shoulders.

They dragged him four, five steps toward the door.

"He has another chip."

They paused.

The adviser, still seated on the couch, still glaring, sneered as if irritated with himself.

"What do you mean?"

"There is a second tracking device embedded behind his right ear. In case anyone ever tried to kidnap him."

Allowing Iko to take the brunt of Kai's weight, Cinder tentatively reached for his drooping head. She brushed his hair out of the way and pressed her fingers into the indent between his spine and skull. Something small and hard rested against the bone.

She nodded at the adviser. "Thank you," she said, ejecting the knife again.

He grunted. "If anything happens to him, Linh-mèi, I will hunt you down and kill you myself."

A DROP OF SWEAT SNAKED ITS WAY DOWN CRESS'S SPINE, BUT her hands were too busy to swipe at it. Her fingers flashed over the screens, skimming along lists and coding, triple-checking her work.

The closed-circuit security system was down, including all cameras, scanners, identity-encoded software, and alarms.

Both backup systems were disabled, and she could find no evidence of a third backup waiting to rise up and ruin all her hard work as soon as she turned away.

The connection to the Lunar spyware had been severed.

She'd ensured that all digital locks in the north tower were disabled, along with any doors in between this security control center and the research facility wing. She'd been extra diligent about disrupting the radar technology embedded in the roof-top's decorative *qilin* sculptures, so they wouldn't detect the Rampion's approach.

All of the elevators were at a standstill except the single elevator in the north tower that was still stationed on the fourteenth floor, waiting for Cinder and Iko to make their escape.

Which was taking *forever.*

She inched her fingers away from the master screen and looked up. The dozens of screens surrounding her had gone black, but for the repeating gray text: SYSTEM ERROR.

"That's it." She sat back. "I think that's it."

No one was around to hear her. The glass wall separating her from Wolf and the rest of Sublevel D was soundproof, bullet-proof, and probably many other types of proof that she didn't even know about. She pushed herself away from the desk.

Wolf was out in the small lobby, leaning against the wall by the stairwell door. At some point he'd removed his tuxedo jacket and bow tie, unbuttoned his collar, and rolled up his sleeves. His hair was no longer neat and tidy, but sticking up at odd angles. He looked bored.

At his feet, scattered across the lobby floor, were at least thirty palace guards.

He met Cress's gaze just as the door to the stairwell burst open and a guard charged through, gun raised.

Cress screamed, but Wolf just grabbed the guard's arm, bent it behind his back, and targeted a precise hit to the side of his neck.

The guard crumpled and Wolf slid him neatly onto the pile of his peers.

Then he held his palms toward Cress, as if to ask what was taking so long.

"Right," she murmured to herself, heart thumping. She inspected the screen with the elevator status reports one more time, and saw that only one elevator was moving. Descending from the fourteenth floor in the north tower.

A smile tickled her lips, but was restrained behind the avalanche of anxiety. Leaning over the control panel, she attached her portscreen to the main input console and set the timer.

DR. ERLAND WATCHED THE SMALL SCREEN ON THE MACHINE'S panel as it spit out a stream of data, documenting the stability of Thorne's stem cells, each step of the automated procedure, and the details of the chemical reaction that was happening on a cellular level inside the tiny plastic vial fitted into place. It was taking ages, but they weren't in any rush. Not yet. Behind him,

Thorne was sitting on the lab table, kicking his heels against the side.

The data stream lit up.

SOLUTION COMPLETE. REVIEW PARAMETERS BELOW.

He made a quick scan of said parameters before allowing himself to feel pleased.

Ejecting the vial, he reached for an eyedropper on the counter. "Finished."

Thorne pulled the blindfold down around his neck. "Just like that?"

"Your immune system will have to do the rest. We'll need to saturate your eyes four times a day for a week or so. Your vision should start returning after, oh, six or seven days, but it will be gradual. Your body is practically engineering a new optical nerve, which doesn't happen overnight. Now—can you be a big boy and do the drops yourself?"

Thorne frowned. "Really? You want us to come all this way just so I can stab myself in the eye?"

Sighing, the doctor dipped the dropper into the vial. "Fine. Tilt your head back and keep your eyes open wide. Three drops in each side."

He reached forward, the clear solution bubbling up at the tip of the dropper and hovering over Thorne's wide-open eyes.

But then Dr. Erland's attention caught on a bruise on the inside of his wrist. He froze and twisted his hand around to examine it.

The bruise had formed around a dark red splotch, like blood puddled beneath the surface of his papery skin.

His stomach dropped.

Suddenly shaking, he inched away from Thorne and set the vial and the dropper on the counter.

Thorne lowered his chin. "What's wrong?"

"Nothing," Dr. Erland murmured as he reached for a drawer and pulled out a face mask, snapping it on over his mouth and nose. "Just . . . double-checking something."

He grabbed a sterilizer wash and wiped down the vial and the eyedropper, then wrapped them up in a cloth. He was feeling weak already, but that was no doubt all in his head.

Even with the mutated disease, victims still survived anywhere from twenty-four to forty-eight hours after showing symptoms. *At least.*

But he was an old man. And he'd been overexerting himself all day, with the walk through the escape tunnels and rushing through the palace. His immune system may already be strained.

He glanced at Thorne, who had begun to whistle to himself.

"I need to take a blood sample."

Thorne groaned. "Please don't tell me something got messed up."

"No. Just taking precautions. Your arm, please."

Thorne didn't look happy about it, but he rolled up his sleeve nevertheless. It was a quick test, one Dr. Erland had done a thousand times—drawing the blood and running it through the diagnostic module to check for letumosis-carrying pathogens—yet he found himself distracted by the warmth of his breaths as they caught inside the face mask.

Thorne. And—if he returned with the others—Cinder.

And his Crescent Moon.

He gripped the side of the counter to keep his hands from

shaking. Why hadn't he told her the truth before? He'd assumed they would have time. He'd believed there would be years, after Selene was crowned and Levana was gone. Years to tell her the truth. To embrace her. To tell her how much he loved her. To apologize again and again for ever letting her go.

He stared down at the bruise-like rash. Only a single bruise so far. It wasn't spreading, at least not on his arms. But his analytical brain, having seen this same rash on the wrists of so many victims, had already set a timer ticking.

He was going to die.

The module dinged, making him jump.

LETUMOSIS RESULTS: NEGATIVE

He shut his eyes in relief.

"How's everything going over there, Doctor?"

He cleared his throat. "I've...I've determined it would be best to let the stem cell solution sit for a few hours. You can apply the drops when you're back on the ship." He picked up a stylus and began to type a message into the portscreen. "I'll put the instructions on this portscreen. Just in case."

"Instructions for who?"

His gut twisted as he wrote. "I won't be returning with you."

There was silence, punctuated by the tapping of the stylus and his own breaths, suddenly labored.

"What are you talking about?"

"I'm too old. I'll just slow you down. When the others arrive, I want you to go on without me."

"Don't be stupid. We have a plan. We're sticking to it."

"No. You'll be leaving me behind."

"Why? So Levana can get her hands on you and torture you for information? Great idea."

"She won't have time to torture me. I'm already dying."

The words pinched something inside him and suddenly his spectacles were steaming up. There wasn't time. After all these years, there was never enough time.

"What are you talking about?"

He didn't respond until he'd finished typing into the portscreen. Shoving the stylus behind his ear, he walked over to the door and peered through the small window into the laboratory corridor.

Outside, dozens of guards had crowded into the hallway, stretching out in each direction with their guns raised.

"All is indeed going according to plan," he muttered.

A hand landed on his shoulder and he pulled away so fast he nearly collapsed into the counter. "Don't touch me."

"What is going on?" said Thorne, growing impatient.

Ducking around him, Dr. Erland paced to the other end of the room. "There is a quarantine room attached to this lab facility. I'll be quarantining myself. Don't worry—no one will dare come in to question me." He removed his spectacles and rubbed the lenses on his shirt. "I've just diagnosed myself with letumosis."

Thorne launched himself away as if he'd been burned, planting his back against the wall so that there couldn't have been any more space between them. Cursing, he wiped the palm that had touched the doctor on his pants.

"Don't worry. Your results are negative. There is a very slim chance that you've caught it in the last two minutes." He slid his spectacles back on. "Your stem cell solution is on the counter to your left, wrapped in a cloth. There is a portscreen beside it. Give them to Cress—she can help you." His voice clogged and he felt for the keypad. The code hadn't changed since he'd left.

As he pulled open the door, the lights in the quarantine flickered on. The window that divided the room was one-way, so that the patients couldn't see the technicians while they were running tests.

He had never been on that side of the glass before.

"Carswell Thorne?"

Glancing back, he saw that Thorne was still plastered against the wall, but the fear had left his expression, replaced with determination, and sympathy. "Yes?"

"Thank you. For keeping her safe in the desert." He knit his brows. "Although you still don't deserve her."

Before Thorne could respond, Dr. Erland stepped into the quarantine and shut himself in. His captivity was instant, airtight and suffocating and final.

Fifty-Three

SHE WAS GLAD THAT WOLF SEEMED TO HAVE MEMORIZED THE palace blueprint better than she had, because with all this running up and down stairwells, around corners, and down countless corridors, Cress was completely lost. Wolf, however, hadn't shown a moment's hesitation as they ran down the abandoned halls.

"Perfect timing," Wolf muttered under his breath as they swung around another corner. He grabbed Cress's elbow and yanked her back before she could collide with Cinder and Iko and the unconscious man hanging between them.

"Well, hello there, strangers," said Iko.

Wolf nodded, first at Cinder, then the unconscious emperor. "I thought that might be his cologne. Need help?"

Neither Cinder nor Iko objected when he stooped down and swung Kai over one shoulder.

If Cress hadn't been panicked and flustered and running on eight quarts of throbbing adrenaline, she would have been much more impressed.

"Labs are this way," Cinder said, taking the lead. Cress picked up her skirt and hurried after her. "Any surprises?"

"Not so far," Cress answered. "You?"

Cinder shook her head as they darted across the sky bridge into the research wing. "Not really. Just a lot of . . . this."

A palace guard appeared in front of them, gripping his gun. "Stop ri—!"

The word became a strangled gasp as his face went blank. His hands fell slack at his sides, the gun dropping to the floor.

Cress gasped, but Cinder pulled her around his dazed form without breaking pace.

"Wow," said Cress between her panting. "Good thing you've been practicing, right?"

"I wish that were the reason it's so easy," she said, shaking her head as they rounded another corner. "With Wolf, at least there was some struggle. Some *effort* involved. But with Earthens . . . it's too easy." She gulped. "If she becomes empress, Earth doesn't stand a chance."

They arrived at an elevator bank and Cress punched in the override code.

"Well then," she said, flashing a weary smile. "Good thing she's not going to be empress."

There seemed to be a mutual sigh as they crowded into the elevator. Cress's nerves were sparking like a million electrodes. Sweat was soaking into the back of her expensive dress. She was frazzled from all the running and the stairs and the panic, but at least they had a brief moment to pause and breathe and prepare themselves for what came next. Cress couldn't help sneaking a curious glance at the man draped over Wolf's shoulder. *The emperor.*

Of all the times she'd imagined meeting him, after years of spying on him and his father, she'd never imagined their first meeting would be quite like this.

Wolf stiffened as the elevator began to slow. "There's a lot of them out there."

"We knew there would be," said Cinder. "Thorne and the doctor had better be ready."

Cress shifted back, happy to keep Cinder and Wolf between her and whatever awaited them in the hall.

Iko bent toward her. "That dress looks *amazing* on you," she said. "Cinder, doesn't she look amazing?"

Cinder sighed as the elevator came to a full stop. "Iko, after this we're going to start working on occasion appropriateness."

The doors slid open and dozens of palace guards in red and gold uniforms stood before them.

"And not an android among them," Cinder muttered. "Kai and I are going to have a long talk about palace security." She marched into the corridor. "*You,*" she ordered, without gesturing to anyone in particular as far as Cress could tell, "are now our personal guard. Form a barrier."

Eight guards shuffled forward and, in robotic unison, formed a wall between them and their peers. Confusion flashed through the eyes of the others.

Cinder held her palm out and one of the guards set a gun into it, handle first.

She aimed it at Kai's head, her expression the picture of cold neutrality. "If anyone thinks of getting in our way, your emperor is dead. Now, move."

With their eight personal guards acting as a protective bubble around them, Cress found herself being herded along with the others toward the lab rooms. When they reached the sixth door, Cinder knocked, using the special rhythm they'd devised.

The door swung open a beat later. Thorne was flushed and

scowling. He had his cane in one hand, a cloth bundle in the other, and his blindfold still on.

"Doctor's not coming," he said.

A hesitation, before Cinder said, "What do you mean he's not coming?"

He gestured toward the back of the lab and they all pushed inside, leaving Cinder's brainwashed puppets to linger, baffled, in the hallway. A window was set into the wall, showing a sterile quarantine room. The doctor was seated on top of a lab table, his head hanging down, his fingers fidgeting with his hat.

With a growl, Cinder marched up to the window and pounded on it with her fist.

The doctor lifted his head, messy gray hair sticking out in all directions.

Grabbing a microphone from the desk, Cinder pushed a button and screamed, "We don't have time for this! Get out here."

The doctor only smiled, sadly.

"Cinder," said Thorne, his tone heavy in a way Cress had rarely heard. "He has the plague."

Cress's stomach dropped, as Cinder reeled back from the window.

The doctor smoothed down his hair. "Has everyone made it back safely?" he asked, his voice coming through some speaker in the wall.

It took Cinder a moment, but then she stammered, "Yes. Everyone but you."

A hand landed on Cress's head. She gasped and recoiled, but Thorne was already wrapping his arm around her shoulders and squeezing her against him. "Just checking it was you," he whispered.

She blinked up at his profile. The hours they'd spent apart suddenly felt like days, and she realized it could as easily have been him that was being left behind, instead of the doctor. She dug herself further into his embrace.

"I am sorry," said Dr. Erland, the words crisply spoken, like he'd been waiting to say them. He looked more fragile than ever sitting on that lab table, his face carved with wrinkles. "Miss Linh. Mr. Wolf." He sighed. "Crescent."

Her eyes widened. No one had called her that since Sybil. How had he even known?

It was a common name on Luna. Perhaps it was a lucky guess.

"I've hurt you all in some way. Been at least partly responsible for some tragedy in your lives. I am sorry."

Cress gulped, feeling a twinge of regret in the base of her stomach. The doctor still wore a bruise on his jaw from where she'd hit him.

"I have made some important discoveries," said the doctor. "How much time can you spare?"

Cinder's hand tightened around the microphone. "Jacin's ETA is in six minutes."

"That will have to suffice." The sorrow on the old man's face hardened. "Is His Majesty with you?"

"He's unconscious," said Cinder.

His eyebrows lifted, almost imperceptibly. "I see. Would you be so kind as to pass on a message to him?" Before Cinder could respond, the doctor pulled on his hat and inhaled a deep breath. "This plague is not a random tragedy. It is biological warfare."

"What?" Cinder planted her hands on the desk. "What do you mean?"

"The Lunar crown has been using antibodies found in the

blood of the ungifted to manufacture an antidote for at least sixteen years, and perhaps much longer. But sixteen years ago, letumosis didn't even exist, unless it, too, had been manufactured in a Lunar laboratory. Lunars wanted to weaken Earth, and to create a dependency on their antidote." He patted his chest, as if looking for something in his pocket, but then seemed to realize it was missing. "Right. I've indicated my findings on the portscreen that is now in Mr. Thorne's possession. Please give it to His Majesty when he is recovered. Earth should know that this war did not start with the recent attacks. This war has been going on beneath our noses for over a decade, and I do fear Earth is losing."

The silence that followed was suffocating.

Cinder leaned down into the microphone. "We're not going to lose."

"I believe you, Miss Linh." The doctor's breath shuddered. "Now, would . . . would Cress come closer, please?"

Cress stiffened. She pressed against Thorne's side as the others all looked at her, and it was only his gentle nudge that unstuck her feet. She crept toward the window that divided them from the quarantine room.

Only now, as she came to stand before the microphone, did she realize it was a one-way window. She could see the doctor, but on the other side he was probably looking at a reflection of himself.

Cinder cleared her throat, not taking her curious gaze off Cress. "She's here."

A pathetic smile tried to climb up the doctor's lips, but failed.

"Crescent. My Crescent Moon."

"How do you know my full name?" she asked, too confused to recognize the harshness of her tone.

But the doctor did not seem fazed, even as his lips began to tremble. "Because I named you."

She shivered, clawing her hands into the folds of her skirt.

"I want you to know that it nearly killed me when I lost you, and I have thought of you every day." His gaze hovered somewhere near the base of the window. "I always wanted to be a father. Even as a young man. But I was recruited into the crown's team of scientists immediately following my education—such an *honor*, you know. My career became everything, and there was no time for a family. I was already in my forties when I married, my wife another scientist whom I had known for many years and never thought I liked very much until she decided that she liked me. She was not much younger than me, and the years passed, and I had given up hope…until, one day, she was pregnant."

A chill slipped down Cress's spine. It felt like listening to an old, sad tale, one that she was removed from. One that she felt she knew the ending to, but denial kept a distance between her and the doctor's words.

"We did all the right things. We decorated a nursery. We planned a celebration. And sometimes at night, she would sing an old lullaby, one that I'd forgotten over the years, and we decided to call you our little Crescent Moon." His voice broke on the last word and he slumped over, scratching at his hat.

Cress gulped. The window, the sterile room, the man with a dark blue rash, all began to blur in front of her.

"Then you were born, and you were a shell." His words slurred. "And Sybil came, and I begged—I begged her not to take you, but there was nothing…she wouldn't…and I thought you were dead. I thought you were dead, and all along you were…if I'd known, Crescent. If I'd known, I never would have left. I would have found a way to save you. I'm so sorry. I'm so sorry for everything." He hid his face as sobs racked his body.

Pressing her lips together, Cress shook her head, wanting to deny it all, but how could she when he knew her name, and she had his eyes, and—

A tear slipped past her eyelashes, rolling hot down her cheek.

Her father was alive.

Her father was dying.

Her father was here, in front of her, almost in arm's reach. But he would be left here to die, and she would never see him again.

Cool metal brushed against her wrist, and Cress jumped.

"I'm so sorry," Cinder said, retracting her hand. "But we have to leave. Dr. Erland . . ."

"I know, y-yes, I know." He swiped hastily to clear his face. When he lifted his head, his cheeks were flushed, his eyes glassy. He looked as weak and frail as a broken bird. "I'm s-so sorry this is how . . . oh, please be careful. Please be safe. My Crescent Moon. I love you. I do love you."

Her lungs hiccupped, as more tears dripped off her jaw, dotting her silk skirt. She opened her mouth, but no words came. *I love you. I love you too.* Words that had been so easy in daydreams, and now seemed impossible.

She believed him, but she didn't know him. She didn't know if she loved him back.

"Cress," said Cinder, tightening her grip. "I'm sorry, but we have to go."

She nodded dumbly.

"Good . . . good-bye," she said, the only word that would come, as she was dragged away from the window.

On the other side of the glass, the doctor sobbed. He did not look up again, but he raised a shaking hand in farewell. The tips of his fingers were shriveled and blue.

Fifty-Four

THEY ABANDONED THEIR ENTOURAGE OF GUARDS IN THE
elevator on the top floor. No one cared that it would be too easy
to deduce where they were heading. Hopefully by the time anyone snapped out of Cinder's brainwashing, they'd be long gone.

The research wing's emergency service elevator was kept on
its own, in an alcove tucked away from the rest of the wing. It was
their final obstacle, and Cress had taken care to ensure it would
be functioning properly when they arrived. She stumbled ahead
of them to punch in the code, emotionally drained. It felt as if her
brain were churning through sludge and it took her a moment to
remember the code at all.

The elevator opened and they crowded inside.

No one spoke—whether out of respect for Dr. Erland, or out
of a tenuous hope that they were so close, so very close . . .

The doors opened onto the rooftop. Dusk was climbing over
the city, glistening off the palace windows and coating the landing pad in purple shadows.

And the Rampion was there, its ramp lowered toward them.

Cress laughed—an abrupt, delirious laugh that felt like it was
being ripped out of her throat.

Iko let out a victorious whoop and ran for the ramp, scream-ing, "We did it!"

Thorne's grip tightened on Cress's arm. "He's here?"

"He's here," she whispered back.

Wolf alone slowed down, baring his teeth. Kai was still draped over his shoulder.

"Jacin—ready for takeoff—now!" Cinder yelled toward the ship. "We're—" Her words fell short and she slowed, then stopped altogether. Cress gasped and locked her hands around Thorne's arm, holding him back.

A figure appeared at the top of the cargo bay ramp. Her white coat and long sleeves made her look like a ghost haunting their ship, blocking their way to freedom.

Cress's instincts screamed at her to run, to hide, to get as far away from Mistress Sybil as she could.

But when she glanced behind her she saw that the thauma-turge wasn't alone. Half a dozen Lunar guards had crowded in behind them, blocking off their path to the elevator. The elevator that wouldn't have worked anyway—she'd programmed it to shut down once they reached the rooftop so that no one could fol-low them. It wouldn't work again until the timer she'd set on the security mainframe ticked down and the system rebooted itself.

Which meant they had no place to run. No place to hide. They were forty steps from their ship, and they were trapped.

CINDER'S MOMENTARY ELATION EVAPORATED AS SHE LOOKED up at the thaumaturge. She should have sensed her immediately, her and the guards, before she'd even stepped off the elevator, but she'd been so distracted with the sensation of success. She'd gotten cocky, and now they were surrounded.

"What a lovely reunion," said Sybil, her sleeves snapping in the rooftop wind. "Had I known you were all going to come to me, I wouldn't have wasted half as much energy attempting to find you."

Cinder tried to keep her focus on Sybil as she took stock of her allies. Wolf was slightly in front of her, snarling as he set Kai on the ground. Though he wasn't showing any pain, she could see a small spot of blood on Wolf's dress shirt—his stitches must have come undone, reopening the wound.

Iko wasn't far from him, the only one of them not panting.

Cress and Thorne were to Cinder's left. Thorne had a cane and, she thought, he might still have his gun too. But he and Wolf could easily become liabilities, weapons to be toyed with by the thaumaturge, unlike Cress and Iko, who couldn't be controlled.

"How many?" Thorne asked.

"Mistress Sybil in front of us," said Cress, "and six Lunar guards behind."

After the slightest hesitation, Thorne nodded. "I accept those odds."

"So charming," said Sybil, tilting her head. "My little protégé has been embraced by cyborgs and androids and criminals—the scum of Earthen society. Quite fitting for a useless shell."

From the corner of her eye, Cinder noticed Thorne easing himself as a shield between Cress and the thaumaturge, but it was Cress who lifted her chin, with a look more confident than Cinder had ever seen on her.

"You mean the useless shell that just disconnected the link to all your palace surveillance equipment?"

Sybil clicked her tongue. "Arrogance doesn't suit you, dear. What do I care if the connection has been severed? Soon this palace will be the home of Queen Levana." She nodded. "Guards, leave His Majesty and the special operative unharmed. Kill the rest."

Cinder heard the thunk of boots, the rustle of uniforms, the click of guns being released from their holsters.

She opened her thoughts to them.

Six Lunar men. Six royal guards who, just like Jacin, had been trained to keep their minds open. Trained to be puppets.

She sought out the electric pulses around them. In unison, all six guards turned toward the edge of the rooftop and threw their guns as hard as they could. Six handguns sailed out of sight, clattering somewhere on the tiled rooftops below.

Sybil let out a screech of laughter, the most unrestrained Cinder had ever witnessed from her. "You have learned a few things since last we saw each other, haven't you?" Sybil paced down the ramp. "Not that controlling a handful of guards is any impressive feat." Her gaze flickered to Wolf.

Abandoning the guards, Cinder reached out for him instead, bracing herself for the sharp burst of pain inside her head that happened every time she took control of Wolf.

But the pain didn't come. Wolf's mind was already closed to her, as if someone had locked his writhing energy up in a vault.

Then he swiveled toward Cinder, his face contorting with a feral hunger.

Cursing, Cinder took half a step back. Her memory flashed to all the duels inside the cargo bay—and then Wolf launched himself at her.

Ducking, Cinder held her hands toward his abdomen and

used his momentum to flip him over her head. He landed lithely on his feet and spun back, aiming a right hook for her jaw. Cinder deflected with her metal fist, but the force drove her off balance and she fell onto the hard asphalt of the landing pad. Planting both hands on the ground, she drove her heel up toward Wolf, catching him in the side—his wounded side. She hated herself for it, but he grunted in pain and stumbled half a step back.

She sprang back to her feet. She was already panting. Warnings flooded her retina display.

Wolf licked his lips as he prepared to charge for her a second time, revealing the glint of his sharp teeth.

Smothering her panic, Cinder tried to reach for him again. If only she could break Sybil's mental hold. If only she'd gotten to him first. She searched for some flicker of the Wolf she knew was encased inside all that fury and bloodlust. Some vulnerable spot in his mind.

She was so distracted by her attempts to dislodge Sybil's control that she didn't notice the roundhouse kick until it had crashed into the side of her head and sent her reeling halfway across the platform.

She lay on her side, dizzy, white sparks flashing in her vision and her left arm burning from skidding across the ground. Breath wouldn't come into her lungs. She couldn't lift her head. Programming diagnostics were going berserk and it took her a moment to remember how to send them away so she could focus.

As her vision cleared, she noticed shapes moving against the twilit sky. People and shadows. Fighting. Brawling. The hazy images were eventually coupled with grunts of pain.

The guards had attacked. Thorne had gotten a knife from somewhere, Cress was wildly swinging his cane, and Iko was using her metal and silicon limbs as best she could to defend herself. But Thorne was blind and Iko wasn't programmed with fighting skills and as soon as one of the guards grabbed the cane out of Cress's hands, she fell to her knees, paralyzed, cowering behind her arms.

As Cinder watched, a guard caught Thorne's wrist and yanked it behind his back. He cried out. The knife fell. Another guard landed a punch to his stomach.

Then Cinder heard a growl. Wolf was crouched, ready to come at her again.

Cinder resisted the urge to close her eyes and brace for impact, instead letting a slow breath out through her nose. She urged her muscles to relax with it.

Your mind and body have to work together.

For a moment, it was like being two people at once. Her eyes were open, focused on Wolf as he lunged for her, and her body—loose and relaxed—instinctively rolled away, before she bounded back to her feet.

At the same time, her Lunar gift sought out the pulses of energy around her, targeted the six guards, and wrapped so tightly around them it was like clasping them in enormous metal fists.

There was a jolt of surprise from the guards. One crashed to his knees. Two fell onto their sides, convulsing.

Cinder dodged another punch, blocked another kick. Her instincts yearned to use the knife inside her finger, but she refused.

Wolf wasn't the enemy.

She landed an uppercut to his jaw—her first solid strike—as those words infiltrated her brain.

Wolf isn't the enemy.

A blur of blue caught her eye. Iko jumped onto Wolf's back

with a battle cry, wrapping her legs around his waist. Her arms surrounded his head, trying to blind or suffocate or distract him any way she could.

She was successful for 2.3 seconds before Wolf reached behind him, grabbed hold of her head, and twisted with such force the skin ripped around her throat. The wiring along her upper spine popped and sparked.

Iko slipped off him, crumpling to the ground. Her legs were twisted awkwardly beneath her. The external plating that protected her collar structure was peeled back on one side, revealing disconnected wires and a torn muscle pad, already leaking thick yellow silicon down her shoulder.

Cinder stumbled and crashed to her knees, staring at the crooked form. Her internal audio latched on to that awful sound and began replaying it over and over—that same brutal snap. That same heavy thud as Iko's body hit the ground.

Her stomach heaved once, but she kept it down as she peeled her gaze away from Iko and looked, not at Wolf, but at Sybil.

The thaumaturge was standing at the base of the ramp now. Her beautiful face was pinched in concentration.

In her distant thoughts, Cinder could tell that the guards were picking themselves off the ground. Rounding on her friends again.

Snarling, she ignored them all. She ignored Wolf.

Sybil was the enemy.

Wolf turned back to face her. His feet pounded on the pavement.

But Cinder was too focused on the bioelectricity rolling off Sybil to care. Sybil's energy was twisted and arrogant and proud, and Cinder had just slipped into the cracks of her thoughts when the impact came.

Wolf crashed into her, knocking her over, but Cinder barely felt it.

While Wolf pinned her to the ground, Cinder was working her way around Sybil's gift. Becoming intimately acquainted with how the energy rippled along her limbs and fingers. How it was so different from the way that same energy churned and throbbed inside her brain.

As Wolf revealed his sharp canines, Cinder discovered where Sybil's gift was boiling hot in her attempts to control Wolf, leaving the rest of her brain cool and vulnerable.

When Wolf lowered his fangs toward Cinder's unprotected throat, Cinder seized Sybil's mind and attacked.

Fifty-Five

CRACK.

Cress glanced up just as Iko slid off Wolf's back, landing broken and mangled on the hard ground. A shudder tore through her. Even from this distance she could see the torn flesh and sparking wires.

"What was that?"

She returned her attention to Thorne. She was still kneeling beside him, trying to steady him as best she could. He'd taken a hard punch to his stomach that had knocked the wind from him, but at least he was breathing and talking again.

"I think we just lost Iko," she said. "Can you stand?"

Thorne groaned, still clasping one hand to his stomach. "Yeah," he said, sounding none too convinced.

Something shuffled. Glancing up, Cress squeaked and dug her fingers into Thorne's arms. The guards, having been paralyzed and empty faced for the past few moments, were twitching. One of them groaned.

Beside her, Thorne pulled himself to his feet. "There. Better," he said, though he was still grimacing. "Do you see my cane anywhere? Or my knife?"

She spotted the cane behind one of the guards, whose furious gaze was no longer empty or harmless.

"Cress?"

"Guards are up again," she said.

Thorne flinched. "All six of them?"

She glanced over her shoulder. "And Cinder's on the ground— she might be unconscious. And Wolf's still under Sybil's control and I . . . I think he's going to . . ." She squeezed Thorne's arm, horrified at the sight of Wolf pinning Cinder to the ground. She wanted to look away, but couldn't, like being stuck in a bad dream.

"That all sounds very dire," said Thorne.

Shivering, she pressed her back against him, wondering how her death was going to come. Her skull crushed against the concrete? Her neck snapped like Iko's?

"I guess it's time."

While Cress's thoughts continued to churn through the horrible things that could happen to her, she felt herself being suddenly spun around and dipped backward, a supportive arm scooping beneath her back. She yelped and caught herself on Thorne's shoulder.

Then he was kissing her.

The battle became a hurricane, with them caught in the eye—his arms cradling her against the wind, her skirt billowing around his legs, his lips gentle but coaxing as if they had all the time in the world.

Warmth overtook her and Cress closed her eyes. She thought her arms wanted to wrap around his neck, but her whole body was vibrating and dizzy and she could barely keep her fingers clutched around the fabric of his shirt.

She had just finished melting when she was suddenly righted again.

The world flipped. Thorne spun, embracing her against his chest with one arm while the other reached for his waist. Cress heard the gunshot and screamed, pressing herself against him, before she realized that Thorne was the one who had fired.

A guard grunted.

Another guard grabbed Thorne by the collar and he turned, elbowing the guard in the jaw.

"Cress, do me a favor." He twirled her around so that her back was against him—she was beginning to feel like a satellite being constantly spun out of orbit, but she had no time to think as Thorne settled his arm on her shoulder. "Make sure I don't shoot anyone we like."

He fired again and the bullet clipped a guard's bicep. The guard barely flinched, and lunged toward them.

Gasping, Cress wrapped her hands around Thorne's and aimed. He fired again, this time hitting the guard in the chest. He stumbled backward and fell.

Cress swiveled, pulling Thorne's hand toward the next guard. Another shot to the chest. A third shot hit the next guard's shoulder. She aimed for the fourth—

Click. Click.

Thorne cursed. "Well, that was fun while it lasted."

The guard laughed. He was tall and made of muscle, with orange-red hair that swept nearly straight up, and he was the only guard that Cress recognized. She'd seen him on the surveillance footage before, usually along with the rest of the queen's entourage, which meant he was probably the highest-ranking guard among them.

"If it's all right with you," he said, "I'll be killing you now."

"Aren't you a gentleman?" Thorne said, pulling Cress behind him and raising his fists.

A scream split through the wind.

Not just a scream, but a scream made up of pain and delirium, torture and agony.

Cress and Thorne both ducked and covered their ears, and at first Cress was terrified that it was Cinder. But when she looked, Mistress Sybil had fallen on the ground and was twitching and digging her nails into her scalp. The scream went on and on as she twisted and flailed, craning her head so fast it smacked against the asphalt, then curling up on herself like a fetus, searching for relief that wasn't coming.

Cinder still appeared unconscious, with Wolf hovering over her. But then he whipped his head like a bedraggled dog and sprang away from Cinder with wild, remorseful eyes.

Cinder stayed corpse-like on the ground.

"Stop!" the red-haired guard yelled. He grabbed Cress, yanking her away from Thorne and wrapping one hand around her throat. She screamed and clawed at his wrists, but he didn't seem to notice. "I said stop, or I'll crush her throat!" Though he was yelling, he could hardly be heard over Sybil, and either Cinder didn't hear him or she didn't care . . . or she couldn't stop. Cress tried to kick behind her, but her legs were too short and already darkness was encroaching on her vision. . . .

Crack.

The guard's fist loosened and he toppled over, unconscious. Cress stumbled away from him, rubbing her neck. Spinning around, she saw Thorne holding his cane like a club.

"I found my cane," he said, tossing it once with a twirl and trying to catch the other end, but missing. The cane clattered to the floor. Thorne flinched. "Are you all right?"

She gulped, ignoring how it burned in her throat. "Y-yes."

"Good." Thorne picked up the cane again. "Now what in the name of spades is all the screaming about?"

"I don't know. Cinder's doing something to Mistress Sybil... something with her gift."

"Well, it's annoying and we're running out of time. Come on."

One of the guards they'd shot reached out for Cress's ankle as she passed, but she kicked at him as they ran for Cinder. Wolf was shaking her, but she wasn't responding. Behind them, Sybil's screams tapered into uncontrollable blubbering as she convulsed on the ground.

"Maybe Cinder has to be rebooted," said Thorne, after Cress had described the situation as well as she could. "That happened once before. Here." He reached beneath Cinder's head and Cress heard a click.

Cinder's eyes popped open and her hand snapped around Thorne's wrist. Crying out, he fell over onto the ground.

Sybil's sobs dwindled to whimpering.

"Don't. Open. My control panel," she said. Releasing Thorne, she shut the plate in her head.

"Then stop going comatose on me!" He stood up. "Can we go now, before the entire Commonwealth military shows up?"

Cinder sat up, blinking. "Iko ..."

"Right. Wolf, could you get the android, please? And the emperor, I trust he's still around here somewhere?"

The emperor. In the chaos, Cress had forgotten all about him.

"Sirens."

Cress looked at Wolf. His head was cocked to one side.

"Heading this direction."

"Which means the military won't be far behind," said Cinder. "I take it there's no sign of Jacin?"

No one responded. There had been no sign of their getaway pilot since the fight had started. Cress licked her lips. Had he betrayed them? Had he told Sybil about their plan?

"Figures," said Cinder. "Thorne, you're with me in the cockpit. Jacin and I practiced takeoffs…once. You can help jog my memory."

Together, they hurried to carry Iko's broken body and Kai, still unconscious, into the cargo bay.

Then they heard laughter. High, strained laughter that dropped ice down Cress's spine.

Sybil was struggling to stand. She made it to her feet and took a couple wobbling steps, before falling back down to one knee. She laughed again and bunched her fists into her long, unruly hair.

Cress was suddenly pushed aside as Wolf trudged down the ramp and grasped Sybil by the front of her white coat, yanking her toward him. Her eyes rolled back into her head. "Where is she?" he yelled. "Is she still alive?"

Even from the top of the ramp, Cress could see the hatred burning in his eyes, overshadowed only by his need to know. To be given any sliver of hope that Scarlet was still out there. That he still had a chance to save her.

But Sybil's head only collapsed to one side. "What—what pretty birds!" she said, before she was overcome with a fit of incoherent giggles.

Wolf snarled, baring his teeth. For a moment, his entire body was shaking and Cress thought he was going to tear her throat out. But then he dropped Sybil to the ground. She fell hard, whimpered from the impact, and rolled onto her back. Then she started to laugh again, staring up at the sky. The sun was just setting, but the full moon had already risen high over the city's skyline.

Turning away from her, Wolf marched up the ramp. He did not meet Cress's gaze as he passed her.

Cress stared, bewildered, as Sybil raised both arms up toward the sky. Cackling. Cackling.

The ramp started to rise, slowly blocking the sight of Sybil and the bleeding guards who were scattered around the rooftop. The roar of the engines soon drowned out both the mad laughter and the sirens blaring beyond the palace walls.

Fifty-Six

TO ANYONE WHO WOULD HAVE SEEN HER, LEVANA WAS A vision of serenity in her ethereal red wedding gown and the sheer gold veil that fell to her wrists. She sat on the settee in her guest quarters, posture perfect, her hands folded in her lap.

Except they were not folded at all, but rather balled into angry fists.

Each one held a wedding band. One that she had worn for far too many years, that she had once believed would bring her love and happiness, but had only ever brought her pain.

The other was supposed to bring her, not the love of a blind, selfish husband, but the love of an entire planet. She should have been wearing it now.

Everything had been going so well. She had been moments away from walking down that aisle. *Moments away.*

She should have been married. She should have been reciting the vows that would make her empress.

When she found out who was responsible for this delay, she would torment their fragile mind until they were a drooling, pathetic idiot, terrified of the sight of their own hands.

A knock cut through the fantasy. Levana shifted her eyes toward the door.

"Enter."

One of her guards entered first, escorting Konn Torin, the young emperor's annoying, perpetually present adviser. She glared at him through her gold veil, though she knew he couldn't see it.

"Your Illustrious Majesty," he said, bowing deeply. The addition of a new adjective combined with the bow slightly lower than usual made the hair prickle on the back of her neck. "I must apologize most severely for the delay, and for the news I have to impart to you. We have been forced, I'm afraid, to postpone the marriage ceremony."

"I do beg your pardon."

He straightened, but kept his gaze respectfully on the floor.

"His Imperial Majesty, Emperor Kaito, has been kidnapped. He was taken from his personal quarters and smuggled onto an untraceable spaceship."

Her fingers curled around the wedding bands. "By whom?"

"Linh Cinder, Your Majesty. The cyborg fugitive from the ball. Along with multiple accomplices, it would appear."

Linh Cinder.

Every time she heard the name she wanted to spit.

"I see," she said, finding it too wearisome to soften the hardness of her anger. "Am I to believe that you did not have any security measures in place for the attempt of such an assault?"

"Our security was compromised."

"*Compromised.*"

"Yes, Your Majesty."

She rose to her feet. The gown swished like a breeze around her hips. The adviser didn't flinch, although he should have.

"You're telling me that this teenage girl has not only escaped from your prison and evaded capture by your highly trained military, but has now invaded your palace and the private quarters of the emperor himself, kidnapped him, and again gotten away with it?"

"Precisely correct, Your Majesty."

"And what are you doing now to retrieve my groom?"

"We have employed every police and military unit at our dispo—"

"NOT GOOD ENOUGH."

This time, he did flinch.

Levana steadied her breathing. "The Commonwealth has failed too many times with regards to Linh Cinder. Beginning now, I will employ my own resources and tactics in finding her. My guards will need to review all your security footage from the past forty-eight hours."

The adviser clasped his hands behind his back. "We are happy to give you access to the security footage we have available. However, we are missing approximately two hours of footage that was compromised this afternoon by the security breach."

She sneered. "*Fine.* Bring me what you do have."

Thaumaturge Aimery Park appeared in the doorway. "Your Majesty. If I may request a word with you, in private."

"With pleasure." She waved a hand at Konn Torin. "You're dismissed, but note that the incompetence of your security team will not be ignored."

With no argument, and another low bow, the adviser left.

As soon as he was gone, Levana whipped the veil off her head and threw it onto the settee. "The young emperor has been kidnapped, and from his own palace. Earthens are pathetic. It's amazing they haven't already become extinct."

"I do not disagree, Your Majesty. I trust Mr. Konn did not inform you of this evening's other interesting development?"

"What development?"

Aimery's eyes danced. "It appears that Dr. Sage Darnel is in this palace, trapped in a quarantine room in the research wing."

"Sage Darnel?" She paused. "Daring to return after he assisted the escape of that wretched girl?"

"No doubt they've been working together, although I've been led to believe that Dr. Darnel won't be around for much longer. It appears he's contracted an unusual strain of letumosis, one that seems to be much faster acting than the common strain. And, of course, he is Lunar."

Her pulse skipped. This did open up some interesting possibilities.

"Take me to him," she said, sliding her true wedding ring back onto her finger. The other, that would cement her to Emperor Kaito, she left behind.

"I must warn you," Aimery said as she followed him into the corridor, "that the elevators throughout the palace are malfunctioning. We'll be forced to take the stairs."

"Earthens," she growled, lifting the hem of her skirt.

It was like traversing an endless labyrinth, but finally they reached the research wing. A crowd of officials had gathered outside the lab and Levana sneered to think that they'd intended to keep this from her when Sage Darnel, like Linh Cinder, was *her* problem to deal with, however it pleased her.

As she entered the lab room, she slipped into the minds of the men and women around her and impressed a strong need to be *elsewhere*.

The room was cleared within seconds, but for her and Aimery.

It was a crisp, chemical-smelling room. All bright lights and hard edges. And on the other side of a tinted window, Dr. Sage Darnel was laid out on a lab table, holding a gray cap against his stomach.

With the exception of the security footage that showed him helping Linh Cinder escape from prison, Levana hadn't seen him since he disappeared over a decade ago. Once, he had been one of her most promising scientists, making grand advances in the development of her lupine soldiers on an almost monthly basis.

But time had not been kind to him. His face had become worn and wrinkled. He was balding, and what was left of his hair was tufted and gray. And then there was the disease. His reptilian skin was covered in bruise-like blotches and a rash that was bubbling up like blisters, piling on top of each other. His fingertips had already begun to turn blue. No, he would not be around much longer.

Levana floated toward the window. A light was on beside a microphone, indicating that communication was open between the two rooms.

"My good Dr. Darnel. I did not think I would ever again have the pleasure."

His eyes opened, still fervently blue behind his spectacles. His attention was locked on the ceiling, and though it occurred to Levana that this was no doubt a one-way window, it annoyed her that he wouldn't bother to face her.

"Your Majesty," he said, his tone brittle. "I thought I might hear your voice one more time."

Beside her, Aimery checked a portscreen at his belt, and excused himself with a low bow.

"I must say, I'm delighted with this irony. You left an honorable position on Luna to come to Earth and devote your last withering years to finding a cure for this disease. A disease that I already have the antidote for. In fact...come to think of it, I might have some samples with me in the palace. I like to keep them on hand in the event something tragic should happen to my betrothed, or someone else necessary to my objectives. I could have the antidote brought to you, but I don't suppose I will."

"Worry not, My Queen. I would not take it from you even if you did, now that I know what lengths you've gone to obtain it."

"The lengths I've gone to? In order to cure a disease that, until this day, did not affect my own people? I do believe that's rather charitable of me, wouldn't you say?"

He slowly, slowly sat up. His head fell to his chest as he tried to recapture his breath, winded from that small exertion. "I've figured it out, My Queen. I truly believed that all shells were killed when you took them from us, but that's not true. Are *any* of them killed, or is it all just a show? A means of putting them into seclusion and harvesting their blood without anyone coming to look for them?"

Her lashes fluttered. "You had a shell child once, didn't you? Remind me—was it a little boy or a little girl? Perhaps when I return home I can find them and tell them how small and pathetic their father was when he died right before my eyes."

"What's most interesting to me," the doctor said, scratching his ear and acting as if he hadn't heard her, "is that the first documented case of letumosis occurred twelve years ago. And yet, you've been collecting antibodies for much longer than that. In fact, it would have been your sister who began the experiments, if my math is correct."

Levana splayed her fingers on the counter. "You have

reminded me why you were such a terrible loss for our team, doctor."

He swiped his arm across his damp forehead. His skin seemed translucent beneath the bright lights. "This disease is all your doing. You've manufactured death to bring Earth to its knees, so that when the time was right, you would be there to save them with your miraculous antidote. One that you'd had stashed away all along."

"You give me too much credit. It was the team working beneath my parents that created the disease, and those beneath my sister who perfected the antidote. I simply implemented their research by determining a means of getting the disease down to Earth."

"By exposing Lunars to it and then sending them here, having no idea what they were carrying."

"Sending them to Earth? Absolutely not. I simply made sure that my security personnel looked the other way when they... *escaped.*" The last word held a bite. She wasn't fond of the idea that some of her people chose to run away from the paradise she'd given them.

"It's biological warfare." Dr. Darnel coughed into his elbow, leaving spots of dark red. "And Earth has no idea."

"And they will continue to have no idea. Because I'm going to stand here and watch you die."

He laughed shrilly. "You honestly think I would carry this secret to my grave?"

A twinge of annoyance traipsed down her spine.

The doctor's eyes were glazing over, but his smile was enormous as he studied the window. "This is a very large mirror I'm looking into. So impossible to hide from what I am... what I've become. My Queen, you would not like to die in this room. I suspect you would tear off your own flesh if forced to stare at it for so long."

She squeezed her hands into fists, digging her nails into the palms of her hands.

"Your Majesty."

Exhaling, she forced her hands to open. Her palms stung.

Aimery had returned with Jerrico, her captain of the guard, looking as though he'd been in an impressive scuffle.

"Finally. Where have you and Sybil been? Report."

Jerrico bowed. "My Queen, Thaumaturge Mira and I, along with five of my top marksmen, managed to surround Linh Cinder and her companions on the emergency landing pad on this tower's rooftop."

Hope warmed her chest. "And you got them? They haven't escaped after all?"

"No, Your Majesty. We failed in our objective. Two of my men are dead, the other three severely injured. I, myself, was unconscious when the spacecraft escaped with the traitors and Emperor Kaito aboard."

Her fury began to claw at her spine again, desperate to be unleashed. "And where is Thaumaturge Mira?"

He respectfully lowered his gaze. "Dead, Your Majesty. Linh Cinder used her gift to torture her mind—I heard her screams myself. Those who were conscious have reported that, after the spacecraft departed, Thaumaturge Mira threw herself from the rooftop. Her body was found in the gardens."

A mad giggling echoed through the room. Levana spun back as the doctor doubled over his knees, kicking his heels against the table. "She deserved it, the snake. After keeping my little golden bird locked up in her cage for so long."

"Your Majesty."

Levana faced Jerrico again. "What?"

"We found one of Linh Cinder's accomplices aboard their ship prior to the confrontation. Her new pilot, it would seem." Jerrico gestured toward the hall. Footsteps clicked, and a moment later, two men entered. Another guard escorting—

Her smile was quick. "Dearest Sir Clay."

Though his wrists were bound behind his back, he stood straight and proper and seemed as healthy as ever. He clearly hadn't been treated like a prisoner aboard Linh Cinder's ship.

"My Queen." He dipped his head.

She scraped her Lunar gift over him, testing for signs of derision or rebellion, but there were none. He was as blank and malleable as ever. "My understanding is that you abandoned your thaumaturge in a pivotal battle in order to side with Linh Cinder against the Lunar crown. Your being here leads me to understand that you are also involved with the kidnapping of my betrothed. You are a traitor to myself and to my throne. How do you plead?"

"Innocent, My Queen."

She laughed. "Of course you are. How can you plead thus?"

He held her gaze without remorse. "During the battle aboard the spaceship, Thaumaturge Mira was consumed with the effort to control a Lunar special operative who has joined the side of the rebels. With my own faculties open, Linh Cinder forced me to comply with her will and fight against my thaumaturge, ultimately leading to her abandoning the ship and leaving me aboard. Realizing this was an opportunity to ingratiate myself to the rebels, I have spent these past weeks acting as a spy with the intention of reporting weaknesses and strategies when I was finally able to return to my queen, who I am most honored to serve."

She smirked. "No doubt your eagerness to return encompassed a desire to see your beloved princess as well."

There—finally. The tiniest ripple of emotion, before the lake was once again still as glass. "I live to serve all members of the Lunar royal family, My Queen."

She smoothed her fingers down her skirt. "How can I believe that you remain loyal to me when you are standing before me in chains, having been dragged from the enemy's own ship?"

"I would hope my actions prove my loyalties. Had I wanted Linh Cinder to succeed in her objectives, I would not have sent Thaumaturge Mira a comm informing her where and when I would be arriving with that ship."

Levana raked her gaze over Jacin before glancing at Jerrico. "Is this true?"

"I can't say. Thaumaturge Mira did seem confident of the location when we went to intercept the traitors, but she didn't say anything about a comm. And she seemed furious when we found Jacin in the cockpit. It was under her order that we took him into custody."

"All due respect," said Jacin. "I did shoot her during our last engagement. And the comm was sent anonymously—she may not have realized I was the one who had sent the tip in the first place."

Levana waved away the statement. "We will investigate further, Sir Clay. But as you claim to have been gathering information for weeks, tell me, what useful things have you learned about our enemies?"

"I've learned that Linh Cinder has the ability to control a Lunar special operative," he said, reciting the information with as much emotion as an Earthen android. "However, she is untrained and lacks focus. She shows no talent for simultaneously engaging in both mental and physical battles."

"Interesting speculation," Levana mused. "In your estimation, would she have the mental focus required to torture an enemy, driving them to the brink of insanity?"

"Absolutely not, Your Majesty."

"*Absolutely* not. Well then. You are either much stupider than I ever suspected, or you are lying, as that is precisely what Linh Cinder did today, against my head thaumaturge herself."

Another spike of emotion announced a sudden bout of nerves, but it was overshadowed by loud thumping from the quarantine.

"Of course he's lying!" the doctor screeched, his voice breaking. He had managed to haul himself off the lab table and was now pounding on the glass with his palms, leaving smears of bloodied spittle. "She's capable of killing your head thaumaturge and all your guards and your entire court. She's Princess Selene, the true heir to the throne. She can kill you all, and she will kill you all. She's coming for you, My Queen, and she will *destroy you!*"

Levana snarled. "Shut up! Shut up, you old man! Why won't you die already?"

He was too busy gasping for breath to hear her. He collapsed to the ground, hands on his chest, his wheezing punctuated with hacking coughs.

Jacin Clay, when she turned back to him, was staring skeptically at the window. But within moments his eyes began to fill with comprehension. His lips twitched, like he was ready to laugh at a joke he just now understood. It was a rare show of emotion that only angered her more. "Take him away. He will undergo a full investigation on Luna."

As Jacin was marched back into the corridor, she faced Thaumaturge Park again, her hands fisted at her sides. "You are hereby promoted. Begin planning our departure immediately, and alert our research team to this new strain of letumosis. Also, initiate mobilizing procedures for our soldiers. Linh Cinder is too afraid to face me herself. The people of Earth will suffer for her cowardice."

"You understand that with the loss of Thaumaturge Mira's programmer, we are not able to transport our ships to Earth without notice?"

"What do I care if Earth sees them coming? I hope it gives them time to beg for mercy before we destroy them."

Aimery bowed. "I will see it done, Your Majesty."

Levana glanced back to see that Dr. Sage Darnel was sprawled out on the floor, his body seizing between his coughs. She watched him writhe and jerk, her blood still boiling at his words.

As far as the people of Luna and Earth knew, Selene had died thirteen years ago.

Levana was going to make sure it stayed that way.

She was the rightful queen of Luna. Of Earth. Of the entire galaxy. No one would take that from her.

Seething, she stepped closer, close enough that she could see the trail of tears left on the doctor's scourged face.

"Sweet Crescent Moon . . . ," he whispered, his lips barely able to form the words. He began to shiver. "Up in the sky..." He hummed a few bars of a song, a lullaby that seemed barely familiar. "You sing your song . . . so sweetly . . . after sunshine passes. . . ."

The last word hovered unspoken as he stopped shuddering and lay still, his blue eyes staring upward like empty marbles.

Fifty-Seven

"SATELLITE AR817.3 . . . DEFLECT TRACKER . . . SET ALTERNATING timer . . . and check. Which should just leave Satellite AR944.1 . . . and . . . that . . . should . . . do it." Cress paused, breathed, and slowly lifted her fingers away from the cockpit's main screen, where she'd spent the last three hours ensuring that any satellites in their path would be conveniently turned away from them as they passed. As long as the Rampion's orbital path held, they shouldn't be detected.

At least, not by satellite or radar.

There was still the problem of visual sightings, and as the Eastern Commonwealth had announced twenty minutes ago that an enormous monetary reward would go to anyone who found the stolen Rampion, every ship between here and Mars would be on the lookout.

They had to be prepared to run if anyone did spot them, which was made extra difficult now that they no longer had a trained pilot onboard. At least, not one who could see. Thorne had managed to talk Cinder through the liftoff procedures, with vast amounts of help from the Rampion's new auto-control system, but it had been a rocky takeoff followed by an immediate switch to neutral orbit. If they were faced with anything requiring more complicated maneuvers before Thorne got his eyesight back, they'd be in trouble.

According to Cinder, they'd be in trouble even when he *did* have his eyesight back.

Cress massaged her neck, attempting to get her thoughts to stop spinning. When she was in the middle of a hack, it tended to fill up her brain until her vision hummed with coding and mathematics, skipping ahead to each necessary task faster than she could complete them. It tended to leave her in a state of drained euphoria.

But for now, at least, the Rampion was safe.

She turned her attention to a yellow light at the base of the screen that had been annoying her since she'd begun, but that she'd been too preoccupied to deal with. As expected, when she prompted the ejection, a small shimmering D-COMM chip popped out from the screen.

The match to the chip that Sybil had taken from her satellite, cutting off any hope that Cress and Thorne had of contacting their friends.

Friends.

She squinted at the chip as she held it up, wondering if that was the right word. It felt like having friends, especially after they'd survived the mission together. But then, she didn't have anything to compare this friendship to.

One thing she knew for sure, though, was that she no longer needed to be rescued.

She looked around for something she could use to destroy the chip, and caught the ghost of a reflection in the cockpit window. Thorne stood in the doorway behind her, hands tucked into his pockets.

She gasped and spun to face him, her full skirt twisting around the chair's base. Though it was dirty and torn in places, she hadn't had the time to change yet, and wasn't entirely sure she wanted to. The gown made her feel like she was still living in a drama, and was perhaps keeping her from going into shock at all that had happened that day. "You scared me!"

Thorne flashed a moderately embarrassed grin. "Sorry?"

"How long have you been standing there?"

He shrugged. "I was listening to you work. It's kind of relaxing. And I like it when you sing."

She flushed. She didn't realize she'd been singing.

Feeling his way forward, Thorne took the copilot's seat, setting the cane across his lap and kicking his boots up on the dash. "Are we invisible again?"

"To radars, for now." She tucked some hair behind her ear. "Could I see your cane?"

He raised an eyebrow, but handed it to her without question. Cress dropped the D-COMM chip to the ground and crushed it beneath the cane's tip. A shiver of empowerment ran through her.

"What was that?" Thorne asked.

"The D-COMM chip you used to contact me before. We won't be needing it again."

"Seems like that was ages ago." Thorne ran his finger along the blindfold. "I'm sorry that you didn't get to see much of Earth while we were down there. And now you're stuck up here again."

"I'm happy to be stuck up here." She twirled the cane absently between her palms. "It's a great ship. Far more spacious than the satellite. And ... much better company."

"I can't argue with that." Grinning, Thorne pulled a small bottle from his pocket. "I came in here to ask if you would help me with this. These are the mystical eyedrops the doctor made.

We're supposed to put three to four drops in each eye, twice a day... or was it two drops, three times?...I don't remember. He wrote down the instructions on the portscreen." Thorne unclipped the port from his belt and handed it to her.

Cress propped the cane against the panel of instruments. "He was probably worried you'd forget, after such a high-stress..." She trailed off, her eye catching on the portscreen text.

Thorne cocked his head. "What's wrong?"

The port had opened to a screen containing instructions for the eyedrops, and also a detailed account of why Dr. Erland believed the plague was a manufactured weapon being used as biological warfare.

But at the top of all that...

"There's a tab labeled with my name." Not Cress. *Crescent Moon Darnel.*

"Oh. It was the doctor's port."

Cress's fingers glided over the screen, and she'd opened the tab before her mind could decide whether it wanted to know what was in it or not.

"A DNA analysis," she said, "and...a paternity confirmation." Standing, she set the port on the control panel. "Let's do your eyedrops."

"Cress." He reached for her, his fingers gathering up the folds of her skirt. "Are you all right?"

"Not really." She looked down at him. Thorne had pulled the blindfold around his neck, revealing a faint tan line around his eyes. Gulping, Cress sank into the pilot's chair again. "I should have told him I loved him. He was dying, and he was right there, and I knew I would never see him again. But I couldn't say it. Am I horrible?"

"Of course not. He may have been your biological father, but you still barely knew him. How could you have loved him?"

"Does it matter? He said he loved *me*. He was dying, and now he's gone, and I'll never..."

"Cress, hey, stop it." Thorne swiveled his chair to face her. He found her wrists, before sliding his hands down to intertwine with her fingers. "You didn't do anything wrong. It all happened so fast, and there was nothing you could do."

She bit her lip. "He took my blood sample that first day, in Farafrah." She squeezed her eyes shut. "He knew all this time—almost a whole *week*. Why didn't he tell me sooner?"

"He probably wanted to wait for the right time. He didn't know he was going to die."

"He knew there was a chance we were all going to die." Her next breath shook inside her diaphragm, and as the tears started, she felt herself being pulled toward Thorne. He drew her into his lap, scooping one arm beneath her legs to keep the enormous skirt from tangling around her. Sobbing, Cress buried her face against his chest and let the tears come. She cried hard at first, the release pouring out of her all at once. But she almost felt guilty when, minutes later, the tears already started to dry up. Her sadness wasn't enough. Her mourning wasn't enough. But it was all she had.

Thorne held her until the sound of his heartbeat became louder than the sound of her crying. He smoothed her hair back from her face, and though it was selfish, Cress was glad that he couldn't see her then, with her red face and puffy eyes and all the unladylike fluids she'd left on his shirt.

"Listen, Cress," he murmured against her hair once her breaths were almost stable. "I'm not an expert by any means, but

I know you didn't do anything wrong today. You shouldn't tell someone you love them unless you mean it."

She sniffed. "But I thought you said you've told lots of girls that you loved them."

"Which is exactly why I'm not an expert. Thing is, I didn't love any of them. I'm honestly not sure I would recognize real love if it was..."

She swiped the back of her hand over her damp cheeks. "If it was what?"

"Nothing." Clearing his throat, Thorne leaned his head against the back of the chair. "Are you all right?"

Sniffing again, she nodded. "I think so. I might still be in a little bit of shock."

"I think we all are, after today."

Cress spotted the bottle of the eyedropper solution, beside the doctor's portscreen. She didn't want to pry herself away from Thorne's arms, but she also didn't want to think about the doctor anymore. The secret he'd kept. The words she couldn't say. "We should probably take care of these eyedrops."

"When you're done shaking," Thorne said. "I don't like shaking things near my eyes."

She laughed weakly and went to pull herself from his lap. Thorne's arms tightened, but only for a moment before he let her go. She forced her guilt back inside. She wouldn't think about it right now.

After reading the doctor's instructions—three drops in each eye, four times a day for one week—she unscrewed the top. Drawing the solution up into the dropper, she moved to stand behind Thorne's chair, her wrinkled gown swaying around her.

Thorne propped his feet on the control panel again and tilted back until his face was turned up to the ceiling. She hadn't seen his eyes in days, but they were as blue as ever.

Cress placed a hand on his brow to steady herself and his cheek twitched. "Here goes," she murmured, squeezing the dropper. He instinctively flinched and blinked, pushing the drops like tears down his temples. Cress brushed them away, unable to resist smoothing a strand of hair off his forehead. Her attention caught on his lips, and suddenly self-conscious, she pulled her fingertips away. "How does that feel?"

He squeezed his eyes shut for a moment. "Like I have water in my eyes." Then he chuckled wryly, opening them again. "Maybe the solution is just water, and the doctor was playing a practical joke on me."

"That would be awful!" she said, twisting the cap back onto the solution. "He wouldn't have done that."

"No, you're right. Not after what we went through to get it." He lifted his head from the back of the chair, tugging at the bandanna knotted around his neck. "Though he did make it pretty clear that he didn't think too highly of me."

"If that's true, it's only because he didn't know you well enough yet."

"True. I would have charmed him eventually."

She smiled. "Of course you would have, in addition to showing him your many other fine qualities," she said, blushing as she set a reminder on the portscreen to go off four times a day. But when she looked at Thorne again, his expression had become serious. "Captain?"

His Adam's apple bobbed. Sitting up straighter, Thorne rubbed his palms together. "I have to tell you something."

"Oh?" Hope skittered through her veins as she claimed the pilot's seat again. The luxurious dress poufed around her.

The rooftop. The kiss.

Had he realized how much he loved her?

"What is it?"

Thorne pulled his feet off the control panel. "Remember when we were in the desert...and I said I didn't want to hurt you? Because you were wrong about me?"

She knotted her fingers together. "When you tried to deny how much of a hero you really are?" She tried to put a hint of teasing into the statement, but her nerves were so jittery it came out as more of a frightened squeak.

"A hero. Exactly." Thorne rubbed a finger between the blindfold and his throat, loosening it. "Here's the thing. That girl that I stood up for when those jerks took her portscreen?"

"Kate Fallow."

"Right, Kate Fallow. Well, she was *really* good at math. And, at the time, I was failing."

The anticipation fluttering through her body turned to ice. Wait—was this his confession? Something to do with...Kate Fallow?

He cleared his throat when she didn't say anything. "I lost the fight and all, but she still let me copy her homework for a month. That's why I did it. Not out of a misplaced desire to be heroic."

"But you said you had a crush on her."

"Cress." He smiled, but it looked strained. "I had a crush on *every* girl. Believe me, it wasn't a big motivator."

She squeezed back against the chair and pulled her knees to her chest. "Why are you telling me this now?"

"I couldn't before. You were so certain that I was this other person, and I kind of liked that you saw me differently than any-one else. Part of me kept thinking that maybe you've been right all along, and it's everyone else who's been wrong about me. That even *I've* been wrong about me." He shrugged. "But even that was just my ego talking, wasn't it? And you deserve to know the truth."

"And you think my entire opinion of you was based on one incident that happened when you were thirteen years old?"

His brow knitted. "I thought I'd done a pretty good job of clarifying all those other incidents, but if you have more, by all means, let me ruin those for you too."

She bit her lip.

The rooftop. The kiss. He'd kept his promise. He'd given her a kiss worth waiting for because she was about to die—they were both about to die. She knew it had been a risk, and probably a stu-pid one. And that was the choice he'd made rather than let her die without experiencing that one perfect moment.

She could think of nothing more heroic.

So why wouldn't he mention it?

Perhaps more important, why couldn't she?

"No," she whispered finally. "I guess I can't think of anything else."

He nodded, though his expression was disappointed. "So given all this new information, you, uh, probably *don't* think you're still in love with me. Do you?"

She shrank into her chair, sure that if he could see her now, he would know. The truth would be evident in every angle of her face.

She loved him more than ever.

And not because she'd scoured file after file of reports and summaries and data and photographs. Not because he was the dreamy, untouchable Carswell Thorne that she'd imagined kissing on the banks of a starlit river while fireworks exploded overhead and violins played in the background.

Now he was the Carswell Thorne who had given her strength in the desert. Who had come for her when she was kidnapped. Who had kissed her when hope was lost and death was imminent.

Thorne awkwardly scratched his ear. "That's what I thought. I figured it was just the fever talking, anyway."

Her heart twisted. "Captain?"

He perked up. "Yeah?"

She picked at the chiffon overlay of her skirt. "Do you think it was destiny that brought us together?"

He squinted and, after a thoughtful moment, shook his head. "No. I'm pretty sure it was Cinder. Why?"

"I guess I have a confession too." She pressed the skirt down around her legs, her face already burning. "I . . . I had a crush on you, before we even met, just from seeing you on the netscreens. I used to believe that you and I were destined to be together, someday, and that we would have this great, epic romance."

One eyebrow ticked upward. "Wow. No pressure or anything."

She squirmed, her body was vibrating with nerves. "I know. I'm sorry. I think you might be right, though. Maybe there isn't such a thing as fate. Maybe it's just the opportunities we're given, and what we do with them. I'm beginning to think that maybe great, epic romances don't just happen. We have to make them ourselves."

Thorne shuffled his feet. "You know, if it was a bad kiss, you can just say so."

She stiffened. "That's not at all what I . . . Wait. Did *you* think it was a bad kiss?"

"No," he said, with an abrupt, clumsy laugh. "I thought it was...um." He cleared his throat. "But there were clearly a lot of expectations, and a lot of pressure, and..." He squirmed in the chair. "We were going to die, you know."

"I know." She squeezed her knees into her chest. "And, no, it wasn't...I didn't think it was a bad kiss."

"Oh, thank the stars." His head fell back against the chair. "Because if I'd ruined that for you, I was going to feel like such a cad."

"Well, don't. It met every expectation. I suppose I should thank you?"

The discomfort melted from his features, and she was jealous as her blush stayed burning hot. Thorne held a hand out toward her and it took every ounce of the courage she'd earned that day to tuck her hand into his.

"Believe me, Cress. The pleasure was all mine."

Fifty-Eight

SHE DREAMED THAT SHE WAS BEING CHASED BY AN ENORMOUS
white wolf, its fangs bared and its eyes flashing beneath a full
moon. She was running through crops thick with mud that
sucked at her shoes, her breath forming clouds of steam. Her
throat stung. Her legs burned. She ran as fast as she could, but
her body became heavier with every step. The shriveled leaves of
sugar beets turned rotten and brittle under her. She spotted a
house in the distance—*her* house. The farmhouse her grandmother had raised her in, the windows beaming with warmth.

The house was safety. The house was home.

But it receded into the distance with each painful step. The
air around her became thick with fog, and the house disappeared
altogether, swallowed whole by the encroaching shadows.

She tripped, landing on her hands and knees. She rolled over,
scrambling and kicking at the ground. Mud clung to her clothes
and hair. The coldness from the ground soaked into her bones.
The wolf prowled closer. Its lean muscles moved gracefully under
the coat of fur. It snarled, eyes lit with hunger.

Her fingers fished around on the ground, searching for a
weapon, anything. They struck something smooth and hard. She

grasped it and pulled it from the squelching mud—an axe, its sharp blade glistening with moonlight.

The wolf leaped, gaping jaws unhinged.

Scarlet lifted the axe. Braced herself. Swung.

The blade cut clean through the beast, cutting it into two pieces from head to tail. Warm blood splattered over Scarlet's face as the two wolf halves landed on either side of her. Her stomach roiled. She was going to throw up.

She dropped the axe and collapsed back on the ground. The mud squished around her ears. Overhead, the moon filled up the whole sky.

Then the wolf halves began to rustle. They gradually rose up, now only the soft outer pelt of the beast, shorn in two. Scarlet could make out vague human-like shapes standing over her, each wearing half of the snow-white pelt.

The fog cleared and Wolf and her grand-mère were before her. Holding their arms out.

Welcoming her home.

Scarlet gasped. Her eyes flew open.

She was met with the sight of steel bars, the earthy smell of ferns and moss, and the chatter of a thousand birds—some trapped in their own elaborate cages, others flocked in the tree branches that entwined around the enormous beams supporting the glass ceiling.

A wolf yipped, sounding both sorrowful and concerned. Scarlet forced herself onto an elbow so she could see the barred enclosure on the other side of the pathway. The white wolf was sitting there, watching her. He howled, just a short, curious sound, not the haunting howls that Scarlet heard in her dreams. She imagined he was asking if she was all right. She might have been screaming or thrashing during the nightmare, and the wolf's pale yellow eyes blinked with worry.

Scarlet tried to gulp, but her mouth was parched, her saliva too thick. She must be going crazy to be carrying on silent conversations with wolves.

"He likes you."

Gasping, Scarlet flipped onto her back.

A stranger, a girl, was sitting cross-legged in her cage, so close Scarlet could have touched her. Scarlet tried to push herself away, but the action sent pain rippling through her bandaged hand. She hissed and fell back onto the ground.

Her hand was the worst of it—the hatchet had taken her left pinky finger to the second knuckle. She had not passed out, though she wished she would have. A Lunar doctor had been waiting to bandage the wound, and he had done it with such precision, Scarlet suspected it was a very common procedure.

But then there were also the scratches on her face and stomach from her time spent in the company of Master Charleson, and countless aches from sleeping on hard floors for—well, she'd lost count of how many nights.

The girl's only reaction to Scarlet's grimace was a long, slow blink.

Clearly, this girl was not another prisoner—or "pet" as the extravagantly dressed Lunars called Scarlet when they passed by her cage, giggling and pointing and making loud remarks on whether or not it was safe to feed the animals.

The girl's clothing was the first indication of her status—a gauzy, silver-white dress that had settled around her shoulders and thighs like snowflakes might settle on a sleepy hillside. Her warm brown skin was flawless and healthy, her fingernails perfectly shaped and clean. Her eyes were bright, the color of melted caramel, but with hints of slate-gray around her pupils. On top of all that, she had silky black hair that curled into perfect spirals, neatly framing her high cheekbones and ruby-red lips.

She was the most beautiful human being Scarlet had ever seen.

Yet, there was one anomaly. Or—three. The right side of the girl's face was marred by three scars that cut down her cheek from the corner of her eye to her jaw. Like perpetual tears. Strangely, the flaws on her skin didn't reduce her beauty, but almost accentuated it. Almost compelled a person to stare at her longer, unable to peel their eyes away.

It was with this thought that Scarlet realized it was a glamour. Which meant this was another trick.

Her expression changed from awestruck and blushing—she despised that she was actually *blushing*—to resentful.

The girl blinked again, drawing attention to her impossibly long, impossibly thick eyelashes.

"Ryu and I are confused," she said. "Was it a very bad dream? Or a very good one?"

Scarlet scowled. The dream had already begun to wisp away, as dreams do, but the question reignited the memory of Wolf and her grandmother before her. Alive and safe.

Which was a cruel joke. Her grandmother was dead, and last she'd seen Wolf, he'd been under the control of a thaumaturge.

"Who are you? And who's Ryu?"

The girl smiled. It was both warm and conspiratorial and it made Scarlet shiver.

Stupid Lunars and their stupid glamours.

"Ryu is the wolf, silly. You've been neighbors for four days now, you know. I'm surprised he hasn't officially introduced himself." Then she leaned forward, dropping her voice to a whisper as if she were about to share a closely guarded secret. "As for me, *I* am your new best friend. But don't tell anyone, because they all think that I'm your master now, and that you are my pet. They don't know that my pets are really my dearest friends. We shall fool them all, you and I."

Scarlet squinted at her. She recognized the girl's voice now, the way she danced through her sentences like each word had to be coaxed off her tongue. This was the girl who had spoken during Scarlet's interrogation.

The girl reached for a strand of filthy hair that had fallen across Scarlet's cheek. Scarlet tensed.

"Your hair is like burning. Does it smell like smoke?" Bending over, the girl pressed the hair against her nose and inhaled. "Not at all. That's good. I wouldn't want you to catch fire."

The girl sat up just as suddenly, pulling a basket toward her that Scarlet hadn't noticed before. It looked like a picnic basket, lined with the same silvery material as her dress.

"I thought today we could play doctor and patient. You'll be the patient." She removed a device from the basket and pressed it against Scarlet's forehead. It beeped and she checked the small screen. "You're not running a fever. Here, let me check your tonsils." She held a thin piece of plastic toward Scarlet's mouth.

Scarlet knocked her away with her uninjured hand and forced herself to sit up. "You're not a doctor."

"No. That's why it's pretend. Aren't you having fun?"

"Fun? I've been mentally and physically tortured for days. I'm starving. I'm thirsty. I'm being kept in a cage in a zoo—"

"Menagerie."

"—and I hurt in places that I didn't know my body even had. And now some crazy person comes in here and is trying to act like we're good pals playing a raucous game of make-believe. Well, no, sorry, I'm *not* having any fun, and I'm not buying whatever chummy trick you're trying to play on me."

The girl's big eyes were blank—neither surprised nor offended by Scarlet's outburst. But then she glanced out toward the pathway that wound between the cages, overgrown with exotic flowers and trees to suggest some semblance of being in a lush jungle.

A guard was standing at the pathway's bend, scowling. Scarlet recognized him. He was one of the guards that regularly brought her bread and water. He was the one who had grabbed her rear end the first time she'd been thrown into this cage. At the time she'd been too exhausted to do anything more than stumble away from him, but if she ever had the chance, she would break every one of his fingers in retaliation.

"We're all right," the girl said, smiling brightly. "We're pretending that I cut off her hair and glued it to my head because I wanted to be a candlestick, and she didn't like that."

While she spoke, the guard's glare never left Scarlet, only narrowed in warning. After a long moment, he meandered away.

When his footsteps had faded, the girl pulled the basket onto her lap and riffled through it. "You shouldn't call me crazy. They don't like that."

Scarlet faced her again, her gaze dragging down the raised scar tissue on her cheek.

"But you are crazy."

"I know." She lifted a small box from the basket. "Do you know how I know?"

Scarlet didn't answer.

"Because the palace walls have been bleeding for years, and no one else sees it." She shrugged, as if this were a perfectly normal thing to say. "No one believes me, but in some corridors, the blood has gotten so thick there's nowhere safe to step. When I have to pass through those places, I leave a trail of bloody footprints for the rest of the day, and then I worry that the queen's soldiers will follow the scent and eat me up while I'm sleeping. Some nights I don't sleep very well." Her voice dropped to a haunted whisper, her eyes taking on a brittle luminescence. "But if the blood was real, the servants would clean it up. Don't you think?"

Scarlet shivered. This girl really *was* crazy.

"This is for you," she said, astoundingly bright once again. "Doctor's orders are to take one pill twice a day." She tilted toward Scarlet. "They wouldn't let me bring you real medication, of course, so it's just candy."

Then she winked, and Scarlet couldn't tell if the wink was to indicate that the box contained candy or not.

"I'm not going to eat it."

The girl listed her head. "Why not? It's a gift, to cement our forever friendship." She pulled the lid off the box, revealing four small candies nestled in a bed of spun sugar. They were round as marbles and bright, glossy red. "Sour apple petites. My personal favorites. Please, take one."

"What do you want from me?"

Her lashes fluttered. "I want us to be friends."

"And all your friendships are based on lies? Wait, of course they are. You're Lunar."

For the first time, the girl deflated a little. "I've only ever had two friends," she said, then glanced quickly at the wolf. Ryu had lain down, resting his head on his paws as he watched them. "Other than the animals, of course. But one of my friends turned into ashes when we were very little. A pile of girl-shaped ashes. The other has gone missing . . . and I don't know if he'll ever come back." A shudder ripped through her, so strong she nearly dropped the box. With goose bumps all down her arms, she set the box on the floor between them and picked mindlessly at her dress. "But I asked the stars to send a sign that he was all right, and they sent me a shooting star across the sky. The next day was a trial, like any trial, except the Earthen girl standing before me had hair like a shooting star. And you'd *seen* him."

"Do you ever make sense?"

The girl pressed her hands onto the ground and leaned forward until her nose was almost touching Scarlet's. Scarlet refused to pull away, though her breath hitched.

"Was he all right? When you saw him last. Sybil said he was still alive, that he may have been used to pilot that ship, but she didn't say if he'd been injured. Do you think he's safe?"

"I don't know what you're—"

The girl pressed her fingertips against Scarlet's mouth.

"Jacin Clay," she whispered. "Sybil's guard, with the blond hair and beautiful eyes and the rising sun in his smile. Please, tell me he's all right."

Scarlet blinked. The girl's fingers were still on her mouth, but it didn't matter. She was too baffled to speak. The battle aboard the Rampion was mostly a blur of screaming and gunshots in her memory, and her focus had been on the thaumaturge then. But she did vaguely recall another person there. A blond-haired guard.

But the rising sun in his smile? *Please.*

She sneered. "I remember two people trying to kill me and my friends."

"Yes, and Jacin was one of them," she said, evidently unconcerned with the whole killing part of Scarlet's statement.

"I guess so. There was a blond guard."

Glee spread over the girl's face. The look had the power to stop hearts and brighten rooms.

But not to Scarlet.

"And how did he look?"

"He looked like he was trying to *kill* me. But I'm sure my friends killed him first. That's usually what we do to people who work for your queen."

The smile vanished and the girl shriveled away, tying her arms around her waist. "You don't mean that."

"I do. And believe me, he deserved it."

The girl was beginning to shake now, like she was on the verge of hyperventilating.

Scarlet decided without much guilt that if that happened, she wouldn't do a thing about it. She wouldn't try to help her. She wouldn't call for the guard.

This stranger was no friend.

Across the aisle, the wolf had climbed onto all fours and was pawing at the base of his enclosure. He began to whimper.

After a few moments, the girl managed to get herself under control. Sliding the lid back onto the candies, she settled them into her basket and stood, hunching in the small cage.

"I see," she said. "That will conclude this visit. I prescribe adequate rest and—" She sobbed and turned away, but paused before she could call for the guard. Slowly, stiffly, she turned back. "I wasn't lying about the walls that bleed. Someday soon, I fear the palace will be soaked through with blood and all of Artemisia Lake will be so red, even the Earthens will be able to see it."

"I'm not interested in your delusions." A sharp, unexpected pain shot up through the arm that Scarlet was using to support herself and she crumpled to the ground, waiting for the pinpricks of pain to fade. She glared up at the girl, angry at how weak and vulnerable she was. Angry at the flash of concern in the girl's eyes that seemed so honest. She snarled up at her. "And I don't care for your mock sympathy, either. Your glamour. Your mind control. You people have built your entire culture on lies, and I want nothing to do with it."

The girl stared at her for so long, Scarlet began to wish she hadn't said anything. But keeping her mouth shut had never been a great talent of hers.

Then, finally, the girl tapped her knuckles against the bars. As the guard's footsteps patted down the pathway, she reached into the basket and retrieved the box again. She set it down at Scarlet's side, tucking it beside her so the guard wouldn't see.

"I haven't used my glamour since I was twelve years old," she whispered, gaze piercing as if it were very important to her that Scarlet understand this. "Not since I was old enough to control it. That's why the visions come to me. That's why I'm going mad."

Behind her, the bolts of the cage door clunked open.

"Your Highness."

She swiveled on her toes and ducked out of the cage, her head lowered so that her thick hair hid both her beauty and her scars.

Your Highness.

Stunned, Scarlet lay on the ground until her tongue began to turn to chalk from thirst. As far as she knew, there was only one Lunar princess. Other than Cinder, of course.

Princess Winter, the queen's stepdaughter.

The unspeakable beauty. The scars that, according to rumor, had been inflicted by the queen herself.

When she glanced back toward the wolf's cage, Ryu had wandered away, toward the back of his enclosure. He had been given much more space to prowl than Scarlet, perhaps a quarter of an acre of dirt and grass, trees, and a fake fallen log that formed a quaint little den.

Sighing, Scarlet looked back up at the glass ceiling, where she could see black sky and countless stars between the tree branches. Her stomach panged, a reminder that her one small meal had been devoured hours ago, and unlike Ryu and the white stag that lived in an enclosure farther down the aisle and the albino peacock that sometimes wandered freely between them, Scarlet wouldn't get another meal until tomorrow.

It took a long time of battling with her weakened willpower, feeling the weight of the candies beside her. She had no reason to trust that girl. She *didn't* trust that girl. But after her stomach had begun to ache from hollowness and her head to spin with hunger, she gave up and pulled the lid off the box.

She pulled out one of the candies. It was glass smooth beneath her teeth. The outer shell cracked easily, giving way to a warm, melty center that burst sweet and sour on her tongue.

She moaned and let her head fall onto the hard floor. Nothing, not even her grandmother's prized tomatoes, had ever tasted so good.

But then, as she was working her tongue around her gums, searching out any missed bits of the candy, a tingling began to warm her throat. It expanded outward, into her chest and through her abdomen and along her limbs, all the way to her missing finger, leaving a trail of comfort in its wake.

When it was gone, Scarlet realized that it had taken her pain with it.

Fifty-Nine

IT WAS LIKE BEING DRAWN SLOWLY FROM THE SERENE darkness, the way one wakes up when they've been having a lovely dream and their subconscious is struggling to hold them there, just a little while longer. Then, with angry resignation, Kai was awake, his eyes wide-open and staring up at unfamiliar slats. The underside of a bunk bed.

He rubbed his eyes, thinking maybe he hadn't awoken entirely yet. His chest was throbbing, and there was a nauseous twist in his stomach. He turned his head to the side and felt an ache in his neck. Reaching up, he discovered a bandage taped beneath his hairline.

But his attention was already moving on, wandering around the room. There was a tiny desk and a utilitarian closet on the other side, though the room was so small he almost could have touched them from where he lay. A dim light had been left on beside the door. The walls were metal and the slightly scratchy blanket he lay on was military brown.

Pulse speeding up, he reached for the bunk overhead to keep himself from hitting his head as he swung his legs over the side. His feet landed on the uncarpeted floor with a thunk and he was surprised to discover he was wearing shoes.

Dress shoes.

And dress slacks.

And his wedding shirt and sash, now wrinkled and untucked.

Great stars. *The wedding.*

Mouth suddenly dry, Kai lurched out of the bed and stumbled toward the small window. He pressed his hands to either side. His stomach dropped in unison with his jaw.

Great stars indeed. He'd never seen so many in all his life, and never so bright. It gave him a strange sensation of vertigo, like he should have been looking up into the night sky, but the gravity was all wrong. Where was the horizon to orient himself? A cold sweat beaded on his forehead as he pressed his cheek to the wall, trying to peer as far down as the small window would let him, and then—

Earth.

Kai shoved himself away from the wall. He nearly fell over, but caught himself on the upper mattress of the bunk. His heartbeat clanked and shuddered.

Mysteries began to click together in his muddled brain. Cinder. A knife. The bandages on his wrist and neck—his tracking chips. Wasn't the chip in his neck supposed to be top secret? And a gun, or something embedded in her hand. The lingering sting beside his sternum.

Had she *shot* him?

Raking a hand through his hair, he turned and wrenched open the door.

He found himself in a narrow hallway, more brightly lit than the room had been. At the far end it opened up into a kitchen of sorts. He could hear voices coming from the other direction. Pulling his shoulders back, he marched toward them.

The hall opened into a huge metal room, cluttered with plastic storage crates. Through a doorway he saw the lights and instruments of a cockpit, and another breathtaking view of Earth.

Two people were seated in the cockpit chairs as he approached.

"Where's Cinder?"

They spun to face him and the girl launched herself to her feet. "Your Majesty!"

The man, a huge grin spreading over his face, was slower to stand, first grabbing a cane from against the wall. "Welcome aboard the Rampion, Your Magesticness. Captain Carswell Thorne, at your service." He bowed.

Kai scowled. "Yeah, I recognize you."

"You do?" The man's smile grew wider and he nudged the girl with his elbow. "He recognizes me."

"Where's Cinder?"

The girl swayed nervously on her heels. "I believe she's in the podship dock, Your Majesty."

Kai turned and marched out toward the cargo bay, and yelped.

Another man was sitting cross-legged on top of a packing crate, shirtless, with a needle in one hand, a thread in his mouth, and a pile of bloodied bandages beside him. His torso was marred by numerous wounds and scars, both old and new. He had a black tattoo stamped on his left arm.

Pulling the needle through a gash on his chest, he let the thread drop from his mouth, and nodded. "Your Majesty."

Choking on his heart, Kai found himself anchored to the floor, expecting the man to leap at him and maul him to death at any moment. He hadn't yet seen one of the queen's wolf soldiers in person, but he'd seen plenty of vids. He knew how fast they were—how deadly.

But after an awkward, silent moment, the man simply returned his attention to his wound.

"Um. Your Majesty?"

Starting, he whipped his gaze back to the blonde girl.

"Would you like me to take you to the podship dock?"

He forced his hands to unclench, reminding himself that he was the ruler of the Eastern Commonwealth and would behave accordingly, even among criminals and monsters.

"Thank you," he gasped. "That would be appreciated."

CINDER CHEWED ON HER LOWER LIP WHILE SHE TWISTED THE wires together, fastening them with a wire connector. "All right, try that."

Iko, flat on her back, cast her gaze downward, then tilted her head to the left. Her eyes brightened and she tried to the right, daring to test the full range of motion. She beamed. "It works!"

Cinder tapped her chin with the end of the fuse pullers. "There's still a little bit of a bend in that third vertebrae, but there's nothing I can do about it now. We'll just have to wait until we can find a replacement piece. Try your fingers again."

Iko wiggled her fingers, then her toes. She lifted her legs until they were perpendicular to the floor, then kept going so that she was practically kissing her knees. Letting out a yelp of delight, she flipped forward, using the momentum to spring up onto her feet. "It works! It all works!"

"Iko, knock it off!" Cinder scrambled up beside her. "I still need to—"

Before she could finish, Iko pulled her against her bosom, squeezing and swaying and trembling with joy.

An android. Trembling with joy.

"You're the best mechanic an android could ever ask for."

"Say that when you don't have an enormous gaping hole in your throat," Cinder said, prying herself out of the embrace.

Iko checked her reflection in the window of the podship and flinched. The paneling from the top of her throat to her sternum was flayed open to give Cinder access to her internal workings. Her central processor, wiring, and mobility mechanics were on full display.

"Oh, yuck," said Iko, trying to cover the hole with both hands. "I hate when my wiring is showing."

"I know the feeling." Cinder pulled a pair of pliers off the wall's magnetic strip. "Come here. I'll see if I can bend some of that external paneling back into place. A lot of your skin fibers are beyond repair, so it's not going to be perfect, but it's all I can do right now. You might have to wear turtlenecks for a while."

Sighing, Iko came to stand beside Cinder. "Figures that as soon as Captain Thorne brings home this marvelous body for me, those stupid Lunars go and ruin everything."

Cinder smirked. "Stop talking for a minute while I do this."

Iko impatiently tapped her fingers against her hips while Cinder warped the external paneling into something that resembled the shape of a clavicle.

Behind her, the door hummed open. "Here she is, Your Majesty."

Cinder stiffened, the pliers still clamped on to Iko's paneling. She heard footsteps and then Iko screeched and shoved Cinder and her tool away. "Don't let him see me this way!" she yelled, diving behind the podship.

Gulping, Cinder tucked the pliers into her back pocket and

slowly turned around. Kai's gaze was dark as it swooped over her to the podship—and Iko's legs beneath it—to the tool chests and power cords fastened to the walls, before landing on Cinder again.

Cress and Thorne hovered curiously by the door.

"You're awake," she stammered. Then, realizing that was a stupid thing to say, she attempted to stand straighter. "How do you feel?"

"*Kidnapped.* How should I feel?"

She rubbed her wrist, tempted to call up a glamour to disguise her cyborg hand. Which was also stupid, of course. And besides, it was something Levana would have done.

"I was hoping maybe you'd feel well rested?" she said, attempting a weak smile.

She was met with no reaction. No smile. No chuckle. Not even a flicker of humor.

She pressed her lips together.

"We need to talk," said Kai.

Thorne let out a slow whistle. "No one ever likes to hear those words."

Cinder glared at him. "Thorne, why don't you go give Iko a tutorial with the cockpit controls?"

"Excellent idea," Cress chirped, nudging Thorne back out the door. "Come on, Iko."

Iko was still hiding, hugging herself self-consciously. "Is he looking?"

Kai raised an eyebrow.

"He's not looking," said Cinder.

A hesitation. "Are you sure?"

Cinder gestured exasperatedly at Kai. "You're *not looking.*"

He cast his eyes to the ceiling. "Oh, for all the stars." Crossing his arms, he turned his back on them.

Cinder waved at Iko. "All clear. We'll finish that up . . . later."

Braids bouncing, Iko darted to join Cress and Thorne in the hallway. "I'm so happy to see you're all right, Your Majesty!" she called to his back.

As the door slipped shut, Iko flashed Cinder an encouraging thumbs-up.

And then they were alone.

Sixty

"I CAN'T BELIEVE YOU KIDNAPPED ME!" KAI YELLED, SPINNING back to face her before Cinder could brace herself. "We're on a spaceship, Cinder. In *space*!" He pointed at the wall. It wasn't actually an exterior wall, but Cinder didn't feel the need to point that out. "I can't be on a spaceship. I have a country to run. I have people who need me. We are on the verge of a war. Do you understand that? *War.* Where people *die.* I cannot be up here, messing around with you and your band of misfits! Do you even know that you are housing one of her mutants up there?"

"Oh, yeah. That's Wolf. He's harmless." She rolled her eyes. "Well, not *harmless*..."

He laughed, but it was sharp and delirious. "I can't—how could—what were you thinking?"

"You're welcome," she muttered, defiantly crossing her arms.

He glowered, rather ungratefully. "Take me back to Earth."

"I can't do that."

"Cinder—" He huffed. Reconsidered. Softened . . . just a bit.

The change put an instant dent in Cinder's defenses, prompting a strange tingle behind her rib cage. She dug her fingertips into her elbows.

"As someone who understands why you did this, and admires your ability to actually accomplish it, I am—*pleading* with you. Cinder. Please. Take me back."

She filled up her lungs. "No."

The softness was gone, instantly. Tipping his head back, Kai strung both hands through his hair. It surprised her how familiar the gesture was.

"When did you become so *frustrating*?"

She scuffed the toe of her boot against the floor.

"Fine! As your emperor, I *command* you to return me to Earth. Immediately."

Cinder rocked on her heels. "Kai...Your Majesty. You may recall that I'm Lunar. And Lunars are forbidden from being granted citizenship in the Eastern Commonwealth. Therefore... you're no longer my emperor."

"This isn't a joke."

She was surprised at how the words stung. Like before, in the palace, indignation reared up fast and burning. "You have no idea how seriously I'm taking this."

"Are you? Do you even know what the consequences are going to be for what you've done?"

"Yes, actually. I know this is a war. I am aware that more people are going to die before this is over. But we didn't have a choice."

"Your choice was to stay out of the way! Your choice was to do nothing! This is my job, my responsibility. I'm the emperor. Let me handle it."

"By letting you *marry* her? That's handling it?"

"It's my decision."

"It's a stupid one!"

Kai spun away, his hands clawed into his hair. Whatever product had been used to style it for the wedding was making it messier than usual, and stars, he looked good.

Cinder smothered the thought, annoyed with herself.

"Please," he said, his voice strained as he faced her again. "Please tell me this isn't some . . . some petty act of jealousy. Please tell me this isn't all because I asked you to the ball, or that time in the elevator, or—"

"Oh, you can't be serious. I hope you don't really think so little of me."

"You *shot* me, Cinder, and then you *kidnapped* me. I honestly don't know what to think."

"Well, believe it or not, we didn't just do this for you. We're trying to save the whole world from your power-crazy fiancée. I refuse to let Levana become empress. I refuse to give her free rein over the Commonwealth. But we need more time."

"More time for what? All you've done is make her angrier, so that when she retaliates, her wrath is going to be that much worse. Was that a part of your master plan, or are you just making this up as you go along?"

Cinder's blood began to boil and she desperately, desperately wished she could tell him that, yes, of course they had a grand master plan that was guaranteed to work. Guaranteed to rid them all of Queen Levana and her tyranny forever. But there was no guarantee. Only a string of hope, and the knowledge that losing wasn't an option.

She swallowed, hard. "I have a plan, to end this for good. But I need your help."

Kai pinched the bridge of his nose. "Cinder. I hate Levana as much as you do. But she's the one pulling the strings here. She has this army . . . it's like nothing I've ever seen before. Those little skirmishes that killed sixteen thousand people a couple weeks ago? Laughable compared to what she's really capable of. Plus she has an antidote to letumosis, and we desperately need it—you know how much we need it. So while the idea of marrying Levana and crowning her empress makes me want to gouge out my own eyes, I don't have a choice."

"Gouge out your own eyes?" she said softly. "She could make you do that, you know."

His expression darkened. "So could you, I'm told."

She looked away. "Kai—Your Majesty—"

He waved his arms through the air. "Kai is fine. I don't care."

Cinder pressed her lips. It felt like a victory, but an unearned one. "You have to trust me. We can defeat her. I know we can."

"How? Even if . . . let's say you did. Let's say you even managed to kill her. There's still a whole posse of thaumaturges ready to take her place, and from what I've seen, they're not much better."

"We'll choose the person to replace her. We . . . already have her replacement, actually."

He snickered. "Ah. I see. Because you think the Lunar people will bow to just any . . . one . . ." He trailed off, eyes widening. And, for a moment, his anger was gone. "Unless . . . wait. You don't mean . . . ?"

She looked at the floor.

He took a single step toward her. "Did you find her? Princess Selene? Is that what this is all about?"

Cinder took the pliers out of her pocket, needing something to fiddle with while her nerves sparked and sputtered. She remembered that her metal hand was still bare, but Kai hadn't glanced at it once through the whole argument.

"Cinder?"

"Yeah," she breathed. "Yeah. I found her."

Kai pointed toward the cargo bay. "Is it that blonde girl?"

She shook her head, and Kai frowned. "The girl from France? What was her name... Scarlet something?"

"No. Not Scarlet." She squeezed the pliers, trying to direct all her frazzled energy into them.

"Then where is she? Is she on this ship? Can I meet her? Or is she still on Earth somewhere? Is she in hiding?"

When Cinder said nothing, Kai frowned. "What's wrong? Is she all right?"

"I have to ask you something, and I want you to be honest."

His eyes narrowed, instantly suspicious, which bothered her more than she cared to admit. She loosened her grip on the pliers. "Do you really think I brainwashed you before? When we met? And all those times, before the ball..."

His shoulders drooped. "Really? You're changing the subject to talk about *this*?"

"It's important to me." She turned away and started gathering the tools she'd used to fix Iko. "I understand if you do. I know how it must have looked."

Kai fidgeted with his ceremonial sash, then, after a moment, pulled it over his head and bunched it up in his fists. "I don't know. I never wanted to believe it, but I've had to wonder. And when you fell, and I saw your glamour... Cinder, do you have any idea how beautiful your glamour is?"

Cinder cringed, knowing that he didn't mean it as a compliment. *Painful to look at* were the words he'd used at the time.

"No," she said, distracting herself by returning each tool to its designated place on the magnetic wall. "I can't see it."

"Well, it's... it was a lot to take in that night. But then, Levana has manipulated me plenty of times, so I know what it feels like. And it never felt like that with you."

She released the last tool.

"Of course, the media wants to think that's what happened. It would be convenient."

"Right." She glanced at him over her shoulder. "A convenient excuse for inviting a cyborg to the ball."

He blinked. "For inviting a Lunar to the ball."

The knot that had been tied up in her stomach for weeks began to unravel, just a little. "Not that it makes a difference what I say, but . . . I never did. Manipulate you, I mean. And I never will." She hesitated. It was a promise that she didn't know if she'd be able to keep. Not if he didn't agree to help them. "And I did try to tell you about being cyborg. I mean, kind of. I'm sure I considered it at least twice."

Kai started to shake his head and she held her breath. "No, you were right before. If you'd told me, I probably never would have spoken to you again." He stared down at the sash twisted between his fists. "Although, I like to think I would act differently now."

He met her gaze and she noticed, with a start, that his ears had gone pink. And then his lips quirked into the faintest of smiles.

It was the smile she'd been waiting for.

It didn't last long.

"Cinder. Look. I am glad I'm not married right now, but this was still a huge mistake. I can't risk angering Levana. Whatever you're planning, you have to leave me out of it."

"I can't. I need your help."

He sighed, but it was shaky, and she could tell his resolve was crumbling.

"You think Selene can overthrow her?"

Biting the inside of her cheek, she nodded. "I do."

"Then I hope she intends to do it soon."

Dragging her hands down her sides, Cinder felt nervousness pressing against her rib cage. "Kai, she may not be exactly what you were hoping for. I don't want you to be disappointed. I know you put a lot into trying to find her and—"

"Why? What's wrong with her?"

Cringing, she knotted her fingers together. Metal and skin. "Well. She was rescued from that fire, but it destroyed a lot of her body. She lost some limbs. And a lot of her skin had to be grafted. And . . . she's just not . . . entirely *whole*."

He furrowed his brow. "What do you mean? Is she in a coma?"

"Not anymore." She braced herself for his reaction. "But she's a cyborg."

His eyes widened, but then his attention was darting around the room as though he couldn't look at Cinder while he adjusted to that information. "I see," he said slowly, before meeting her gaze again. "But . . . is she all right?"

The question caught her by surprise and she couldn't help a startled laugh. "Oh, yeah, she's great. I mean, half the people in the world want to kill her and the other half want to chain her to a throne on the moon, which is just what she's always wanted. So she's *fantastic*."

He stared at her like he was once again questioning her sanity. "What?"

Cinder shut her eyes and tried to bury her mounting panic. Opening them again, she spread her hands, placating. Hesitated.

She looked at the ceiling.

Took in a breath.

Met his gaze again.

"It's me, Kai. I'm Princess Selene."

Sixty-One

KAI'S FACE WAS MADE UP OF CONFUSION, LIKE SHE'D SPOKEN gibberish. His wedding sash slipped out of his hands and drifted to the floor.

When the silence slipped toward awkward, Cinder cleared her throat. "And in case you weren't sure, I was being sarcastic before about all that 'great' stuff. Not that, I mean—I know you have your own things to worry about, so you don't need to . . . I don't . . . I'm fine, really. It's just been a rough few weeks with the whole"—she circled her hands wildly through the air—"Peony-ball-Levana-wedding thing. And now Dr. Erland is dead and Scarlet is gone and Thorne is blind and Wolf . . . I'm not sure. He's so *still* these days and I'm really starting to worry about him. But I've got it under control. I can do this. I'm—"

"Stop. Please stop talking."

She clamped her mouth shut.

The silence dragged on.

Cinder opened her mouth, but Kai held up his hand. She shut it again. Bit her lip.

"You?" he finally said. "*You* are Princess Selene?"

Grimacing, she rubbed at her wrist. "Surprise?"

"All this time?"

She ducked her head, suddenly uncomfortable at the way he was looking at her. "Um, yeah, technically. Dr. Erland figured it out first, when I was taken in for the cyborg draft. He ran my DNA and . . . yeah. But he decided not to tell me until I was locked up in prison, which complicated a few things."

Kai guffawed, but not in a mean way. Inhaling a shaky breath, he rubbed the palms of his hands into his eyes. Then, as quickly as his disbelief had come, the comprehension came faster. "Oh, stars. Levana knows, doesn't she? That's why she hates you so much. That's why she's so determined to find you."

"Yeah, she knows."

"And it was you. This whole time, it was *you*."

"You're actually taking this better than I thought you would."

He dragged both hands down his face. "No, you know, it almost makes sense. Kind of." He scraped his gaze over her. "Although . . . somehow, I always pictured the princess . . . I don't know. In a dress."

Cinder laughed.

"And I always thought that when I found her, it would be so easy. We would just . . . present her to the world and announce her as the true queen, and Levana would crawl away to some hole. I never imagined that Levana would already know. That she would be *fighting* it."

She quirked an eyebrow. "I'm beginning to think you may not know your fiancée very well."

He scowled at her. "That's it, Cinder. No more secrets. I don't know if I can survive any more big reveals from you, so if you have anything else to tell me, out with it. Right now."

Cinder rocked back on her heels, pondering.

Cyborg. Lunar. Princess.

No more secrets. No more lies.

Well, just one.

She thought she might be a tiny bit in love with him.

But there was no way she could tell him *that*.

"I can't cry," she whispered instead, hunching her shoulders.

Kai blinked, twice, then scratched his ear and looked away. "I already knew that."

"What? How?"

"Your guardian may have said something about it. And I . . . I've seen your medical records."

"My—" Her eyes widened. "You've seen . . . you know . . . ?"

"You were a fugitive and I needed to know more about you and I . . . I'm sorry."

She squeezed her eyes shut. She'd seen the diagram of her cyborg implants. Every wire. Every synthetic organ. Every manufactured panel. Thinking about it made her feel nauseous. She couldn't imagine what someone else would think when they saw it. What Kai must have thought.

"No, it's all right," she said. "No more secrets."

He took a step toward her. "Your eyes . . . are they really . . . ?"

"Synthetic," she murmured, when he couldn't say the word himself.

"And that's why you can't cry?"

She nodded, unable to look up at him, even as he came to stand not two steps in front of her. "I don't need the tear ducts for lubrication, and they were getting in the way of . . . um." She tapped a finger against her temple. "I have a retina scanner and display in my eye. It's like a really small netscreen, so there's a lot of wiring. Oh, stars, I can't believe I'm telling you this." She buried her face in her hands.

"It's kind of brilliant," said Kai.

She nearly choked on her own laugh.

Kai reached for her wrists. "Can I see?"

She groaned, knowing that if she had the ability to blush, her face would be as red as his wedding sash.

Mortified and resigned, she let him pull her hands away and struggled to hold his gaze. He stared into her eyes like he could see through to her control panel, but then, after a moment, he shook his head.

"You'd never even know."

Trying not to fidget, Cinder raised her eyes to the ceiling, hating herself a little bit for what she was about to do. But what did it matter now? He would never again be fooled into thinking she was human.

"Watch the bottom of my left iris," she whispered. She turned on the retina display, pulling up a newsfeed she'd been watching before they got to New Beijing—news from the African Union. An anchor was talking, but Cinder didn't bother to turn on the audio.

Kai dipped his head. It took a moment, but then his lips parted. "There's . . . is that . . . ?"

"Newsfeed."

"It's so small. Just a dot, really."

"It looks a lot bigger to me." A tingle traipsed down her spine at how he was studying her, almost in childish awe, and how he was so close, and how he was still holding her wrists.

He seemed to realize it at the same time. His expression changed suddenly, and she knew he wasn't looking at the retina display anymore, or even her synthetic eyes. He was looking at *her*.

Her heart pattered.

Kai licked his lips. "I'm sorry I had you arrested. But I'm glad you're all right."

"Really? You don't hate me for . . . shooting you?"

His lips twitched and he glanced down. Taking her cyborg hand into both of his, he lifted it between them, eyeing the metal fingers. "I don't remember that medical diagram saying anything about a gun. My security team probably would have found that to be useful information."

"I like to maintain an air of mystery."

"I've noticed."

She watched his thumb trace the length of her fingers, finding it hard to breathe, impossible to move. "The hand is new," she whispered.

"It appears to be excellent craftsmanship." His voice, too, had dropped.

"It's plated with one-hundred percent titanium." She didn't know why she said it. Hardly knew what she'd said at all.

Bending his head, Kai pressed his lips to her knuckles. The plating had no nerve endings, and yet the touch sent a tingle of electricity along her arm.

"Cinder?"

"Mm?"

He lifted his gaze. "Just to be clear, you're not using your mind powers on me right now, are you?"

She blinked. "Of course not."

"Just checking."

Then he slid his arms around her waist and kissed her.

Cinder gasped, pressing her palms against his chest. Kai pulled her closer.

Seconds later, her brain began registering all the new chemicals flooding her system. INCREASED LEVELS OF DOPAMINE AND ENDORPHINS, REDUCED AMOUNTS OF CORTISOL, ERRATIC PULSE, RISING BLOOD PRESSURE . . .

Leaning into him, Cinder sent the messages away. Her hands tentatively made their way to his shoulders, before stringing around his neck.

Then, somewhere in the rush of sensations, Cinder's attention snagged on the retina display, alone against the darkness of her eyelids. At first, it was only a dim, annoyed awareness. But then—

FARAFRAH.
LUNARS.
MASSACRE.

Her eyes snapped open. She pulled herself away.

Kai started. "Wha—"

"I'm sorry."

She started to tremble, still focused on the newsfeed.

A moment passed in which she was watching the feed with horror, and then Kai cleared his throat. His voice had gone heavy. "No. No, I'm sorry. I shouldn't have—"

"No!" She grabbed his shirt before he could pull away from her. "It's not—It's Levana."

His expression turned cold.

"She's . . . she's retaliated. She attacked . . ." Cursing, she tore her hands away from Kai, covering her face while she digested the news. A swarm of Lunar soldiers attacked the oasis town not two hours ago, before disappearing into the desert as fast as they'd come. They murdered both the civilians and the Commonwealth soldiers who had been sent to question them.

Pictures flashed across the scene.

Blood. *So much blood.*

"Cinder—*where?* Where did she strike?"

"Africa. The town . . ." She gulped. "The people that helped us."

Something snapped in her head. Screaming, Cinder reached for the strip of tools, seized a wrench, and threw it at the far wall. It clattered harmlessly to the floor. She grabbed a screwdriver next, but Kai just as quickly lifted it from her hand.

"Has she put forth any demands?" he said, absurdly calm.

She clenched her empty fists. "I don't know. I just know they're all dead. Because of me. Because they helped *me.*" She fell into a crouch, covering her head. Her entire body was burning up with fury.

At Levana.

But mostly at herself. At her own decisions.

Because she'd known this would happen. She'd made the choice anyway.

"Cinder."

"This is my fault."

A hand settled on her back. "You didn't kill them."

"I might as well have."

"Did they know the risk they were taking when they helped you? The danger they'd be in?"

She turned her head away from him.

"Maybe they did it because they believed in you. Because they thought the risk was worth it."

"Is this supposed to be helping?"

"Cinder—"

"You want to know another secret? The biggest secret?" She sat, splaying her legs like a broken doll in front of her. "I'm *scared,*

Kai. I'm so scared." She thought it might feel better, to say the words out loud, but instead they only made her feel pathetic and weak. She wrapped her arms around her waist. "I'm scared of her, and her army, and what she can do. And everyone expects me to be strong and brave, but I don't know what I'm doing. I have no idea how to overthrow her. And even if I succeed, I have no idea how to be a queen. There are so many people relying on me, people who don't even *know* they're relying on me, and now they're dying, all because of some ridiculous fantasy that I can help them, that *I can save them*, but what if I can't?"

A headache began to throb against her temples, a reminder that she would be crying right now. If she were normal.

Arms wrapped around her.

Cinder pressed her face against his silk shirt. There was some sort of cologne or maybe soap there—so faint she hadn't picked up on it before.

"I know exactly how you feel," Kai said.

She squeezed her eyes shut. "Not exactly."

"I think pretty close."

She shook her head. "No, you don't understand. More than anything, I'm afraid that . . . the more I fight her and the stronger I become, the more I'm turning into her."

Sitting back on his heels, Kai pulled away just enough to look into her face without releasing her. "You're not turning into Levana."

"Are you sure about that? Because I manipulated your adviser today, and countless guards. I manipulated Wolf. I . . . I killed a police officer, in France, and I would have killed more people if I'd had to, people in your own military, and I don't even know if I would feel bad about it, because there are always ways to justify it. It's for the good of everyone, isn't it? Sacrifices have to be made. And then there are the mirrors, such a stupid, stupid thing, but they—I'm beginning to get it. Why she hates them so much. And then—" She shuddered. "Today, I tortured her thaumaturge. I didn't just manipulate her. I *tortured* her. And I almost *enjoyed* it."

"Cinder, look at me." He cupped her face. "I know you're scared, and you have every right to be. But you are not turning into Queen Levana."

"You can't know that."

"But I do."

"She's my aunt, you know."

He smoothed back her hair. "Yeah, well, my great-grandfather signed the Cyborg Protection Act. And yet, here we are."

She bit her lip. *Here they were.*

"Now, let's never talk about you being related to her again. Because I'm technically still engaged to her, and that's really weird."

Cinder couldn't help laughing, even exhaustedly, even just to cover up the screaming inside, as he bound her up in his arms again. Her headache began to fade, replaced with the strength of his heartbeat and the way she felt almost delicate when she was pressed up against him like this.

Almost fragile.

Almost safe.

Almost like a princess.

"You won't tell anyone, will you?" she murmured.

"I won't."

"And if it turns out I make a terrible princess?"

He shrugged against her. "The people of Luna don't need a princess. They need a revolutionary."

Cinder furrowed her brow. "A revolutionary," she repeated. She liked that a lot better than *princess*.

The door zipped open.

Cinder and Kai jumped apart, Kai scrambling to his feet.

Cress, breathless and flushed, paused in the doorway.

"I'm sorry," she said. "But the newsfeeds—Levana—"

"I know," said Cinder, forcing herself to stand. "I know about Farafrah."

Cress shook her head, wild-eyed. "It isn't just Farafrah. Their ships are swarming Earth, every continent. Thousands of soldiers are invading the cities. Her other soldiers." She shuddered so hard she had to grasp the door frame. "They're like animals, like predators."

"What is Earth doing?" asked Kai, and Cinder recognized his leader voice. "Are we defending ourselves?"

"They're trying. All six countries have declared a state of war. Evacuations are being ordered, military is assembling—"

"All six?"

Cress pushed her hair off her brow. "Konn Torin has temporarily assumed the role of leader of the Commonwealth . . . until your return."

A heavy silence pressed against Cinder's chest. Then Kai turned to face her, and she could feel the gravity of his emotions without looking at him.

"I think it's about time you told me about this plan," he said.

Cinder curled her hands into tight fists. The possibility of their success had seemed so faint that she'd hardly considered what would come next. She'd hoped they would have some time, at least a day or two, but she saw now that there would be no such respite.

War had begun.

"You said yourself that the people of Luna need a revolution-ary." She lifted her chin, holding his gaze. "So I'm going to Luna, and I'm going to start a revolution."

Acknowledgments

Where, oh where, to begin.

The marvelous team at the Macmillan Children's Publishing Group continues to amaze me with their brilliance, creativity, and enthusiasm. My editor, Liz Szabla, my publisher, Jean Feiwel, along with Lauren Burniac, Rich Deas, Lucy Del Priore, Elizabeth Fithian, Courtney Griffin, Anna Roberto, Allison Verost, Emily Waters-Curley, Ksenia Winnicki, and no doubt countless others who work tirelessly behind the scenes to bring these books out into the world—you are all awesome. Thank you.

My agency team—Jill Grinberg, Cheryl Pientka, and Katelyn Detweiler—is a constant source of comfort and encouragement. I am so grateful for everything you do.

I'm lucky to have amazing beta readers who have given me priceless feedback on this series since day one. Tamara Felsinger, Jennifer Johnson, and Meghan Stone-Burgess, I really couldn't do it without you. And thanks to the rest of the UM Girls, who are so clever and hilarious and supportive, and to Tuxedo Mask, for bringing us together.

Thanks to blog readers Melissa Anne and Mark Murata, along with Kasey Andrews, Brittney, Chantalle, Elisabeth, Megan, and Miniwriter12 from Goodreads, who helped me develop the discussion questions for *Scarlet*, a task no author should have to conquer alone.

Last, but never, ever least, a thousand thank-yous to my husband, my parents, my family, and my friends who have helped me plan launch parties (thanks, Mom!), designed swag (thanks, Leilani!), styled my hair for a book tour (thanks, Chelsea!), kept me from going crazy on said tour (thanks, honey!), and who smile knowingly when I space out during a conversation because I just had a really great idea for The Book. I love you guys.

Turn the page for

bonus materials. . . .

An interview (and other random shenanigans)

between

Marissa Meyer

and the author of *Storm Siren*,

Mary Weber

*Includes a bonus question with Jay Asher!

Mary Weber (MW): Okay, so my first question is regarding *Cress*'s gorgeous book cover! I mean, I think I'm not alone in noting how much the picture of Cress looks like the backside of David Bowie's amazing head (if he had hair extensions). Knowing your obsession with dear David, can you, in fact, confirm the rumor that he modeled for the cover?

Marissa Meyer (MM): I can neither confirm nor deny the involvement of one David Bowie in the making of this book. *shifty eyes*

Oh, look at that. One question into this interview and I'm already Googling pictures of David Bowie's hair. How is it always so *fabulous*? Okay, focus.

MW: *raises eyebrow and smirks* Uh, can you pardon me a moment? *quickly types confirmation into interweb news sources that "Marissa says YES to David Bowie on cover"* Annnnd as a onetime rabid cosplayer, have YOU ever had fabulous-looking hair extensions?

MM: Yes! Well, sort of. Not like *real* ones, but I did have to attach these awful wig things to my hair when I cosplayed Princess Zelda at Anime Expo years ago. They were such a tangled mess by the end of the day, I think I tore out half of my real hair trying to un-attach them, ugh. But look how pretty!

MW: *dies* That is FANTASTIC! (And you look lovely!!) Ohmygoodness my eight-year-old son is officially your biggest fan (Zelda!). Speaking of biggest fan, one of my favorite characters in the Lunar Chronicles series is Kai's betrothed, Queen Levana with her hawt glamour. It's so deceptively dangerous. Which is why after reading *Cress* (and curling up in a ball because that ENDING), something has begun nagging at me. . . . What if *you* are actually Levana in disguise and this whole "Marissa Meyer" persona is just a ploy to destroy reader hearts with swoony love and cliff-hangers. *squints at you* So . . . are you Levana?

MM: Let's not be hasty with the accusations! First, let's take a look at the evidence. Queen Levana is an evil mastermind who has the patience required to bring the most fiendish of plots to fruition. She's not averse to doing horrible things to Cinder and the Rampion's band of rebels so long as it serves her own purposes. Oh, and she's completely obsessed with marrying Prince Kai.

Whereas I, on the other hand . . .

I'm . . .

Um.

cough

Next question?

MW: A-HA! Exactly. *GLARES AT YOU* Quick, what's one thing only the REAL Marissa Meyer would know?

MM: The real Marissa Meyer knows . . . how the series is going to end.

BWA HA HA HA.

Okay, wow, that didn't help my point *at all.*

Can we talk about David Bowie some more?

MW: Uh-huh. *types confirmation into webnews that *"Marissa admits to being Levana AND David Bowie"** **Okay, moving on . . . If you could have one of Cinder's cyborg qualities, what would it be?**

MM: The Google Brain! That's total wish fulfillment for me. Of course, now we all have our smartphones, which is just one step removed from the Google Brain, but still—imagine being able to just *think* a question and have the answer appear to you. Genius!

I think it's going to happen someday, too. The science is almost there. Sign me up!

What about you, Miss Mary? Any cyborg upgrades you would or wouldn't volunteer for?

MW: Definitely Cinder's finger darts! I could use them when fighting zombie-monkeys or kidnapping super-attractive futuristic rulers or robbing a Chia Pet store. I mean, how cool! As far as your Google Brain wish fulfillment, I like it! (And serious upside—you could Google David's hair all day long.) So when you write certain scenes, do you ever find yourself acting out a movement in order to get it "just right"? You know, such as shooting those darts from Cinder's finger or maybe kissing Captain Thorne hottie-pants?

MM: True Author Confessions: I sometimes practice kissing the back of my hand when I'm writing a kissing scene. *ACK!* I can't believe I just admitted that.

But yes, sometimes you have to act things out to get a feel for how actions fit together, and how best to transcribe those actions onto the page. I do it a lot with big battle scenes, too, especially when there are a lot of characters involved. I'll put on some intense music and clear some space in the living room and plot it out step by step.

On a related note, fight scenes are *hard.*

MW: I am not even kidding that coffee may have just shot out of my nose at that kissing-hand comment. Hahahahaha! Er . . . hold on a sec. *discreetly wipes off laptop screen* Ahem. Now, where were we? Oh, yes. QUESTIONS. Here goes. Writing the middle books in a series is notoriously difficult, and yet you completely rocked it (like a freaking BOSS) with *Cress*. So, let's see . . . how can I put this simply? HOW are you such a genius? And what were the hardest/easiest aspects of hashing out the story of *Cress*?

MM: Why, thank you. It's not easy being an evil mastermind, I mean, a genius. *hair flip*
(Mary's insertion: *"See?* I knew it.")

Some of the easiest scenes for me are the ones where a bunch of the characters are all together—talking. Which probably sounds boring, but I love the banter! I was really inspired by Joss Whedon's *Firefly* in that regard—the idea of throwing a bunch of opposing personalities onto a spaceship and then seeing what happens. *Cress* was the first time I really got to play with that, because now I have a whole bunch of characters together all at once and I finally get to see how they interact.

I also really enjoyed writing the last quarter of the book, because it felt like writing a spy thriller. I'm a huge sucker for spy movies. I had James Bond theme songs in my head for, like, a month.

As for the more difficult aspects of hashing out the plot, I'd say the biggest ongoing challenge is trying to strike a balance between the various plotlines. It took a lot of rearranging of the chapters to feel like I had good pacing for each storyline, and trying to keep each one engaging, and finding good places to break up one plot and switch to another. I don't really have any magic tricks for it, though. Shuffle things around, re-read, shuffle around again, rewrite, shuffle around, revise . . . over and over until it feels right.

MW: You just mentioned Joss Whedon, *Firefly*, and James Bond all in the same response. I'm pretty sure the swoon universe has finally exploded somewhere. And seriously—your method for plot-shuffling is unbelievable. I'm always following your "how-to" blog posts and my brain just dissolves. And not simply due to the plot, but because of how wonderfully ALL of your characters play off each other. Were these interactions based on relationships in your own life? (Like, for instance, maybe a certain super-nerdy fangirl/author. *looks coy*)

MM: It *is* odd how sometimes in real life you meet someone and you just *click!* Unfortunately, my characters don't have David Bowie and Han Solo to geek out over together (*nerdy fist bump*). But they do have other things to bond over, like overthrowing wicked queens and . . . trying not to get killed. And stuff. Of course, the most fun interactions to write are the ones where the characters are a little at odds with each other. I really loved writing the scenes between Cinder and Jacin in *Cress* because Jacin's motives are pretty questionable, but they have no choice but to work together. I know many readers don't care a whole lot for Jacin in this book, but he's become one of my personal favorites. It's refreshing to write someone with more dubious morals once in a while!

MW: Aww, Marissa clicks with me! *preens* And Jacin . . .*sighs* Although, admittedly, even more than your morally dubious men, it's your strong female lead characters which are my favorite aspect of the Lunar Chronicles (and a huge inspiration for my own stories). How did you go about developing them? Did you start the series with each of their personalities already in mind?

MM: Aw, thank you! I really loved Nym and Breck in *Storm Siren*, so that's such a great compliment!

Cinder and Cress were both pretty easy for me to figure out. They both knew who they were from the very beginning and their voices came to me really easily. (*Sailor Moon* fangirl insert here—my original inspiration for Cinder's character was Sailor Jupiter. She's tough and tomboyish, but also yearns for love and acceptance, and I loved how she wasn't just a stereotype.)

Scarlet, on the other hand, gave me a lot more trouble. She was kind of a wimp in early drafts and it took a while for her to develop into the stubborn, headstrong, independent girl she eventually became. When I'm struggling with a character, I'll often find that I'm trying to force them to behave one way, and it doesn't feel authentic. I have to step aside and let them be who *they* want to be, and that's when they start to come alive.

It's not the most scientific approach. . . .

MW: (AHHH! She likes Nym and Breck!!!!) I actually love that you don't base your characterizations on a scientific approach when it comes to Cinder, Cress, and Scarlet. It's their authenticity and "realness" that makes me adore those girls.

However . . . I DO have a scientific-type question for you. Picture this with me:

You, Captain Thorne, and Cress are hanging out in Mos Eisley (at a *Firefly* TV show reunion) and Iko is seriously busting out the karaoke when Levana (and entourage) pull up in an AT-AT and threaten to purge the world of cute cats and Joss Whedon pics. Do you:

(A) have Thorne and Cress bust sweet dance moves that stun Levana while you flirt with Han Solo, so he'll rescue said cats and pics

(B) have Cress pick Thorne up from fainting on the floor while you shoot finger darts full of cat-hater serum

(C) forget the cats and Joss! Have Iko crank up the volume until Levana's ears bleed, then steal her AT-AT for a joyride

(D) none of the above

MM: I'm sorry, I think I tuned out everything after "Flirt with Han Solo." YES. YES, I CHOOSE THAT ONE!

While I'm otherwise occupied, I guess I'll have to pass the responsibility of saving the day over to you. Have at it, Mary!

MW: *laughs* Can I have *Firefly*'s Mal Reynolds there? Because he and I will shoot first and ask crabby-type questions later while Iko croons away. Speaking of Iko, I adore that girl in the same way I adore *Harry Potter*'s Dobby. So, here's what I NEED TO KNOW. Does she have a happy ending in the series? Please say yes. If not, LIE TO ME.

MM: I have *big plans* for Iko. Like, BIG plans. *vanishes into the cave of vagueness*

MW: EEP!!! Yaaaaay!! But wait, WHAT ARE THE PLANS? *follows you into cave only to trip on someone's laptop cord while yelling after you* Just tell me—has anyone ever commented on the similarities between Prince Kai and EVERY HOT GUY EVER?

MM: Mostly, Kai gets compared to Tuxedo Mask from *Sailor Moon*, which wasn't intentional on my part, but you know—Hot Future Prince of Earth, meet Other Hot Future Prince of Earth. What can I say? I'll take it!

He also gets compared to this guy from the Korean pop band EXO. His name is *also* Kai (like in real life!) and he looks really similar to how I imagined my Kai, so it's kind of surreal. Lots of people send me his picture and ask if he was the inspiration for Kai's character and I'm like, "Nope, I'd never heard of him before writing this series—but I do appreciate the eye candy!"

MW: I totally know who that other Kai is (not that I, like, follow him or anything, what?), and ohmygosh, he's EXACTLY how I picture Prince Kai!!!!!! And seeing as you mentioned *Sailor Moon*, which personality are YOU most similar to and why?!

MM: In high school, my friends called me Usagi-chan, which was Sailor Moon's name in Japan, because I dressed up as her once for Halloween. (Usagi means "bunny.") But really, I'm probably more like Sailor Mercury. I'm a perfectionist and a neurotic overachiever, but I also like to think that I place high value on friendships and doing the right thing.

Side note: Are you watching *Sailor Moon Crystal*?! *fangirls*

MW: Can we still be friends if I confess to you I have NEVER seen a single *Sailor Moon* episode? I thought about remedying that after how much you tweet about it, but then was like, "Wait, is that stalkerish of me? That's probably stalkerish of me."

MM: WHA?? Never seen *Sailor Moon*! *astonished*

Well, no one's perfect. (But if we're ever at a book conference together, we are marathoning that show like nobody's business!)

MW: Deal. Sooo, anyhoooo . . . Let's talk about the storyline of *Cress*. It's based on the Rapunzel fairy tale, but can you share which aspects heavily influenced you as you wrote?

I knew early on that there were elements from the fairy tale that I definitely wanted to incorporate—such as Rapunzel's tower, being held captive by the witch, the prince being blinded by *thorns* (get it??), and Rapunzel being cast out into a great desert. So, those elements acted as a framework for me to then start expanding off of. The tower became a satellite, but then I had to figure out why Cress was stuck in a satellite in the first place. What were Sybil's motives for keeping her prisoner? How and why would Thorne get involved? And most important, how does it fit into the larger conflict between Cinder, Kai, and Levana?

I love that part of writing, though. How you can have all of these ideas that don't really feel like they go together, but then you start figuring out how to puzzle-piece them into one story and it becomes a big challenge, almost like a game. It's so rewarding when things start to come together and feel like they were always meant to happen that way.

MW: I love that! And it's rewarding for your readers, as well. (Especially when the kissing stuff starts happening.) So, what's been your favorite thing to develop in regards to the worldbuilding in the series?

MM: Luna! You get to see a lot more of Luna in both *Fairest* and *Winter*, and it was really fun for me to build an entirely new society. I had to give a lot of thought not only to the logistics of living on the moon (oxygen, gravity, agriculture, etc.), but also to how their society functions and how it would look beneath Levana's totalitarian regime. I got to nerd out with my research on space colonization and oppressive governments and all sorts of things, and it was fun for me to expand on my very, very early ideas for the Lunars (i.e., people who live on the moon with *magic powers!*) and see it grow into a society that, I hope, feels rich and authentic. Of course, the readers will be the final judge of that.

MW: Oh, ME ME!!! *raises hand* I'll be a judge for that! Just send me the early draft and I'll let you know if it's as fantastic as we all suspect.

Also, on a totally random weird Lunar-world note, I keep meaning to tell you that, while I laughed out loud repeatedly in *Cress*, my absolute favorite thing was when Dr. Erland considered how he'd "always been fond of the rumor that Sybil Mira's cheekbones were made out of recycled plumbing pipes." Is this true? Were they?

MM: Well, Luna's resources are severely limited, so they do recycle *everything.* . . .

MW: YES! *hurriedly types note to interweb news saying that "*I totally called that one!*"* Okay, so here's my almost-last question. You may or may not know that food is my thing. Which is why I need to ask—while writing *Cress*, were there any specific foodie items you just HAD to have?

MM: I go through a stage with each book where I really want to immerse myself in the location (as much as I can if traveling there isn't an option), so I ate a lot of Asian cuisine when I was writing *Cinder*, and became obsessed with croque madame sandwiches when I was writing *Scarlet* (YUM), and with *Cress*, I made some curries and Moroccan stews. I really, really wanted to try tamarind juice, which is the beverage Jamal gives Thorne in the hotel room. It sounds delicious, but I can't find it anywhere! It's on my someday wish list.

I also have this fantasy of having, like, a Lunar Chronicles tasting party someday, and cooking a bunch of the foods that are mentioned in the books. I have an obsession with writing food descriptions, but a lot of them end up getting cut from the final book (sad, I know), so I thought a food party would be a fun way to show off all the things I've learned.

I'll invite you, Mary, but you'll have to bring a dish, too!

MW: Excuse me while I have an Iko moment (AHHHHHHH!!! A PARTYYYY!!!!! What shoes will I wear?!!!!!) Also, I just Googled "tamarind juice" and apparently, it's both sweet and sour, and used in making certain poisonous vegetables safe to eat. So clearly, that's what I'll bring.

MM: Excellent. I will make sure to have some poisonous vegetables on hand.

MW: And finally . . . my Flash Fangirl–questions:

Han Solo or *Firefly*'s Mal Reynolds?

Han—he was my first true love.

Harry Potter or Ron?

Neville! **(Mary's insertion: *Oh, you win all the wins for that answer.*)**

Cake or sushi?

Sushi . . . then cake?

Unicorns or zombies?

Zombies.

Two food items you can't live without?

Cheese and peanut butter. Not together, though. Gross.

laughs And that wraps up our epic random shenanigan interview

with one of my very favorite authors. Thank you for the laughter and rabid fun, dear Marissa!!!!!!!

Wait—hold the phone! Look who just walked into this interview! Our friend Mr. Jay Asher, *New York Times*–bestselling author of *Thirteen Reasons Why.*

MM: No way! *fangirl* *fangirl*

BONUS QUESTION with JAY ASHER

JA: Just butting in for a quick question! Marissa, you're the perfect person to ask advice on this. Okay, so there's this author I'm thinking of who's known more for his . . . or her! . . . realistic stuff. But maybe he or she has a really cool idea for a sort of sci-fi/futuristic/fantasy/fairy tale book. What would be your suggestion for totally nailing that? Or maybe a pitfall to avoid? Seriously, anything will help him . . . or her.

MM: Thank you so much for popping in, Jay! I'm thinking that this guy (or gal?) should definitely come join the crazy, genre-mash-up party. We have disco-dancing robots and Butterbeer!

As for nailing a genre-blending novel, I would suggest that your realistic-writing friend focus on worldbuilding. Obviously, every novel, including contemporary realism, requires worldbuilding to some degree, but I think it's a different beast when writing science fiction or fantasy or a combination of the two. We want to create a world that feels authentic and believable to the reader, and this requires giving some thought to things like politics, culture, history, and traditions. If we make a decision about our world (say—that the planet Earth has been divided into just six peaceful nations), we need to have an explanation to offer for that decision. Why are there only six nations now and how did that come to be and what are their political relations like and how have they maintained world peace and how do they share resources and what is travel like between them and how much have their cultures blended and/or stayed separate?

Of course, we don't want the story to read like a textbook and bore our readers to tears, so a lot of the super-smart explanations you—er, your friend—come up with might not make it into the book at all. But I think that's part of the fun! I love finding ways to convey the world that the characters live in through small, interesting details: the aromas of street food at a festival. The texture of silk brocade on a gown. The remnants of spent fireworks after a celebration. The hum of magnets under the street. Symbolic bats painted onto the side of a spaceship . . .

Hopefully, the reader will walk away from the book not only feeling that they understand the world, but that they've just been visiting it.

MW: And thus concludes our epic random shenanigan interview with one of my very favorite authors. Thank you for the laughter and rabid fun, dear Marissa!!!

MM: And thank *you*, Mary and Jay, for making this interview such a blast!

Mary Weber is a ridiculously uncoordinated girl plotting to take over make-believe worlds through books, handstands, and imaginary throwing knives. In her spare time, she feeds unicorns, sings '80s hair-band songs to her three muggle children, and ogles her husband, who looks strikingly like Wolverine. They live in California, which is perfect for stalking L.A. bands, Joss Whedon, and the ocean. You can geek out with her on Facebook and Twitter (@mchristineweber), as well as over the fact that *Storm Siren*, book one in her debut YA trilogy, was recently endorsed by Marissa Meyer as a "rich and inventive fantasy [with] one seriously jaw-dropping finale!"

Mirror, mirror, on the wall.
Who is the Fairest of them all?

Fans of the Lunar Chronicles know Levana as a wicked queen who will stop at nothing to rule Earth. But long before she crossed paths with Cinder, Scarlet, and Cress, Levana lived a very different story—a story that has never been told ... until now.

Turn the page for the next exciting installment of
The Lunar Chronicles

Mirror, mirror, on the wall.
Who is the Fairest of them all?

Come close and I shall tell you a tale—
My Queen's dark secrets I've longed to unveil.

Her greed may have led her to steal and to kill,
While her wickedness drove her to break a man's will

But the greatest tragedy I've yet to expose
Is that she did it all for love . . .

so our story goes.

Should my portrayal of the Queen you ever wish to deny,
Know that I'm naught, but a mirror. I cannot lie.

SHE WAS LYING ON A BURNING PYRE, HOT COALS BENEATH her back. White sparks floated in her vision but the mercy of unconsciousness wouldn't come. Her throat was hoarse from screaming. The smell of her own burning flesh invaded her nostrils. Smoke stung her eyes. Blisters burbled across her skin, and entire swaths of flesh peeled away, revealing raw tissue underneath.

The pain was relentless, the agony never ending. She pleaded for death, but it never came.

She reached out with her one hand, trying to drag her body from the fire, but the bed of coals crushed and collapsed under her weight, burying her, dragging her deeper into the embers and the smoke.

Through the haze she caught a glimpse of kind eyes. A warm smile. A finger curled toward her. *Come here, baby sister . . .*

Levana gasped and jolted upward, limbs tangled in her heavy blankets. Her sheets were damp and cold from her sweat, but her skin was still burning hot from the dream. Her throat felt scratched raw. She struggled to swallow, but her saliva tasted like smoke and made her cringe. She sat in the faint morning light shuddering, trying to will away the nightmare. The same nightmare that had plagued her for too many years, that she could never seem to escape.

She rubbed her hands repeatedly over her arms and sides until she was certain the fire wasn't real. She was not burning alive. She was safe and alone in her chambers.

With a trembling breath, she scooted to the other side of the mattress, away from the sweat-stained sheets, and lay back down. Afraid to close her eyes, she stared up at the canopy and practiced her slow breathing until her heartbeat steadied.

She tried to distract herself by planning who she would be that day.

A thousand possibilities floated before her. She would be beautiful, but there were many types of beauty. Skin tone, hair texture, the shape of one's eyes, the length of a neck, a well-placed freckle, a certain grace in the way one walked.

Levana knew a great deal about beauty, just as she knew a great deal about ugliness.

Which was when she remembered that today was the funeral.

She groaned at the thought. How exhausting it would be to hold a glamour all day long, in front of so many. She didn't want to go, but she would have no choice.

It was an inconvenient day for her focus to be shaken by nightmares. Perhaps it would be best to choose something familiar.

As the dream receded into her subconscious, Levana toyed with the idea of being her mother that day. Not as Queen Jannali had been when she died, but perhaps as a fifteen-year-old version of her. It would be a sort of homage to attend the funeral wearing her mother's cheekbones and the vivid violet eyes that everyone knew were glamour-made, though no one would have dared say so aloud.

She spent a few minutes imagining what her mother might have looked like at her age, and she let the glamour settle over her. Moon-blonde hair sleekly pulled into a low knot. Skin as pale as a sheet of ice. A little shorter than she would become full grown. Pale pink lips, so as not to detract from the vibrancy of those eyes.

It calmed her, sinking into the glamour. But no sooner had she tested the look than she felt the wrongness of it.

She did not want to go to her parents' funeral in the garb of a girl-now-dead.

A tap fluttered at the door, interrupting her thoughts.

Levana sighed, and quickly fell into another costume that she'd dreamt up days before. Olive skin, a graceful slope to her nose, and raven-black hair cut adorably short. She shifted through a few eye colors before landing on a striking gray-blue, topped off with smoldering black lashes.

Before she could second-guess herself, she embedded a silver jewel into the flesh beneath her right eye.

A teardrop. To prove that she was in mourning.

"Come in," she called, opening her eyes.

A servant entered carrying a breakfast tray. The girl curtsied in the doorway, not lifting her gaze from the floor— which rendered Levana's glamour unnecessary—before approaching the bed.

"Good morning, Your Highness."

Sitting up, Levana allowed the servant to set the tray across her lap and tuck a cloth napkin around her. The servant poured jasmine tea into a hand-painted porcelain cup that had been imported from Earth several generations ago, and garnished it with two small mint leaves and a drizzle of honey. Levana said nothing as the servant uncovered a tray of tiny cream-filled pastries, so that Levana could see what they looked like whole, before using a silver knife to saw them into even tinier bite-size pieces. While the servant worked, Levana eyed the dish of bright-colored fruits: a soft-fuzzed peach set into a halo of black and red berries, all dusted with powdered sugar.

"Is there anything else I can bring for you, Your Highness?"

"No, that will be all. But send the other one up in twenty minutes to prepare my mourning dress."

"Of course, Your Highness," she answered, although they both knew there was no *other one.* Every servant in the palace was *the other one.* It didn't matter to Levana who the girl sent up, so long as whoever it was could properly stitch her into the sleek gray gown the seamstress had delivered the day before. Levana didn't want to bother with glamouring her dress today in addition to her face, not with so many other thoughts in her head.

With another curtsy, the servant ducked out of the room, leaving Levana to stare down at her breakfast tray. Only now did she realize how very un-hungry she was. There was an ache in her stomach, perhaps left over from the horrible dream. Or she supposed it could have been sadness, but that was doubtful.

She felt no great loss at the death of her parents, who had been gone now for half the long day. Eight artificial nights. Their deaths were terribly gory, assassinated by a shell who used his invincibility against the Lunar gift to sneak into the palace. The man had shot two royal guards in the head before making his way to her parents' bedroom on the third floor, killing three more guards, and slitting her mother's throat so deeply the knife severed part of her spine. He had then gone down the hallway to where her father was lying with one of his mistresses and stabbed him sixteen times in the chest.

The mistress was still screaming, blood spurts across her face, when two royal guards found them.

The shell murderer was still stabbing.

Levana had not seen the bodies, but she had seen the bedrooms the next morning, and her first thought was that all that blood would make for a very pretty rouge on her lips.

She knew it was not the proper thing to think, but she also did not think her parents would have thought anything better had it been *her* murdered instead of them.

Levana had managed to eat three-quarters of a pastry and five small berries when her bedroom door opened again. Her first thought was anger at the intrusion—the servant was early. Her second thought was to check that her glamour was still in place. This, she knew, was the wrong order of concern.

But it was her sister, not one of the faceless servants, who swept into her bedroom. "Channary!" Levana barked, pushing the tray away from her. The tea slopped over the sides of the cup, pooling in the saucer beneath. "I have not given you permission to enter."

"Then perhaps you should lock your door," said Channary, sliding like an eel across the carpet. "There are murderers about, you know."

She said it with a smile, wholly unconcerned. And why shouldn't she be? The murderer had been promptly executed when the guards found him, bloodied knife still in hand.

Not that Levana didn't think there could be more shells out there, angry enough and crazy enough to attempt another attack. Channary was a fool if she thought otherwise.

Which was part of the problem. Channary was simply a fool.

She was a beautiful fool, though, which was the worst kind. Her sister had lovely tanned skin and dark chestnut hair and eyes that tilted up just right at the corners so that she looked like she was smiling even when she wasn't. Levana was convinced that her sister's beauty was glamour-made, certain that no one as horrible on the inside could be so lovely on the outside, but Channary would never confess one way or the other. If there was a chink in her illusion of beauty, Levana had yet to find it. The stupid girl wasn't even bothered by mirrors.

Channary was already dressed for the funeral, though

the dull gray color of the fabric was the only indication that it was made for mourning. The netted skirt jutted out nearly perpendicular to her thighs, like a dancer's costume, and the body-hugging top was inset with thousands of silver sparkles. Her arms were painted with wide gray stripes spiraling up each limb, then coming together to form a heart on her chest. Inside the heart, someone had scrawled, *You will be missed.*

Altogether, the look made Levana want to gag.

"What do you want?" asked Levana, swinging her legs out from beneath the blankets.

"To see that you won't be embarrassing me by your appearance today." Reaching forward, Channary tugged at the flesh beneath Levana's eye, an experiment to see if the embedded gemstone would hold. Flinching, Levana knocked her hand away.

Channary smirked. "Thoughtful touch."

"Less fraudulent than claiming you're going to miss them," said Levana, glaring at the painted heart.

"Fraudulent? To the contrary. I shall miss them a great deal. Especially the parties that Father used to throw during the full Earth. And being able to borrow Mother's dresses when I was going shopping in AR-4." She hesitated. "Though I suppose now I can simply take her seamstress as my own, so perhaps that is no great loss after all." With a giggle, she sat down on the edge of the bed and snatched a berry from the breakfast tray, popping it onto her tongue. "You should be prepared to say a few words at the funeral today."

"*Me?*" It was an appalling idea. Everyone would be watching her, judging just how sad she was. She didn't think she could fake it well enough.

"You're their daughter too. And—" Suddenly, inexplicably choked up, Channary dabbed at the corner of her eye. "I don't think I'm strong enough to do it all on my own. I'll be overwhelmed by grief. Perhaps I will faint and require a guard to carry me to someplace dark and quiet to recover." She snorted, all signs of sadness vanishing as quickly as they had come. "That's an intriguing idea. Perhaps I can stage it to happen next to that new young one with the curly hair. He seems quite . . . obliging."

Levana scowled. "You're going to leave me alone to guide the entire kingdom in mourning, so that you can frolic with one of the guards?"

"Oh, stop it," said Channary, covering her ears. "You're so annoying when you whine."

"You're going to be *queen*, Channary. You're going to have to make speeches and important decisions that will affect everyone on Luna. Don't you think it's time you took that seriously?"

Laughing, Channary sucked at the grains of sugar left on her fingertips. "Like our parents took it so seriously?"

"Our parents are *dead*. Killed by a citizen who must not have thought they were doing a very good job."

Channary waved her hand through the air. "Being queen is a right, little sister. A right that comes with an endless supply of men and servants and beautiful dresses. Let the court and the thaumaturges deal with all the boring details. As for *me*, I am going to be known throughout history as the queen who never stopped laughing." Tossing her hair off her shoulder, she surveyed the bedroom, its gold-papered walls and hand-embroidered draperies. "Why aren't there any mirrors in here? I want to see how beautiful I look for my tear-filled performance."

Crawling from the bed, Levana pulled on a robe that had been laid out on the sitting chair. "You know very well why there aren't any mirrors."

To which Channary's grin widened. She hopped up from the bed as well. "Oh, yes, that's right. Your glamours are so becoming these days I'd almost forgotten."

Then, quick as a viper, Channary backhanded Levana across the face, sending her stumbling into one of the bedposts. Levana cried out, the shock causing her to lose control of her glamour.

"Ah, there's my ugly duckling," Channary cooed. Stepping closer, she grabbed Levana's chin, squeezing tight before Levana could raise her hand to soothe her already-flaming cheek. "I suggest you remember this the next time you think to contradict one of my orders. As you have so kindly reminded me, I am going to be queen, and I will not tolerate my commands being questioned, especially by my pathetic little sister. You *will* be speaking for me at the funeral."

Turning away, Levana blinked back the tears that had sprung up and scrambled to reinstate her illusion. To hide her disfigurements. To pretend that she was beautiful too.

Spotting movement in the corner of her eye, she saw a maid frozen in the doorway. Channary hadn't closed it upon entering, and Levana was quite certain the maid had seen everything.

Smartly, the servant lowered her gaze and curtsied.

Releasing Levana's chin, Channary stepped back. "Put on your mourning dress, little sister," she said, once again wearing her pretty smile. "We have a very big day ahead of us."

Wandering the Pages, Oh, the Books!, Fairy Tale Fandom, Cammminbookland, Tessellated Tales, Mackin Books in Bloom, Effortlessly Reading, Katie's Book Blog, My Friends Are Fiction, Scott Reads It!, Pivot Book Reviews, Words of Mystery, The Daily Prophecy, Books Take You Places, The Artsy Reader Girl, The Attic, The Art of Escapism, What Mrs. Light is Reading, Bang Bang BOOK Blog, Oh, For the Love of Books!, In Libris Veritas, Howdy YAL!, {Krista's Dust Jacket}, Snuggly Oranges, Musings of a YA Reader, Gone with the Words, Consumed by Books, YA Bibliophile, Gypsy Reviews, Michelle and Leslie's Book Picks, Words With Sarah, Young Adult Hollywood, YA Reading Club, Writer of Wrongs, On a Book Bender, Mostly YA Book Obsessed, My Life in Books, Novels by G. Donald Cribbs, Carina's Books, thebookheap, Let the Ink Run Free, Bibliopunkk, Greyland Reviews, Lisa is Busy Nerding, LizzieLovesBooks, Quality Fangirls, Unlucky Primes, A Trail of Books Left Behind, Love is not a triangle, Stacked, Christina Reads YA, Ageless Pages Reviews, A World of Reviews, Awkwordly Emma, The Cheap Reader, Paper Cuts, Paperback'd Reviews, Nose Graze, Touch the Night, A GREAT read, OriginiquEquanimity, Tripping Over Books, The Book Addict's Guide, Mermaid Vision Books

Alexa Loves Books, Novel Views, Ohana Reads, The Midnight Garden, Swept Away By Books, Retracted Light Reviews, Great Imaginations, ForeverBookish A Fan-girls Unique Critique, The Starry-Eyed Revue, Romancing the Laser Pistol, Wholly Books! YA Book Queen, MissFictional's World of YA Books, A Reader of Fictions

In Starships and Dragonwings, An Ally's Book Blog, Gone Pecan, The Book Butterfly, kaBOOKs, IceyBooks, The Book Swarm, The Book Sphere, My, Snow Monkeys, Made Flower, The Daily Prophecy, Book Labyrinth, Fic Fare, In Love With Handmade, Emilie's Book World, A Perfection Called Books, Our Shelf Lives, Follow the Yellow Book Road, Book Badger, Reading Teen, Chapter Break, Cuddlebuggery, Book Blog Bake, Lunar Rainbows, YA Books Central, Book Badger, The Lib...ary Canary, Mundie Moms, Her Reviews, Fiction Folio, Lili's Reflections, Paper Riot, Tabitha's Book Blog, A Class of Wri..., Ravens and Writing Desks, Chapter Break, Cuddlebuggery, Read My Breath Away, Fangirling Over Books, Mundie Moms

Thank you, bloggers, for all your support!

Marissa Meyer's first three novels in the Lunar Chronicles—*Cinder*, *Scarlet*, and *Cress*—all debuted on the *New York Times* bestseller list. She lives in Tacoma, Washington, with her husband and their three cats. Visit her online at marissameyer.com.